The Earth is Flat: Tales from the Flat Earth and Elsewhere
By Tanith Lee

Cover art by Lauren Gornik

D1264377

Special thanks to Allison Rich and the Cushing Library at Texas A&M for their assistance.
For more information on Tanith Lee, visit Daughter of the Night: An Annotated Tanith Lee Bibliography.
http://daughterofthenight.com/

"The Origin of Snow" originally appeared in December, 2002 on Tanith Lee's now-defunct website.

"The Man Who Stole the Moon" originally appeared in the February, 2001 issue of *Realms of Fantasy*.

"The Snake" originally appeared in the June, 2008 issue of *Realms of Fantasy*.

"The Pain of Glass" originally appeared in *Clockwork Phoenix 2* (Norilana Books, 2009).

"I Bring You Forever" originally appeared in the June, 1998 issue of *Realms of Fantasy*.

"Foolish, Clever, Wicked and Kind" originally appeared in *Arabesques: More Tales of the Arabian Nights* (Avon, 1988).

"Blue Vase of Ghosts" originally appeared in the Winter, 1983 issue of *Dragonfields*.

"After I Killed Her" originally appeared in the July, 1997 issue of *Asimov's Science Fiction*.

"Cold Spell" originally appeared in *Young Winter's Tales 7* (Macmillan, 1976).

"Beauty is the Beast" originally appeared in the Fall, 1986 issue of *American Fantasy*.

"Into Gold" originally appeared in the March, 1986 issue of *Isaac Asimov's Science Fiction Magazine*.

"The Truce" originally appeared in *The DAW Science Fiction Reader* (DAW Books, 1976).

"The God Orkrem" originally appeared in the March, 2011 issue of *Fantasy Magazine*.

"The Kingdoms of the Air" originally appeared in the Summer, 1988 issue of *Weird Tales*.

TABLE OF CONTENTS

Tales from the Flat Earth

Tales from Elsewhere

ALSO AVAILABLE

The Empress of Dreams by Tanith Lee – Sixteen tales of swords and sorcery by the Crown Princess of Heroic Fantasy!

Arminius, Bane of Eagles by Adrian Cole - Set in an alternative Romano-Celtic Europe, Arminius, the Germanic tribal leader and destroyer of three entire Roman legions in the Teutoburger forest, and Germanicus, ambitious Roman conqueror and potential heir to the Empire, avoid assassination attempts and set out on a course that will eventually see them clash in a war that will shake the foundations of their world. Sorcery and elemental forces collide with the Roman war machine!

Samhain Sorceries - Just in time for Halloween, DMR Books presents ten haunting tales of swords and sorcery. On Samhain, the dead will rise, dark rituals will be performed, and gateways to the afterworld will open. One of the more notable tales in this anthology is "Night of the Burning Ghost" by Keith Taylor, which features Felimid mac Fal, hero of the classic *Bard* series. *Samhain Sorceries* also includes stories by Adrian Cole, Matthew Pungitore, Harry Piper, and more.

Far Away & Never by Ramsey Campbell - Through these eight tales of swords and sorcery—four of which feature the inexhaustible swordsman Ryre—the reader is taken on a ride through different times and unlike worlds, all filled with the fantastic creatures and thrilling action one would expect to come from Campbell's imagination while writing in this realm. Twenty-five years after its original publication, *Far Away & Never* is now back in print, with one additional story included.

Tales from the Flat Earth

The Origin of Snow

Over the midnight desert they rode. One from the north, and one from the south, and one from the west. He from the north was white-skinned and clothed in gold, and thirty men rode behind him, musicians and priests. He from the south was smoky-skinned and clothed in scarlet, and fifty men rode behind him, armed to their teeth—which were also capped by steel. He from the west was black, and clothed in silver, and what rode behind him were not men, more like great cats, though they too carried musical instruments and weapons.

At the edges of the scene, the mountains crowded, and above the sky was full of stars.

The three riders met.

"Are were here for the same reason?"

Which of them spoke? All three, and each in a different language. But all three too were scholars, and all three understood all three.

Then they stared upward at the sky.

"From there?" asked White-and-Gold.

"It must be from there. From the country of the gods," avowed Smoke-and-Scarlet.

Meanwhile, Black-and-Silver, who had the keenest sight, added, "But who is this, now, coming from the east?"

The one from the east did not ride, he walked. However, with every stride, it seemed he covered half a mile or more. No man, no *thing* accompanied him—and yet, the whole night seemed to do so. He was pale of skin, black of hair. His garments were black, and a great cloak blew all about him like a storm, though there was no wind. His beauty was—unreasonable.

They did not know him. Though, being wise, they knew of his kind.

"He is a demon."

"He is, without doubt, from their high caste, the Vazdru."

"*We* must be wary."

"Greetings," they said.

The Vazdru stood looking up at them. Never before had any of the three been looked *up* at, by one standing *below* on the ground, who seemed in fact to look *down*.

At last, he spoke.

"Your threefold journeys made some noise across the ceilings beneath."

"Your pardon, sir," said Black-and-Silver. "We did not mean disturb you, or your people in the fair city of Druhim Vanashta underground."

"But here we are," said White-and-Gold, "to attend the arrival of a new god—or at least a mighty magus…"

"Or most holy messenger," said Smoke-and-Scarlet.

"The advent has been predicted," they said. "He is to fall from heaven like a star."

Azhrarn, the Vazdru, who—at that time—was not yet *Prince* of demons, laughed softly. Never had music more wonderful been heard, or with such a knife-like edge.

"Neither god nor mage, nor, for that, messenger, will fall. The gods keep to themselves."

"Handsome sir, the constellations, whose movements we study, tell us otherwise. Tonight, a great wonder will occur."

"The stars do not move," said Azhrarn. "They hang like diamonds, from roots of air."

Perturbed, the three riders glanced at each other.

Eventually Black-and-Silver said, "Then we are ahead of our time. Perhaps this gift from heaven is due in some other age."

"If so," said Azhrarn, "the earth will then no longer be flat, as now it is. And the gods will be otherwise, for now they have no interest in mankind. Save sometimes they are disgusted by you."

As the three riders frowned in disappointed and uneasy silence, the demon vanished. Instead a coil of shadowy sand drifted away—but whether north, south, west or east—none of those three wise men could tell.

Azhrarn, mere prince among princes, waited alone on a rock in the desert, and gazed towards the mountains, pondering.

At length, he leapt forward, and in another moment was instead on the highest peak of the furthest crag. Here a cave opened, within whose darkness burned a flicker of emerald fire.

"Who are you?" demanded the dragon, when Azhrarn appeared in its lair. "No matter," it graciously conceded, "you are a most fascinating creature and I shall enjoy dining on your flesh."

Jaws full of points like swords clashed. Azhrarn stood smiling a little, as the dragon regained its balance.

"Give up. I am no prey of yours."

The dragon took no notice. It flapped its wings about him some minutes, hawking up fire, snapping and rending—and achieving nothing. Then finally Azhrarn struck it across the head.

The dragon collapsed, stunned. Rather than hurt, the blow had been exquisite...

"Now," said Azhrarn, "you will carry me to the Upperearth."

The dragon snorted and regained its confidence. "Though you are glamorous and a magician, I will do no such thing."

"You have seen some of my powers. Do this, and I will give you a reward."

"What? What can you give me?"

"Your recompense shall be in proportion to your work."

Up through the night sky, past a rising crescent moon, who seemed to avert her gaze in a veil of cloud. Up through the starry gardens, whose stars now did swing on their roots at the gust of dragon wings—perhaps causing more astrological predictions below.

In through the gates, invisible, un*actual*, the doorway of Upperearth, the country of the gods, they flew.

Though night lay beneath, and all across the plate of the Flat Earth, it was always morning in Upperearth. Cold and shining blue, the polished and almost empty landscape, where also mountains distantly gleamed, rimmed with adamantine. In those days—a memory even long ago—groves of strange trees existed there, thin and long and silver-golden, and in their branches sat weird elementals, that the gods then kept as (neglected) pets.

These showed some interest in Azhrarn, but mostly in the dragon. The dragon sank down.

"The weight of the magnetic gravity of this place exhausts me. You must go on alone."

Azhrarn, indifferent to most gravities, left it in the groves, among the whizz of tiny chirping steams and atoms.

He walked over the plain of heaven.

In one area stood a well of glass, filled with some sort of sludge. Three guardians lay muffled and asleep on a bench. He ignored such trivia.[1]

Whatever else, Azhrarn, from the moment he had heard the hoofs galloping above Druhim Vanashta, had known this night was pregnant with some bizarre event.

Curious, prescient, untender, he reached a godly palace, like a shaft of sunlight changed to crystal.

A god was inside. (Flawless, fly in amber.)

There he poised, the god, in the even-then moronically self-absorbed over-intellectualism of these particular deities. They made Man, then lost interest in him. But demons they had *not* made. The demons had made themselves—and very marvelously too. *Their* design was much better.

Azhrarn touched the glassy sunbeam. It shivered but did not give way. The god however shot him a look.

Through the god's transparent skin and mirror eyes, violet ichors dimly showed. He (or she) was perfectly lovely, and in a way that was, frankly, repulsive.

"What do you want?"

Gods did not speak. They did something, however, which we must believe amounted to speech, since the stories are sometimes full of their chatter.

Azhrarn heard the question. He said, "Mankind has smelled something cooking up here. What is it?"

"Nothing. It is nothing," said the god.

By his, or her—or *its* (only the gods themselves might know what gender they were) *denial*, proof was given to Azhrarn. Such beings would never deny what was not a fact.

*A*zhrarn ran. He raced across the plain. All types of indescribable and ridiculous god-stuff flashed by—pavilions, gardens, *devices*—fruitless to attempt to see, let alone consider them.

He came to a square of open land (if it was land). The square was of a colour the earth did not, and never would, have. Nor does it now. A group of gods were here, and they unwound together a long, long parchment. And as they did this, they fed it into the mouth of a hideous but also—be glad—quite indescribable object. Perhaps it was animal,

[1] Actually, the Well of Immortality, as he would later know.

perhaps machine, or vegetable, even. In any event, it ate the parchment up and swallowed it down.

Azhrarn asked no further questions. Truly there *was* an aroma, a smell like burning. He knew instantly what they were at.

The endless scroll was the writing of fate. That was, a fate not yet made accessible[2]. Inchoate and free-flowing, still it contained, obviously, many predictions, a whole rota of events that must and would occur.

Azhrarn leaned forward, trying to see what was written there. He noted only one awful sentence, in letters no human could decipher: *One day the earth's flatness will be roundness.*

The gods were still young enough at this hour that they were by then trying to block his view.

"Humanity snuffling after this like a dog—three troublemakers in the desert—Man the cockroach must not learn too much—such matters must be hidden..." voicelessly they screamed.

And he, Azhrarn, still only a prince among princes, did not know *not* to reach out and snatch...

In that glimpse, he saw that every letter written there was unlike any other...

Then the parchment—which smelled of burning—burnt him, savagely. It was like clutching the whitest, hottest fire. But he bore it, and he tore that fragment away. And in that instant the furious gods, still capable, in their elderly youth, of real annoyance, evicted him from heaven.

The glacial blue cracked. Through the sudden gap Azhrarn was cast—and fell.

He fell like a dark star. Like a premonition of many other things to come. Yet in his hands he retained the smouldering fire of parchment.

This, meeting the atmosphere of the Flat Earth, became abruptly a white and splintering whirlwind.

Only then did Azhrarn let go. He took charge of himself in contrast, and stopped his fall. On an island of cloud close by the moon, he found the dragon, which had, it seemed, left heaven of its own accord, irritated beyond endurance by the attentions of the eager pet atomies.

Together, they watched the shreds of fate's scroll scatter down

---

[2] Or manlike—later in the stories Fate will be Kheshmet, one of the Lords of Darkness.

11

towards earth.

"The gods will punish you," opined the dragon.

"I tremble," said Azhrarn, idly.

"You have burnt your hand."

"That is your reward, then, for taking me there," said Azhrarn. "You may lick the roasted meat of demonkind."

The dragon pleated its scaly forehead in a scowl. Then duly licked the alluring scorch.

Down on the desert, the three wise men saw the flakes of white begin to descend.

"What is that?"

"It burns…"

"No… it is cold…"

On the tops of far-off earthly mountains, white fire-flakes of unreadable fate gathered in sparkling hoods of ice. Elsewhere, upon forests and rivers, upon the shores and hills of the world, glittering like tears of sorrow or laughter, in they came.

While in his high tower, a fourth wise man, who had analysed the stars more carefully, and had not left his city, caught on one finger a single fleck of the falling white.

Through a magnifying lens he examined it. Then another, and another. Each was of wondrous pattern. Each was unique unlike all the rest.

Across the face of the Flat Earth, mankind at its windows and doors, staring.

"What is this? Are all the stars falling? They *burn*—no, they are cold— what shall we call this thing?"

Azhrarn, young on his cloud, looked silently and named the fluttering white *Broken Letters*.

In his tower the fourth wise man named the phenomenon *Flowers*.

A king's favourite wife called it *White Bread*—but the king's favourite slave called it by a different, saucier name.

Everywhere, it *was* named. And by naming, made perpetual, since words are magic, then, now.

Letters, stars, flowers, bread, *seed*… One day, perhaps, we of this foretold and altered earth will decode them. And so learn the rules of Fate in this secret alphabet of snowflakes.

The Man Who Stole the Moon

everal tales are told concerning the Moon of the Flat Earth. Some say that this Moon, perhaps, was a hollow globe, within which lay lands and seas, having even their own cool Sun. However, there are other stories.

One evening, Jaqir the accomplished thief rose from a bed of love and said to his mistress, "Alas, sweetheart, we must part now forever."

Jaqir's mistress looked at him in surprise and shook out her bright hair. "You are mistaken. My husband, the old merchant, is miles off again, buying silk and other stuff, and besides suspects nothing. And I am well satisfied with you."

"Dear heart," said Jaqir, as he dressed his handsome self swiftly, "neither of these things is the stumbling block to our romance. It is only this. I have grown tired of you."

"Tired of me!" cried the lady, springing from the bed.

"Yes, though indeed you are toothsome in all respects, I am inconstant and easily bored. You must forgive me."

"Forgive you!" screamed the lady, picking up a handy vase.

Jaqir ducked the vase and swung nimbly out of the high window, an action to which he was quite accustomed, from his trade. "Although a deceiver in my work, honesty in my private life is always my preferred method," he added, as he dropped quickly down through the vine to the street below. Once there he was gone in a flash, and just in time to miss the jar of piddle the lady that moment upended from the window. However, three of the king's guard, next second passing beneath, were not so fortunate.

"A curse upon all bladders," howled they, wringing out their cloaks and hair. Then looking up, they beheld the now no-longer mistress of Jaqir, and asked her loudly what she meant by it.

"Pardon me, splendid sirs," said she. "The befoulment was not intended for you, but for that devilish thief, Jaqir, who even now runs through that alley there toward a hiding place he keeps in the House of the Thin Door."

t the mention of Jaqir, who was both celebrated and notorious in that city, the soldiers forgot their inconvenience and gave instant chase. Never before had any been able to lay hands on Jaqir, who, it was said, could steal the egg from beneath a sleeping pigeon. Now, thanks to the enragement of his discarded lover, the guard knew not only of Jaqir's proximity, but his destination. Presently then they came up with him by the House of the Thin Door.

"Is it he?"

"So it is, for I have heard, when not in disguise, he dresses like a lord, like this one, and, like this one, his hair is black as a panther's fur."

At this they strode up to Jaqir and surrounded him.

"Good evening, my friends," said Jaqir. "You are fine fellows, despite your smell."

"That smell is not our own, but the product of a night-jar emptied on us. And the one who did this also told us where to find the thief Jaqir."

"Fate has been kind to you. I will not therefore detain you further."

"No, it is you who shall be detained."

"I?" asked Jaqir modestly.

But within the hour he discovered himself in chains in the king's dungeons.

"Ah, Jaqir." said he to himself, "a life of crime has taught you nothing. For have the gods not always rewarded your dishonesty—and now you are chastised for being truthful."

Although of course the indifferent, useless gods had nothing to do with any of it.

A month or so later, the king got to hear that Jaqir the Prince of Thieves languished in the prison, awaiting trial.

"I will see to it," said the king. "Bring him before me."

So Jaqir was brought before the king. But, despite being in jail, being also what he was, Jaqir had somehow stolen a gold piece from one jailor and gifted it to another, and so arrived in the king's sight certainly in chains, but additionally bathed, barbered, and anointed, dressed in finery, and with a cup of wine in his hand.

Seeing this, the king laughed. He was a young king and not without a sense of the humorous. In addition, he knew that Jaqir, while he had stolen from everyone he might, had never harmed a hair of their heads, while his skills of disguise and escape were much admired by any he had not annoyed.

"Now then, Prince of Thieves, may a mere king invite you to sit? Shall I strike off your chains?" added the king.

"Your majesty," said one of the king's advisers, "pray do not unchain him, or he will be away over the roofs. Look, he has already stolen two of my gold rings—and see, many others have lost items."

This was a fact. All up and down the palace hall, those who had gathered to see Jaqir on trial were exclaiming over pieces of jewelry suddenly missing. And one lady had even lost her little dog, which abruptly, and with a smile, Jaqir let out of an inner compartment in his shirt, though it seemed quite sorry to leave him.

"Then I shall not unchain you," said the king. "'Restore at once all you have filched."

Jaqir rose, shook himself somewhat, and an abundance of gold and gems cascaded from his person.

"Regrettably, lord king, I could not resist the chance to display my skills."

"Rather you should deny your skills. For you have been employed in my city seven years, and lived like the prince you call yourself. But the punishment for such things is death."

Jaqir's face fell, then he shrugged. He said, "I see you are a greater thief, sir, than I. For I only presume to rob men of their goods. You are bold enough to burgle me of my life."

At that the court made a noise, but the king grew silent and thoughtful. Eventually he said, "I note you will debate the matter. But I do not believe you can excuse your acts."

"There you are wrong. If I were a beggar calling for charity on the street you would not think me guilty of anything but ill luck or indigence. Or, if I were a seller of figs you would not even notice me as I took the coins of men in exchange for my wares."

"Come," said the king. "You neither beg nor sell. You thieve."

"A beggar," said Jaqir, "takes men's money and other alms, and gives nothing in return but a blessing. Please believe me, I heap blessings on the heads of all I rob, and thank them in my prayers for their charity. Had I begged it, I might, it is true, not have received so great a portion. How much nobler and blessed are they then, that they have given over to me the more generous amount? Nor do they give up their coins for nothing. For what they buy of me, when it is *I* who steal from them, is a dramatic tale to tell. And indeed, lord king, have you never heard any boast of how they were robbed by me?"

The king frowned, for now and then he had heard this very thing, some rich noble or other reciting the story of how he had been despoiled of this or that treasure by the nimble Jaqir, the only thief able to take it. And once or twice, there were women, too, who said, "When I woke, I found my rings were gone, but on my pillow lay a crimson rose. Oh, would he had stayed a while to steal some other prize."

"I am not," declared Jaqir, "a common thief. I purloin from none who cannot afford the loss. I deduct nothing that has genuine sentimental or talismanic weight. I harm none. Besides, I am an artist in what I do. I come and go like a shadow, and vanish like the dawn into the day. You will have been told, I can abstract the egg of a pigeon from beneath the sleeping bird and never wake it."

The king frowned deeply. He said, "Yet with all this vaunted knack, you did not, till today, leave my dungeons."

Jaqir bowed. "That was because, lord king, I did not wish to miss my chance of meeting you."

"Truly? I think rather it was the bolts and bars and keys, the numerous guards—who granted you wine, but not an open door. You seem a touch pale."

"Who can tell?" idly answered pale Jaqir.

But the king only said, "I will go apart and think about all this." And so he did, but the court lingered, looking at Jaqir, and some of the ladies and young men came and spoke to him, but trying always not to get near enough to be robbed. Yet even so, now and then, he would courteously hand them back an emerald or amethyst he had removed from their persons.

Meanwhile the king walked up and down a private chamber where, on pedestals of marble, jewel-colored parrots sat watching him.

"He is clever," said the king, "handsome, well mannered, and decorative. One likes him at once, despite his nefarious career. Why cast such a man out of the state of life? We have callous villains and nonentities enough. Must every shining star be snuffed?"

Then a scarlet parrot spoke to him.

"O king, if you do not have Jaqir executed, they will say you are partial, and not worthy to be trusted with the office of judge."

"Yes," said the king, "this I know."

At this another parrot, whose feathers shone like a pale-blue sky, also spoke out. "But if you kill him, O king, men may rather say you were jealous of him. And no king must envy any man."

16

"This is also apt," said the king, pacing about.

Then a parrot spoke, which was greener than jade.

"O king, is Jaqir not a thief? Does he not brag of it? Set him then a test of thieving, and make this test as impossible as may be. And say to him, 'If you can do this, then indeed your skill is that of a poet, an artist, a warrior, a prince. But if you fail you must die.'"

Then the king laughed again. "Well said. But what test?"

At that a small gray parrot flew from its pedestal, and standing on his shoulder, spoke in the king's ear with a jet-black beak.

The king said, "O wisest of all my councilors."

In the palace hall Jaqir sat among the grouped courtiers, being pleasant and easy with them in his chains, like a king. But then the king entered and spoke as follows:

"Now, Jaqir, you may have heard, in my private rooms four angels live, that have taken another form. With these four I have discussed your case. And here is the verdict. I shall set you now a task that, should you succeed at it, must make you a hero and a legend among men—which happy state you will live to enjoy, since also I will pardon all your previous crimes. Such shall be your fame then, that hardly need you try to take anything by stealth. A million doors shall be thrown wide for you, and men will load you with riches, so astonishing will your name have become."

Jaqir had donned a look of flattering attention.

"The task then. You claim yourself a paragon among thieves. You must steal that which is itself a paragon. And as you say you have never taken anything which may be really missed, on this occasion I say you will have to thieve something all mankind shall miss and mourn."

The court stood waiting on the king's words. Jaqir stood waiting, perforce. And all about, as at such times it must, (still must,) the world stood waiting, hushing the tongues of sea and wind, the whispers of forests and sands, the thunder of a thousand voiceless things.

"Jaqir, Prince of Thieves, for your life, fly up and steal the Moon from the sky. The task being what it is, I give you a year to do it."

Nine magicians bound Jaqir. He felt the chains they put on him as he had scarcely felt the other chains of iron, thinking optimistically as he had been, that he would soon be out of them.

But the new chains emerged from a haze of iridescent smokes and a rumble of incantations, and had forms like whips and lions, thorns and bears. Meeting his flesh, they disappeared, but he felt them sink in, painless knives, and fasten on his bones and brain and mind.

"You may go where you wish and do what you will and suffer nothing. But if you should attempt, in any way, to abscond, then you will feel the talons and the fangs of that which has bound you, wrapped gnawing inside your body. And should you persist in your evasion, these restraints shall accordingly devour you from within. Run where you choose, seek what help you may, you will die in horrible agony, and soon. Only when you return to the king, your task accomplished fully, and clearly proven, will these strictures lapse—but that at once. Success, success alone, spells your freedom."

So then Jaqir was let go, and it was true enough, honesty being the keynote to his tale so far, that he had no trouble, and could travel about as he wanted. Nor did any idea enter his mind concerning escape. Of all he was or was not, Jaqir was seldom a fool. And he had, in the matter of his arrest, surely spent sufficient foolishness to last a lifetime.

Since he was *not* a fool, Jaqir, from the moment the king had put the bargain to him, had been puzzling how he might do what was demanded.

In the past, many difficult enterprises had come Jaqir's way, and he had solved the problem of each. But it is to be remembered, on none of these had his very existence depended. Nor had it been so strange. One thing must be said, too, the world being no longer as then it was—Jaqir did not at any point contest the notion on the grounds that it was either absurd or unconscionable. Plainly sorcery existed, was everywhere about, and seldom doubted. Plainly the Moon, every night gaudily on show, might be accessible, even to men, for there were legends of such goings on. Thus Jaqir never said to himself, *What madness have I been saddled with?* Only: *How can I effect this extraordinary deed?*

So he went up and down in the city, and later through the landscape beyond, walking mostly, to aid his concentration. Sometimes he would spend the night at an inn, or in some rich house he had never professionally bothered but which had heard of him. And occasionally men did know of him to recognize him, and some knew what had been laid upon him. And unfortunately, the nicest of them would tend to a similar, irritating act. Which was, as the Moon habitually rose in the east, to mock or rant at him. "Aiee, Jaqir. Have you not stolen her *yet?*"

18

Because the Earth was then flat, the Moon journeyed over and around it, dipping, after moonset, into the restorative seas of chaos that lay beneath the basement of the world. Nor was the Moon of the Flat Earth so very big in circumference (although the size of the Moon varied, influenced by who told—or tells—the tales).

"What *is* the Moon?" pondered Jaqir at a wayside tavern, sipping sherbet.

"Of what is the Moon *made?*" murmured Jaqir, courting sleep, for novelty, in an olive grove.

"Is it heavy or light? What makes it, or she, glow so vividly? *Is* it a she? How," muttered Jaqir, striding at evening between fields of silver barley, "am I to get hold of the damnable thing?"

Just then the Moon willfully and unkindly rose again, unstolen, over the fields. Jaqir presently lay down on his back among the barley stalks, gazing up at her as she lifted herself higher and higher. Until at length she reached the apex of heaven, where she seemed for a while to stand still, like one white lily on a stem of stars.

"Oh, Moon of my despair," said Jaqir softly, "I fear I shall not master this riddle. I would do better to spend my last year of life—of which I find only nine months remain!—in pleasure, and forget the hopeless task."

At that moment Jaqir heard the stalks rustling a short way off, and sitting up, he saw through the darkness how two figures wandered between the barley. They were a young man and a girl, and from their conduct, lovers in search of a secret bed. With a rueful nod at the ironies of Fate, Jaqir got up and meant to go quietly away. But just then he heard the maiden say, "Not here, the barley is trampled—we must lie where the stalks are thicker, or we may be heard."

"Heard?" asked the youth. "There is no one about."

"Not up in the fields," replied the girl, "but down *below* the fields the demons may be listening in the Underearth."

"Ho," said the youth (another fool), "I do not believe in demons."

"Hush! They exist and are powerful. They love the world by night, as they must avoid the daylight, and like moonlit nights especially, for they are enamored of the Moon, and have made ships and horses with wings in order to reach it. And they say, besides, the nasty magician, Paztak, who lives only a mile along the road from this very place, is nightly visited by the demon Drin, who serve him in return for disgusting rewards."

By now the lovers were a distance off, and only Jaqir's sharp ears had picked up the ends of their talk after which there was silence, save for the sound of moonlight dripping on the barley. But Jaqir went back to the road. His face had become quite purposeful, and perhaps even the Moon, since she watched everything so intently, saw that too.

Now Paztak the magician did indeed live nearby, in his high, brazen tower, shielded by a thicket of tall and not ordinary laurels. Hearing a noise of breakage among these, Paztak undid a window and peered down at Jaqir, who stood below with drawn knife.

"What are you at, unruly felon?" snapped Paztak.

"Defending myself, wise sir, as your bushes bite."

"Then leave them alone. My name is Paztak the Unsociable. Be off, or I shall conjure worse things—to attack you."

"Merciful mage, my life is in the balance. I seek your help, and must loiter till you give it."

The mage clapped his hands, and three yellow, slavering dogs leaped from thin air and also tried to tear Jaqir into bite-size pieces. But avoiding them, Jaqir sprang at the tower and, since he was clever at such athletics, began climbing up it.

"Wretch!" howled Paztak. And then Jaqir found a creature, part wolverine and part snake, had roped the tower and was striving to wind him as well in its coils. But Jaqir slid free, kicked shut its clashing jaws, and vaulted over its head onto Paztak's windowsill.

"Consider me desperate rather than impolite."

"I consider you *elsewhere*," remarked Paztak with a new and ominous calm.

Next instant Jaqir found himself in a whirlwind, which turned him over and over, and cast him down at last in the depths of a forest.

"So much for the mage," said Jaqir, wiping snake-wolverine, dog, and laurel saliva from his boots. "And so much for me. I have had, in my life, an unfair quantity of good luck, and evidently it is all used up."

"Now, now," said a voice from the darkness, "let me get a proper look at you, and see if it is."

And from the shadows shouldered out a dwarf of such incredible hideousness that he might be seen to possess a kind of beauty.

Staring in awe at him then, from his appearance, and the fabulous jewelry with which he was adorned, Jaqir knew him for a Drin.

"Now, now," repeated the Drin, whose coal-black, luxuriant hair swept the forest floor. And he struck a light by the simple means of running his talonous nails—which were painted indigo—along the trunk of a tree. Holding up his now flaming hand, the Drin inspected Jaqir, gave a leer and smacked his lips. "Handsome fellow," said the Drin. "What will you offer me if I assist you?"

* * *

Jaqir knew a little of the Drin, the lowest caste of demonkind, who were metalsmiths and artisans of impossible and supernatural ability. He knew, too, as the girl had said, that the Drin required, in exchange for any service to mortals, recompense frequently of a censorable nature. Nor did this Drin seem an exception to the rule.

"Estimable sir," said Jaqir, "did you suppose I needed assistance?"

"I have no doubt of it," said the Drin. "Sometimes I visit the old pest Paztak, and was just now idling in his garden, in chat with a most fascinating woodlouse, when I heard your entreaties, and soon beheld you hurled into this wood. Thinking you more interesting than the mage, I followed. And here I am. What would you have?"

"What would *you* have?" asked Jaqir uneasily.

"Nothing you are not equipped to give."

"Well," said Jaqir resignedly, "we will leave that for the moment. Let *me* first see if you are as cunning as the stories say." And Jaqir thought, pragmatically, *After all, what is a little foul and horrible dreadfulness, if it will save me death?*

Then he told the Drin of the king's edict, and how he, Jaqir the thief, must thieve the Moon.

When he had done speaking, the Drin fell to the ground and rolled amid the fern, laughing, and honking like a goose, in the most repellent manner.

"You cannot do it," assumed Jaqir.

The Drin arose, and shook out his collar and loin-guard of rubies.

"Know me. I am Yulba, pride of my race, revered even among our demonic high castes of Eshva and Vazdru. Yulba, that the matchless lord, Azhrarn the Beautiful, has petted seven hundred times during his walkings up and down in the Underearth."

21

"You are to be envied," said Jaqir prudently. He had heard, too, as who had not who had ever heard tales about the demons, of the Prince of Demons, Azhrarn. "But that does not mean you are able to assist me."

"Pish," said the Drin. "It is a fact, no mortal thing, not even the birds of the air, might fly so high as the Moon, let alone any *man* essay it. But I am Yulba. What cannot Yulba do?"

Three nights Jaqir waited in the forest for Yulba to return. On the third night Yulba appeared out of the trunk of a cedar tree, and after him he hauled a loose, glimmering, almost-silky bundle, that clanked and clacketed as it came.

"Thus," said the Drin, and threw it down.

"What is that?"

"Have you no eyes? A carpet I have created, with the help of some elegant spinners of the eight-legged sort, but reinforced with metals fashioned by myself. Everything as delicate as the wings of bees, strong as the scales of dragons. Imbued by me with spells and vapors of the Underearth, as it is," bragged on the Drin, "the carpet is sorcerous, and will naturally fly. Even as far as the gardens of the stars, from where, though a puny mortal, you may then inspect your quarry, the Moon."

Jaqir, himself an arch-boaster, regarded Yulba narrowly. But then, Jaqir thought, a boaster might also boast truthfully, as he had himself. So as Yulba undid the carpet and spread it out, Jaqir walked on there. The next second Yulba also bounded aboard. At which the carpet, with no effort, rose straight up between the trees of the forest and into the sky of night.

"Now what do you say?" prompted the Drin.

All the demon race were susceptible to flattery. Jaqir spoke many winning sentences of praise, all the while being careful to keep the breadth of the carpet between them.

Up and up the carpet flew. It was indeed very lovely, all woven of blue metals and red metals, and threaded by silk, and here and there set with countless tiny diamonds that spangled like the stars themselves.

But Jaqir was mostly absorbed by the view of the Earth he now had. Far below, itself like a carpet, unrolled the dark forest and then the silvery fields, cut by a river like black mirror. And as they flew higher yet, Jaqir came to see the distant city of the king, like a flower garden of pale lights, and farther again, lay mountains, and the edges of another country. "How small," mused Jaqir, "has been my life. It occurs to me the gods could never understand men's joy or tribulation, for from the height of their dwelling, how tiny we are to them, less than ants."

"Ants have their own recommendations," answered Yulba.

But the Moon was already standing high in the eastern heaven, still round in appearance, and sheerest white as only white could be.

No command needed be given the carpet. Obviously Yulba had already primed it to its destination. It now veered and soared, straight as an arrow, toward the Moon, and as it did so, Jaqir felt the tinsel roots of the lowest stars brush over his forehead.

* * *

And what was the Moon of the Flat Earth, that it might be approached and flown about on a magic carpet? It was, as has been said, maybe a globe containing other lands, but also it was said to be not a globe at all, but, like the Earth itself, a flat disk, yet placed sidelong in the sky, and presenting always a circular wheel of face to the world. And that this globe or disk altered its shape was due to the passage of its own internal sun, now lighting a quarter or a half or a whole of it—or, to the interference of some invisible body coming between it and some other (invisible) light, or to the fact that the Moon was simply a skittish shapechanger, making itself now round, and now a sliver like the paring of a nail.

As they drew ever nearer, Jaqir learned one thing, which in the many stories is a constant—that heat came from the Moon. But (in Jaqir's story) it was an appealing heat, quite welcome in the chilly upper sky. Above, the stars hung, some of them quite close, and they were of all types of shape and shade, all brilliant, but some blindingly so. Of the closer ones, their sparkling roots trailed as if floating in a pond, nourished on some unknown substance. While below, the world seemed only an enormous smudge.

The Drin himself, black eyes glassy, was plainly enraptured by the Moon. Jaqir was caught between wonder and speculation.

Soon enough, the vast luminescence enveloped them, and the heat of the Moon was now like that of a summer morning. Jaqir estimated that the disk might be only the size of a large city, so in his story, that is the size of the Moon.

But Jaqir, as the carpet began obediently to circle round the lunar orb, gazed at it with a proper burglar's care. Soon he could make out details of the surface, which was like nothing so much as an impeccable plate of white porcelain, yet here and there cratered, perhaps by the infrequent fall of a star. And these craters had a dim blue ghostly sheen, like that of a blue beryl.

When the carpet swooped yet nearer in, Jaqir next saw that the plate of the Moon had actually a sort of landscape, for there were kinds of smooth, low, blanched hills, and here and there something which might be a carven watercourse, though without any water in it. And there were also strewn boulders, and other stones, which must be prodigious in girth, but they were all like the rarest pearls.

Jaqir was seized by a desire to touch the surface of the hot, white Moon.

He voiced this.

Yulba scowled, disturbed in his rapturous trance.

"O ignorant man, even my inspired carpet may go no closer, or the magnetic pull of the Moon will tug, and we crash down there."

As he spoke, they passed slowly around the globe, and began moving across the *back* of the Moon, which, until that minute, few mortals had ever seen.

This side lay in a deep violet shadow, turned from the Earth, and tilted upward somewhat at the vault of the sky. It was cooler here, and Jaqir fancied he could hear a strange sound, like harps playing softly, but nothing was to be seen. His hands itched to have something away.

"Peerless Yulba, in order to make a plan of assault, I shall need to get, for reference, some keepsake of the Moon."

"You ask too much," grumbled Yulba.

"Can you not do it? But you are *Yulba*," smarmed Jaqir, "lord among Drin, favorite of the Prince of Demons. What is there Yulba *cannot* do? And, I thought we were to be friends…"

Yulba cast a look at Jaqir, then the Drin frowned at the Moon with such appalling ugliness, Jaqir turned his head.

"I have a certain immense power over stones," said the Drin, "seeing my kind work with them. If I can call you a stone from the Moon, what is it worth?"

Jaqir, who was not above the art of lying either, lied imaginatively at some length, until Yulba lumbered across the carpet and seemed about to demonstrate affection. "*Not* however," declared Jaqir, "any of this, until my task is completed. Do you expect me to be able to concentrate on such events, when my life still hangs by a thread?"

Yulba withdrew once more to the carpet's border. He began a horrible whistling, which set on edge not only Jaqir's teeth but every bone in his body. Nevertheless, in a while, a single pebble, only about the size of an apricot, came flying up and struck Yulba in the eye.

"See—I am blinded!"" screeched Yulba, thrashing on the carpet, but he was not. Nor would he then give up the pebble. But soon enough, as their transport—which by now was apparently tiring—sank away from the Moon, Jaqir rolled a moment against the Drin, as if losing his balance. Thereafter the moon-pebble was in Jaqir's pocket.

What a time they had been on their travels. Even as the carpet flopped, wearily and bumpily now, toward the Earth, a blossoming of rose pink appeared in the east.

This pretty sight, of course, greatly upset Yulba, for demons feared the Sun, and with good reason, it could burn them to ashes.

"Down, down, make haste, accursed flea-bag of a carpet!" ranted he, and so they rapidly fell, and next landed with a splashy thump in a swamp, from which green monkeys and red parakeets erupted at their arrival.

"I shall return at dusk. Remember what I have risked for you!" growled Yulba.

"It is graven on my brain."

Then the Drin vanished into the ground, taking with him the carpet. The Sun rose, and the amazing Moon, now once more far away, faded and set like a dying lamp.

By midday Jaqir had forced a path from the swamp. He sat beneath a mango tree and ate some of the ripe fruit, and stared at the moon-pebble. It shone, even in the daylight, like a milky flame. "You are more wonderful than anything I have ever thieved. But still I do not see how I can rob the sky of that other jewel, the Moon."

Then he considered, for one rash moment, running away. And the safeguarding bonds of the king's magicians twanged around his skeleton. Jaqir desisted, and lay back to sleep.

In sleep, a troop of tormenters paraded.

The cast-off mistress who had betrayed him slapped his face with a wet fish. Yulba strutted, seeming hopeful. Next came men who cried, "Of what worth is this stupid Jaqjr, who has claimed he can steal an egg from beneath a sleeping bird."

Affronted in his slumber, Jaqir truthfully replied that he had done that very thing. But the mockers were gone.

In the dream then Jaqir sat up, and looked once more at the shining pebble lying in his hand.

"Although I might steal a million eggs from beneath a million birds, what use to try for this? I am doomed and shall give in."

Just then something fluttered from the mango tree, which was also there in the dream. It was a small gray parrot. Flying down, it settled directly upon the opalescent stone in Jaqir's palm and put out its light.

"Well, my fine bird, this is no egg for you to hatch."

The parrot spoke. "Think, Jaqir, what you see, and what you say."

Jaqir thought. "Is it possible?"

And at that he woke a second time.

The Sun was high above, and over and over across it and the sky, birds flew about, distinct as black writing on the blue.

"No bird of the air can fly so high as the Moon," said Jaqir. He added, "but the Drin have a mythic knack with magical artifacts and clockworks."

Later, the Sun lowered itself and went down. Yulba came bouncing from the ground, coyly clad in extra rubies, with a garland of lotuses in his hair.

"Now, now," commenced Yulba, lurching forward.

Sternly spoke Jaqir, "I am not yet at liberty, as you are aware. However, I have a scheme. And knowing your unassailable wisdom and authority, only you, the mighty Yulba, best and first among Drin, can manage it."

* * *

In Underearth it was an exquisite dusk. It was always dusk there, or a form of dusk. As clear as day in the upper world, it was said, yet more radiantly somber. Sunless, naturally, for the reasons given above.

Druhim Vanashta, the peerless city of demonkind, stretched in a noose of shimmering nonsolar brilliance, out of which pierced, like needles, chiseled towers of burnished steel and polished corundum, domes of faceted crystal. While about the gem-paved streets and sable parks strolled or paced or strode or lingered the demons. Night-black of hair and eye, snow-frozen-white of complexion, the high-caste Vazdru and their mystic servants, the Eshva. All of whom were so painfully beautiful, it amounted to an insult.

Presently, along an avenue, there passed Azhrarn, Prince of Demons, riding a black horse, whose mane and tail was hyacinth blue. And if the beauty of the Eshva and Vazdru amounted to an insult, that of Azhrarn was like the stroke of death.

He seemed himself idle enough, Azhrarn. He seemed, too, musing on something as he slowly rode, oblivious, it appeared, to those who bowed to the pavement at his approach, whose eyes had spilled, at sight of him, looks of adoration. They were all in love with Azhrarn. A voice spoke from nowhere at all.

"Azhrarn, Lord Wickedness, you gave up the world, but the world does not give up you. O Azhrarn, Master of Night, what are the Drin doing by their turgid lake, hammering and hammering?"

Azhrarn had reined in the demon horse. He glanced leisurely about.

Minutes elapsed. He too spoke, and his vocality was like the rest of him. "The Drin do hammer at things. That is how the Drin pass most of eternity."

"Yet how," said the voice, "do *you* pass eternity, Lord Wickedness?"

"Who speaks to me?" softly said Azhrarn.

The voice replied, "Perhaps merely yourself, the part of you that you discard, the part of you which yearns after the world."

"Oh," said Azhrarn. "The world."

The voice did not pronounce another syllable, but along an adjacent wall a slight mark appeared, rather like a scorch.

Azhrarn rode on. The avenue ended at a park, where willows of liquid amber let down their watery resinous hair, to a mercury pool. Black peacocks with seeing eyes of turquoise and emerald in their tails turned their heads and all their feathers to gaze at him.

From between the trees came three Eshva, who obeised themselves.

"What," said Azhrarn, "are the Drin making by their lake?"

The Eshva sighed voluptuously. The sighs said (for the Eshva never used ordinary speech), "The Drin are making metal birds."

"Why?" said Azhrarn.

The Eshva grew downcast; they did not know. Melancholy enfolded them among the tall black grasses of the lawn, and then one of the Vazdru princes came walking through the garden.

"Yes?" said Azhrarn.

"My Prince, there is a Drin who was to fashion for me a ring, which he has neglected," said the Vazdru. "He is at some labor for a human man he is partial to. They are *all* at this labor."

Azhrarn, interested, was, for a moment, more truly revealed. The garden waxed dangerously brighter, the mercury in the pool boiled. The amber hardened and the peacocks shut every one of their four hundred fifty eyes.

"Yes?" Azhrarn murmured again.

"The Drin, who is called Yulba, has lied to them all. He has told them you yourself, my matchless lord, require a million clockwork birds that can fly as high as the Earth's Moon. Because of *this*, they work ceaselessly. This Yulba is a nuisance. When he is found out, they will savage him, then bury him in some cavern, walling it up with rocks, leaving him there a million years for his million birds. And so I shall not receive my ring."

Azhrarn smiled. Cut by the smile, as if by the slice of a sword, leaves scattered from the trees. It was suddenly autumn in the garden. When autumn stopped, Azhrarn had gone away.

Chang-thrang went the Drin hammers by the lake outside Druhim Vanashta. *Whirr* and *pling* went the uncanny mechanisms of half-formed sorcerous birds of cinnabar, bronze, and iron. Already-finished sorcerous birds hopped and flapped about the lakeshore, frightening the beetles and snakes. Mechanical birds flew over in curious formations, like demented swallows, darkening the Underearth's gleaming day-dusk, now and then letting fall droppings of a peculiar sort.

Eshva came and went, drifting on Vazdru errands. Speechless inquiries wafted to the Drin caves: Where is the necklace of rain vowed for the Princess Vasht? Where is the singing book reserved for the Prince Hazrond?

"We are busy elsewhere at Azhrarn's order," chirped the Drin.

They were all dwarfs, all hideous, and each one lethal, ridiculous, and a genius. Yulba strode among them, criticizing their work, so now and then there was also a fight for the flying omnipresent birds to unburden their bowels upon.

How had Yulba fooled the Drin? He was no more Azhrarn's favorite than any of them. All the Drin boasted as Yulba had. Perhaps it was only this: Turning his shoulder to the world of mankind, Azhrarn had forced the jilted world to pursue him underground. In ways both graphic and insidious, the rejected one permeated Underearth. Are you tired of me? moaned the world to Azhrarn. Do you hate me? Do I bore you? See how inventive I am. See how I can still ensnare you fast.

But Azhrarn did not go to the noisy lake. He did not summon Yulba. And Yulba, puffed with his own cleverness, obsessively eager to hold Jaqir to his bargain, had forgotten all accounts have a reckoning. *Chung-clungk* went the hammers. *Brakk* went the thick heads of the Drin, banged together by critical, unwise Yulba.

Then at last the noise ended.

The hammering and clamoring were over.

Of the few Vazdru who had come to stare at the birds, less than a few remarked that the birds had vanished.

* * *

The Drin were noted skulking about their normal toil again, constructing wondrous jewelry and toys for the upper demons. If they waited breathlessly for Azhrarn to compliment them on their bird-work, they did so in vain. But such omissions had happened in the past, the never-ceasing past-present-future of Underearth.

Just as they might have pictured him, Azhrarn stood in a high window of Druhim Vanashta, looking at his city of needles and crystals.

Perhaps it was seven mortal days after the voice had spoken to him. Perhaps three months.

He heard a sound within his mind. It was not from his city, nor was it unreal. Nor actual. Presently he sought a magical glass that would show him the neglected world.

How ferocious, the stars, how huge and cruelly glittering, like daggers. How they exalted, unrivaled now.

The young king went one by one to all the windows of his palace. Like Azhrarn miles below (although he did not know it), the young king looked a long while at his city. But mostly he looked up into the awful sky.

29

Thirty-three nights had come and gone, without the rising of the Moon.

In the king's city there had been at first shouts of bewildered amazement. Then prayers. Then, a silence fell which was as loud as screaming.

If the world had lost the Sun, the world would have perished and died. But losing the Moon, it was as if the soul of this world had been put out.

Oh those black nights, blacker than blackness, those yowling spikes of stars dancing in their vitriolic glory—which gave so little light.

What murders and rapes and worser crimes were committed under cover of such a dark? As if a similar darkness had been called up from the mental guts of mankind, like subservient to like. While earth-over, priests offered to the gods, who never noticed.

The courtiers who had applauded, amused, the judgment of the witty young king, now shrank from him. He moved alone through the excessively lamped and benighted palace, wondering if he was now notorious through all the world for his thoughtless error. And so wondering, he entered the room where, on their marble pedestals, perched his angels.

"What have you done?" said the king.

Not a feather stirred. Not an eye winked.

"By the gods—may they forgive me—what? What did you make *me* do?"

"You are king," said the scarlet parrot. "It is your word, not ours, which is law."

And the blue parrot said, "We are parrots, why name us angels? We have been taught to speak, that is all. What do you expect?"

And the jade parrot said, "I forget now what it was you asked of us." And put its head under its wing.

Then the king turned to the gray parrot. "What do you have to say? It was your final advice which drove me to demand the Moon be stolen—as if I thought any man might do it."

"King," said the gray parrot, "it was your sport to call four parrots, angels. Your sport to offer a man an impossible task as the alternative to certain death. You have lived as if living is a silly game. But you are mortal, and a king."

"You shame me," said the king.

30

"We are, of course," said the gray parrot, "truly angels, disguised. To shame men is part of our duty."

"What must I do?"

The gray parrot said, "Go down, for Jaqir, Thief of Thieves, has returned to your gate. And he is followed by his shadow."

"Are not all men so followed?" asked the king perplexedly.

The parrot did not speak again.

L et it be said, Jaqir, who now entered the palace, between the glaring, staring guards of the king, was himself in terrible awe at what he had achieved. Ever since succeeding at his task, he had not left off trembling inwardly. However, outwardly he was all smiles, and in his best attire.

"See, the wretch's garments are as fine as a lord's. His rings are gold. Even his shadow looks well dressed! And this miscreant it is who has stolen the Moon and ruined the world with blackest night."

The king stood waiting, with the court about him.

Jaqir bowed low. But that was all he did, after which *he* stood waiting, meeting the king's eyes with his own.

"Well," said the king. "It seems you have done what was asked of you."

"So it does seem," said Jaqir calmly.

"Was it then easy?"

"As easy," said Jaqir, "as stealing an egg."

"But," said the king. He paused, and a shudder ran over the hall, a shuddering of men and women, and also of the flames in all the countless lamps.

"But?" pressed haughty Jaqir.

"It might be said by some, that the Moon—which is surely not an egg—has disappeared, and another than you may have removed it. After all," said the king stonily, "if one assumes the Moon may be pilfered at all, how am I to be certain the robber is yourself? Maybe others are capable of it. Or, too, a natural disaster has simply overcome the orb, a coincidence most convenient for you."

"Sir," said Jaqir, "were you not the king, I would answer you in other words that I do. But king you are. And I have proof."

And then Jaqir took out from his embroidered shirt the moon-pebble, which even in the light of the lamps blazed with a perfect whiteness. And so like the Moon it was for radiance that many at once shed tears of nostalgia on seeing it. While at Jaqir's left shoulder, his night-black shadow seemed for an instant also to flicker with fire.

As for the king, now he trembled too. But like Jaqir, he did not show it.

"Then," said the king, "be pardoned of your crimes. You have surmounted the test, and are directly loosed from those psychic bonds my magicians set on you, therefore entirely physically at liberty, and besides, a legendary hero. One last thing…"

"Yes?" asked Jaqir.

"Where have you put it?"

"What?" said Jaqir, rather stupidly.

"That which you stole."

"It was not a part of our bargain, to tell you this. You have seen by the proof of this stone I have got the Moon. Behold, the sky is black."

The king said quietly, "You do not mean to keep it."

"Generally I do keep what I take."

"I will give you great wealth, Jaqir, which I think anyway you do not need, for they say you are as rich as I. Also, I will give you a title to rival my own. You can have what you wish. Now swear you will return the Moon to the sky."

Jaqir lowered his eyes.

"I must consider this."

"Look," they whispered, the court of the king, "even his shadow listens to him."

Jaqir, too, felt his shadow listening at his shoulder.

He turned, and found the shadow had eyes.

Then the shadow spoke, more quietly than the king, and not one in the hall did not hear it. While every flame in every lamp spun like a coin, died, revived, and continued burning upside down.

"King, you are a fool. Jaqir, you are another fool. And who and what am I?"

Times had changed. There are always stories, but they are not always memorized. Only the king, and Jaqir the thief, had the understanding to plummet to their knees. And they cried as one, *"Azhrarn!"*

"Walk upon the terrace with me," said Azhrarn. "We will admire the beauty of the leaden night."

The king and Jaqir found that they got up, and went on to the terrace, and no one else stirred, not even hand or eye.

Around the terrace stood some guards like statues. At the terrace's center stood a chariot that seemed constructed of black and silver lava, and drawn by similarly laval dragons.

"Here is our conveyance," said Azhrarn, charmingly. "Get in."

In they got, the king and the thief. Azhrarn also sprang up, and took and shook the reins of the dragons, and these great ebony lizards hissed and shook out in turn their wings, which clapped against the black night and seemed to strike off bits from it. Then the chariot dove up into the air, shaking off the Earth entire, and green sparks streamed from the chariot-wheels.

Neither the king nor Jaqir had stamina—or idiocy—enough to question Azhrarn. They waited meekly as two children in the chariot's back, gaping now at Azhrarn's black eagle wings of cloak, that every so often buffeted them, almost breaking their ribs, or at the world falling down and down below like something dropped.

But then, high in the wild, tipsy-making upper air, Jaqir did speak, if not to Azhrarn.

"King, I tricked you. I did not steal the Moon."

"Who then stole it?"

"No one."

"A riddle."

At which they saw Azhrarn had partly turned. They glimpsed his profile, and a single eye that seemed more like the night than the night itself was. And they shut their mouths.

On raced the dragons.

Below raced the world.

Then everything came to a halt. Combing the sky with claws and wheels, dragons and chariot stood static on the dark.

Azhrarn let go the jewelry reins.

All around spangled the stars. These now appeared less certain of themselves. The brighter ones had dimmed their glow, the lesser hid behind the vapors of night. Otherwise, everywhere lay blackness, only that.

In the long, musician's fingers of the Prince of Demons was a silver pipe, shaped like some sort of slender bone. Azhrarn blew upon the pipe.

There was no sound, yet something seemed to pass through the skulls

33

of the king and of Jaqir, as if a barbed thread had been pulled through from ear to ear. The king swooned—he was only a king. Jaqir rubbed his temples and stayed upright—he was a professional of the working classes.

And so it was Jaqir who saw, in reverse, that which he had already seen happen the other way about.

He beheld a black cloud rising (where before it had settled) and behind the cloud, suddenly something incandescent blinked and dazzled. He beheld how the cloud, breaking free of these blinks of palest fire (where before it had obscured said fire) ceased to be one entity, and became instead one million separate flying pieces. He saw, as he had seen before when first they burst up from the ground in front of him, and rushed into the sky, that these were a million curious birds. They had feathers of cinnabar and bronze, sinews of brass; they had clockworks of iron and steel.

Between the insane crowded battering of their wings, Jaqir watched the Moon reappear, where previously (scanning the night, as he stood by Yulba in a meadow) he had watched the Moon *put out,* all the birds flew down against her, covering and smothering her.

Unbroken by their landing on her surface, they had roosted there, drawn to and liking the warmth, as Yulba had directed them with his sorcery.

But now Azhrarn had negated Yulba's powers—which were little enough among demons. The mechanical birds swarmed round and round the chariot, aggravating the dragons somewhat. The birds had no eyes, Jaqir noticed. They gave off great heat where the Moon had toasted their metals. Jaqir looked at them as if for the first, hated them, and grew deeply embarrassed.

Yet the Moon—oh, the Moon. Uncovered and alight, how brilliantly it or she blazed now. Had she ever been so bright? Had her sojourn in darkness done her good?

End to end, she poured her flame over the Earth below. Not a mountain that did not have its spire of silver, not a river its highlight of diamond. The seas lashed and struggled with joy, leaping to catch her snows upon the crests of waves and dancing dolphins. And in the windows of mankind, the lamps were doused, and like the waves, men leaned upward to wash their faces in the Moon.

Then gradually, a murmur, a thunder, a roar, a gushing sigh rose swirling from the depths of the Flat Earth, as if at last the world had stopped holding its breath.

"What did you promise Yulba," asked Azhrarn of Jaqir, mild as a killing frost, "in exchange for this slight art?"

"The traditional favor," muttered Jaqir.

"Did he receive payment?"

"I prevaricated. Not yet, lord Prince."

"You are spared then. Part of his punishment shall be permanently to avoid your company. But what punishment for you, thief? And what punishment for your king?"

Jaqir did not speak. Nor did the king, though he had recovered his senses.

Both men were educated in the tales, the king more so. Both men turned ashen, and the king accordingly more ashen.

Then Azhrarn addressed the clockwork birds in one of the demon tongues, and they were immediately gone. And only the white banner of the moonlight was there across the night.

Now Azhrarn, by some called also Lord of Liars, was not perhaps above lying in his own heart. It seems so. Yet maybe tonight he looked upon the Moon, and saw in the Moon's own heart, the woman that once he had loved, the woman who had been named for the Moon. Because of her, and all that had followed, Azhrarn had turned his back upon the world—or attempted to turn it.

And even so here he was, high in the vault of the world's heaven, drenched in earthly moonshine, contemplating the chastisement of mortal creatures whose lives, to his immortal life, were like the green sparks which had flashed and withered on the chariot-wheels.

The chariot plunged. The atmosphere scalded at the speed of its descent. It touched the skin of the Earth more slightly than a cobweb. The mortal king and the mortal thief found themselves rolling away downhill, toward fields of barley and a river. The chariot, too, was gone. Although in their ears as they rolled, equal in their rolling as never before, and soon never to be again, king and thief heard Azhrarn's extraordinary voice, which said, "Your punishment you have already. You are human. I cannot improve upon that."

Thus, the Moon shone in the skies of night, interrupted only by an infrequent cloud. The king resumed his throne. The four angels—

35

who were or were not parrots—or only meddlers—sat on their perches waiting to give advice, or to avoid giving it. And Jaqir—Jaqir went away to another city.

Here, under a different name, he lived on his extreme wealth, in a fine house with gardens. Until one day he was robbed of all his gold (and even of the moon-pebble) by a talented thief. "Is it the gods who exact their price at last, or Another, who dwells farther down?" But by then Jaqir was older, for mortal lives moved and move swiftly. He had lost his taste for his work by then. So he returned to the king's city, and to the door of the merchant's wife who had been his mistress. "I am sorry for what I said to you," said Jaqir. "I am sorry for what I did to you," said she. The traveling merchant had recently departed on another, more prolonged journey, to make himself, reincarnation-wise, a new life after death. Meanwhile, though the legend of a moon-thief remained, men had by then forgotten Jaqir. So he married the lady and they existed not unhappily, which shows their flexible natures.

But miles below, Yulba did not fare so well.

For Azhrarn had returned to the Underearth on the night of the Moon's rescue, and said to him, "Bad little Drin. Here are your million birds. Since you are so proud of them, be one of them." And in this way Azhrarn demonstrated that the world no longer mattered to him a jot, only his own kind mattered enough that he would make their lives Hell-under-Earth. Or, so it would seem.

But Yulba had changed to a clockwork bird, number one million and one. Eyeless, still able to see, flapping over the melanic vistas of the demon country, blotting up the luminous twilight, cawing, clicking, letting fall droppings, yearning for the warmth of the Moon, yearning to be a Drin again, yearning for Azhrarn, and for Jaqir—who by that hour had already passed himself from the world, for demon time was not the time of mortals.

As for the *story*, that of Jaqir and Yulba and the Moon, it had become as it had and has become, or *un*-become. And who knows but that, in another little while, it will be forgotten, as most things are. Even the Moon is no longer *that* Moon, nor the Earth, nor the sky. The centuries fly, eternity is endless.

The Snake

The snake lay under a low, flowering tree, at the side of the forest path. The snake seemed like a small spill of amber that the sun had firmed and coined with scales.

A woman passed, on broad, bare feet. The snake watched from eyes like darts, but did not change its position. Later a scholar wandered by, gazing at this and that. He paused some while to inhale the perfume of the flowers, leaning into the lower branches of the tree, but his mind was so fixed on the minutiae of esoteric things, he never glimpsed the snake. The snake however saw the scholar, and watched him, yet did not stir, made no move either to strike at him or to retreat. Eventually the scholar wandered off into the forest, thinking of stars and gods and other lives he had lived.

An hour later a young man came riding along the path on the back of a jet-black horse. It was adorned with golden bells and had a garland round its neck, and the rider was elegantly dressed in satin and silk, with boots of fine blond leather. He was handsome also, and seemed happy, looking up into the sky as if he saw in it all sorts of kind and generous creatures, each of whom smiled lovingly back at him.

The snake suddenly flickered its amber tail.

Though small, the snake by its action caused the lower and most flowery branches of the tree to begin shaking. *Swish-swish* they went— and the rider glanced down at them.

"The favorite flower!" he exclaimed. And dismounting gracefully at once, he reached into the tree to snap off the largest bloom. In less than a second the snake uncoiled all its length and rose upright on its tail. Its shining head shot forward. A single hiss escaped its jaws—and its poisonous fangs stabbed deep into the young man's palm.

As gleaming death spilled from his fingers he stood transfixed. He stared at his hand, then upward at the sky that, moments before, had been so crowded with sweetness, yet now seemed filled with fire and doom. For him it was. He stiffened, choked. Tears poured from his eyes. Rigid as a stone statue he crashed to the ground, where two or three inadvertent stony ripples ran over his body, after which he was motionless, and dead as yesterday.

The horse, frightened, galloped off along the path. The snake too had vanished.

Perhaps three hundred heartbeats after, a noise of music and laughter began to be audible, and then a large company of riders, all richly clad and mounted on horses strung with bells, came dancingly into view.

Instantly an awful cry went up. The cavalcade was halted.

Living men bent over the dead man on the path.

"Look, see there, the marks on his palm. Already he is turning black with venom."

"And the flower beside him," said one, "he went to the tree and plucked it for her, since this one is her favorite. But he disturbed a snake—"

"The gods," said another, "can never be trusted."

Zerezel waited among her maidens, on the terrace before her father's palace, all morning, and through the flame of noon, the thick gilt of afternoon. At first they joked: Had the handsome prince met another he preferred on the very road to his wedding? And they were amused, for they, and she, knew he loved only Zerezel, while even the patterns of the stars had confirmed this. Then more serious things were said—the great forest was full of tigers and lynx, robbers, ghosts—but certainly the young prince was brave and intelligent enough to defeat or elude all such dangers. Besides, he had ridden that way before, and now as always traveled with a vast company of men and servants. Perhaps he might have ridden a little ahead, impatient to reach his lover, but only by three hundred heartbeats, or four hundred heartbeats—no more.

When the gilded afternoon turned to jasper and swung low into the western sky, the old prince, Zerezel's father, sent some of his soldiers out along the road.

Then the maidens began to weep. It was Zerezel who calmed them. She moved among them gently, with her long hair that was the color of the western sky, her slender wrists ringed by pearl. "All will be well." But there began to be a shadow on her beautiful face. For now it was the time for shadows. They rose up full length and stood on their tails among the carved and painted trees of columns, they spread like poisonous stains over the patterned floors. And then the shadows burst out of the forest, shouting and calling, and making too a sound like that sound a heart makes, when it falls down through some inner chamber of the body, and into a place of blackness under the earth which men say does not exist, and which does *not*, yet which any who have ever suffered

38

know, and have visited often.

"He is dead, Princess. He is dead."

"*Is* he dead?" she asked. "Why, then, so is the world."

And so for her the world died. And she went in and lay down, and the edges of her bridal robes, and her marigold hair, poured like tears along the floor, and the darkness could come up from the hell under the earth, and veil it all in black.

"**S**he will die too."
This was what they said.

It was known by then also that her betrothed had plucked a flower for her, her favorite flower that did not anymore grow in his own land. And that was how he met the snake and death. She lay in her apartment, on a floor, and drank nothing and nibbled at the air. She heard no one speak to her. She said not a word. Only the medicinal spells of sages kept her in her body, and this barely.

A month passed from the calendar.

Another month began to pass.

"Send," her father said, "to the four corners of the earth, send to the tops of mountains and the cellars of the seas, to deserts of sand or wind or snow. Tell any there anything I can give them I will render, to one that can save my daughter."

The messengers rode out. They scattered like thrown grains of rice along the world.

They had a great many adventures on their various journeys, each of which, probably, would crowd a whole book. But there was one among them, Keshom by name, who traveled northward and then farther north, beyond the limit of any then-drawn map.

Gradually, the land turned cold, and white. Keshom assumed this was from that fabled element known as "snow," which clothed the heights of the tallest mountains—apparently. Yet here, the land was not so tall. It went up and down, and the *white,* which was like marble, or purified cream, was combed all over it. Here and there too Keshom seemed to see some word or other, even now and then—if only when he was very tired—whole sentences decoratively written on it... Most strange.

After a while, however, the terrain did rise consistently. So Keshom,

39

of course, rode upward with it.

All at once he came over a kind of ridge—and there before him stretched what he took at first to be some giant's smashed mirror of corrupt and misted glass. From its center lifted a curious tower, very black, but with veins of a glistening red.

Presently he realized, as if reason only now returned to him, that the area of broken glass ahead was a lake, seemingly frozen.

Meanwhile a red light had burgeoned at the apex of the tower.

Exactly then there occurred a snowfall.

Keshom sat his horse, and he and it observed how this snow dropped everywhere. The messenger put out his hand and caught one flake, and peered at it in dismay. For there *was* a word on it, and so it seemed to him, written clearly, and he read it. *Thus,* it said. But then snowflake and word melted together. Keshom was glad.

He did not advance until the snowfall ended. But when it did, he picked toward the tower.

"Does some mage live there?"

Prudently, rather than cross the ice, Keshom rode around the lake, and after perhaps three-tenths of an hour, he reached a causeway of high snowy stone, which led out to the tower. Nothing marked this but for a great skull at its beginning, which Keshom took to be that of a tiger or leopard. It was black.

From the vantage of the causeway he could see a single window that burned with a cool gray light, and matched the heavy sky now settling to evening.

Keshom went along the causeway and arrived at the base of the tower.

Above in the gray window nothing had been, or was to be seen, and there was no indication of a door whereon to knock, let alone to enter by.

But Keshom raised his well-trained voice.

"My prince sends me, as one of his messengers, to all four corners of the earth, to mountaintops and sea cellars, to deserts of sand, wind, and snow. I am to tell you, he will give anything he can render to one that can save his daughter."

"What is this daughter's name?" said another male voice.

It seemed to speak directly in Keshom's ear, and was both quiet and overwhelming at the same time.

40

Keshom shook his head to clear it of the sound. He thought, *This one has power.*

He answered, "Zerezel."

At this a huge panel slid back in the tower-side. Beyond, Keshom saw a dimness, lit only by the failing light of evening. Yet through the dim appeared a flight of cranky steps.

"Enter," said the other voice, more softly and even more distinctly now.

Keshom hesitated. "Great sir," said he, "may I ask *your* name?"

"Thus," said the voice.

And on the stair a line of gray tapers lit, to indicate, needlessly, the way.

𝕴n the far country where Zerezel lay suspended between life and death, albeit with one of her narrow feet already well across death's threshold, a full year had been sloughed from the calendar.

The old prince had aged not one but a hundred years. His complexion and hair were white as any supernatural snow. And if a word were written on *him* it was *Despair,* plain for all to see. He paced about night and day. Only once at each dawn and once at each moonrise would he step into his daughter's chamber, where by now they had laid her on a couch. She herself was beyond all human contact. Her slenderness had grown thin, and in her bright hair too some strands of white had appeared. Her eyes were shut. She did not speak, and only a physician's glass could show she breathed. She had no awareness of the world that had died for her, nor of any person in it. She had lost everything but one thing, and that was her beauty, which still clothed her like wedding finery, impervious. Only magic kept her alive, and this was *all* it could do. And often now, gazing at her actually lifeless deathlessness, her father would chide himself, and believe he should order the safeguards removed, that she could fully die and have peace. For perhaps in the waste of the deadlands she might find her beloved again. But the old prince had never been certain any afterlife existed, despite the teachings of the priests. For if it did, and was worth anything, why had the gods themselves preferred to be immortal?

And perhaps one can be found who will save her...

But few of the messengers had returned, and those that had brought no help. In every country they had encountered not a single man or woman of power who had reckoned themselves able to assist. "We can part oceans and topple stars," they would say, "but Lord Death we may not bargain with. And since only her lover, restored to life, would bring your princess from her deadly state, save her we cannot. Nor none can. Such a love as hers, broken, slays those who otherwise would not die. For such a love is greater than death. Go home then. We offer nothing but to pull down another star."

There was an evening when it was to be a night of no moon. On such a night the old prince spared himself a visit to Zerezel's chamber. As he sat alone, a servant came to him and told him the messenger Keshom waited nearby.

Soon Keshom knelt before the prince.

"Sir, I bring news."

The old man stared at him with a heart that quailed. Keshom looked stern and troubled. But then he spoke:

"In the farthest north, among the dry white snows, I chanced on a magician of extraordinary power. For name he takes only the word *Thus*. But he has said to me he alone can rid your daughter, exquisite Zerezel, of her killing sorrow. And I was convinced." Keshom's face, during these sentences, had altered. He seemed merely earnest now, and perhaps his former look had been due to exhaustion.

The old prince rose to his feet. He summoned his court to hear what Keshom had said, and what else he had to say. Keshom continued:

Having left his horse at the base of the tower, he climbed the stair in the half-light for several minutes, until he emerged directly into a vast stone space, lit with a sort of dusk, above which, in the ceiling, burned a nonilluminating red glow like that of a setting sun.

No other was to be seen, though on all sides were cabinets stacked with scrolls of vellum, and large books bound in ebony and horn, or else in what seemed to be black or white human skin. The whole area was round and had no corners. But at the walls, equidistant from each other, were four stone beasts. One was like a griffen, and one an alligator, one a man with the head of a dog, and one a fox with the face of a child. Each of these creatures had in its forehead a jewel. The eagle brow of the griffen had a jaundiced topaz, and that of the alligator a sable pearl; the dog-headed man bore a dull purplish spinel, but the child-faced fox wore a gem Keshom had neither seen before nor heard of—it was the color of decay. From the jaws of each beast there curled out vapor. But this was odorless and faint, neither increasing nor ceasing.

Keshom had paused, rather terrified, yet in command of himself, for he had been well trained in his duties.

At length the disembodied and inimical voice he had heard outside spoke to him again from the air.

"Shall I appear?"

"That would be welcome," said Keshom.

"Do you suppose so?" the voice asked ominously.

Abruptly a cloud-like fog filled the space. It did not issue from the mouths of the four beasts, but simply straight down from the redness above.

It swirled then cleared, and when it had done so a tawny leopard crouched there, in the chamber's center. It snarled at Keshom too, showing off its fangs and its blood-red mouth. But Keshom did nothing. He waited.

Then the pelt of the leopard wrinkled and poured off, and it stood upright and became a tall and slender man, whose golden hair flowed from his head over his wide shoulders. He was clothed in velvet. His face, as Keshom currently told the old prince, was of a wonderful handsomeness. Never, said Keshom, had he seen any man, nor even a woman, aside from Zerezel, whose beauty was as noble, or as instantaneously persuasive.

"Now, besides knowing the name I use, you behold my true human likeness," said the paragon to Keshom.

Keshom bowed low. "Sir," he said, "the sun has set on the world. I must ask if you are one of the Demonkind? Even if you are their lord, Azhrarn himself?"

["Indeed," murmured several of the prince's court when they heard this, "and was he as beautiful as *that?*"]

But the man, the magician, had only smiled a little at Keshom's inquiry. "Unlike that of any demon, my hair is yellow," said he, playfully quite underestimating the glamour of his hair. "Besides, note that I wear golden rings, as no demon could, or would deign to do. No, I am not one of Azhrarn's fine troupe, though others now and then have made the same error as yourself." Keshom once more bowed low. The magician resumed. "I know of your master's daughter, Princess Zerezel. She is said to be the fairest maiden now living. What therefore ails her that she must be saved from it?"

43

Keshom punctually related the tragic events. He added that she lay now close to death, while her father, and all the land, mourned.

"And can none of your own scholars offer rescue?"

"None. Nor any other I have met with, despite great ability. For they say love is stronger than death. And such a love it is that slays her."

A change passed over the face of he who named himself solely *Thus*. While across the room, the stone beast that resembled a child-faced fox blinked both its eyes—even Keshom gasped—and the mortifying jewel in its forehead gleamed for an instant coldly green.

"I have heard this said before," murmured the magician, "this of love and death. Very well. Return to your prince. Tell him I alone can save Zerezel. But my price shall be high."

"He would give you his *own* life, great magus, I assure you, in payment."

"And so I should," agreed the old prince now. "Oh, can it be possible her savior is at hand? But," he added, "where is he? Surely he has traveled with you."

"No, sir. He said he would remain in his northern tower until your answer."

"Alas! The way is so long, never now will he reach us in time—for despite any magic woven about her, I can no longer blind myself—she sinks and fades like guttering candleshine."

Outside a wind blew along the terraces of the palace, and the forest trees bowed down as it went by. A vague smoke for a moment seemed to hide the stars.

"Fear nothing," said a voice at the old prince's ear. "I am already with you."

And there he was, the magician, tall and fabulous as Keshom had described him, or more so perhaps, much more.

The Prince spoke to him without faltering, also well trained in his duties. "Lord Magus, you are welcome as summer. But how am I to call you?"

"As your slave did. *Thus*. For that is my name."

It had not, however, always been his name.

Some twenty odd years before that moonless night, the magnificent and puissant magus, Thus, was only a spindly youth, drab of skin and shaven-headed, who drove camels for an unkind master, and went by the name of Drahn—which meant, in those regions, *Hardship*.

Drahn had been sold to camel work, at the age of six, by his mother, who demonstrably had not wanted him. If anything, she had been more unkind even than his owner, who through the ten years of their acquaintance simply half-starved him, and whipped him if he transgressed—only punching and kicking him groundlessly during bouts of drunken wrath. The camels were also harsh with Drahn, being themselves ill-treated. They too kicked him, and stinkingly spat at him. One morning, the most violent of them, a huge red animal, kicked Drahn so cruelly he lost his senses. And when he woke again, the caravan had moved on, either not noticing they had mislaid Drahn, or reckoning him worth less than other rubbish shed along the route.

Where Drahn had dropped was in the middle of a desert—this one not of snow but *salt*.

Here for two or three blazing days, and the cold nights between, he staggered or crawled about, croaking with thirst and fear.

Finally he tumbled down a slope and fetched up by a horrible little pond of black, salty liquid. Nevertheless, partially crazed, Drahn attempted to drink it. The result was ungood.

After this episode he abandoned himself to death.

He was accordingly amazed to be woken by a tall, ancient man, who held a flask of clean water to Drahn's lips, and firstly prevented him from drinking too much, which after the dearth, would have killed him more certainly than his thirst.

One salt-preserved tree grew by the pond. It had a whitish trunk and even leaves, these like strips of fossilized gum.

Here the ancient man sat sheltering, and Drahn beside him, while the blade of the sun sliced its slow agony from east to west.

Drahn had little social chat.

Neither had the ancient one. *He* spoke only facts.

"I am glad to have met with you, Drahn," he said, "since Lord Fate decrees I must perish here of old age, and all my mighty magecraft cannot prevent it."

"Pah! What magecraft, you old goat?" politely inquired Drahn, who of course had learnt his manners from sadists and camels.

"Why, lad. Such as this—"

At which the filthy pond-puddle changed to a pool of crystal water, and the salted-down tree to a towering palm, pineapple-trunked, with fronds like malachite.

"Ahhh!" screamed Drahn.

"Yes, yes. But to continue. I have been caught unawares by my own demise—which I confess I had not bothered to predict, which prediction in any case is an inexact science, just as King Death himself does not always know when he must rise up and strike us down. Unawares, I say, I despaired of finding any to whom I might pass on such quantities of power as I contain. (For you must understand, I possess also the knack of gifting my brilliance to anyone, at my death.) However, despair begone! Here *you* are! And yes, poor boy, you are such a ghastly specimen, ugly, brainless, and vile, that I shall be able to fill you to the brim with greatness, glory, strength, and genius, not to mention vast physical beauty, and magery beyond all dreams. *You* will far excel even myself. For I was cultured, a clever and educated man at the hour these attributes came to me, and handsome too. Which left less room for improvement. With *you,* the tide of power will work in unimpeded transfer. The dreary vacant vessel which is yourself will be flooded, and so enlarge. After all, it is always better to gather water in an empty jar. Or write on a blank page." (Drahn snorted and gobbled in confusion.) Taking no notice, the sage finalized: "Now brace yourself for the torrent of benefits. Also for extreme amounts of time in which to exercise and enjoy them. For though this cannot make you either invulnerable or immortal, and one day you, as I, must die (and should be careful meanwhile of accidents), with reasonable care longevity is yours. I myself have lived hundreds of years. But death encroaches. I feel his hand upon me—therefore, receive all—*Thus!*"

Then the sage stretched out his own hand, and as one finger of it touched Drahn, a blow far more conclusive than that of a camel's hoof threw him into oblivion.

Waking the gods knew how much later, he found himself in a luxurious oasis of palms, dates, and orange trees, where wholesome fountains sparkled, and deer and hyenas drank together in harmony at the lustrous pool. The sage had vanished. Only some bones, picked pristine, lay along the pool's rim.

And Drahn? Drahn was gone.

The *he* that had woken was not the *he* that he had been.

In the water, he saw the new *he* that he now was.

And presently, without effort translocating himself from the oasis to some other spot miles off, he laughed aloud and renamed himself: for the last word he had heard when in mundane human form.

𝕿he old prince and his court conducted the Magician Thus solemnly up the winding ways of the palace, to the life-death chamber of Princess Zerezel.

All were afraid—but the magician.

They flung open the doors—an *act* of fear.

Beyond the extended teardrops of windows, the moonless night hung black as a curtain, torn and fanged with stars.

In the glimmer of a solitary lamp, a single couch. And on the couch lay Zerezel. Hair of sunset and winter frost. Skin of silk and silence. Beauty of the world, *despising* the world. Alive. Dead. In her wedding garments of baffled, thwarted love.

Not a word, let alone a phrase, was spoken by any of them.

Not even Thus spoke in his mage's voice.

Keshom though, who had come up to the chamber with the rest, glanced at the magician warily. And saw that in the magus' face the skull stood out like a knife.

Then he alone moved forward, the magician Thus, and standing by her bed, he looked directly down at her. If never before had he seen her, surely even like this, he must love her now. If ever before he *had* seen Zerezel, he must have loved her then.

He was, it was a fact, much handsomer than the man she had adored and meant to wed. Thus truly did possess the perfect gorgeousness credited to demons.

And when he bent toward her, and his mane of hair, in the lamp's low gleam like a rush of volcanic rain, furled round her, who could not believe that these moments had been preordained. As, in a way, they had.

𝕿he sage's tower, when Drahn-now-Thus had first came to it, rose from a lake of glassy water, amid a plain of blowing grass. It was, the tower, of marble, and veined with luminous rainbow colors. Imbued with the learning, wisdom, sorcerous genius, and memory of the sage, Drahn-Thus recognized the tower instantly, and entered it.

A white stair went up to the sage's library, which was sunny both day and night. The walls were lined with scrolls and books, cased or bound in covers of precious materials, none of which seemed earthly in origin. Above in the ceiling beamed a constant sunlight. Equidistant from each other, four marble beasts guarded the chamber. They were a feathered lion, a graceful lizard, a smooth-coated dog, and a little child with butterfly wings. On the forehead of each shone a gem. The lion had a sky-blue topaz, the lizard a silvery pearl, the dog a crimson spinel. But the child's jewel was clear and flashing as water. It was a diamond.

Knowing how, Thus made his home in the tower.

From the tower, also knowing how, he came to rule all the land about.

In his brain was the memory of the mage-sage. The sage had been benign, gentle, and trusted. Wherever therefore that Thus took himself, he was greeted with gladness, and at once recognized the sage's heir.

For one bred to abject slavery and misuse, lessoned only in cruelty, to one unattractive, mindless, and foul, such happenings were a tonic.

Years passed, on bare broad feet. Decades wandered by, scholastically gazing at this and that.

From the mouths of the four beings in the tower faint smokes began to issue. They could tell Thus of so many matters, and he questioned them very often, determined to learn, to understand and grasp. He had indeed been empty, was greedy now.

The sage had known, seeing Drahn in the desert of salt, that to give him too much water too swiftly in his great thirst would physically ruin and destroy him. Yet this careful sage had also deluged Drahn with psychic power, not even thinking twice.

He did not set a hand on her, the woman who lay before him. All saw this, the throng in the lamplit chamber.

Yet, despite the brazen rainfall of his hair, it was obvious to them that he bent toward Zerezel like a stooping hawk. Most realized next, with a sudden start, he had placed his lips upon hers.

He kissed her.

He kissed her, and from the night all about a composite sigh, a breath, winged up.

For *kindness* kisses. Honor kisses. *Love* kisses.

He did not linger then, but raised his head, and stood above the lovely spill of her body.

Soundlessness followed the sigh, and stasis, and in the solitary lamp the flame faltered as if it must go out—before leaping high, filling the whole chamber with light.

Where had she been to, Zerezel? Oh, she did not think or know or care. Somewhere, nowhere. Where the beaten soul will drag itself, wishing it too should die.

Yet there, after millennia, something brushed against her, as a leaf may glance across a sleeping hand.

It was more than that. Weightless, formless, yet it had to it a peerless bittersweetness, and an *edge* like honed steel. It had the sort of *voice* which called more loudly than any trumpet note, more subtly than any murmur uttered either side of life.

She lifted her face from the ashes of nothingness. Sightless and deaf, she waited to see and hear again this *thing*. At a loss. And when the summons did not come again, still she turned and broke the surface of the ash entire, and she flew out like a bird toward the sun—outward, upward, into the living world.

In the chamber with the lamp it was as if a glass screen shattered.

She had seemed dead, the prince's daughter. Now in one movement she rose straight up from the couch, kneeled there on it, and death fell from her like a veil.

Her eyes were wide and full of a vital searching.

She spoke hoarsely, for her voice had been dumb some while.

She spoke only to one.

"How?" she asked. "How? How have *you* done this?"

Then the magician flaunted himself before her. It was his vanity, and few could miss it. (Did she?) But after all why should he not be vain, when he had worked such a miracle?

How *had* he done it? Through his great power, evidently, his force of charisma.

But "I have done it," he told Zerezel, "through love."

"Then," she whispered, *"I love you."*

After which she fell back on the couch, too weak to offer anything other. Which hardly mattered, she had offered all. And her eyes anyway stayed open, and burned on the magician. It was noted, by some regretfully and by others in approval, that never had she gazed with such hypnotized fashion at her former bridegroom, even though his death had nearly slain her.

The palace rang with celebration. Flags of scarlet and saffron dripped from ledges. Firecrackers were being made ready to fill the sky with arcs and orbs and showers of rose-red stars.

Keshom entered the princess' apartment.

How changed everything was. The floors and walls dazzled with polishing and sunshine. Most burnished of all, the young woman who stood before him. She had given orders and the couch was taken away on which she had lain so long. It was an emblem of sadness and ill-omen, and had been burned.

Now Zerezel's *eyes* burned. The fire in them was very bright, all her sorrow seemingly consumed there.

She spoke at once. "Tell me of him."

Of course, Keshom had no doubt of whom she wished to hear. Yet it was quite curious, for in another day and evening, that same man and she were to be married. This was the price Thus had demanded of her father—Zerezel herself. The old prince had been glad to pay it. As for the girl, she had already consented, for had she not whispered before them all *I love you*.

"Lady," said Keshom, "what would you know? I was with him only that one hour inside his room of magic."

"Tell me of that, then," said Zerezel.

So Keshom described again what he had seen, and what had been said and done.

She listened attentively, occasionally nodding. And as he spoke, Keshom saw how she was strong and well, a bloom of health on her from the magician's healing kiss, even the white that had come in her hair disguised and colored over. One would not know, to look at her now, she had suffered any loss.

When Keshom concluded his account, she said, "And after? What did you learn *then*, when you had left him?"

Keshom frowned.

"That is," she said, "when you traveled back from the tower. You will have passed through the lands best known to the Lord Thus. Surely they talked of him there?"

Keshom frowned worse. It was true enough, the magician *was* talked of, if one should ask about him, as Keshom had during his return journey.

"They praised his erudition, lady, and his looks. They told of wonders he had performed, incredible feats of marvel. Although…"

"Although?"

"They were afraid of him too." Keshom lowered his eyes, for now *her* eyes blazed only with great anger. Certainly she must think he slighted her second suitor. Quickly Keshom added, "Such power as his may terrify. As I have said, even to me he showed himself as a leopard. He is able to assume such forms, and it would be impossible not to be afraid of it. Besides, I have heard the stone creatures in his tower tell and show him everything he desires. He is like a god on earth. One may adore and admire and *also* fear such prowess."

"Yet, though long-lived, he is not an immortal, nor invulnerable," said Zerezel, rather doubtfully. "So I have heard. Can this be so?"

She dreads she will lose him like her last lover, thought Keshom. And he said, "So too I heard—that he is vulnerable and mortal both. Yet, we concede, so mighty in power, he is well equipped to defend himself." After which Keshom bit his tongue, for he wished the magician might not be so armed in his own defense, that he *might* be lost to Zerezel, and to the palace, and to the whole earth.

For Keshom *had* asked for stories in those lands of the Magus Thus, and first he was only given the most fulsome praise of him. Royal messenger as he was, Keshom had known this at once for the subterfuge of pure terror. And gradually he weaned some of them to mutter the truth, or scraps of it. And these tiny scraps were like huge blots of filth soon smeared all over the image of the magician. Thus was to the people round about his tower a beast, not only in his shapeshifting, but in his inhuman cruelties and viciousness, his greed and evil-doing. They had another name for him, too. Here and there Keshom had seen, or been shown it, scratched into some wall or fence as a warning, and the magician had not, lion as he was there, bothered to smite the scratches away. *Drahk,* that was the harsh name the people of those regions gave him. *Drahk.*

Keshom himself had known but too well he could not cross such a mortal demon. (Demonkind might have been nicer to deal with. They had their own oblique codes, and would sometimes make bargains.)

The monster however would merely kill him, and worse, vent his displeasure on those who spoke ill of him. And therefore Keshom had come home and delivered the magician's message, and all the rest followed.

Much alarmed, only one item *perplexed* Keshom at this point. That a being of such enormous and unfastidious power should trouble to save Zerezel, let alone require to wed her.

The princess meanwhile nodded. Her eyes were dark. Was she then content with what he had said? Approaching Keshom, she gave him a silver ring with a white gem in it. "You are a good man, Keshom."

He thanked her and went away, and raged at himself that he had not confessed the horror to her. But it would have been no use. Thus—or *Drahk*—had each of them in his thrall. And she, poor maiden—*loved* him.

The wedding day arrived.
Dawn till sunfall they rejoiced.

Birds were loosed in multicolored drifts; incenses spiraled upward; night closed and was undone with fireworks.

After the banquet, with garlands and singing, Zerezel went up to her bridal bower. Never had any woman looked so lovely, or so glad. Presently her husband, the magician, followed her. Never had any man looked so godlike. Or so sure.

Priests blessed the bed, the rafters, the doorway, and all nine windows of the room. Wine and perfume were spilled. A guard of attendance waited in the antechamber as custom decreed. Three maidens chosen for their virtues, and three gentlemen chosen likewise for theirs. It seemed Zerezel had asked that Keshom be one of these. It was a bestowal of much favor, for which he was envied. He would, needless to say, rather have been placed in a dungeon for the night.

Outside, beyond the festive gardens, the forest hushed and rustled, asking itself perhaps what went on now in that huge lighted house, where, for a year, only lament and silence had visited. And perhaps too certain trees asked each other, or the sky above to which they prayed with the upraised wooden fingers of their branches. *Has she forgotten him so soon? Has she forgotten her beloved one? He that died against our feet from the bite of a little golden snake?* But to that, neither the trees nor the sky gave answer.

Drahk who was Thus. Thus who was Drahk. Years he ruled that land the kind, pompous sage had governed, and that had expected something similar from Drahk. But Drahk had been Drahn and Drahn

52

had been scum. And for every particle of mystic brilliance that entered his brain, still Drahn lurked too in there, skulking like a venomous insect in the corner of a golden palace filled by lights. Or, as a poisonous snake might do, of course.

People and lands were soiled and spoiled. The landscape was altered to a desert, and then came the scourges of winds, and then the snow dropped dry and adamant, white, like salt. The lake too froze and broke and froze. The ethereal rainbow marble of the tower went black and seemed to run with blood, the blood of those savaged by Drahk who was still Drahn, and taught by camel-kicks and the fists of dead-souled human *things*.

The sage, dying, for all his genius forgot his common sense. He knew not to give a man perishing of thirst too much water. He did not consider that this might apply also to the giving of flawless knowledge and magecraft to one dehydrated of all goodness, thought, and heart. Oh, that power—

In it had gushed.

Another receiving it would have died. Alas, Drahn-Drahk lived on. And on and on, for though not invulnerable, as Keshom remarked, Drahk's cunning and defenses, once marshalled, were never overcome.

So he ruled his ruined lands. And when he grew bored with his sin, he asked questions of the wise stone beasts, the feathered lion and giant lizard, the dog, the child with butterfly wings. And the topics he asked to hear of and see converted those arcane creatures to a predatory griffen, an alligator, a man with a dog's head—and the child lost its beautiful wings.

But then there came a night when Drahk considered he had seen and learned and done all that could interest him. And boredom gnawed. So then he said to all four beasts: "I am the best of men. I am master of the earth. I therefore disdain to conquer and rule more of it than these few miles, for it is all the same. Instead I will have something else. For any woman I have seen that I have wanted—I took. They were all dross. Yet maybe there is one who is not dross. A virgin, and the most glorious. Find and show me that one. The fairest woman on earth, as I am easily the most handsome among men."

Vanity, always that, with him. He had had nothing, now had, could have, it all. Boasted and wanted to partner his grandeur. A moon to his sun, a satellite to his world.

The beasts obliged. That was their fate.

The griffen revealed a wondrous woman in the east, but she was too old for Drahk. The alligator revealed a more wondrous and younger woman in the west, but she was a harlot. The dog-man revealed one younger and more wondrous still, but she was newly deceased, and had lain three days in her tomb. Drahk cursed his servants. Then he said to the wingless child, "Now, you. And be sure *you* do not fail me."

And the child revealed Zerezel, in the far south, and she was young and virgin and the most beautiful woman living on earth. But she loved another man and was due to wed him.

Drahk said, "If *I* go to her, she will instantly forget the fool. She will want only me."

But the child answered softly, "No, lord magician. For true love is blind. True love can only love. Such love is a sword, stronger even than death—therefore beware of it!"

At these words Drahk, entirely at last frustrated, felt the sword of true love pierce *him*, through the heart he had never properly had, either as Drahn or Drahk. And so he cursed the stone child too, whose wings had already been ripped away.

From his curses the jewels of all four creatures were muddied. But the child's turned a dreadful shade. Yet as the child was also robbed of its form, becoming a fox with only a child's face left to it, it *laughed,* though this seemed just the barking of the fox.

And here now is the puzzle of the magician.

Evil and ignorant he was. Fantastically enlightened and made a genius as well. And in that way his spirit was at war with nature within him. Though *he* wished only to exercise his vileness, the power that had become his mind yearned for sanity and goodness, and pulled and struggled and rent at him. Because of this he had hoped to find some way to outwit his better side, to blind it in one eye—which was that of the intellect and soul.

And unfortunately the matter was to hand. Arch-mage that he had become, could he not shapeshift?

Like one donning another coat, Drahk had put on him the form of a leopard, and went out to kill and rape and raven. Or he wore another mantle for it, that of the bear, or of the unicorn, or the shape of a tiger or the wolverine. So he indulged his pleasures, so he outwitted him*self.*

And this method did not, even in his new ecstasy of love, desert him.

The clean power always refused to allow him the act of murder, but once no longer human he was without conscience. And he was used, by then, to splitting himself in twain. It was surprisingly very easy.

He had obsessively studied Zerezel some while. He knew, amongst other things, her favorite flowers.

Drahk blighted all of them in her lover's country, and instead grew a tree of them beside a forest path, along which her betrothed would travel, a little ahead of his retinue, as Drahk had seen he always did.

Drahk then contemplated, and selected the most fitting alternate form to put on. He assumed it. And lay under the tree of flowers, and waited patiently.

hen the bridegroom entered the bedchamber, his bride stood before him. She was clothed as if in silken mist and her hair was like a waterfall.

Her eyes rested on him with the most profound hunger.

How could she help but love him? And he loved her.

He knew this.

Love stronger than death.

He had used up so much carnal passion in unspeakable scenarios, that now he paused a minute, gazing at her, wanting to delve in himself for some wholesome dream of lust, of longing, and certain he did so.

Zerezel seemed faultlessly to suit herself to his mood. Only after some time did she address him.

"My beloved lord," she said, "you brought me from the outskirts of death's kingdom. And you are the mightiest mage known upon earth. How can it be you—*you*—a god among mankind, have chosen *me?*"

"Ah," he said. A fakery of dismissal.

"Beloved," she said, "I do not deserve you."

Something struck a spark then in his vain, divided mind.

With a hint of—was it *petulance?*—he said, "Nor I you, it seems. Since you loved and would have wed another."

"He is *nothing,*" said the woman immediately. And her eyes revealed without doubt that only Drahk (Thus) filled her thoughts.

"You did not reckon him nothing once," said Drahk. "Nor myself anything at all."

"How might I? I had never looked on you. Nor had you beheld me either."

"Suppose," said Drahk quietly, "I were to tell you that, even before that man's untimely end, I *had* seen, and *had* desired you?"

Was she stunned by this? It seemed so. "My lord—I must ask you why then you hesitated? For if you had come to me then, and I had seen *you*, could I have wanted any other?" (And beyond the windows the forest rustled and hushed, lifting its praying wooden arms to the sky.)

Drahk mused. "Could you not? But if you had loved me better, what then of your betrothed? The contract was too firm to break."

She grew deadly pale and answered, "I should have despised him, having looked on you. I would have begged that someone kill him and rid me of him instantly."

"One did kill him and rid you of him."

"A snake, they say. How I wish I might see that snake! I would have them make a temple to its glory."

Drahk preened himself. "Oh, I could show it to you."

"What, can you summon it?"

"In a way. I could take on its form."

She laughed then. It was a melody, her laughter, played only for one man. "I know, lord, you are a shape-changer. But, beloved love, lord of earth and forever, a leopard is your form, or a lion—some kingly beast— or an eagle, a dragon—never a snake. How could you become such?"

Drahk smiled. Was his smile playful too, or very dangerous? "Do you doubt it?" he inquired. "Are you unable to picture it?"

She lowered her beautiful and fiery eyes.

𝕴t was midnight.

A moon had risen late.

The amber debris of the firecrackers still clouded the forest, and the moon itself smoldered like a ruby, even when it reached the apex of the sky.

It was then that Keshom heard a voice call to him, and only to him, from Zerezel's inner chamber.

The other five attendants had fallen asleep. Only he, burdened with his misery, had not.

Nor could he tell, disoriented as he had become, quite whose voice it was that called, whether that of male or female, or even if it were that of some ghost which wailed from the forest.

He rapped on the door, and his hand was cold.

"Enter," said the voice. *"Thus."*

The magician had not, even as the sage had not, been able to predict all things. That Zerezel would almost die, for example, had not entered his calculations. But that her father must thereafter send for help was nearly traditional. And by some kind of influence too, Drahk had then made sure one messenger at least should find him.

A single question however remained outstanding.

The fox child in the tower had warned Drahk that Zerezel could not love him, could only love her first lover—even dead. And since these stone creatures were all-knowing, even vain, self-blinded Drahk could believe it, and accordingly *slew* her first lover. Why then and how had Drahk's own kiss *restored* Zerezel to life, let alone to utter instant love of *him*—a love that even denied the former lover, forgot or wanted him slain? She, who had been so faithful. Love stronger than death—

Now the answer to that lingering question lay before Keshom. Though he did not quite see it yet.

He saw only the room, the marriage bed—untouched, unused—and Zerezel the maiden, who stood there wrapped in a silken shawl, the ends of which were pooled over and around her feet. The lamps were out, but red moonlight filled the room from three of nine windows. No other was present. The Magician Thus, or Drahk, was not to be seen.

"I wish to thank you, Keshom," said Zerezel in a mild, low tone, "for bringing him to me. For delivering him up to me. This man who, in the form of a little, yellow snake, slew my beloved with his venom."

"Lady—" cried Keshom, galvanized, "I failed you, rather. For I told you nothing of my suspicion of him. Let alone that he had killed your prince—for I swear that *this* I never guessed."

"You need tell me nothing. You had only, as you did, to confirm the mage was facile in the craft of shapeshift. And vulnerable, too. Capable of dying." (Outside the forest made no sound, listening with all its million million leaves. And the moon, like Keshom, stared with an amazed wild face.)

"I had learned who was the murderer—yes, even in the oblivious nothing where I wandered. And also how the murder had been done. I knew from the moment I felt the touch of his lips. For *on* his lips I tasted the skin of my one true love, and mingled with the unique fragrance of his flesh—the taint of some dire poison. It seems my lover's body was the last human element the magician had touched with his mouth, before

57

that mouth kissed mine. Oh," she said, and from her eyes the moon-hot tears fell out like blood, "at once I woke and flung back to regain the world and view the assassin. I gazed at him with burning loathing, and with deep hunger for his death—which others, and even he, mistook for *love*. And when he came to me tonight I wooed and coaxed him to put on the shape he used to work his crime. Boastfully he did so. And when he coiled there on the floor, slender and little and scaled and venomous, I went to him with cries of praise and delight, and *see*—" she let drop the shawl and slid it away—*"how I rewarded him."*

And there on the floor in the strange light, spine-snapped and crushed in one second under her heel, lay a golden snake, dead as yesterday, unmade as tomorrow.

The Pain of Glass

1. The Third Fragment

That very afternoon a caravan had entered the city. It had journeyed from the Great Purple Sea, which lay far to the west and was so named for the preponderance of purplish weed that massed its waters, and at certain seasons dyed them. After the coast, the caravan negotiated many lands. It had crossed serpentine rivers, dagger-like mountains, and finally the Vast Harsh Desert, renowned for waterless and unobliging terrain. Small wonder then that the caravan might be supposed to bring with it much valuable stuff, not to mention travellers' tales, whose vividity was matched only by their tallness.

Prince Razved stood on a balcony of his palace, staring out over high walls and lengthening shadows, to the marketplace.

"Oh, to be merely a merchant," sighed the Prince. "Oh, to have no destiny but the discovery of new things, adventure and commerce."

He did not mean this. What he actually meant, and partly he knew it, was that he yearned to be freed from the direly irksome situation into which Lord Fate had thrust him. For though he ruled the city, he might enjoy neither it nor his full power in it. A single awful obstacle kept him always from his rights.

Just then a voice arose at his back. It was wild, quavering, and disrespectful.

"Are they *here?* Are they *near?*"

The Prince clenched his jaw and his fists. He paled white as fresh ivory. Young though he was, the weight of extra decades slumped upon his shoulders.

There in the chamber behind the balcony stood a filthy and dishevelled old man. Two hundred years of age he looked, and the colourless thin wires of his hair rained round his face, which was like that of a demented hawk. He was mad as the word, and none could help him. Now too he began to weep and scream. Razved locked his fists together behind his back and bellowed for assistance.

It came instantly in the person of three men, frenzied with dismay, who rushed into the room, where they flung themselves on their faces before the Prince.

But Razved only said to them, in tones of steel, "He has got out again. How has he done this? Are you not meant to care for and contain him?"

"Mighty Master—only a moment was the door undone…"

"Only ever is it undone for a moment," replied Razved, his tone now composed of stifled rage and black despair. "Or it is the window-lattice. Or some other pretext. Take him away. *Hide* him from me. If you transgress again, you will meet the doom those of his last retinue suffered."

Whispering shrieks of terror, the jailor-retinue leapt to their feet and gathered in the mad old man, bearing him instantly off, crying and calling, along the corridor to renewed detention.

But Razved could not rid himself of the memory of the encounter, which had been so often repeated through countless years. He strode to another chamber. There he donned a disguise he sometimes employed when wandering about the city. Razved believed none of the citizens had ever penetrated this. And although, of course, many of them had, and did, none were recently foolish enough to confess to him.

As the sun burned down behind the palace, the Prince also descended. Before the first star blinked, he was in the marketplace.

Soon the whole market, infused by the caravan and lighted with torches, was like a lamp against the blue night.

Razved strolled from place to place, forgetting for a while his plight. He beheld an indigo snake of extreme size and patterned with gold, that danced to the intricate beat of drums. It twisted itself into hoops and spirals, coils and knots, that each time seemed impossible for it ever to unravel—yet always it did so, rising and bowing to the crowd. They threw coins, which the snake caught in its mouth. And there was a silk from the edge of the Purple Sea, coloured—with the purple weed-dye, and this material seemed to burn with sapphires in the shadows and rubies in the torchlight. Also Razved tasted bizarre fruits with thick cream skins, that had no juice but gave up the flavour of honey. Elsewhere stood books the height of a man and twice his width, with covers of hammered bronze, and pages of blond wood incised with silver—but often what they said was nonsense. Or there were birds which could recite poetry in the voices of beautiful boys or women, tiny, exquisite models of temples and shrines cut from green pearls, wines which were black and scented with roses, swords both straight and curved, in the blades of which were supernaturally-written spells of invincible power…

After a while Razved grew weary. He sat down by the booth of a seller of glass and drank some black wine.

Behind him the Prince could hear how the glass-seller was complaining, some tale of half his wares, including the most expensive mirrors, being broken, the fault apparently of a vulture-like desert witch. Razved paid little heed, only thinking, *the man does not know his luck. He has only loss of trade, and poverty to fear. While I…* And once more he clenched his fists, pondering how the full rule of the city might never come to him, nor the title of King. Dwelling too upon the awful haunt of the insane old man in the palace. *I shall never get what I am owed. I shall never be free of him. Would not death be preferable?*

But despite his bitter thoughts, Razved was not yet ready to make the close acquaintance of Lord Death. And presently he turned his head to glare at the complaining glass-seller.

At once the man broke into smiles. "Best sir, what might I show you, that may tempt? It is true, many of my finest articles were destroyed as I travelled here, but even so certain elegancies remain which, though quite unworthy of your discerning gaze, may yet briefly amuse you."

Razved yawned. He passed a jaundiced look over a surviving mirror so liquid it suggested a tear from the full moon, and a curious magnifying glass that stared back at him like an elemental eye.

"Well," said Razved, with unencouragement, "what is your finest *remaining* piece?"

The glass-seller, whose name was Jandur, bowed his head as if in thought. He had heard rumours concerning the city, and of a strange delaying fate which hung over its King-in-waiting. Jandur had also been told that sometimes this Prince went about the streets in disguise, but was easily recognisable, the disguise being a sloppy one and the Prince himself equally brooding, ill-tempered, and unmissably regal in his manner. Yet those who gave away their recognition, the rumour added, were normally found deceased not long after. Jandur now guessed that here sat the very man. To be cautious was therefore prudent. To make a *sale*, however, must be a prize. Besides, there was too another matter.

"Wise sir," said Jandur, after a moment, "one item there is that I feel inclined to show you—though I am uneasy at doing so."

"Come," snapped Razved, "your task is to sell, is it not?"

"Quite so, intelligent sir. My unease rests on two counts. Firstly, I hope you will pardon me—but I perceive from your garb you are neither rich nor high-born…"

Razved seemed coquettishly pleased. "You speak honestly."

"…yet," continued cunning Jandur, "what strikes me forcefully is a great refinement of spirit and judgement immediately apparent about your person. Because of these qualities I would wish to reveal a treasure. Yet again…"

"Yet again!" Razved had now risen and was impatient to be shown.

"…I am loath to part with the thing. It is charming, and unusual beyond all my other wares, yes, even those exquisites smashed to bits amid the desert sands of the Vast Harsh."

"Come," said Razved, with a dangerous glint in his eye. Life had baulked his wishes, this pedlar should not.

Jandur gauged all perfectly and now exclaimed, "You shall see the wonder! Pray follow me, illumined sir, into the back premises of the booth."

In the dark beyond the light beyond the dark, then—that was, the shadowed space inside the lighted market and city, which themselves rested in the dish of night—the ultimate inner brilliance shone. It was very small.

As Jandur lit the candle to display it, Razved peered. What did he see?

"Only that?" he said, in ominous disappointment.

The object was a little drinking vessel, about as tall as the length of a woman's hand. The stem was slender, and the cup wide, like the bowl of an open flower, but it would hold, Razved believed, less than three gulps of wine. "And this is your most astonishing vendible, is it? Your brain must be as cracked as your broken mirrors."

"Pray examine the item."

Razved sullenly reached out and wondered somewhat why he bothered to do so. But then his fingers met the texture of the glass. As they did this, the candlelight caught all the vessel's surfaces, and for a second it seemed to the Prince he held in his hand a mote of softest living flame—it was like phosphorescence on water, or like fireflies glimmering on a marble trellis. The colours of the goblet woke, shifted and merged, now dawn-pink, now flamingo-red, next a limpid golden green. Not meaning to, not knowing quite what he did, Razved touched his other fingers to the lip of the cup. Instantly there came the sweetest and most poignant note of music, slender as sheer silk passed through a silver ring. And in that moment, standing in the cramped booth felt within his hands not the glass of a vessel—but two perfect breasts—crystalline, silken—that sang back against his palms, while on his lips he tasted the glass-girt wine of a longed-for lover's kiss.

Jandur, who had predicted with some cause an intriguing result at contact, stepped swiftly forward, and steadied both Razved and the precious goblet, though Jandur wrapped the latter in his sleeve.

Razved seemed nearly in a swoon. Jandur sat him on a bench and replaced the foremost treasure of his stock safely out of reach.

"What occurred?" eventually Razved asked. He no longer had the voice of a Prince, he sounded like a child. "Is the cup ensorcelled?"

"I cannot definitely tell you," Jandur answered. It was a fact, he could not.

"It is—*what* is it?"

"Alas. I cannot say. Mystical and magical certainly."

"Does it affect all—who—touch it?"

"In various ways, it does. Some weep. Some blush. Some begin to sing."

"And *you*," said Razved, with another warning note suddenly entering his voice: that of jealousy, "what do *you* feel when you take hold of it?"

"Fear," Jandur replied simply.

"Ah," said Razved. "It is not meant for *you*, then."

For a while after this exchange, neither man spoke or moved. Jandur stood in the dark beyond the candle, thinking his own thoughts. The Prince, still physically overwhelmed, his manhood urgently upright and his blood tingling and thundering, slumped on the bench. At length however, he bethought himself of his status, and drew himself together.

"Well, an astonishing trifle," said he, with the most ludicrous dismissal. "But what price do you set on it?"

Jandur now realised his peak of cunning bravado.

"I will confess, sir, I am so taken with admiration for your natural gifts that, while acknowledging your obvious penury, I believe you may after all be able to summon the amount. For surely such a man as yourself will have *another* admirer from whom you will command the present of the vessel—an admirer even more smitten than I. The value I require is seventy sevens of white gold."

Razved snorted piggishly. He now cared, it seemed, less for his deception. "You are astute, glass-vendor. Just such a sum was handed me by a lover, in order I might buy myself a trinket." And reaching into his poor man's apparel, he drew forth a bag and spilled the contents at Jandur's feet. "Wrap the thing in a cloth," he commanded in a feverish undertone.

Jandur, ostensibly ignoring, even stepping on the spilled money, did as he was bid, he himself taking great care not to touch the goblet once. In a few more minutes the King-in-waiting had hurried from the booth, and any who noted his rushing figure saw it fly off around the high outer wall of the palace.

But Jandur sat down on the bench and murmured a prayer of thanks to a god of his own country—both for the riches Razved had given him, and for his release from proximity to the glass goblet.

Deep in the dark thereafter, Prince Razved repaired alone to his most isolate chamber. Not even the moon might look in, save through the sombre vitreous of thick windows clad in gauze.

Dark was in the flagon, too, the black wine aromatic of roses, which he had had his servants bring him.

The haunting madman had been locked away, shackled tonight for good measure. Not only were merchants prudent, after all.

Razved, bathed in hot water and spices, clad in loose and sensuous garments, unwrapped at last the goblet. Holding it only through a piece of fine embroidered cloth, he set it on the table by his couch.

Despite the lack of light, even so the faintest and most mellifluous tinctures of colour began at once to flutter to and fro in the glass.

They were like birds in a cloud, or fish in a ghostly pool. Dilute crimson melded to opalescent rose—to amber—to emerald. All this—just from his touch through cloth, his hungry gaze upon it.

In a while he leant forward and filled the vessel full of inky wine. Rather than dim the spectrum in the glass, the blackness seemed to bring it out. Gold shot through the other tints like benign lightning.

Razved sighed. He had put away his woes.

He placed his fingers upon the rim of the goblet. At once, it sang for him. He could hear again a woman's voice in the notes, clear as a silver bell, and as he kept just one finger on the vessel, the melody—and melody it was—went on and on. Razved was not afraid.

Unlike the shoddy glass-seller, he was royal, a warrior of a warlike and powerful line—although he had never ridden to battle, nor seen what battle may produce aside from valour. The glass was neither evil nor any threat. It was enchanted, and enchanting. It was a delicious toy the gods had sent him, in recompense for all the other frustrations of his days.

Unable any longer to detain himself, the Prince now put both his hands on the goblet. Intoxicating heat raced through his arms and filled his body, as he drew the brim towards his lips. He drained the wine, and the act of drinking became instead the act of kissing, while the singing notes entered his brain, and floated there like iridium feathers.

He found he had lain back, the cup held firm against his heart. And then it seemed the cup too had taken hold of *him*. Female arms, slender and strong, encircled his body. For an instant he glimpsed, lifted above him, a maiden made of flames and waters, flowing down on him in waves and foam and sparks, more sinuous than any serpent. Then a mouth famished as his own fastened on his lips, a tongue like smoothest myrrh and ice-hot quicksilver, drank deeply. Against him in his delirium he felt the movement of a frame that was softness and succulence, pliable and limber as a young cat's—but all this, the plains of skin, the pressure of slim muscle, the downfall of shining hair—even the narrow hands whose tips were like bees, the flawless breasts whose tips were like buds—all this was cool and composite, and made all, *all* of it, of *glass*.

Yet still Razved feared nothing. As his hands swept over the crystal curves of a phantasmal yet actual shape, as he drowned in the silver notes of a song that had, as yet, no words, as he began to ride in the primal race of desire, not one qualm interrupted Razved's intense and scalding pleasure. For it did not trouble him *she* was all of glass, and that *she* flamed with shades of flowers and gems, and her tongue was of glass, her lips and hair, her little feet that gripped him, glass that kissed, caressed, and sang in ecstasy. Even her centre, the core of her glory, that too, where now he lay, fixed and explosive as a sun, *that* was formed of glass. And it rippled and embraced and grew molten, better than any human vessel; wine and darkness; jasper, asphodel: fire, ash, sand.

2. The Second Fragment

That very morning, they had entered the expanse of the terrible desert known as the Vast Harsh, Jandur the glass-seller received an omen. He did not, at the hour, much consider it, but later it came to him he had been awarded one of those useless portents the gods tended to throw before mankind. What the omen presumably was, had been a solitary black vulture crouched on a sycamore, which weirdly held upright in its beak a shard of glass. This caught the light and flashed, amusing many who saw it. But they, and Jandur, soon forgot, since a mile or so later the desert began.

There lay before the caravan now countless miles of that inimical landscape, which separated the more abundant lands from the towns and cities of the north and east. And though provided with all necessities, none of the travellers viewed the desert prospect with much joy. The Harsh was famed not only for its personal cruelties, but for those of various men driven out there, and making their desperate livelihoods by the robbery and murder of passing human traffic. Well-armed guards had joined the caravan at Marah, the last town on the desert's edge.

The Harsh opened to receive them, grinning.

Jandur journeyed glumly among the rest.

By day the caravan wended, though sheltering sometimes at noon, when the predatory eye of the sun centred the sky. Once there it turned both heaven and earth into a furnace any glass-maker might have valued. *Perhaps,* thought Jandur then, *the gods also are glass-makers. The earth is their kiln and we, mortals of siliceous sand, suffer, turn and burn in this sun fire, and likewise the flames of pain and sorrow, in order to become creatures as pure and beautiful as glass.*

But really he was well aware that people rarely grew beautiful or pure through suffering and burning. Normally ill-treatment made them worse, and wicked. Those who did achieve virtue no doubt might have become just as wonderful, even if they had *not* had to suffer, or to burn.

At night the caravan spread itself out like an exhausted yet demanding beast. It lit torches and fires, cooked its meals, sometimes told stories or danced, frequently bickered, argued, or even came to blows. Above, the myriad stars blazed bright. *If each were a glass,* thought Jandur, *what a fortune they would make for those that formed them. But alas, when they fall,* he added to himself, seeing one which did, *they shatter.*

Jandur had himself never made a single piece of glass. He only sold glass, but that in quantities. In the very next town they would come to, which was called Burab, and which still lay ninety days and nights across the Harsh, Jandur's brother-in-law had charge of the family's second glass-makery. He was a quarrelsome brute, dark red from heat, and scarred all over with the white bites of burns. But Jandur had already enough stock and thought he would not need to trouble his brother-in-law. Which thought cheered Jandur in the desert, even when jackals howled, or the dust-winds blew.

Despite the reputation of the Harsh, they met no robbers. Probably any robbers spied them first and found their numbers, and their armed escort, off-putting. Meanwhile, on a certain evening, they reached one of the few oases that served the waste.

This was a poor enough specimen. A handful of spindly trees led to a well no bigger than a washtub, the margin spiked with black rushes that discontentedly chittered.

Leaving his servant to go for fresh water, Jandur dismounted from his mule and took a walk among the stunted trees. The sun was already low and veiled in sandy gold, and a reluctant breeze smoked along the dunes. The impromptu caravanserai was being settled for the night, cookfires breaking into red blossom. Jandur went up to a little rise, idly following the prints of some now-absent, small desert animal. From here he looked about at the world, as mortals did and yet do, both pleased and displeased with it, suspended in the quiet melancholy of dusk.

"Where is the glass-maker?" shouted a baleful voice behind him.

"I do not know," muttered Jandur. But he turned nonetheless. And there on the rise with him perched a most ungainly and uncouth female figure. She was clad in a mantle of vulture feathers. More, her long and ragged hair, lucklessly dark as was the hair, they said, of demons, was stuck with other such feathers. On her wrists and at her long, thin neck were ornaments of what Jandur, not illogically, concluded to be vulture bones. She smelled of vultures too, a smell that was of chickens, and of carrion.

If he had been going to admit to an acquaintance with glassware, perhaps now he thought better of it. But this was all in vain. For she announced immediately, "You are *he*. You are the one named Janpur or Jinkor, a glass-maker and vendor of such."

"What, assuming I am he, would you have with him?" inquired Jandur.

The female ruffled her feathers. It was difficult to be sure, when she did this, if rather than a mantle, they were not actually growing from her skin. "I am Morjhas. I perambulate the desert. I have no trepidation in the Harsh, for my powers bring me all I need."

67

She was a witch. Jandur nodded politely.

But she reached forward and thrust her skinny talon of a finger at his breast. "Come you with me. I will show you a strangeness. I am bound to do this, for my talent carries with it a certain onus. A strangeness, I say. And what you do thereupon I shall advise you."

"I may not leave the caravan," protested Jandur. "If you are often here, you will know the place abounds in villains."

"What care I for villains? They are all afraid of Morjhas—and rightly. Those who annoy me," she added, fixing Jandur with a tar-black eye, "regret it. If you behave, you will be safe enough in my company."

They flew.

He had not, and maybe he might have done, expected this. But the bird-hag lifted him straight off his feet and bore him away. He suspected he screamed, but none heard him over the din of the caravan; twilight doubtless screened the view. And she—she spread her wings and rushed both of them on.

However, they did not travel a very great way. The 'strangeness' Morjhas meant to reveal lay only some half mile from the camp.

At first, having been landed, Jandur gaped about him. No trace of sun remained, only the huge, translucent, violet dome of nightfall, where they were lighting the million cobalt, ferrous, and pewter cookfires and torches of the stars.

The vulture witch pointed with her eldritch claw.

"See there."

Some sixty or seventy paces off rose a mesa, scorched black by weather, and below, as elsewhere around, lay sand, slightly patched paler or darker, denoting seemingly depth, variance of consistency, or only shadows.

"At what do I look? That rock?"

"Hush, fool. Look and listen and learn."

So there they stood, and the night gathered all about, glowing as always in such open places, yet also black behind the stars. And coldness came too, for the desert, even the Vast Harsh, presented two faces, furnace by day and iceberg by night.

Jandur was frightened, but not out of his wits. He stared at the patch of sand below the mesa that his unwanted guide had indicated, and in a while he started to note a disturbance in it. A dust devil appeared to be at work there, but one which did not move from its origins. And after a time, the motes which circled upward and round and round commenced also to shine.

"Is it a ghost?" asked Jandur in a whisper.

"Hush," said the witch.

And exactly then the spinning busyness began to chime. An eerie carillon it was, bereft and lorn, like the cries of the wolves and jackals which prevailed in the desert. Yet too it had profound beauty, an insistent music. Like song it seemed, lacking words, though once perhaps words had belonged to it, a song of longing and loss that only a poet might create, and a human throat emit.

This uncanny and emotive recital continued for several minutes. Then came the night wind, and breathed on the spot, as a mother might with a weeping child. And the song ended, and the dust of the sand drifted down. It slept, whatever it had been, whatever it was. And silence returned, composed of the shift of the dunes, the sigh of the flimsy wind.

Morjhas spoke. "There, then."

"But *what* then?" asked Jandur.

"I cannot tell you. I, even I, do not know. But it cries out, does it not? I cannot ignore that cry, nor shall you."

"But what am I to do with it?"

"Fool of a *fool, son* of fools to seventeen generations, *father* of fools and *grandsire* of *imbeciles!"* ranted the vulture-witch. "Are you a glass-maker? Gather up the sand there, take and make it into glass, for glass is made with sand and fire. Take it and shape it and see what *then,* it does—for long enough it has lain and lamented here, unheard by any but myself and now you, O *fool."*

"Take and make…" cried Jandur in horror, for he did not want any part of this scheme.

"Take and make. For my powers are generous and I must be kind in turn to the tragedies of the Harsh. But you I will punish if you fail in this. Heed me, Jumduk, if so you are named. Either scoop up the sand there and have it worked, or I will send my minions to smash every item of your saleable glass, even within the cosy caravan. I will begin, O *fool,* with a certain mirror…" Here the vulture held up her wing and gave a screech, and from far away—about half a mile in fact—the appalled merchant seemed to detect a glacial splintering. "I will smash all and

69

everything, until you have dug up that place of sand which sings and sobs. Go now. Hasten back to the camp and get your slaves and your spades, for with every second you delay, another delicacy *breaks*. Be assured also, that if the sand is not then rendered to glassware before three more months elapse, I will break anything you may have left, or thereafter acquire! You had best believe this."

Jandur was uncertain if he had only gone mad, but he credited every word. He bolted for the camp, and endlessly along the route as he ran, he heard the shattering of glass—the whole while becoming louder and louder.

𝕴ndeed, Jandur's bivouac lay in some confusion when he reached it. People stood about amazed, and bits of glass lay around sparkling prettily in the firelight, but there was a deal of shrieking and praying too. "Vile winged shadows fell upon your wagon, Jandur!" some explained, hurrying gladly to convey bad news. "We heard the vandalism upon your wares but dare not enter! No other among us is attacked—only you, poor Jandur. Whatever can you have done to incur this supernatural wrath?" While as a background to their verbiage, yet other breakages sounded.

But Jandur paid no heed. Seizing his servant, two spades and some sacks, Jandur pelted back again, now on foot, across the desert. Regaining the spot where the dust had lifted and sung, the two men dug and transposed sand for all they were worth, until they had filled the sacks.

No sign of the vulture-witch remained, and truly the general site was so unremarkable that, saving the mesa, it was probable Jandur would not have found it again. A large dug hole now marked the dunes. Yet soon enough the sands would refill it.

"Hark," said Jandur. "Does it seem the wrecking has ceased?"

Presently he and the servant were agreed, any noises of destruction had stopped.

They trudged back to the caravan then and loaded the sacks into the wagon, where there was now some space for them, Jandur having lost a fair portion of his most valuable goods.

𝕹o other event of any moment befell the caravan, or Jandur, until they had entirely crossed the Harsh, and reached the town of

Burab.

Jandur went, albeit with no delight, to the house of his brother-in-law, Tesh the glass-maker, which lay behind the smoking chimney of the makery. Here Jandur's sister, Tesh's wife, greeted Jandur with affection tempered only by her husband's censure. Tesh himself banged in and out of the place, upbraiding Jandur for the loss of his goods... "A witch broke them? Ha! A likely tale. Your donkey of a servant packed them improperly, either that or *you* lost them at gambling. What a simpleton you are, Jandur. Your father must whirl in his grave at your incompetence."

"Nevertheless," said Jandur, gravely, "I have collected in the desert a most fascinating sand, and this I would request you put to use instantly. Fashion some fresh articles that I may sell them in the great city markets."

Tesh was not the man to be given orders by such as Jandur. He made a colossal fuss, shouted at his wife, tried to kick the dog—which eluded him without effort, being well-practiced in the skill—and rained curses on the earth in general. However, since Tesh had had no items in the original wagon-load, and might now get profit from future sales, he eventually complied, making out that he did Jandur the sort of favour that was known, in those parts, as a 'Full day's holiday, with a feast at its end.'

Jandur then retired exhausted to his bed. The caravan would not quit Burab for some while, and there was time enough. The sand had filled three sacks to the top, and he expected several pieces to result. Unease he put from him. If the sand were possessed by some supramundane force, Jandur himself had had no choice but to take it on. What the resultant glass might be, or do or cause, Jandur did not permit himself to consider.

The next morning the chimney of the makery gouted, as always, thunders of smoke and sparkling cinders.

Jandur busied himself about the town, buying presents for his sister and the dog.

Evening fell and the smouldering chimney cooled. A little after the regular hour, in came Tesh—both Jandur and Tesh's wife jumped up in startlement.

The red-hot man was pale as one of his burn-scars, and glassy tears trembled from his eyes.

"My darling wife," said he, and she so addressed almost fainted with the shock, "can you forgive me for my temper and my foulness?"

"Are you ill?" she cried in panic. "What ails you?"

"Alas," wept Tesh, and gentle as a lamb he went and knelt before her, burying his face in her skirts. And when the dog came worriedly to sniff him, Tesh, without looking, stroked its head and murmured, "Poor boy, you shall have a bone, you shall have a dish of meat. I will buy you a collar that reads: *Faithful Under Duress.*" After which his words were drowned in his tears.

As she embraced this strange, new-made husband, Jandur's sister said urgently to Jandur, "Go to the makery and see what has gone on!"

And Jandur did as she asked, his mind buzzing between curiosity, amusement, pity—and sheer fright.

The makery was a significant and hellish area. It rose up on many levels, that were dominated by the dark yet fiery hulks of kilns and braziers, and silvered stoops and founts of water, and all the while the crackle and bubble, the trickle and shiver, the rush and gush and whoosh and push—things altering, melting, expanding, blooming or dying. And always, even now, the ebb and flow of fire flickering on walls and roof, the glycerine riveting and drip of molten glass, the stench of hot metal and clay and combustion, and gaseousness, the nasal glitters and sumps of stone-dust, silica, calcium, and black natron.

Below on benches sat Tesh's work-gang. One was nursing a blowing pipe, three or four some smallish empty moulds. These fellows seemed bemused beyond speech. At a table sat one, though, who was polishing little beakers with the rubbing stone. He glanced up and said to Jandur, "I will tell it. There has been a peculiarity here. Either you have brought us bad luck—or good luck. We are not sure as yet."

Jandur put a substantial coin before the man. "I hope you will all take some wine to comfort you. But for now, go on."

"The sand," said the stone-rubber, "when emptied, was only enough for a single slight item."

"But it had filled three sacks!"

"So we thought, too. But opening and emptying them, all that was there was this miniature amount. Be sure, Master Tesh ranted he would waste none of his *other* sand to pad it out, and next he made oaths worthy of the demonkind. But by then he must make something else of it than vulgar language, so we set to work. Then, when all goes in the

72

crucible, a wild scent comes from the mix."

"A scent of what?"

"Of women's sweet skin and garments and young clean hair… so *then* we are all afeared, but Tesh rants on, so on we make. Then when he comes to blow the piece, soft light shines up above the brazier. Like green iron, or the rose-red that comes from glue-of-gold. But Tesh blows on, and then the vessel comes from the fire and is finished and firmed with a speed not very usual."

"What had been made?" demanded Jandur.

"One slender goblet with a flower-like drinking-bowl."

"And then?"

"Master touches it," put in one of the other men. "And his face goes rapt, as if he saw the gods. And then white. And then he staggers out to his house."

Jandur collected his wits. "Where is the goblet?"

"He took it with him."

When Jandur pelted back in at the house door, he halted as if he struck a buffer of some sort.

For there sat his sister, with Tesh adoringly leaning on her, and the dog with its head on Tesh's knee. And Jandur's sister sang in a light and lovely voice, an evening song. And in her hand Jandur beheld a glass drinking cup, no *longer* than a woman's hand, and full of mutable colours, as the stone-rubber had said. But just then the servant girl came in, and singing, Jandur's sister handed her the cup.

In consternation and excitement, Jandur watched the girl, to see what her reaction to the goblet might be.

For a moment she only stood quite still and gazed at it. She was not more than thirteen years, and next she turned away, rather as a child would who has found out a secret. Jandur though saw she smiled, and her face blushed like one of the tints in the glass.

Jandur went to her and softly said, "What is it you feel?"

"Oh," said the girl, without either shyness or boldness, "only that one day I shall be in love."

"You must give me the cup," said Jandur. "It is mine."

Without any hesitation the girl did so, but the smile did not leave her, just as Tesh was yet affectionate, and his wife yet sang to him.

When Jandur took the cup he braced himself, thinking all manner of insanities or ecstasies might overwhelm him, and that despite them he

73

must not let it fall and break. But all he felt was a speechless fear, the very same which had already visited him on the goblet's account.

He walked out into the little garden of the house. The moon was rising over the wall, where a mulberry tree grew, its leaves tarnished by exhalations of the makery. Jandur raised the glass, and the moon shone through it, grey and silent, telling nothing.

What shall I do with you? Jandur thought. *You may work miracles or do much harm. I will take you with me because it seems I must, and in the first city I will sell you, if such is possible. If I am wrong in that, forgive me, spirit of sand and glass. I have no other notion what is to be done.*

Then the wind blew through the mulberry leaves, and the wind said *Yes,* as sometimes, they reported, it did. *Yes,* said the wind among the leaves. So Jandur wrapped the goblet carefully and placed it in a box. A handful of time later he bore it to the city, where Prince Razved was King-in-waiting, and the Prince bought the goblet at the price of all the other broken glass. And after that Jandur took his own way through the world again, in prosperity or misfortune, as each man must.

3. The First Fragment

That very night, years before, the King of another country was to enter the town of Marah.

In the south, on the coast of the Great Purple Sea, there had been a war and much skirmishing, and this King, whose own city lay north of the desert, had brought his troops to assist a southern ally. The battles done, and victory secured, now the young King was returning home. The bulk of his army had marched ahead of him, but he himself stopped here and there on his route. That he should honour Marah was a source to the town of pride and pandemonium.

Most of the townspeople too were knife-keen to view the King. He was said to have that rare combination, pronounced beauty of person, intelligence of mind, and goodness of heart.

Marah, however, was not then as it would come to be in the time of Jandur's maturity—which time was yet some two decades in its future. Preparations were frantic and extreme.

Came the night, the young northern King rode through the main avenue of the town. In the glare of many hundred torches, it was seen that while his black horse was caparisoned in silk from the Purple Coast, which burned sapphire in shade but like ruby in the light, the King was dressed well but plainly, and his only jewel was the ring that signified his kingship. In himself though, he was jewel enough. His hair was like darkly gilded bronze, his face and figure were so handsome he might have been some wonderful statue come to life.

All about exclamations rose, and sighs, and after these—dumbness. How lucky was that northern city, to be ruled by such a paragon? How lucky his young wife, who had already borne him a son? How lucky his son, in such a father? How lucky the very sky there, and the air itself, to be seen by *him,* and breathed into *his* lungs?

Her name was Qirisn. She was by trade a musician, adopted and trained by an ancient school of the town, for her parents had died when she was only an infant. Marah, and the desert beyond, were all Qirisn knew, or supposedly. Since also she knew music, and knew it flawlessly, for she possessed great natural talent both as a player of stringed instruments, and as a singer. Music had, it seemed, taught her that incredible elements lay beyond the mere facts of existence, and far outside the scope of human law and rational thought. A fine and feral inner landscape existed within the brain and spirit of Qirisn, and something of it showed in the night-blue of her eyes, though few noticed her until she sang. Her voice was of an almost supernal quality, very flexible and silken, and superlative from its lowest to its highest notes. "So stars must sing," her last tutor had remarked of her, although not in her hearing. But she did not need to be made either modest or vain. She knew her worth and where it lay; it made her happy, and others happy also: there are few greater gifts than such genius.

It had been arranged that the best musicians of Marah should entertain the northern King, but they would do so, as was the custom then in the town, behind a screen. That being so, they went out on a little terrace above the street to watch, with various others, the monarch's arrival at the hall of banqueting.

Among these witnesses there was no change of opinion from that of all the rest who had glimpsed him.

"How fair he is!" they said. "Better than sunrise."

Only Qirisn did not say a word.

She was not, certainly, the only one to look upon the King and love him instantly, but with her the blow sank much deeper. Not simply had she never experienced the lightning strike of physical love before, she had, conversely, when involved in making or listening to music, experienced the phenomenon over and over, never then having a point of reference. It had seemed to her always until this moment, that the passion of her inner sight was impossible to realise in the outer world. Now she found otherwise. Panes like ice shattered before her. Her heart itself seemed to break like a mirror. To her, love was the most familiar and least known of any emotion. She went in to play and sing, moving in a trance, aware solely that he would hear her music. As of course he must, since now he would be the cause of it, and even in the past, before ever she looked at him, he had been so. It was plain to her, if in the most dreamlike way, she had known him elsewhere, in some other life perhaps, or on the outer fringes of this one. Or else, she had known him forever. And yet, in her current sphere, they would never meet.

The banquet began, the lamps burned bright, flowers and incenses released their perfumes. The diners were regaled by performances of magic and mystery. Doves burst from bottles and flew away, lions spoke riddles and could not be answered, diamond rain fell dry and cool as the moon's kisses.

The musicians played and sang too. If they were noticed above the general hubbub, who could be sure? Yet, when Qirisn sang, and tonight it seemed she sang more exquisitely than ever before, some did fall quiet to listen. And the King? It was noted he turned his head a fraction and, for a second, he frowned. But he was not unkind, not capricious, not heartless. Perhaps only he did not much care for music?

n the following day, the King resumed his journey, which, having once left Marah, must take him out over the boiled shield of the Vast Harsh.

He had, naturally, no concern for robbers, his retinue of servants and soldiers were more than enough to make cautious the most vulpine robber band. Nevertheless, he himself led forays among those bandit strongholds which were sighted, wiping many felons from the desert's face with efficient economy.

Otherwise, the King seemed somewhat preoccupied. He had trouble sleeping, and restlessly walked about the nightly encampments, chatting with the guards. Or he might write a letter to his wife—a foolish exercise since he would see her in a pair more months.

A sunset happened which was the colour of a damson. The King stood watching it, and then he turned to one of his officers, a man who had been close to him during the recent campaign.

"Did you hear ever, Nassib, was there much witchcraft in that last town?"

"In Marah, my lord? No, rather the opposite. Some of them talked of a witch who will shape-change to a vulture, but she is a desert hag and who knows, may only be a vulture and nothing more, save in a story."

"Quite so."

"Why do you ask, sir?"

"Oh, a little matter." The King watched the last of the sun's disc as it hid itself in some slot of the horizon. He added rather slowly, "I heard a girl sing at Marah, one of the musicians at the dinner. She had a lovely voice. But it is more than that."

"You fancied her, my lord? Surely you might have had her brought to you?"

"Well, but I never saw her even. And I do not wish to force any woman."

The officer laughed, between approval and envy, for very few women would not desire the King.

Returning to his tent, the King however wrote on the paper he had left ready for another letter, only these words: *In Marah, at the desert's brink, I heard a girl sweetly sing. And ever since that night, her voice has stayed with me. I do not know why. It seems I have been much disturbed by her song.*

The crossing of the desert, what with the forays upon bandits, and the King's mood, lasted longer than it might have otherwise.

But they lay over at a small oasis when the King called Nassib to him.

"Listen, my friend, I have a task for you if you will accept it."

Nassib declared he would willingly do so.

"Wait first to hear the commission. If you wish to refuse, I will find another to undertake it. You know I have been wed these past three years, and my wife has given me a healthy son."

Nassib agreed he did know this.

"Custom allows me to take other women, and also to wed them, but I have never thought either act necessary since my marriage. Now I am in love. I am in love with a *voice* and—oh, Nassib, you will think me insane—with a vision I see of her in sleep, or awake, when sunlight falls a certain way, or a cloud scarfs the stars. Am I bewitched? I do not know, nor any longer care. Go back if you will to Marah and seek out there the woman with the voice of silk and crystal. Though never having seen her, I can tell you how she is. Little and slender, with light hair, and eyes like blue midnight. If you doubt, ask her to sing a single note. Then you may be sure. Give her this ring with a crimson stone. Tell her, you will bring her to me, if she will go with you. I think she will. Her soul calls out to mine, Nassib, as mine to hers. Long ago, on some other earth, we have been lovers. More, we have been two halves of a solitary whole, and so remain. Tell her she shall be my second queen. Tell her," and here the King's face assumed such a look of bliss, his words rang strangely with it, "tell her I am dead without her, and wish to come alive."

Nassib stood bereft of speech. He was shocked beyond calculation at his own response. For it was as if all this while he had known the King uttered only the truth, and there could be no other choice.

But "My regrets, Nassib," said the King, taking his hand. "No, I do not think I am mad. I am at the sanest moment of my life. If you will trust me, do what I ask. If not, remain my friend, and I will send another. For she must be brought with some subterfuge to the city. There will be many obstacles to overcome, both of courtesy and faction. There may be dangers."

"My lord," said Nassib humbly, "I believe the gods have taken you and she into their hand. I cannot gainsay the gods. I will do everything you ask, as best I am able."

Before moonrise Nassib, accompanied by eight hand-picked men, was racing back across the Harsh to Marah.

She had dreamed of him every night, as he had of her. Awake, in changes of light she had seen him, in the faces of others or the faces of statues, or in the pouring of water, or the dazzle of sun on the strings of an instrument.

Qirisn grieved yet, seeing him so often, still she did not lose her quite unfounded hope. She could be nothing to him—yet surely she was. They could never meet—yet surely they would.

Some months after the night of the banquet, a young man, garbed like a desert wanderer, sought her in the court of the musicians' school.

He asked her if her name was Qirisn, and if she had sung in the hall when the King of the northern city dined there. He looked intently at her soft hair and small frame, and long into her eyes.

He asked she sing him one single note. She sang it. "I am Qirisn," she replied.

"Yes, so you are," said he. Then he gave a savage laugh. Then he begged her pardon for it. "When he was here in Marah, did you see the King?"

Qirisn assented. She was very calm, long-trained in means of control, as the musician must be, but pale, so her eyes seemed black rather than blue.

Nassib took a breath, and asked her, "Would you see the King again?"

To which Qirisn quietly answered, "I would give my life to do so."

Then the rest of the message was detailed, and the ring of rose-red topaz pressed into her hand. And she carried it to her lips and kissed it. Nassib next told her how they would leave the town before sunset, and start out over the desert, he and his eight men her escort. She nodded but asked nothing at all, only the colour of her eyes came back and filled Nassib's mind with a kind of blank serenity, and after this all was easy to do.

How easy indeed it was, as it had been easy to say to him, as she had, she would give her life to see the King once more.

And thus, while Qirisn and Nassib were crossing the waste, at long last the King reached his city.

Near to evening he entered the palace, and his wife the Queen came to meet him, her look radiant, her glorious hair twined with hyacinthine zircons. He greeted her publicly with great affection, and then they went away into their private apartments, and here, after a slight interval, during which the radiance faded from her, the young King spoke of his love and respect for her, but then told his wife what had befallen him, and what presently must come to be.

She paid close attention. When he had finished, she raised her face, now like a paper never written on.

"What of your son, the Prince?"

"He shall continue as my heir. I will love him always—love does not cast out love, only increases it. He shall reign as King long after me."

"And I," she said.

"You will ever be my first wife, First Queen, and I will hold you dear. You need be afraid of nothing."

"Need I not," she said. And then, "Well, my lord. I wish you every felicity in your life with this second queen, who is your highest love, your spiritual mate through time. After the aeons you have waited to regain her, how marvellous will be your reunion." And rising she bowed to him and went away.

The Queen paced slowly to her own rooms, and there she drew off her body every rich thing which she had gained through her marriage. She called in the nurse, and gazed at her son, less than one year of age. "Be blessed, my darling," she said to her child, and gave the nurse seven zircons from her hair. Alone again, the Queen went into her compartment of bathing, and there she lay down on the marble floor and cut the vein of her left arm. Some while she watched the white stone alter to topaz red. She said to it, "He has not broken my heart, he has broken my soul." But then she fell asleep, and soon thereafter she died.

Such was the rejoicing at the King's return, no one discovered what had gone on until that night had passed. The King himself did not receive the news until noon of the next day. When he did, he wept. It was proper that he should, and his court and subjects revered him for his tender sorrow. The Queen meanwhile they reviled for a madwoman. Even those who knew the truth avowed he had not meant to hurt her, she was unreasonable. And of course he had *not* meant to, for no man wants, unless an utter monster or fool, to saddle himself with such a dreadful scourge of guilt. Yet through the anguish of his tears and remorse, his love for Qirisn stayed like a pearl within contaminated water. The days of mourning would be long and scrupulously he would attend and mark each one. Beyond them, heaven-upon-earth awaited him. He could endure till then.

A storm was coming to the desert, it blew from the north. Lightning flared through the clouds, littering them with thin fissures of grey-gold. The thunder drummed on the sky's skin, as if to break through and plummet to the ground below in heavy chunks like granite, and each larger than a city. No rain fell. The dunes lit white, then brass, flickered to black, seemed to vanish underfoot.

To begin with they rode on, the escort of nine men on their horses, the girl in the little open carriage, she and its driver protected only by a canopy. But in another hour a strong wind gusted from the mouth of the storm, smelling of metal and salt. Soon enough it had the horses staggering and snapped the posts so the canopy flew up to join the roiling cumulus above.

Nassib came to the carriage.

"There are tall rocks there. We must shelter, Qirisn-to-be-queen. No other way can we keep you safe."

They sought the rocks then, a narrow mesa like one segment of the backbone of a dead dragon.

Lightning carved about them still, and the thunder rolled. Men and animals waited, stark or trembling, and only Qirisn was composed, afraid of nothing since her fate had found her, and she had trusted it.

Eventually another sound grew audible. It was that of men, unlike all others. Around the rocky hill came a cavalcade of sorts. They had lighted lamps too, and they were jolly, smiling and calling out invitingly to those who took shelter at the mesa's foot.

One of Nassib's men spoke in a voice of death.

"In number there are at least thirty of them. They are bandits. This is their stronghold. The gods have abandoned us."

Nassib drew his sword. It made a rasping, jeering noise, as if it mocked them. "While we may, we fight. Do not let them take you living." He had seemingly forgotten the girl. If he had remembered, he would have turned and offered to slay her at once. He could see his men had no chance, and nor would she have any, since these felons were everywhere noted for their profligate viciousness.

After this the bandits sprang from their donkeys and rushing up they killed every other man that was there, Nassib too, the bandits grabbing and their leader beheading him at one blow. They recalled Nassib from the King's forays on their kind, but tonight they lost none of their own.

When even the carriage-driver had been slaughtered, they drew the valuable northern horses aside. That done, the leader went swaggering and laughing to Qirisn. "And what are you? Not much, for sure. Yet a woman, I will grant you that."

Perhaps she had gone mad in those minutes. Perhaps she had only been mad from the instant she fell in love.

She addressed the bandit reasonably, without fear or anger. "You cannot touch me. I am meant for a king."

"Are you? His loss, then. You shall have me and my lads instead."

The storm watched, missing no detail of what was next enacted at the foot of the dragon's backbone. In the lightning, flesh blazed white, or golden, or grew invisible; blood ran like blackest adders, or inks of

81

scarlet or green. Cries became only another melodic cadence for the thunder and the gale. Storms frequently carried, and carry yet, such crying. Who can say if it is only imagined, or if it is the faithful report of the elements which, since time's start, have overheard such things?

At length, no one was there beneath the rock, but for the dead and Qirisn. In her, one ultimate wisp of life remained, although swiftly it was ebbing. *Come away,* life whispered to her urgently, *come away, for you and I are done with all this now.*

But Qirisn's eyes fixed on the sky of storm. The gods had forsaken her, love had, truth had. Worse than all these, she must now forsake *him.*

Something in her screamed in mute violence, a wordless, unthought prayer to the sky. Which, pausing, seemed to hear.

The cacophony of the cloud settled to a kind of stasis. The flutter of the lightning fashioned for itself another shape, that of an electrum knot. From this, long strands extended themselves, like searching arms. Long-fingered hands, resembling tentacles, reached as if most delicately to clasp the world. Then, from the core of heaven, a levin bolt shot downward. A flaming sword, the white of another spectrum, struck deep into the ground, at the spot where Qirisn lay dying. And after this it stood, the bolt, joining heaven to earth, pulsing with a regular muscular golden spasm. It fused all matter, sand and soil and dust, body and bone and blood, together in a disbanded union of change. Then the sword diluted and was gone. Everything was gone. And darkness sank into the space which was all the heaven-fire had left.

It is said, and possibly only Jandur, those twenty years later, propagated such a tale—for he was secretly a romantic—that hours on, when the storm had melted, demons came up onto the Harsh to enjoy its refreshment under a waning moon.

Passing the spot, those beautiful dreamers, the Eshva, paused only to sigh, before wandering away. If Vazdru princes passed, they paid no attention. But two Drin, the dwarvish, ugly and talented artisans of Underearth, did halt beside the silicate residues of Qirisn's death.

"Something is here worth looking at!"

But a desert hare, a female, gleaming platinum under the watery moon, and with ears like lilies, galloped over the dunes. And lust stirred up the Drin at such loveliness, and they vacated the area to pursue her. Such a master was love, then, for demons, and for men.

That very moment, as he entered the highest vortex of pleasure, Razved heard his phantasmal partner call out his name in her joy. It was not a moment otherwise for anything, let alone for thought. Nevertheless, it seemed not inappropriate she should know his name. Then the colossal wave bore him through the gate and dashed him among stars, and after that flat on his back again amid the pillows, with a maiden of glass gripped in his arms.

Only now did he unwillingly feel the chill and ungiving texture of her unflesh, and sense the folly, and maybe the *error* of what had just been done.

Only *now* also did he understand it was, after all, not exactly *his* name that she had called aloud in her voice of glass.

No, not *Razved,* that was not the name she had uttered. It had been Raz Vedey. *Raz Vedey, my beloved lord.*

Drained by ecstasy, stupefied by confusion, Razved lay there. There rushed through his befuddled mind a memory of his mother, who had slain herself before ever he had known her, and of an old man locked up and enchained in a dirty room below. Down there, amid the irons and the skittering of rats, that was where *Raz Vedey* might be located.

In his mind, Razved asked of himself, *whatever she is, what would she have with my father?*

Because, of course, the mad old man, who constantly escaped his imprisonment, but who haunted Razved even when safely stashed away, was that father, that very Raz Vedey.

Razved himself knew well that, along with a disgraced mother who had cut her wrist and died, he had a male parent who, while yet young and strong, the victor in a southern war, had one night, during a galvanic storm, started up shouting that his soul had perished in the Vast Harsh. And who, despite the subsequent care and attention of the best physicians and maguses, quickly became and stayed entirely lunatic. Razved, growing to maturity, was reared sternly by tutors, and when only thirteen made the regent of his father. Since then Razved had ruled the city, but without full authority and without the essential title of *King.* For did the King not still live? The city's moral code forbade his removal save through natural decease, and crazed though he was, the King ungraciously refused to die. Razved, to be sure, had engineered a clutch of clandestine attempts upon the wretch's life. All of these had failed. Yes, even the strong poison, or the block of stone cast from an upper roof. It was as if, Razved had long decided, his devilish sire awaited some news, or even arrival, and would not himself depart the world until assured of it. His constant wail: "Are they *here?* Are they *near?*" seemed infuriatingly—or pitiably—to confirm this last suspicion.

The Prince's eyes now remained tightly closed. He was partly afraid to open them, for the fragile weight of *her* still lay over him. What would he see? What must he do?

"Remove yourself from me," he muttered, but there was no reaction.

Instead his brain brimmed suddenly with uncanny images—a glassy girl, shimmering green and rose, who drifted through the chamber on feet of glass, and her eyes, curiously, were dark, and gazed at him and did not see him. Perhaps they saw nothing, for they were made—not of eyes, nor of glass—but of *pain,* of *agony,* and of despair. A bride, brought forth from the carcass of the Harsh Desert, the true meaning of whose title was *The Illegitimate Vessel,* a bride who had died in horror and waited in blind lament for two decades, next entering the city of her lover, her beloved, and mistaking for him one who *was* flesh of his flesh, if *never* spirit of his spirit. Where now then for her? Where else was there to seek or to fly?

On Razved's skin the glacial glass turned to ice, and with a howl he burst from his trance.

He bounded off the couch, slinging the succubus-creature from him, and opened wide his eyes. And in that instant, he saw and heard a shattering of glass—as if a million crystal windows had blown in and whirled about him.

"Help me!" yowled Razved, King-in-waiting, descendant of warrior-lords, spraying his robe with the waters of his bladder. "Assassins! Demons!"

But when his terrified servants entered, they found him quite alone, not a mark upon him, and on the floor by his couch only one little plain drinking goblet, smashed into bits like sugar.

Qirisn was now finally and fully dead. Free therefore, she glided through the wall of the prison-chamber and stole quietly to King Raz Vedey. She touched his ravelled face, and looking up he saw her, her light hair and blue-midnight eyes; he saw her soul. And shedding his ruined mind and form, he came out to her, strong and young and beautiful as he had been in Marah, and kissed her hands and her lips. After which they went away together, wherever it was and is that lovers go, after physical death, when they are two halves of a faultless solitary whole.

But in the red dawn, when someone came to tell the Prince that his father had abruptly departed the world, Razved buried his head in the pillows and wept, over and over: "At last, at last, *I am the King!*"

I Bring You Forever

Did the sages not say, in Jeshlah, each human thing is but a little place of life, surrounded by the desert? Just so, the palace towered upon its rock like the back of a lion, and all about, the town, pinned to the Earth by towering trees and stems of water. But beyond—beyond, the great lakes of dust, whose close hot breath is the desert wind. Gardens falling like green steps. A fountain that sprinkles, by night, the water drops of the stars. But beyond, beyond, the hot white Moon that has the face of the skull of a gazelle. There are bones under the dusk. And bones in Heaven, too.

When she was a year old, the king saw his daughter for the first time. He had been at war, triumphed, and come home. Three beautiful wives had already given him several strong sons. But his favorite wife, the fourth, had borne during his absence a female child. The woman approached, her soft hair falling to her waist and filled with tiny golden bells that made a placating noise. Her lambent eyes were downcast. (A nurse held the child sidelong, as if to hide it.)

"Forgive me," said the fourth wife.

"I shall only," said the king, catching her to him, "not forgive you for thinking me such a savage. Forgive you for what? For bearing me another such as you, to charm the hearts of men like music?"

Presently he took the girl child, who smiled and waved little fists, trying to snatch his jeweled earring. "See, she wants this." The king removed the costly earring, broke off the sharp hook by which it had held to his ear, and gave it to his daughter. "She must have everything she wants," he said, warm with victory, homecoming, lust, and simple happiness. "Always."

They had not named the child, for fear he would not want it to have even a name.

So the king named her Zulmeh, which in that tongue meant Diamond—the gem she had reached for.

The Diamond child grew up. A clear child, like cool water slenderly poured. And her hair was like dark copper, and her eyes a smoky green, like jade.

As she grew, so grew the town of the desert king. Long channels were made to conduct the water of the oasis, enamel roofs arose, and towers and lions of white stone.

By the day she was, Zulmeh, ten years of age, the king was called the Great King. And by the year she was thirteen, he was dead. A tomb was built for him that the desert people said was a wonder of the earth, and traveled far to see. Pillars and stairs raised it up to Heaven, showing it to the sky and the gods above, as if to ask them, what have you done?

But the Princess Zulmeh was only thirteen. What was death to her? It was true she wept beautifully as she followed the king's bier among the flowers of his weeping women. But it was only that the sad songs made her cry. She had scarcely known him. He had always been away at war, and in the end war had claimed him utterly, with the spear that pierced his vitals.

Her mother had died too, somewhere in those years. But her mother had not meant very much either. Her mother belonged to the Great King.

Only one thing Zulmeh knew for sure. That whatever she asked for she was given. How strange, perhaps, she never thought to ask, as another child would, for her father or her mother. She must have learned very early, perhaps even that morning in the arms of the king, that she would be given bright and shining things, valuable things, mystical and longed for. Hard, too. Hard as diamond. But nothing easy. Nothing that was hers—by right?

It would seem then she was a demanding child. Not so. She learned also, and quickly, to choose with care what she would have.

At seven years, asking for a particular beast, which she had been told of, she saw a caravan dispatched to a foreign land, to fetch it. One year later they returned, those who that had survived the dreadful trek, and they brought her, stiff and stuffed, the animal she had wanted, since it too had perished on the journey. One more lesson. Hard lesson. Diamond lesson.

When she was fifteen, Zulmeh's brothers fell to fighting among themselves for the crown of the Great King. Their armies clashed out in the desert, and from a place high on the city walls, one might see a flash of swords and arrows, over and over, and the dust rising like a purple column to uphold the indifferent sky.

The victor presently returned. His name was Hazd.

He swept the city like a broom, and settled on the golden lion throne, and called them all to admire him there. He asked who the girl was, the royal girl with dark red hair. They told him. Hazd said he would marry this girl, to uphold his claim to his father's throne. They were only half-brother and sister, he and the Diamond, and Hazd was a bastard.

Strangely, again, for one taught she might have anything she asked for, Zulmeh must have known not to ask to be spared her half-brother. But then, he was ebony-skinned, with corded hair that fell to his knees, lion-strong, a warrior and a poet. And she had never known him as brother, as she had never known, let us be exact, father or mother.

They were wed, and he led her to a pavilion high on the palace roofs, and from there he showed her the enormous desert of dust in the settling dusk of evening.

"What do you see, Zulmeh?"

"The Great Sands," she answered.

"No, you see my kingdom. Soon that absence of life will be covered by the life of my city."

But then they sat drinking sweet wine, and he played a melody for her on a lap-harp of ivory. He sang a song he had made for her. It compared her to the Moon, now lifting over the desert. But Hazd did not say the Moon was a skull. No, it was a young girl, whose eyes were green, if only one might see them. Of all his fine songs, this was, at that time, the most beautiful.

Zulmeh listened. Perhaps she thought, if she had not already, "I want and must have this man—"

At midnight, colored birds were uncaged above the roofs of the palace, where, behind the highest lighted windows, the city knew that Hazd and his bride had mated and made one.

Their love was glorious. He told of it in his songs, carved into the stone pylons of the city, beside his lion songs of war. But Zulmeh left no record of this love. For some reason she did not conceive his child. He would have assured her not to mind it. He had plenty of women who could do that in her stead.

Was there ever a night or a morning then, standing in the high place, when Zulmeh invoked magic from the stars or those strange otherworlds, the planets, or the gods, or the Sun or the Moon, saying: I want and must have the child of Hazd—I—I—No. There never was. She had learned her lesson, had she not. No father nor mother. No child. And, at last, no lover-husband either. Zulmeh was seventeen years, when one brother returned across the desert, a true son of their father. His name was Hroor. He slew Hazd in single combat, before the gates of Jeshlah. Did she see? Yes. But she was high up on the walls. Such little figures—so far off. Did she ask the gods for his life? Perhaps she thought of the exquisite living animal brought dead and mummified and laid before her. Perhaps she asked a moment too late—even as Hazd fell, dying—but by then her request would have been only a denial, Oh, let it be not so. A prayer must always be framed, the sages tell us, in the positive mode. Never do not, but only Let it be so.

If she thought she would be given to Hroor, the victor, with the other wives, she was correct. But Hroor was not a man for women, and did not trouble any of them. Also, not being a man for women, he was kind to them. Seeing Zulmeh stand alone, white as ivory in her red hair, dry-eyed green among the wailing queens of Hazd, Hroor asked who she was.

Then, "Ah," said Hroor. "The Diamond. I remember well my father's decree. Take heed, all of you. Give her always what she wants."

She never wept when others were by, not for grief, she who had always softly and publicly wept at melancholy music.

She sat alone, high up in the women's courts, in her own luxurious pavilion, which Hroor had not taken from her. She gazed away over the desert. Once or twice someone will have asked Zulmeh what she desired. She will have answered, "Nothing."

Hroor ruled three years.

One warm evening, with a Moon like a bow in the sky, the faction that had risen against him took their omen, and shot him full of arrows.

He lay unburied in the street, flighted like some old dead bird, while the sections of Jeshlah fought together. When the fighting was done, in the hour before dawn, men came to Zulmeh's pavilion.

They kneeled down to her.

"You," said they, "are the last descendant left living of the blood of the Great King. Only you, our Diamond, are now fit to rule."

She saw their smiling, crafty, blood-streaked faces. She would be Queen, but they would rule through her, for a woman was only an ornament, as the Moon only gave light.

But it was not a time to argue or declare what instead one wanted. She acquiesced meekly.

So Queen Zulmeh took the throne of Jeshlah.

And sages tell us, wisdom comes with the years, as with pain. We are scourged in the school of life that we memorize the lessons. To rule, even as a puppet and a woman, was dangerous, and so Zulmeh now encouraged, secretly, her own faction, those who revered her true royal blood, or were struck by her beauty and her sorrowful widowhood. Those too who liked power, but preferred it second-hand, the natural captains of a king.

When the fruit was ripe, Zulmeh the Diamond addressed them. It was a night of feasting in her private apartments. Cloth-of-gold, velvets strewn, tame birds with long tails of amethyst that stalked about, perfume playing in the fountains. The gold cups were raised high to praise the Queen and the gods.

Zulmeh spoke. "Never compare me to Heaven. They are perfect and eternal, and I have only my little span of being, which any moment may be wrenched away."

Then they cried out that they would serve her with their very lives. What did she wish of them?

She said: "I want safe rule in Jeshlah. I want the crown of Jeshlah and not its shadow. I must be rescued from those who, today or tomorrow, will cast me down, and all you with me, in a grave. I must have their heads."

The color crimson was on the room, crimson, purple, and gold. Before the lamps failed, on golden trays they brought her, her faithful men, twenty-four severed heads, dyed in their own red-purple blood.

Then Zulmeh was truly Queen in Jeshlah. And she had been given what she wanted.

Seven years passed, and the city grew like a natural thing, until it filled the horizon on four sides. Then Jeshlah was called the Great City, and the Queen of it, Zulmeh, the Diamond, the Moon of Jeshlah. Whatever she wanted, she was given. A thousand towns and cities paid tribute to her. From the four corners of a horizon beyond the horizon of the Great City, came the merchandise of the world. Silk and sandalwood, precious jewels and priceless stones, trees of resin and cedar, baths of oil and wine. Men came there too, mighty soldiers and princes, musicians and poets, acrobats, magicians and scholars. All to the white wheel of the

Moon of Jeshlah, wrapped in her copper cloud.

Feasts and shows of great extravagance were continually arranged. Here men fought to display their skill rather than to kill each other (although, quite often, kill each other they did). But also sorceries were worked of incredible kinds, to thrill and astound. And there were competitions for music and the making of songs. Jeshlah was civilized. Towers of books stacked scroll on scroll, volume on volume, the height of many tall men. Instruments that made a hundred ravishing sounds.

Zulmeh was in her thirtieth year. Among the poor such an age was a crone's age, but among the royal kindred it was not much.

A competition there was to be at which the best songs of all the world, as the world was known, were to be sung before her. Judges would award the prize not to the singer, but to the poet who had made the winning song.

As Zulmeh was carried to her stadium of music, she glittered flawlessly on her people. She had earned her name, they said, she blazed so bright with riches they could hardly bear to look at her. Her face, too, might have been cut from diamond, they said. So pure and radiant. (So hard?)

She sat and heard the songs. If her mind wandered now and then, no one could be sure. If she wanted anything, everyone might see it, a cup of wine, green figs or honey, the breeze of fans, and these things were given her at once.

Then a whispering began all about that did not quite center on the Queen. If she had been thinking of other things, this noise recalled her. A man waited below, tuning a little lap-harp modestly. Presently he sang.

His voice was fair, but it was the song which held the stadium.

The song told how a poet had seen a woman, and thought her at once a harp of ivory, but strung with his own black hair. By herself, this harp could sound him, as if he had been will-less. Yet without the strength of her strings, these long black strands, her music must be dumb.

When the song ended, the world seemed itself made dumb.

Zulmeh inclined her head, on which an unaccountable fortune flamed and spangled. Who could miss the flash of these fires, like swords at work in the desert far away.

he was not unloved, but the love had come with her station, the accessory of her rank. Doubtless what they had devised had been meant to please her, honor her, to be, even, kind. When finally the judges rose, the sky was red. But if any other songs had been sung, Zulmeh at least had not heard them. There was no deliberation. Naturally not. The judges declaimed their verdict to the stadium, which roared back its approval. Perhaps it was truly the best of all the songs, for Hazd had made it for Zulmeh, in the first year of their marriage.

It was the custom at such a festival, after the announcement of the winner, for the victorious poet to be called by a herald, three times. Nor did they omit this custom.

Loudly the name of Hazd was called, once, and then again, and then again.

And then all that stadium packed with people cried aloud for Hazd, and the noise rocked the sky, as if it were one huge bell of ruby glass.

Yet after the tumult, a silence fell, profound and terrible. The silence of a grave.

The Queen alone spoke softly, and none heard her. It was a silly childish thing she said. "He cannot take his prize. He is dead."

Darkness swept over the stadium. And all the kindled lights became little hopeless wisps beneath it. Anything might snuff them out. And nothing light up the black of the sky but the careless stars.

Zulmeh raised her face to these stars, and the tears glinted on her cheeks, and were, of course, taken for yet more jewels by the crowd. It must be said, if they heard what she uttered, they would have taken the words for the moistureless wit of kings.

But if they had thought to please or honor or be kind, they failed. They had only taught her one more lesson. For though she had known in her mind for ten full years that Hazd was dead, only now did she know it. So long it took the message to sink home, like a slow, slow knife.

All that night she walked about the palace's high places. She touched the birds upon their gold stands, so they trilled or spoke, the leaves of exotic shrubs, so they gave off a myriad scents. She looked through the magnifying lenses of her mages, and saw the stars more closely, tinted rose and sapphire and bronze.

Later she whispered, "But even the stars go out."

And she gazed to the edges of the city, to the desert that surrounded all things.

Her counselors were anxious. They stood in anterooms, puzzling, planning, yet not plotting.

At first light she came back among them all.

She had no appearance of madness, rather she was implacable, as some had seen her father, the Great King. They bowed to the ground.

"Now I will tell you," said Queen Zulmeh, the Diamond, "what I must have. What I will have. What you must get for me." Never had they heard her so clear, so sure.

They waited in instinctive terror.

They were wise.

"Bring to me," said Zulmeh, "immortality."

Only one year passes now, perhaps more swiftly than all the others. Experiments of all sorts took place in Jeshlah, acts of magic and religion, of devotion, of cruelty, elixirs, mythology, drugs, philosophy, poison. Men died, so that the Diamond might learn how to live.

Yet she did not learn. None learned, save only a few old tales which none could credit. All lessons require canny teachers.

Of her punishments for failure little is recorded. Possibly she was merciful. Only her looks of disappointment killed.

At the year's end, the city stood in its magnificence, yet about it hung a kind of smoke. And this inchoate thing towered up to the sky, like a pillar, a tomb. As if to ask the gods, What have you done?

"O great Moon," cried the girl, casting herself down before the Queen, "someone has come to the palace."

Zulmeh lifted her head, she stared, her green eyes fixed as a hawk's upon far distant prey. "Who now?"

The girl replied rapidly. "An old man, from the desert. But he says that he has heard of your quest—and has the remedy."

It was the hour of lamp-lighting. But the slaves stopped still and the tapers blew out in their hands.

"Bring him to me!" cried the Queen.

She rose up, thin and white and gleaming. Hard, hard, hard. Diamond lasts, but they scratch scars on things, even merely by looking from their burnished eyes.

And the appalled girl rushes away, and then returns, with the man from the desert, evenly flanked by twelve guards. (Strangely. One for every full year since the death of her love.)

Others had come, of course, to Jeshlah, promising they could find the way to get the Queen what she wanted. Perhaps none had said so decidedly that he possessed the goods already.

He was a tall old man, narrow as a stick, but straight and strong, sunburned, with a life carved on his face. Much scarred by years, he seemed unwary of the Diamond's scratch. But he was anomalous. So ancient a creature, to hold the secret of ageless eternity?

His clothes were ragged hides. He had no adornment but for his silver hair and the blackest black of his eyes. Such as he wandered the deserts, living in caves, feeding on sand, and drinking the dew. So poor a beggar to hold a secret that might have made him rich as any king?

"Kneel, old man," said the nearest guard. "On your knees before the Moon Queen of the Great City of Jeshlah."

At this, the old man smiled. Then he knelt with surprising agility on the tiled floor.

"Are you of this land?" asked the Queen's steward.

"Am I of any land?" asked the old man.

"What is your name?" frowningly asked the Queen's steward.

"What is a name?" smilingly asked the old man.

The steward indicated that the guard might strike the old man. Who laughed. And Zulmeh spoke to prevent the blow.

Then she ordered every one of her people from the room, and stayed alone there with the old man who kneeled, smiling, on the floor. One so old and so poor and so arrogant and so unafraid must hold some secret, after all.

Then a while passed. A fly might be heard crawling on the wall.

At last the Queen herself instructed the old man: "Speak."

He rose, and his smile was gone. He looked into her eyes and said, "I bring you forever."

It seemed to Zulmeh then, that all the lights that had been lit faltered and went dark. But a moment after, they burned up again, bright as before. As if time itself had blinked.

"What must you do," said Zulmeh the Diamond, "to make this so?"

"What indeed?"

"Tell me," she said.

"I have told. And I have done."

"Is it done then? But—is this all?"

"It is everything," said the old man.

He had stepped farther off, although she had not seen him do so. Maybe in that moment of the blinking of light and time. He seemed in shadow now, and the black of his eyes was almost violet—or red, a red-violet burning through the fabric of him, from within.

"Well," said the Queen, "you shall remain as my guest. There must be trials to be made, to see."

But across the room a curtain turned to a wind and blew, and he was gone in it, gone away, gone out like a lamp that did not rekindle.

The Diamond stood alone, and touched her face with her smooth fingers. (And how smooth they felt.) Am I changed?

* * *

The Moon of Jeshlah ruled in her city. "She is the Diamond," they said, "see how smooth and burnished-bright she is, graceful and slender, her metallic hair and expensive eyes. Not a mark on her. Always the same." But they squinted as if also they beheld that now each day was for her like each previous day. And each night all other nights. One eternal day and one night of forever.

Times unravels, samenesses, changes...

All the days and nights the same. Where do they go to? Changing into what?

Zulmeh left her bed early, and her women brought her a cordial of roses and mint. As she drank it, she saw them changed and changing. There a pale young girl, but now more sallow than pale. And there a voluptuous girl, whose figure drooped. And there, and there, a thread of gray in the silken hair, or hair too colorful, dyed to hide the gray.

When they laughed or sulked, Zulmeh saw the cracks time made in their enamels.

They clothed her and brought her jewels. Their hands were not so deft as they had been. Their perfume not so fresh.

Zulmeh gave an audience. Gnarled hands on yellowing papers... chipped voices... Now Zulmeh walked in her gardens. On the green steps, places opened slyly in the arbors. The white marble of the seat, as she sat admiring it, realizing that it had lost its glow. Flowers had burned themselves out. The vines were ancient and the grapes, that hung to be plucked, no longer tempting. Green droplets of juice shriveled to raisins.

Zulmeh looked aside into the palace courts. Children had become stubborn adults, and moved grumbling and fussing there. Already their shoulders were bowed. Their tones coarsened.

The sun rushes to the apex. She was left behind it.

She reenters a great pavilion—

She ate a meal in one of the great pavilions, among her nobles and captains. The gray is creeping in their hair. Rheumatic hands, old wounds that hurt them. The dogs were thin, with filmy eyes. Young dogs stand up on wild ungainly legs—steadied, and began at once to stiffen like the beautiful dead mummy brought her once across the world.

The lilies that had been wound in the garlands crumbled away. The bread has a taste of mildew.

Zulmeh gives another audience. Over the floor, feverish ambassador, the Sun hurries, moving so fast.

Old men paraded before her who had entered the palace young men. The tribute of sparkling veils spread for her delight were fraying at their edges. Only the hard jewels dimly shone.

Soon the palace and the city slept in the heat of afternoon. The Queen prowls like a panther up and down.

Over the Earth the Sun now shuffled. The Sun was old, and surely had lost some of its light. The sunset burned out like the dullest flower.

Zulmeh bathed once more and was dressed once more. Morning? Night? Old women tended her, she sees the bones behind their faces, their breasts are fallen empty bags.

The tiles in the floor had been rubbed almost clean of their pictures.

Time flew, flies, has flown. It flew, flies, had flown, over and over, circling the dish of the world. Like the blinking of the lamps, the sunrise and sunset, the flicker of the black-blue eyelids of night.

A dead bird lay on the terrace. It always lay there, lies there, or another bird. No more songs.

Zulmeh looked out to the four corners of the horizon, and her powerful city was laid like a carpet before her. But the wind and Sun had pared away the colors of the city. The old trees leaned or had fallen or been cut down. An axe strikes. There, another will fall, falls, fell.

At last, one day, some day, Zulmeh has them bring her carriage, and was carried through the streets. She watched the elderly people bowing to her, painfully, and the children stand taller and gain their first true balance—and stiffening there at once to statues of pallid wax. She watched the lights die in their eyes already long ago, heard their shrill bright savage voices tamed to monotonous regret.

Dead flowers littered the carriage, thrown in alive. Thrown in, yesterday, tomorrow?

"How wonderful is the Queen-who-is-a-Moon," she heard the fissured voices croak, "she has not aged one hour." Or do they only mutter against her, that she is a witch?

The guards marched by the carriage, and their breathing rasped, their footfalls rang heavily, exhaustedly.

Now the buildings of the Great City of Jeshlah are and were partly ruinous, with stones fall-fallen out. The inhabitants crouched in hovels made from bits. The dust of the desert had come in and covered everything it could, thick as yellow flour.

There was a huge gateway, a gate of triumph inlaid with blue lapis, and guarded by two lions higher than the towers around. But the lions had lost, one, his forepaws, the other, his head. And the lapis rains out of doors. Had rained out of doors. Here and there a blue petal of lapis lay and lies, in the dust. One petal that would not fade. Already fading.

Zulmeh left the carriage.

The ancient men in their tarnished armor stared at her with half-blind eyes. When the Queen said that she would walk a little in the desert beyond Jeshlah, they remonstrated, but feebly.

"Rest," said Zulmeh. "Rest a while."

She thought that when she turned back to them they must be skeletons, fallen or propped on their shields and spears.

It seemed to her she moved like a slim white knife and cut a way through dust and age and time, and as she cut, her own cutting made her sore. And conversely the rush of everything toward death, leaving her behind as did the Sun and the Moon and the stars, rubbed on her, grazed her. But a Diamond is polished finer by abrasion. So they say and said.

When her feet, in priceless sandals (of which the straps now gave way), met the flame-harsh grit of the desert's back, Zulmeh paused a moment.

"This I know," said the Queen. "For you are made by the grinding up of all else, as now, it seems, am I."

So she walks among the sloping dunes.

The racing hound of the Sun ran more slowly yet, aging, losing

97

ground.

Zulmeh stared after its bled-out shape, all wrapped in a distant storm of dust. She would, then, outlive the Sun? She would outlive the world? She, and the desert.

The frayed veils of dust, the desert's tribute, furled over the city, which seemed finally like a mirage. Soon every tower would drop down. Every wall collapse. Jackals would howl among the wreck—for a moment, only a moment. The Moon would set behind the Sun and darkness would come, but not the dark of night. Night too will have died, with all the stars, for she has said before, the stars go out.

Zulmeh walked, and the Sun came and went, comes and goes, and night likewise, and she reached and reaches a little place of life surrounded by the desert.

Two trees rose above a pool. A deer was drinking there, and seeing the blown white brilliance of the Queen, the deer sprang away. But as it touched the Earth again, it lost its vivid momentum. Through the flesh, Zulmeh saw its Moon-skull stare at her.

The Queen of Jeshlah sat down by the pool of the oasis. She thought she must be thirsty, and so cradled some water in her hands and drank it, before the pool should dry up and shrink away.

From two trees spread a shade that seemed cold, and almost still. Zulmeh sat down there. But, as she spread her hand in the shade, the shade seeps off, as soon, surely, the pool must do.

Zulmeh sat beneath the trees, and the shade came and went, comes, goes, the cool of it, never staying long, the heat. Somehow the pool was replenished from some fountain under the ground. She thought achingly of Jeshlah. But Jeshlah must now be dust. A place of bones.

"Time moves so fast," said Zulmeh to the desert, "but only adds to you, and never diminishes me."

Winds blew, hot as the sting of a scorpion, and burnished the Diamond more.

"I wish," said Zulmeh, "how I wish I do not have forever. How I wish that I am dead." (The denying prayer that does no good.)

Then she lay down in the moment of the shade under the trees, to sleep. For she seemed not to have slept at all, for many hundreds of years. And after she had slept, this once, she might never sleep again. Although, when she woke, she knew the Earth too might have vanished, will have done, dashed and rushed down into the bottomless abyss of nothing. Opening her eyes, she would find only the desert and the darkness left, and the cry of the soulless winds of immortality, the music of unforgiving forever. (No more songs.)

But, even so—even so, she slept, she sleeps.

Zulmeh dreamed. For the sages said, even the eternal gods have dreams.

A man was walking over the sand, in the dream, and Queen Zulmeh got up and followed him. He was changeable, this man. First he was black as her lost lover, Hazd, or blacker perhaps, but his hair was not black. Then he seemed goldhaired, but also grayhaired. And then he had no hair, his head was smooth as a brown nut. And then his hair was black, and then silver. And then his hair was a wave or a wind which blew the world sideways.

However, changeable as he was, he did not dash only one way, toward the pit of silence and dissolving.

Halting, Zulmeh thought he was, after all, the forever-bringing man from the desert, who must be a mage, and so quite capable of constant change.

"I will give you all I have," said Zulmeh, no longer running at his back but standing deadly still, "if you will take your curse from me."

"Did I curse you?"

"Yes. With your venomous blessing."

"I only gave you, Diamond," he said, "what you wanted."

"No one," said the Diamond, "ever gave me that."

Then he laughs, and turns and faces her. She cannot see at all who he is, for he is all shapes, all colors, coming and going, chaotic, elastic—terrible. Yet, his voice is like a song.

"My father," said the Diamond, "gave me a gem in place of my mother. The animal I loved they brought me made into wood, with cold hard fur, and eyes of vitreous. They gave me the heads of men in a pond of blood. They gave me the heavy crown of Jeshlah. Only one thing I never did ask for, and that was my marriage to my husband. And this was the only thing I ever wanted. Yet I did not know I wished for it till he was by my side."

"Hazd is gone," said the whirlwind upon the sand.

"Hazd is dead. I wish for death."

"You asked for never-ending life. Wished for and wanted it."

The Diamond said, "Did I not tell you. It has always been my way to ask for and receive that which I do not want?"

"You are a fool," said the thing before her. "Go back to Jeshlah."

"Jeshlah has fallen," said Zulmeh. "I have lived on, and centuries have passed. I have felt every one of them drag over me as it went. It has been centuries."

"Fool," said the thing which had given her forever, "it has only been thirty days. The number of years of your little human life."

Zulmeh opened wide her eyes. "Then have you not—" said she, "made me an immortal?"

"I gave you forever in thirty days. I did not promise you your wish, but its remedy."

Zulmeh opens wide her eyes once more, and this time wakes. The night is spread above, black and still, the stars fixed in their places, each sparkling hard and enduring as any diamond.

They say, it is true, that Zulmeh returned to her city, over the desert. She was very strong and not old. But the rumor of her journey, and her brief (it had been brief) sojourn in the waste, became a legend of that land.

When she came near the city, peasants at a well saw her walking toward them, and knew her as the Queen. They brought her milk in a clay cup, and she clasped their hands, those of young and old alike, laughing like a girl, so they laughed too. She petted the goats of their wild herds as if goats were quite new to her. The herders said, never was there a king like this.

But for Zulmeh, what? The frantic race of time, which she had only imagined, or been spelled to see, or spelled herself to see, had ceased. What she had witnessed in her sensation of eternity, the line beside the mouth, the fallen stone, were those intimations that all men, and all women too, will notice now and then. But not as she had done.

For had she ever noted a gray hair in the black harp-ropes of Hazd? No, never. But they were there, since he had been many years older than she. Had she thought the Sun ran across Heaven? Never, until she was given forever. (The remedy.)

Nothing is forever, unless, like the demon creature in her dream, it changes. Youth to age. Age to death. Death to birth to youth—

Reentering the gate of her city, it stood high as Heaven and full of its blue petals, the lions proud, their paws and peerless heads only a little worn. While on the avenue her soldiers raised their spears in salute, young men, mature men, strong and valid. And beyond, the people called for her, and the children timelessly played, and roses fell, firm and fragrant, the color of a sunset that was not blood, nor decay, but like a young girl's blush.

And in the city, the towers and the walls, they soared up. And in her private rooms, her lovely maidens welcomed her, peaches, jasmin, with teeth like pearls.

Zulmeh had seen what immortality might entail. Now she saw again what mortals see, dancing together on the floor of life, whose tiles are whole and perfect. Yet never would she forget her vision, her thirty days in a wilderness, static, and about her the whole wheel of time revolving and revolving. Poor child, she saw what men should never see. Wise child, she learned, and left it and came away, and lived. Hard lesson. Last lesson, perhaps.

In Jeshlah, Zulmeh the Diamond raised a pylon, which at midday held the Sun upon its tip. She would watch this phenomenon through a lens, a third jade eye. It always took the proper time. By night she traced the measured progress of the planets.

Also, in her thirty-first year, she married again a prince of another land. He was not black, but the color of honey. She bore for him, and for herself, three children, who ruled the city when Zulmeh's mortal time was done.

Long, long before that hour had struck, one night, near dawn, there was a shooting star. It flashed like a jewel across the firmament.

Zulmeh's lover-husband kissed her, and he said, "If you wanted it, I would give you that brilliant thing—if I could. I cannot. But I will love you forever."

The Diamond said, as the sages record, "We love. But nothing is forever, as forever is nothing. Forever is this moment. The world in a grain of sand."

Tales from Elsewhere

Foolish, Clever, Wicked and Kind

Death, the unmaker of men, came one sunrise to visit a noble man in the city of Baghdad. The nobleman's fine house stood on the east bank of the Tigris, set round with rose gardens and groves of pomegranate trees, but this did not hinder Death, who passed by the pools and over the lawns and in at the portals, without a second glance. Death was much-travelled and had seen many things, and beside was not inclined to dawdle, having several appointments in the City before midday prayers.

The nobleman lay unsleeping on his pillows. Two slaves, who had tended him through the night, for their part slumbered exhaustedly at the bed's foot. The nobleman did not rouse them. He turned his eyes toward the doorway and beheld, unsurprised, the figure standing there.

"Is it you?"

"It is I," said Death.

"I am not sorry to see you," replied the nobleman. "But for a single item I should be ready to depart."

"There is always something," remarked Death.

"I have vast wealth, and three sons," said the nobleman.

"Not all men are so fortunate," answered Death severely.

"This is true. But I have a presentiment now. With my passing there will be discord and quarreling. Disaster hovers over the roof like a vulture."

"Just so," said Death, not unkindly, "did your own father whisper to me, on the evening I called upon him."

The nobleman sighed. "You are wise. It is a fact. There is no hope nor help save Allah. My sons must take their chance as do all men, in the shadow of Fate. Therefore, I am ready. Let us be going."

It had happened that Khassim, the nobleman's eldest son, was hunting on the plains beyond the City. Though messengers sought his camp, they could not find him. Thus, after some days, when he returned home, it was to discover the house in mourning and his father already buried.

Khassim rent his clothes and flung away his turban. He told his servants to burn the skins of the beasts he had killed, two of which were the coats of lion. He called the barber to shave his face, saying, "It is not fit I should wear the aspect of a man, seeing I was not here at my father's end."

When he had been shaved, Khassim shut himself up and wept guiltily. To the second brother, Shireef, who—in the eldest son's absence—had carried out the funerary duties, Khassim had barely been able to bring himself to speak. (Although to the youngest son, Ahmed, he paid no heed, for it was the habit of both elder brothers to discount him always.)

At last Khassim came from his chamber with a cloud if not a beard about his face. Calling two or three of his servants, he vowed to ride that moment to the tomb of his father, and on the uncanny spot to keep a vigil through the night, praying to God, and expressing his sorrow and respect.

Shireef, watching him depart in the hour of evening prayers, murmured, "It is the cock who crows at the sun's rise, and the donkey who brays after it."

Then Shireef, handsome as bronze, smiled and went to walk among the roses.

* * *

The night sky was clear and dyed with darkest blue, and all the stars burned in it, when Khassim entered the cemetery and approached his father's tomb. He was alone, for his servants he had permitted to remain outside the graveyard gate.

Standing before the great mausoleum, the eldest son bowed his head and began his devotions, and the stars slowly wheeled across the canopy of heaven.

Presently Khassim yawned. A mighty weariness had overcome him. He glanced at the sky. The moon was only just now rising and it was many hours yet till dawn.

"O my father," said Khassim, "my misery has worn me out. Allow me to lie down on the ground and sleep awhile. These stones will make only a comfortless couch, of which I am most deserving. And soon I will be somewhat refreshed and may continue my vigil."

This declaration delivered, Khassim stretched himself on the earth at the tomb's foot, with his sash for a pillow. He fell immediately asleep.

When he waked it was with a dreadful start.

Nothing seemed stirring, however, save for a melancholy night bird which sat nearby in a bush and occasionally called. But the sky was growing pale, and among the stars the unseen Hand of God was discernable, snuffing their lights one by one.

"There is no strength save in Allah," said Khassim. And standing up he resumed his sash and would have commenced praying once more, when his attention was diverted. Between the graves close by, some persons were slowly walking, carrying lit tapers in their hands. Arriving before a large white tomb, this procession halted, and there stood forth the figure of a woman.

She was dressed in some splendour, and veiled, and when she raised her slender hands, jewels gleamed on them.

"My dear lord," she cried, in the direction of the white tomb, "as usual I have fasted and prayed, and watched all night under the wall. Now I approach to rain upon the ground the water of sorrow. Three full years I have mourned you, nor wed another, nor found any other man indeed that might replace you in my heart, so perfect were your virtues and accomplishments. Alas, alas, the sight of this burial place is now the only sweet I have."

Now here is true devotion, thought Khassim with sullen admiration.

And at that moment the woman cast aside her veil that she might kiss the surface of the tomb. Even in the dimness it was evident that she was beautiful, and, when the glow of the tapers covered her, that she was also young.

Seeing her loveliness and her grief in the loneliness of morning twilight, Khassim was impelled to step forward.

As he appeared the young woman uttered a low cry and stared at him with her large wild eyes.

"Pardon me, lady," said Khassim, "and do not tremble. I am no ifreet that haunts the cemetery, but a human man, who like yourself is here to mourn among the graves."

The young woman in her turn took a step towards him, and then another, her eyes still fixed upon his face. As for her attendants, they made no move at all.

"Tell me your name," said she.

Khassim told her his name, and, for good measure, his lineage.

Then she wept again, most beautifully, the teardrops spilling from her eyes like oval crystals.

"Although it is a sin, I had wished you a ghost," she said. "For you are the image of he that I lost, my dead husband, dearer to me than all the world."

Then she turned from him, and summoning her maids, she leaned on them, and went with a halting, graceful tread, away.

But Khassim apprehended one of the male servants.

"Tell me your lady's name, by the Faith."

The man was not loath.

"This is the Lady Nadina, a widow known throughout Baghdad for her misfortune, charm, and wealth. She was wife but three days. Yet, since her loss—for three years—thrice in every month save Ramadan—she fasts and keeps watch, then comes near dawn to embrace her dead lord's tomb."

"But had he no kindred to care for her?" asked Khassim.

"None. And as for offers of marriage, she would have spurned and fled from them, so precious is the one memory to her."

"And it is a fact," began Khassim, "that I—"

"You are his living likeness, sir," announced the servant, bowing low. "Such is Fate, and only Allah is God."

Just as the man was proceeding after his mistress, Khassim once more caught up to him, and offered him a generous sum of money.

"Although she is famed in Baghdad, I have never before heard of her. Where is her house?"

"Upon the west bank of the river, in the Street of Happiness beside the Fountain of the Ivory Pigeons."

Such absolute directions even Khassim was unlikely to mislay.

"What is amiss with you, elder brother?" inquired Shireef of Khassim in the late afternoon of that following day.

"Nothing at all. Everything is well."

"You have been closeted in the library, next in the bath and with the barber. Surely, after your vigil at our father's tomb, you are in need of slumber and rest?"

"No, rather invigorated."

"And where are you going now, in such glory?"

"To pray and to give alms to the poor."

He is not generally so pious, thought Shireef to himself. *Allah grant he has not gone mad and is about to squander all our inheritance.* Then Shireef called one of his own slaves, a mute Circassian pale as lime, and instructed him to follow Khassim and his retinue, and observe where they went and what they did.

Sunset came and rushed away, and night, and the evening prayers, and the moon stood high above Baghdad, staring upon the palaces and gardens of men as if to say, *What passing foolishness is this?*

Not until the hours of earliest morning did the Circassian return, and entering the apartments of Shireef, tell him in a language of signs known only to themselves, what had gone on.

R eaching the Street of Happiness, Khassim had halted at the Fountain of Ivory Pigeons, where his retainers erected a costly awning. All sat down upon cushions of silk. Musicians made music, and incenses were burned.

"Who is this fellow blocking up the street?" demanded the passersby. They approached, and Khassim's servants informed them that here was a doctor, versed in mathematics, medicine, and philosophy, who might be consulted upon any matter, but especially in ways of alleviating great grief of the heart.

However, when the traffic of the street sought to consult this learned man, his servants pushed them aside. "What? You have lost all your gold in a night? Your only son has been bitten by an asp? Tush! These items are too trivial to trouble our master with them."

Presently an old woman came pushing through the crowd. Going up to Khassim's servants she exclaimed, "My mistress lives in that fine house there. Her first grief is famous throughout Baghdad. Now a second grief has been added. Can your master do anything for her?"

"Why certainly," said Khassim's steward, "if it happens the lady's name is Nadina."

"Such perspicacity," remarked the old woman.

They conducted her to Khassim, who, muffled in a false beard, and trembling from beard to foot, affected nonchalance and questioned her.

"My mistress lost her husband to Death's long sleep after three days and nights, but such was their quality that she has mourned him three years. Last night, at his graveside, she met with a man who so resembled her dead lord, she has gone into a fit of sorrow sufficiently dreadful we despair of her life."

"I know the very cure," said Khassim. "Find some means that I may come to her."

"Only allow me," said the old woman eagerly, leering and pinching his arm, "space to get back in the house. I will leave a little side door ajar. Within waits a porter. You cannot mistake him, he is coal-black. He will take you to my mistress."

Khassim gave the old woman some money and ordered his servants to disperse the crowd.

It was by now sunset, and there came the call to prayer. In a short while, when the street had grown quiet, Khassim rose from his cushions and hastened to the side door of the house. Sure enough, it stood ajar. Khassim hesitated, looking for the porter. Suddenly there sounded the flap of wings. On a golden perch was a falcon, black as coal. This, having fixed Khassim with a glittering eye, flew up and away into the house. Khassim followed, and the door swung shut.

Now it may be supposed the Circassian slave of Shireef would be baulked by the shutting of this door. But that was not the case. Limber as a snake, the pale slave found the means to climb the house-wall by a vine which flourished there. Coming on to the roof, he next detected a lighted window and, wriggling like a serpent, got a purchase to peer in at the lattice. What should be in the room but a veiled young woman reclining on a couch. Next moment in ran Khassim.

He had no more than stammered a beneficence, than the young woman threw off her veil, and raising her lovely face and hands, entreated him.

"My sadness is unsupportable—help me, learned doctor!"

Khassim, who had perused ancient scrolls to ascertain the best and most proper form in which to deceive and have his way, was now overcome by compunction.

"Lady, I am modest in the profession—"

"The seat of my pain is here," cried the lady, touching her heart. "Since you are a philosopher, and plainly an aged man—to have grown such a great grey beard—there can be no wrong in revealing myself to you. Pray examine me, for I must be cured, or die." And so saying she threw off every stitch of clothing, and stood before Khassim naked as the young moon. Her skin was fragrant and supple, her contours rounded and her waist slender. At her wrists and ankles sparkled brilliant jewels, and her black hair flowed about her to her knees.

Khassim dropped at her feet.

As he did so, the hideous beard was dislodged and fell from his shaven face.

Nadina gave a cry.

"Alas! How I am shamed. What wicked trick has Satan put into your head, dishonourable man. Woe to me that ever I loved you, or mistook you for another, whose virtues and honesty were beyond all question."

Khassim commenced kissing her toes.

"Lady," bleated he, "I will wed you. There will be no shame. I will marry you in the sight of the City. Only appease me now."

Nadina made a move towards him, then seemed to recollect herself. "You must repeat your promise before my witnesses."

"Yes, yes, gladly. Be it only swift."

The woman clapped her hands and in came some of her servants, one of whom was bundled in the mantle of the old woman who had first got Khassim access to the house—and yet who now seemed ill-fitted by her garment. In his haste, Khassim took small note of this, and boldly made his vows once more. Nadina then dismissed the retainers and took Khassim to her bosom, enjoining him to have his way. Which, with much energy and outcry, he did.

Near morning, appeased and exhausted, the young man sank into a profound sleep. No sooner had he done so than his bedmate left the couch and gave him a box on the ear. It did not wake him. She then left the room and passed into an adjoining chamber.

Now this chamber had no windows, and was unlit. Thus, the watchful Circassian who, until this instant, had not once lost sight of either Khassim or the woman, now did lose sight at least of the latter. Nevertheless he made out faint whispers and a low and bitter laugh. Presently, back into the lighted room stepped the widow, clad and combed, and bearing the black falcon on her wrist. Apprehending she might come to the window, the Circassian prudently hid himself.

Nadina spoke to the falcon.

"Go now to our lord the magician," said she, "and tell him, this fish is hooked."

Then the falcon came darting straight out of the window.

The bird winged away across the City sky, where night was waning, until, far off in the pearl-pale height above the river, it vanished, a black speck, in at the top of a tall, black tower.

And with this news, the Circassian returned to Shireef.

The wedding of Khassim and Nadina lasted many days and nights. What quantities of precious gums were burned, and firecrackers exploded and filled the dark with jewelry rain. Music and song, feasting and delight, made loud the mansion.

The moon waned, and began again to wax, the guests departed, and there came an evening when Khassim called his brothers to a private dinner. Or, he called Shireef. To the youngest brother, Ahmed, it was made apparent that, although invited, he need not bother to present himself.

Khassim's wedding had not, for a wonder, depleted the kitchens. Many sumptuous dishes were served, while musicians plucked melody from the gunibry and Nubian kissar, and maidens danced with bells at their waists and ankles.

At length, Khassim turned to Shireef and embraced him fondly, having tears in his eyes.

"Dearest brother Shireef! How I shall miss your company when you are no longer in my house."

Shireef smiled. "Then I am due to be elsewhere?"

"Certainly. You know tradition recommends it."

"That the younger brothers be ousted once the eldest is wed?"

Khassim sighed. His beard was now of natural luxuriance, but the role of bridegroom had but increased his girth and balconied his eyes. "Dearest brother Shireef," said this smug bolster, "you shall be given your portion—which though small is lavish as I may spare. I stand as father to you now, and believe me, it is not good to be idle. What better work could you have, than the management of your estates?"

Shireef mused upon his estates, reduced by his neglect to some slight areas of dust disdained even by locust and jackal.

"Or," postulated Khassim, "undertake the holiest of all journeys—travel to Mecca. Though I cannot afford to finance the enterprise, be sure my sincerest wishes would go with you. Indeed I should envy you your days of fasting and prayer, your proximity to the sacred shrine... all that you would learn from hardship on the road."

Shireef mused upon Mecca and hardship.

"Yes, Khassim," he answered. "You are as sage as you are generous."

A nightingale sang in the gardens, her song so beautiful that men could no longer make out the words: Blessed is God, who created the seven heavens. His work is faultless. Turn your eyes upward to the sky: Can you detect a single flaw?

But the veiled and mantled form which approached Shireef under an almond tree said only:

"I represent my mistress. What is it, lord, you would say to her?"

"Oh," said Shireef, "can it be that you are that old hag who attends her, the one who claims herself to be named *Nadina*? She that has taken to impertinent grinning at me as if she is privy to some secret about me. She that I would have whipped?"

"I do not believe that I am the hag that you refer to, lord. But I ask again, what you would say to my mistress."

"I would not say much. Only that I have put a watch on her comings and goings, and on the venturings of her slaves. And so have learned a thing or two."

"What things can these be?"

"Why, that she serves a magician in a black tower. That Khassim is her dupe. But mostly," amended Shireef, eyeing the figure narrowly, "I have learned her beauty intoxicates me, and my life is worthless to me unless I make her my own."

The mantled one let slip a fold of the silk, and the liquid eyes of Nadina the widow-wife looked coldly on Shireef.

"You have gathered your bricks," said she. "What house would you build?"

"Rather than aid the stupid Khassim, I would myself take on the luscious lady, and myself serve her mage-master. *I* am no fool, but I have thoughts of power. Let us be rid of the idiot and ally together, fairest love."

Then Nadina discarded the silk from her face entirely, and stared at Shireef as if she measured metal on a scales.

"It is a fact," said Nadina, "I have no liking for Khassim. But do you mean I should, by my arts, kill him?"

"Let us not incur the full wrath of Allah," said Shireef. "Let us only anger God a little. It would be amusing, would it not, if you are able—to turn Khassim into the likeness of what he is: A fat, saddled donkey."

Nadina, catching the smile of Shireef as if by contagion, curved her lovely mouth as the sickle moon is curved, or the sword.

"A donkey. And thereafter?"

"He shall be reported dead on a journey to Mecca. I shall wed you.

Your wealth and status you shall keep, and I practice at your side your master magician's will. Between whiles, we shall extravagantly couple."

Finding her yet smiling, Shireef leaned to bring their smiling mouths together. But Nadina slowly drew back.

"Say that I agree. First, at the feet of my master, you must be proved."

"I am ready."

Nadina clapped her hands. From the boughs of the almond tree shot downward the black falcon. As it came it screeched once, and the nightingale fell silent, and all the garden hushed.

But the falcon dropped upon Shireef's arm and gashed his hand with its beak so the blood flowed and he cursed it.

"Be wary, beloved, whom it is you offer oaths," said Nadina. Going up to him, she showed him a feather no bigger than a rose petal. "Put this beneath your tongue instead. Take care when you loose it out again."

Shireef now frowned, but he put the feather into his mouth.

Next second he was changed. His body compressed itself, he was bereft of arms, and reins of fire sprang from his heart through his backbone. His vision was cleft. Then he leapt upwards, and he was a falcon, dark as bronze in the light of the stars, his wings outflung and his beak firmly clasped to hold in the talisman as he flew over the mansion's top.

Two others sped before him, one black, one grey, but they went westward, and he followed them.

Below rushed the roofs and walls of Baghdad, the river like the rusted belt of fluted Basra steel, fretted with sleeping ships. But on the west bank there ran up in the air to meet them a black needle with an eye of cold yellow.

Towards the needle's eye they were pulled in like a triple thread. And through the eye they pierced, one, two, three, and Shireef was the third, and cast themselves down in the precincts of the magician.

Immediately a huge voice, like a brass bell, boomed through the chamber. The words were of an unintelligible language. But no sooner had the voice pronounced than the feather fell out of Shireef's mouth. And at once he was a man again, and beside him was the woman, his brother's wife. (Although the black falcon did not alter itself, but only perched in the window embrasure like a thing of jet.)

Then a pair of doors at the chamber's other end burst open, and the

114

mage entered the room.

He was tall, and clad in robes both fabulous and curious, many jewels and rings flashed on the fingers of his left hand, sulphurous, bloody, white and blue. His face was itself like that of a bird of prey, but with gluttonous lips.

"I have brought this one, lord," murmured the woman Nadina, on her knees, "as you foretold me I should."

The magician glared at Shireef, and Shireef's cool heart quailed. But he said, "I am at your disposal, mighty one. If you have judged I would come to you, you will know what wishes I have carried here in my soul."

"Never doubt I do," replied the mage. "You are a child of the planet Marikh, of the fellowship of envy, war and murder."

Once these sentences had been spoken, Shireef felt the floor of the tower give under him. He was whirled away before he could so much as cry aloud.

When the tumult settled, Shireef found himself on a great bare plain, and above stormed a sky like fire, where copper-colored eagles fought and tore at each other. Near at hand grew a solitary plant, with flowers of scarlet. But no sooner had Shireef observed it than the stony soil under the plant cracked open and there heaved up from the earth beneath an enormous scorpion, which turned instantly and began to move towards him.

Shireef stood his ground. He stared into the red eyes of the beast, the sting of which surged high above him.

The scorpion spoke.

"Get upon my carapace, little man."

And Shireef noted that between its eyestalks there was the mark of King Sulayman, which had bound it to the magician's will. So Shireef got himself up on the scorpion's back, and it scuttled off with him, over the desert plain under the sky of fire, until they arrived at a deep well, the bottom of which was not to be seen.

"Unwind your turban, little man," said the scorpion, "and tie the end to my foreclaw. Then lower yourself into the pit."

Shireef did not waste words, but obeyed the scorpion, though he doubted there was enough silk in one man's turban to support him all the distance into the well's depths.

The scorpion crouched over the well-head, as Shireef, hand under hand, climbed down into the sightless gloom below. After a time, even the shrieks of the battling eagles grew dim, but still there was enough of the turban left to bear him. And when Shireef suddenly reached the end of the silk, lowering his feet, he touched a floor with their tips.

Another voice spoke out of the dark.

"Come here and embrace me."

Shireef had no more than looked about when the dark became manifest. An enormous serpent had upreared itself, and next coiled him round. And he saw it plainly for it was itself luminous. But he did not struggle when the scaly mask approached him and the blood-red eyes beamed on him. On its brow was the mage's mark.

"Thus you have passed, without flinching, all the tests but one," said the serpent. "Now you have only to answer the riddle I will pose you. But if you cannot, you shall be slain."

"I await the riddle," said Shireef (though he shuddered once).

"I am subtle," said the serpent, "I am cruel. Put into me pure gold and you will get back dross. Feed me and I will shrivel. Starve me and my poison will swell and increase. I am to all men a hollow coffer to be filled and a shut door that will not be opened. What is my name?"

The nobleman's second son smiled once more, there in the dark, in the serpent's clutch.

"Your name," said he, "is Shireef."

The serpent sighed. "There is none stronger for good or ill than he that knows himself." But its words and breath became then the whirlwind, which tossed up Shireef the subtle, the cruel, the hollow coffer, the closed door, through toils of pitch and flame, and out into the magician's tower.

As the eyes of Shireef cleared, he beheld this mighty sorcerer standing before him touching his forehead with the point of a strangely shining sword. It burnt Shireef, but he made no complaint.

"Now you are my slave," said the mage. "But to other men, a prince you will be, and a tyrant. Only if you fail me, you will fall, and then the tiniest beetle, crushed beneath a beggar's heel, even that will pity you."

"So be it," said Shireef.

The porters of the dawn uplifted and bore off the silver-studded lid of night. There poured over the City the call to prayer, and in the stables of the mansions above the Tigris, one raised himself and bethought him of offering worship to God. But such was not possible.

"Allah is merciful! Now what is this?" gasped the unfortunate one. But from his mouth issued other sounds entirely.

Presently grooms came to the stall, and leading out the fat ungainly donkey, which heaved forth unusual moans, and stumbled over its four hoofs continuously, they took it off to be sold in the market.

However, as the donkey was led away, one of its sideways eyes glimpsed, behind a high window, two round smooth arms (upon which familiar bracelets sparkled), encircling the neck of a man whose name was not Khassim. And then the donkey lamented indeed, but what it got for its pains was a kick.

All this while, it may be remembered, there had existed a third son, the nobleman's youngest, Ahmed. Since his elder brothers quite discounted him, he had not much figured in their lives. He had, nevertheless, attended his dying father, and mourned him, observed Khassim's courtship of a young widow, and the wedding, and at length received his order to quit the household with no vast astonishment, nor any demur.

It was true, Ahmed, of all his kin, had the least in the way of resources. And it might be said he had been careless of what he had. For he had spent much of his slight riches on entertainments and gifts for his friends, and given most of the rest away in alms.

This very day, indeed, on a street of the City, Ahmed might be perceived handing his last coins to a beggar, who blessed him. But another person, coming on the scene, upbraided Ahmed. "Young fellow, I know your situation. What do you mean by it, leaving yourself with nothing, in this feckless manner?"

"Only three things are sure," remarked Ahmed pleasantly. (He was in all forms very pleasant, not least to the eye and the ear.) "God is above us. Fate surrounds us, and one day, every man must die."

"That does not justify the prodigal," chid the other.

"Perhaps you are right," conceded Ahmed with grace. "But it seems to me that I will put my trust in Allah the All-Wise. Being human, I am, at my best, liable to fault. But God is perfect. A man has only to be patient, to be shown his path."

Now the one who had been questioning and chiding Ahmed was a stranger, very tall, and clad in white, and the hood of his mantle hid his face. Yet as they talked, the white of him seemed to become ever

117

brighter, until Ahmed could hardly keep his eyes on it. Moreover the tones of the stranger, which at the start had been irritant, now turned musical, kingly, and profound.

"Perhaps," said this interesting man, "you should go to the houses of your friends. When you were wealthy, you were unceasingly kind to them, and no doubt they would be glad to help you at this hour."

"It is considerate of you to advise me," said Ahmed. "But I would rather my friends were left in peace. None of them is rich, and all have burdens of their own. For myself, I am lighthearted, and besides, consider this an adventure. Who knows what God may put in my way? For if a child asks his father for bread or a fish, what father will give him a stone?"

"There are many fish," said the stranger, then, "in the river."

And that said, he turned aside into a walk between the walls of two buildings, and there his white brilliance faded abruptly, so he was not to be seen.

But Ahmed thought to himself, *That is as good a path as another.*

And so he went down through Baghdad, that great and enterprising City, to the rim of the brown river Tigris.

On the banks, at a spot where the fishermen were setting to work with their nets, Ahmed paused. After a time, seeing a handsome and well-dressed youth gazing at them attentively, some of the fishermen left off their toil and came to ask his desire.

Ahmed replied that he was of a mind to learn the trade of a fisher.

The fishermen scoffed.

"Do not mock us, high-born boy. This life is not for you."

So then he asked their permission to merely observe them, and what they did. To that they agreed, and resumed their labours, now and then jesting at his expense.

But Ahmed did watch very closely, and after midday prayers, he went on along the shore, and finding a fisherman sleeping beneath an awning, roused him and acquired from him his mended net, in exchange for a silver ring. (This fisherman, not believing his luck and thinking Ahmed to be addled, went scampering off in haste.)

Ahmed waited a space, until the time of day and state of the water seemed propitious, then wading out, he cast the net.

At the first try, nothing came up but some weed from the mud. And at the second try a rotted piece of timber. But Ahmed only laughed and said, "The river is joking with me. I can hardly blame her. How many thousands of years she has taken her way, here, but I shall come and go like a gnat across the surface."

All day he cast, but with no results, though never losing heart.

Then, well into the afternoon, the upper air grew thick with birds. This seemed to auger well, and he cast the net a final time.

Almost at once it turned heavy, but from the movement of the cord in his hands, he could tell something live had been snared.

Ahmed hauled on the net, and his catch resisted him. The sun had come down low over the river, glowing between the walls of the farther bank and making on the water a spill of gold. And up out of this molten gold there suddenly burst the net. Its captive was a large fish, gleaming like nacre, with a crest of golden filigree and emerald upon its head. And this fish lay in its cage in the sunset, staring at Ahmed sorrowfully from the most beautiful eyes.

"Why," said Ahmed, "though I have hoped all day for a catch, you I cannot keep. Surely you are the queen of fishes? Trust me. I will cut the net and let you go."

And without another thought, he drew his knife and cut the net. Out swam the remarkable fish, but it did not at once dive down under the river. Instead it circled Ahmed, round and round, lifting its face from the water and gazing up at him, and then, taking the edge of his coat in its lips, it began to tug and pull at him in turn.

"Dear fish," said he, perplexed, "be wary of those circling birds above me." And when it did not heed them, "Where is it you would take me?"

The fish vanished under the surface, but still keeping the edge of his garment in its mouth. Ahmed was amazed. The fish reappeared, and stared at him once more with imploring eyes.

"If I follow, I shall surely drown," said Ahmed.

The fish loosed his coat and spoke to him with the voice of a girl.

"Do you believe you hear me speak?"

Ahmed, startled, answered: "Yes!"

"Believe then also that, through my friendship, you will not drown under the river."

And that said, she pulled again at his garment. Ahmed, bowing to the east, murmured, "Most wonderful is God, who has made all things, and of such variety!" And then he dived after the fish into the depths of the

Tigris, leaving only the broken ripples of gold to mark their going down.

𝕌nder the river was darkness, but the magical fish gave off a light of her own, and moved like a swift lamp before him. As she had promised, Ahmed found that he could breathe without difficulty, although he had no inkling by what means.

Shortly, the fish led him amongst a forest or town of ancient, foundered ships, merchantmen and fishing-craft both, anchored where the flow of the river had left them, and plastered over with a black slime. Beyond this place lay a valley like a cauldron of pale sand, lit by a faint luminescence whose source was not to be seen. And here rested one last ship, a magnificent vessel, as it looked only newly sunk. Her sails were reefed, and the carving and paint on her sides stayed vivid.

To this ship the fish hurried, and darting up, disappeared over the rail. Ahmed swam after, and no sooner had he gained the deck, than he met a sight which halted him.

Three maidens of great loveliness, clad like princesses, obeised themselves to him, their draperies and veils blowing softly at the motions of the water. Then one, rising up like a flower opening in the dawn, conducted him along the deck, to a cabin, the inlaid doors of which stood wide.

Within the cabin, gilded lamps set with carbuncles burned with sorcerous fire, and carpets of Samarkhand hung, dyes unimpaired, upon the walls. And in the splendour there waited a maiden whose loveliness was, to the loveliness of her servants, that of a peerless rose amid jasmin. She was dressed in clothing of nacre silk, and wore a headdress of golden filigree adorned with chains of emeralds. And the eyes of the maiden were like a world of midnight skies, so lustrous they were, and so heavenly.

"Behold me, as I really am," invited the maiden. "But know, that only here, sheltered by the contrivance of my father on this sunken ship, may I take my proper form."

Then Ahmed said to her, "Lady, even in the guise of a fish, it seems I knew you. Did I not call you queen of your kind?"

"So you did, and set me free. Woe had been your lot if you had dealt otherwise, for even in the shape of a fish, my father had left for me some protection."

"If I had harmed you, I should have deserved nothing better than woe."

Then the lady bade him be seated, and the charming maids entered and served for them a feast of rare delicacies from the earth's four corners.

And while they feasted, they spoke of trivial and gentle things but when they had finished with the feast, the maidens brought perfumes and honey and sweetmeats, and the juices of fruits, and crystalline water, all of which was miraculously possible in the river's depths, nor did the river in any way taint anything. Then, on tortoise-shell harps, the maidens made silvery music. And to the sound of it, in a voice also of silver, the lady recounted to Ahmed her story.

Her name, she said, was Jehaneh. Her father, a rich man, a scholar, and something of a mage, had also been a traveler through inclination. And in his maturer years he had settled on the City of Baghdad for a domicile, and even on the wife he would take there. Accordingly he set out, with all his household and his only daughter (the child of a previous union which Death himself had dissolved). Many months of exotic travel ensued, until they entered the mouth of the mighty Tigris.

Now the ship was a possession of the scholar's, and the captain a former servant of his. The voyage had been of the pleasantest, and perhaps, entering the homeward stretch, they had grown too trustful of Fate, seeing it had been good to them.

Some miles below the City, where the arid shores came down lion-like to drink at the river, the ship's watch spied a floating raft and a man lying on it who feebly hailed them.

The flotsam was grappled and the unfortunate brought on board.

Being revived, he explained that he was a journeying noble from a distant land, who had fallen prey to the plot of his enemies. His slaves, corrupted by these men, had turned on him, robbed and abused him, and left him for a corpse in the desert. He had struggled to the riverbank nevertheless, and fashioned the flimsy raft, but, his strength then giving way, he abandoned himself to the will of God.

Jehaneh's father, finding the man to be, like himself, a traveler, and erudite, soon took to him. But not so Jehaneh herself, who had been privy to some of their talk behind a screen. Her father, however, fondly put by her doubts and would hear no talk against the man.

It happened that the father of Jehaneh, in his youth, had gained possession of a very extraordinary ring. It contained a perfect sapphire, the gem of the planet Mushtar, ruler of justice and strength, and it had, besides keeping the wearer in fortune and health, certain sorcerous properties. The scholar for a fact never, since getting hold of it, removed the jewel from his finger, and by now flesh and metal had all but become one.

In the midst of the night, as the ship lay at anchor, and each save the watch might be supposed asleep, Jehaneh woke from an anxious doze, thinking she heard her father call to her. Her maids still slumbered, and the whole ship seemed doused in a velvet gloom, unleavened by stars or lamps.

Proceeding to the curtain and screen that marked off the scholar's portion of the cabin, Jehaneh called to him in turn. "It is nothing of any import," replied the scholar. "Only that I was having a peculiar dream."

"Pray tell it me, my father."

Then the scholar ruefully recounted that in the dream he had felt something plucking urgently at the sapphire ring, but starting up awake he found matters otherwise. "And surely no one," he added, "could take the ring from me unless they have the finger with it."

At his words Jehaneh was filled with terror, but she did not speak. Being courageous, she drew a dagger which she kept for her own protection, and sat all the remainder of the night by the screen, listening and alert, in vigil over her father's slumber. But not a sight nor another sound, nor any disturbance, occurred throughout the last hours of darkness.

Then the dawn began to bloom on sky and river, and in the first soft moments of the light, a loud and fearful cry galvanized the ship.

All who might rushed out on to the deck, and there they came on the ship's watchman, gibbering with fright. When once he could bring himself to utter, he declared that, just as the darkness was fading, he had perceived a slender stream of mist curling out from a passenger's cabin. This, swirling upright, put on a shape so awful that it had almost deprived the observer of reason. Questioned as to the nature of this shape, the man answered that it had been a giant thing, somewhat resembling a man, but three times at least man's height, tusked like an elephant, and with the claws of a lion.

"It is a jinn!" exclaimed the crew, virtually as one.

"Truly, I think it may be so," said Jehaneh's father, and she saw that he had turned deadly pale. Motioning her to follow him, he went back instantly to the cabin. Seating her before him there, he spoke thus: "I have been stubborn in not heeding your instincts, when earlier you warned me. See now what has befallen." And he showed her his hand. Jehaneh was struck by horror. There was not a mark on the flesh, but the finger which had worn the sapphire had shrunk down and wasted away until it was no bigger than the digit of a three-day infant. The ring itself was gone.

Even at that moment, a shadow seemed to cover the ship, as if the dark of night were returning.

"That one is a powerful and evil sorcerer, there can be no doubt," continued the scholar. "Perhaps some misfortune did indeed chance upon him, so he requires the virtue of the ring, or perhaps he is only greedy and a player of games. Whatever, we are in much danger still. Dearest daughter, he can intend only wickedness, and I possess one method alone by which to protect you, and the innocent maidens who are yours. There are spells I know of transformation, and this ship being mine, I have also long since fitted it with uncanny means and benefits, for one can be sure of nothing save the omniscience of God."

Then the father told his child that, if she would suffer it, he would transform her and her maidens into fishes, and send the ship to the bottom of the river. For the captain and the crew another remedy should be found. The scholar alone would brave, as best he might, the schemes and rage of the magician. Should he survive, he would seek and free Jehaneh—and he would have said more to her, but that second the door rushed open and there stood the wretch they had succoured, grinning at them, with the stolen sapphire on his hand. Behind him the sky was black as in eclipse, an inky cloud had enveloped the ship, and the sailors might be heard calling on Allah.

"See where your generosity has delivered you," said this evil man. "Now you are my slaves, and your treasure and goods shall be at my service too, and this dear daughter I will have for my pleasure."

But the scholar rose to his feet, and shouted aloud a spell of such substance the river boiled and the black sky seemed to crack.

Immediately all the crew of the ship, and the captain, were flung up in the air, and there they found themselves a flock of birds, mewing and soaring. For Jehaneh and her maidens, their peerless skin and silken garments turned to the sheerest scales, and they were cast away into the water like four pearls beyond price.

The evil magician stood in anger, cursing all things, until he was moved to take the scholar by the throat. Even as he did so, with a colossal shudder, the great ship sprang a hundred vents, took water, and began to go down.

"So all escape but you! Then you must pay for all."

"For that reason I have remained," responded the scholar.

And these were the last words and sight Jehaneh had of her father as the spell dashed her away into the river's depths.

"Therefore you see me, most unhappy of women," said Jehaneh at her tale's conclusion. "Bereft of the father that I loved, and held safe from the vengeance of his foe solely by a form which, save here, I am unable to relinquish. The ability of speech too I have retained, though I have learned that few can hear me. For most, being convinced fish cannot talk in the tongue of men, cry out to them as I may, they stay deaf to me. Other safeguards my wise father placed on me also, for once or twice I or my maidens have been trapped in the net of a fisher who would not free us. But before we came ashore, the strands of the net would part and change to serpents, and strike at him, and the man would run away screaming with pain and fear. But such things are small consolation. As you will have noted, my father's own powers are such that he must certainly have escaped himself, had he not deemed it needful to linger to deflect the sorcerer's spite, and in itself this argues ill for his survival. Three years have passed since that black dawning. Yet always I have hoped that I should some day come on a man who is both clever and kind, who would have the wit to hear and to credit me. (For the ability to breathe beneath the water that I possess in woman's shape, is extended to any who keep me company, whether I am woman or fish.) Tell me therefore, if in you, as I pray I have, I discover a champion?"

Ahmed, who was bemused, though not at all displeasingly so, replied, "If you wish it, it shall be my wish also. What would you have me do?"

"Against all wisdom, my heart tells me my father is living yet— though, lacking the ring, in thrall to the sorcerer. I am not able, but you if you would might search for him, and, if it is written, effect his release."

"For that, I must overcome the magician."

"It is undeniable. I must not ask you to put yourself in such peril."

"There is no need to ask me," said Ahmed, "for it is my only desire in the world, to bring you happiness."

124

$\mathfrak{F}$or some months then, Ahmed was in the service of the fish-maiden. By day and by night, he hunted the City, going here and there, and falling into chat with whomsoever he could, but learning nothing much. For his purpose, and also having generally sparse funds, he assumed the attire of a beggar. That fraternity, many of whom recalled his charity in better days, were considerate of him, and often enough he shared the edible tidbits of their profession, or slept under their protection beneath the walls and wells of Baghdad the bountiful. But now and again, Ahmed might have a piece of silver or a goblet of ribbed glass, and these things he would sell, and distribute the money, keeping for himself what was necessary and no more. And such items were the gifts of Jehaneh.

Rising from the river on the nights of the new and full moon, a shimmering fish, she would greet Ahmed with tender looks and gracious thanks, for all he had no news to return her. (Sometimes a flock of birds overhung their meetings, black on the moon, and so high up their likeness was not to be discerned. Ahmed presumed these birds must represent the crew of the sunken ship, transformed by the scholar's protective spell.) But whatever the magical atmosphere of their meetings, the young man would not go down again with Jehaneh into the river, to feast with her on the ship or to review once more her human beauty, saying he had not yet earned this reward.

$\mathfrak{O}$ne dusk, just after the call to prayer, the figure of a tall man stepped into the path of Ahmed, who was hastening to the mosque. The ethereal summons was dying like dim music in an ember sky, but Ahmed courteously stopped, and asked his interrupter how he could serve him. To that the man replied: "Do not go by this road, but rather take that alley, there."

Now Ahmed could not but notice that the alley was a less convenient route to the mosque, and some idea of the robbers of the west bank went over his mind. Yet the tall one, clad in white, had so commanding and benign a presence, Ahmed merely thanked him and obeyed. And in those instants, Ahmed recollected the stranger of the white mantle, who had sent him to the river to fish, and in that way brought him together with the exquisite Jehaneh. A minute more and such reveries were swept from his brain by an appalling din which was going on in the alley behind a pot-seller's shop. From the yard there burst oaths and the thud of blows, the smash of pots, and frantic braying. Ahmed looked into the yard.

"Satan take the beast!" cried the potter, as he wrestled with a donkey among the breakages. "The creature is possessed, I am sure of it."

"How can you think it?" inquired Ahmed.

"Because, having no business to, it inclines to worship Allah. And that is very well, but I am not a rich man, and I have lost a great many pots through the predilection of this animal for throwing itself down on the ground, with its hairy nose toward Mecca, at every cry to prayer. I have had the beast for seven days, and it has already cost me a fortune. I got it from a seller of gourds who, I now realize, had had the same trouble but spared me the information, saying his fruit had been bruised by camels." And that revealed, the potter laid about the donkey again with his stick. "What is more," affirmed the potter, between smitings, "at sunset tonight a lord and his retinue rode by on horses, going to a banquet, and this spawn of the Devil began to roar and prance, and ran after them along the street, to the very gates of a mansion there, and more of my wares perished in this excursion. A thousand ills drop on the beast!"

"Stay your hand," said Ahmed, helping the potter to do so. "Here are some silver coins. Will you accept them in exchange for your donkey?"

"In exchange for such a curse I can accept nothing. How can I cheat you as I was cheated? It is a worthless animal inhabited by ifreets."

"Nevertheless," said Ahmed, "pray take the dirhems and rest your stick."

So the potter agreed, thinking privately that the handsome youth was touched, and gave the donkey's rope into his hand.

Out into the dark street they went then, Ahmed and the donkey, both demure and silent. But when Ahmed set his hand on the donkey's head, it shook him off peevishly. Ahmed murmured, "Since you wish to pray, I will take you to the gate of the mosque. There you may feel free to worship as you required."

This Ahmed did, going to the mosque and halting the donkey at the gate. Sure enough, the donkey instantly obeised itself, and mumbled the softest and most pious of brays. Ahmed prayed beside the donkey, seeing nothing wrong in that, for it seemed to him a creature that had the wit to praise God was better companion than many of his fellow men.

When they had finished their prayers, Ahmed, turning to the donkey, saw that it was weeping. The round tears coursed down its face and fell like heavy rain into the dust.

"Be comforted, O donkey," said Ahmed. "No man shall beat you ever again, or deny you your religion, or force you to bear a load. While I live I will care for you, and feed you, and if I cannot we will go hungry together. Come, God made you and holds the world in his arms. Fear nothing. You shall be my brother."

At these words, the donkey came up to Ahmed and hung its head, like one ashamed. But no sooner had Ahmed stretched out his hand again, than the animal was off, running along the street, but looking back constantly, sometimes pausing and stamping with its hoofs, until Ahmed hastened after. And while this was happening, Ahmed bethought him of Jehaneh once again, and wondered if here too was one enchanted out of human shape.

Where the street ended, there stood the high walls of a mansion, the boughs of whose scented garden trees seemed to lift the moon in their branches. But above the trees and higher at this hour even than the moon, there arose a straight black tower with a solitary cold light ablaze in it.

Having reached the mansion's wall, the donkey slunk into the shadow of an archway.

"Whose house is this?" asked Ahmed of the donkey's ear. "Someone who has wronged you, it seems to me."

He was consumed by curiosity, and securing the donkey, Ahmed pulled his ragged beggar's garb about him, and went around the wall until he arrived at a great door, which was of ebony studded with grotesque faces of brass.

Ahmed rapped upon the door.

Presently it was opened by a Nubian porter clothed in a leopard pelt. But the eyes of the Nubian were milky fires—which not every man would have seen, but Ahmed saw them.

"Who knocks?" asked the jinn, and the teeth of it were all pointed.

"A poor beggar," groveled Ahmed. "Alms, for the love of Allah."

At that, the jinn grimaced, and reaching into a bag tied at its waist, threw down a loaf before Ahmed.

"Blessing and honor stifle and smother you, lordly one," said Ahmed. "And who is your master, that I may bless him also?"

The jinn needlessly showed yet more of its fangs, and pointed away into the house.

"Look there. That is my master."

And Ahmed, gazing through the lamplit vestibule, saw a feast going on in an inner court. But though he perceived the dancing of girls like roses on amber stalks, and the thrill of fountains gushing wine, and golden stuffs that glowed, and over all heard loud laughter and the clash of cymbals, he could not be certain of any face, or catch any voice or name.

"Well then," said Ahmed, "I will bless him as the Lord of the Black Tower."

"Do so," said the jinn playfully, picking its teeth with a large dagger. "By that title he comes to be known in your City. Or else they call him the Mage of Birds. Or, the Master of the Four Rings."

Ahmed hesitated. Then he said merrily, "Yes, I have heard of him. The rings are all great diamonds, are they not?"

"Tush!" said the jinn. "What could you know? One is a diamond. And one a topaz and another a ruby. These three are old friends of his."

"That is only three rings," said Ahmed. "You misnamed him then, since he masters only those."

"Recently he has acquired a fourth ring," said the jinn. "A sapphire, if the likes of you know even what such a thing can be. Now get off with you, or you shall be bitten!"

Ahmed removed himself from the portal and the door was slammed. Ahmed returned to share the loaf with the donkey, saying to it only, "Brother, your enemy is also mine."

But near midnight, when the feast began to end in the mansion of the black tower, Ahmed and the donkey went down to another place of shadows to see who left the house.

And in that fashion, after some watching, they beheld, both of them, he that had ridden past the potter's shop formerly, arrayed like a king and mounted on a horse of snow: Brother Shireef.

"Welcome, matchless husband," said Nadina, bowing like the lily. "It is late," said he.

"Wisdom glitters in your every word."

"My meaning is, it being late, why then are you here, paragon of wives?"

"Only to salute you, and to promote your health and vigour with this herbal drink I have prepared."

Shireef regarded the cup which had just been borne in by Nadina's old servant woman. (This crone had become something of a trial to him, as she was constantly peeking and leering at him. And this very minute, having set the cup by the window, she gave him such a ribald look and wink that Shireef was moved to strike her—but before he could do it she had waddled out.) For the drink, it was jewel-clear and delicious-smelling.

"I may not yet seek my bed," announced Shireef. "Our master has bidden me back, in the guise we use, one hour from this."

"He tries you sorely," said Nadina. "Nevertheless, drink, dear husband. It will increase your mental capacity."

Saying this, Nadina went to the table and took up the cup, which she brought to Shireef. But as her back was to the window, there suddenly appeared there a pale ghostly apparition, which dolefully shook its head. This was the Circassian mute, Shireef's slave, who being bidden ever to spy on any of his mistress' mixings and fermentations, had proved this one to be a narcotic of unusual potence.

Something in Shireef's demeanour caused his wife to glance behind her at the window, but the Circassian was already gone into the branches of a benighted tree.

Shireef accepted the cup, but said, "Why will you try these tricks? Is it to make a fool of me before the magician, or to make me seem disobedient to him? Or is the drug slower, that it should seize on me in flight, and opening my mouth in a yawn, the talisman will be lost, and I tumble to oblivion?"

"You mistake me," said Nadina.

"Then swallow the syrup yourself." And with one hand he offered her the goblet, while with the other he drew the dagger from his sash.

Nadina's eyes flashed like swords, but she sheathed them with her lids. She took the cup and sipped at it. It fell from her grip and she after it, to lie still as marble that breathed.

"Witch," said Shireef, "I have informed your master several times of the pest you become to me. I shall be rid of you soon enough, when once he too is bored with you."

Striding to the table, he picked up a small feather which lay there. Placing this under his tongue, he was transformed at once into a bronze-brown falcon. Exactly then, in through the window came bounding a tattered beggar, who, with a whoop, caught the falcon in a snare of rags,

129

and grasping the bird by the neck, forced open its beak. Out dropped the magical feather of the metamorphosis, and there lay Shireef upon the ground, with his younger brother Ahmed kneeling upon him.

"Here is my own knife, freshly sharpened," said Ahmed, "and by you, the spillage of the drugged drink. I offer you the same choice as you offered your wife. Lap the one or endure the steel of the other."

"What crankiness is this?" rasped Shireef, half-choked and greatly discommoded.

"Nor will your albino servant come to your aid," confided Ahmed, "since, finding him occupying the tree I had climbed as I listened to your connubial conversation, I have tied him there that he may enjoy it better. Come now, no delay, for I gather your mage-master is expecting you."

Shireef lay snarling, but the knife now pressed on his windpipe. He turned away and sucked up some of the opiate from the floor. Ahmed encouraged him to take more.

"The sun rose," said Shireef, when he had done drinking, "and the sun declared, *It is day*. But later the night returned. Be you warned."

"Hush, go to sleep, my brother," said Ahmed.

And Shireef discovered he must.

Ahmed threw off his beggar's trim, and stripping his brother, put on instead Shireef's glories of the banquet. Clad in this raiment, Ahmed much resembled Shireef, for they were close kin. Next, taking the feather, Ahmed put it under his tongue. Another second and he was in the air, up and out through the window he went, across the gardens, and west over the City towards the sorcerer's tower.

As the falcon-Ahmed approached the tower, he saw, flying about it, another of falcon-kind, blacker than the night. But this bird, having circled him once, gave a thin cry and winged away.

One more slave of the mage's, no doubt, thought Ahmed, and he went in at the window of the sorcerous chamber.

Here lamps yet burned, and even as he flew among them a huge voice of brass boomed out in some unknown language. The feather fell from Ahmed's mouth and he was a man again, albeit in the likeness of his brother.

A pair of doors opened and the magician entered, in his occult robes. Ahmed bowed to the floor. But as he did it, he heeded the four great rings on the mage's left hand, a topaz, a ruby, a diamond, and a sapphire.

"You return promptly, Shireef," said the magician. "And you have cause. Every day my influence in the City expands, and such as yourself have value for me, but not of a bottomless sort. Be ever diligent, or I will slough you. There are those that you sat at dinner with tonight in my hall, who—waxing careless—shortly shall be cast down, where worms and flies shall pity them."

"Master and lord," said Ahmed coolly, and in the tones of Shireef, "almost I was prevented from attending you. That daughter of sheep, the woman Nadina, this very night would have drugged me and kept me from your service."

"Yes, she grows stupid," said the mage, seeming to ponder. "But as I have intimated, she has her grievance."

Ahmed prudently forebore to comment. The mage toyed with an ebony wand, and the huge jewels flared and snapped on his fingers.

Presently, Ahmed, lowering his voice into an icier vein, inquired, "Will you not grant me leave to slay the woman?" And going nearer the magician, he drew out his own knife mildly, as if to display the weapon's sharpness. "See, I have whetted the edge of this for her throat."

"Stay your annoyance a season more," said the sorcerer. "There is other commerce to be seen first. But perchance I will give you the gift before too long."

At that Ahmed clasped the sorcerer's hand, with its garland of rings, and pressed to it his kiss. Then, raising both his head and his knife, with all his strength he dealt the mage a terrible blow. The whetted metal sheared through the sorcerer's wrist. The blood flushed forth and stained the robes of both, and the floor of the chamber and its furnishings. But Ahmed sprang away, the severed hand held fast in his.

"What have you done?" screamed the sorcerer.

"Do you not know, lord?" asked Ahmed. "Why, I believe I have removed your powers from you. For they are in these jewels, are they not? Each one renders you facility in something, and the sapphire here completes the whole."

The magician foamed at the lips. Lightnings whipped about the chamber, and the lamps went out.

"Not all my powers, not all!" raged he. And pointing at Ahmed he thundered like the storm: "Go you to the outer heaven of your planet, ascendant at your birth, and be imprisoned there." And then he added words in the unknown language of sorcery.

At that Ahmed was in the midst of a whirling, as if the earth erupted and the sky fell. He was plunged away, holding yet the dripping knife and the severed hand.

Once the tumult ceased, Ahmed uncovered his face, got up and looked about him. He stood upon turf smooth as that of his father's lawns, but of a violet hue, and with blue flowers breaking. Close by was a lake of opalescent water whose muted ripples came constantly to play among the gem-like pebbles lying there. Above hung a sky of hyacinth and rose, over which, sometimes, white doves went drifting.

Ahmed was sustained by his amazement, and so serene was the environment, any fear left him.

(The sorcerer, thinking his assailant to be Shireef, had condemned him to the outer heaven of his birth planet, Marikh, pictured formerly. But as it was to Ahmed that he hexed in this way, he had sent him to another spot, that of his personal planet, Aspiroz, the ruler of beauty and healing.)

The young man wandered dreamily a while along the shore of the translucent lake, until at length he came to a pasture where milk-white bulls were grazing on the flowers. One of these animals came walking over to Ahmed, and addressed him in the mortal tongue.

"Throw down your knife," said the white bull. And on its forehead he saw there was the mark of balance.

So Ahmed, charmed by the gracious creature, threw down the knife, which changed immediately into a flowering bush.

"For that other loathsome thing you hold, regard the jewels that are on it, then throw it down also."

Ahmed again did as the bull suggested. The severed hand, when it struck the earth, shattered into a hundred fragments, and these became smooth opaline pebbles that rolled away toward the hem of the water. But the rings flamed on in the grass.

"The topaz," said the bull, "you must rub to make warm. The ruby, spit on, to make moist. The diamond turn three times eastward. The sapphire you must admonish by its secret name, which few men know, but if you wish, I will tell you."

"I thank you for these clues to power," said Ahmed. "But it is not my destiny to become a sorcerer. There is one I have been told of, in whose possession such baubles might be well and virtuously utilized. For myself, I wish only to win home to my City, be rid of an enemy there, and finally to set free the father of she I mean to make my bride."

"Both last intentions will be a simple matter," said the white bull. "The second is even now being seen to. But for the first, you must rub the topaz. Only remain courageous and speak boldly, and you will have your way."

Ahmed thanked the bull, which galloped off so weightlessly that the young man perceived at last that it was winged.

Then, bracing himself, he gathered up the four rings and rubbed the topaz.

Soon it grew hot to the touch and began to coruscate like burning sulphur. Next, out of the rosy air there tore seven fearsome beings, palpably jinn, each one towering up higher than three elephants together. One had tusks and claws and the mane of a lion, another was like a Nubian, but with pointed fangs and a leopard's tail, a third had blotched skin of black and white, like a goat's, a fourth had four pairs of arms, and the three others were of such an aspect they were actually indescribable. But each had also the mark of Sulayman on his forehead. And as it appeared, each groveled and moaned at Ahmed, calling him *Master,* and asking what he craved.

"Return me instantly to the sorcerer's black tower in Baghdad!"

And no sooner said—than done.

𝕴n the tower chamber a single lamp had been lit. By its radiance, stretched upon the ground was visible the body of the magician. He had been slaughtered, stabbed, and his eyes plucked from his head. On his breast a black falcon perched, fanning with its wings and mewing shrilly. Before the lamp stood a woman, a dagger lying at her feet. It was Nadina. As Ahmed was whirled into the chamber, with the seven jinn in attendance upon him, she fell to her knees and hid her face in her veil.

Ahmed dismissed the jinn, which vanished. But he had pushed the rings onto his fingers, and these he showed to Nadina. "Know I have at my beck a strong army."

"Lord," said Nadina, "will you not reckon how I adore the mage, by my own act on him with that dagger? And will you grant me room to tell my story?"

Ahmed assented.

Then Nadina told him this, as follows:

Some years before, her own father, having glimpsed Death idling at

133

his gate and practicing his knock, arranged for Nadina a marriage. The man was a friend of her father's youth, not young, therefore, but hale and wise, and possessed of wealth, and very learned. Nadina had, besides, seen him when she was but a child, and always kept for him a great partiality. At that time, he was situated in a distant country, where previously he had wed and buried a wife, who had borne him one daughter.

The bridegroom was already making onwards towards the City and his new union, when Nadina's father happened upon Death in the garden, and Death, as is his wont, would not take No for an answer. Left unprotected in her sorrow, Nadina prayed that her husband would quickly reach her side. It was not to be. Even as he sailed the river towards Baghdad, an evil sorcerer was in pursuit of him and a magical ring in his keeping. And this one succeeded in his malign plans, had the ring, and enslaved the scholar.

Now Nadina would have learned no detail of this, if it had not been for the scholar's former servant, the captain of the ship. The scholar had turned him into a black falcon to save him from the magician's spleen. And the bird, having earlier been told the road to Nadina's house, flew there. Being herself something versed in occult art, Nadina was able to decipher some of what he would relay to her. All in all, the plight of her betrothed.

Nadina was overwhelmed by distress, but taking no measure of her own danger, she sought out the abode of the sorcerer, and went there to beg for the liberation of the scholar and his daughter—whom she also supposed the mage's prisoner.

"Young woman, I will enlighten you. Her, the stingy father altered into a fish, and hid her in the river, where she may waste her fishy, chilly life as she desires. But in the case of the scholar, maybe I will let him go, if you permit me, with proper compliance, your favors."

"And if I do that, lord," had answered Nadina, "I will be ruined."

"It is all one to me," said the mage, licking his fat lips. "Either way, you will not have your wedding. But if you please me, then the scholar shall live."

So then Nadina said she would do what he wanted, and arranged to visit the tower during the secrecy of night. Returning to her house, she summoned an old woman servant, who had been with her all her life, and who indeed had nursed her as a child. To this crone, Nadina made a proposal. By her own sorcerous skill, Nadina would throw over the old woman an image of Nadina's self, a form young and fair, exact in every point. The hag would then go into the mage, who would enjoy her, supposing it was Nadina he violated, while Nadina would be at some distance secure in her virginity and honor. The old servant cackled with glee at the plot, and said she was not averse to this bargain for, though the magician was wicked, she had heard he was lusty enough, and it was some while since she had had a chance at such sport.

The exchange settled, the crone (to every appearance and sense Nadina, equipped even with her dulcet voice), betook herself to the magician's tower, and spent there a night of many adventures. So she at least was no loser. But when the true Nadina presently sued again for the freedom of her husband-to-be, the magician had this to say to her: "Because of the satisfaction you gave me, I will spare his life. But since you are so winsome, I am not yet done with you, and you will, besides, be of use to me as a snare. Therefore, I shall keep your scholar secure, and so he shall remain unless you go against me. Then I will send him head over heels out of the world."

And to that end he showed her the scholar, where he had shut him up, and Nadina grieved, for looking on the man she loved him freshly, as she had not known to love when a child. But the mage continued, "You shall be a widow, though never were you a wife." And next he sent the scholar into a deathly sleep, and incarcerated him in a large white tomb in a cemetery of the city. "Go mourn him there with extravagance. And when men marvel and make eyes at you, lead them on and say they resemble your mortified lord."

In that way Nadina and her household were coerced into the practice of wrongdoing, even the same which she exercised on Khassim, in order the magician might tangle the rich and the eminent in his web. But Khassim was too foolish, and it had come to wicked Shireef to take his place. Until, growing quite desperate, Nadina had vowed she would kill her tormentor the mage. She prepared a narcotic to see Shireef from her way. He learning of the ruse, she only pretended to drink the drug and to swoon, and next seeing Ahmed also intent upon the sorcerer's overthrow, she had put on the falcon-form the mage loaned her, and hurried after.

When she reached the tower, what should she find but that Ahmed had completed half the task before his exile. Weakened by the loss of his rings and by his wound, the sorcerer was outmatched. For there came at him a black falcon that had only feigned subservience that it might wait for just such an opportunity, and a young woman armed with a dagger and all the ferocity of outrage.

"If you do not accept my words," said Nadina now, kneeling at Ahmed's feet, "then slay and be done with me. But go you after to the white tomb, hard by your father's resting-place, and break in. The sapphire ring, put on my bridegroom's finger, will restore him. Of his chaste and noble daughter, alas, I have no news."

Ahmed laughed. "Trust me, lady, but I do. Come, get up and be at peace. What the law has seen to cannot be undone, but you shall be to me my honored sister, my brother Khassim's wife."

"Never," cried Nadina, rising angrily. "That donkey? It is the one bad thing I have done without excuse, and do not regret. For the rest, my old servant woman has taken on my offices with each of those lechers, the fool and the cruel. And it is she, not I—though it is a fact she bears the name Nadina as I do—who is wed to each of your brothers. I am yet as God made me, and have known no man, nor will I do so, save the man for whom I was meant, whose graces are to all others the sun above dying lamps."

"I congratulate you," said Ahmed. "But which donkey is it you refer to?"

As if in answer, a miserable but insistent braying clamored over the mansion's walls.

Thus, in the earliest waking of day, there was much going up and down and to and fro about the west and east banks of the Tigris. In the cemetery there came the ill-omened sound of mallets and picks ringing on mortar, a trespass inside a tomb, and at last a man emerging into the light, giving thanks to God and his rescuers, and on his hand a sapphire ring, and three others to neighbor it, of topaz, ruby, and diamond. And thereafter a black falcon was transformed into a ship's captain, and a whole flock of birds, swooping down, into a shouting and gesticulating crew. While from the deep of the brown river, a splendid vessel was brought up solely by the means of words, and on the deck were seen some pretty maidens, and one other whose beauty and joy outshone the day.

Following on these things, one wicked brother was removed where harsh punishment might complement harsh crimes. And one sillier brother emerged from the hide of a pack-beast. And he, seeing his prayers had been heard even over the potter's blows and breakages, went swiftly seeking the sacred city of Mecca, there to circle seven times the shrine, to touch the holy stone—and left behind him a wife old enough to be his grandmother, who yet hoped he might gain some wisdom on his road.

While for marriages, there were two more of them. The nights were made into pure gold by the blaze of torches and firecrackers, and the songs were so sweet and the sighs so profound, who could hear the nightingale now as she sang on her branch in the nobleman's garden.

But sing she did, and this was her message: Behold how the desert is reborn when Allah sends to it the rain. He that gives life will give back life again, even to the dead.

But Death himself did hear this, as he was passing, on other business, the mansion's gate.

And Death nodded resignedly, for he had seen a second passerby at the garden's edge among the roses, an angel in blinding white, who was not beyond nurturing the happiness of men.

But nevertheless, thought Death, *the resurrection is far off.* To this house, as to all houses, he would return, some other evening.

Blue Vase of Ghosts

1. Subyrus, the Magician

Above, the evening sky; dark blue, transparent and raining stars. Below, the evening-coloured land, also blue to the depths of its hills, its river-carven valley, blue to its horizon, where a dusting of gold freckles revealed the lights of the city of Vaim.

Between, a bare hillside with two objects on it: a curious stone pavilion and a frightened man.

The cause of the man's fear, evidently, was the pavilion, or what it signified. Nevertheless, he had advanced to the open door and was peering inside.

The entire landscape had assumed the romantic air of faint menace that attends twilight, all outlines darkening and melting in the mysterious smoke of dusk. The pavilion appeared no more sinister than everything else. About eight feet in height, with a flat roof set on five walls of rough-hewn slabs, its only truly occult area lay over the square step and through the square door mouth—a matched square of black shadow.

Until: "I seek the Magician-Lord Subyrus," the frightened man exclaimed aloud, and the black shadow vanished in an ominous brazen glare.

The man gasped. Not so much in fear, as in uneasy recognition of something expected. Nor did he cry out, turn to run, or fall on his knees when, in the middle of the glare, there stood an unnatural figure. It was a great toad, large as a dog and made of brass, which parted its jaws with a creaking of metal hinges, and asked: *"Who* seeks Subyrus, Master of the Ten Mechanicae?"

"My name is not important," quavered the man. "My mission is. Lord Subyrus is interested in purchasing rarities of magic. I bring him one."

Galaxies glinted and wheeled in bulbous amphibian eyes.

"Very well," the toad said. "My maker hears. You are invited in. Enter."

At which the whole floor of the pavilion rushed upwards, with the monster squatting impassively atop it. Revealed beneath was a sort of metal cage, big enough to contain a man. Into this cage all visitors must step, and the frightened visitor knew as much.

Just as he had known of the hill, the pavilion, the glare of unseen lamps and the horrendous brazen guardian. For down the trade roads and throughout the river ports of Vaim, word of these wonders had spread, along with the news that Subyrus, Master of the Ten Mechanicae, would buy with gold objects of sorcery—providing they were fabulous, bizarre and, preferably, unique.

The visitor entered the cage, which was the second of the Ten Mechanicae (the toad being the first). The cage instantly plunged into the hollow hill.

His entrails seemingly left plastered to the pavilion roof by the rapid descent, this visitor clutched to himself the leather satchel he had brought, and thought alternately of riches and death.

Subyrus sat in a chair of green quartz in a hall hung with drapes the colours of charred roses and black panthers. A clear pink fire burned on the wide hearth that gave off the slight persuasive scent of strawberries. Subyrus studied the fire quietly with deep-lidded dark eyes. He had the face of a beautiful skull, long hands and a long leopardine body to concur with that image. The robe of murky murderous crimson threw into exotic relief his luminous and unblemished pallor, and the strange dull bronze of his long hair that seemed carved rather than combed.

When the cage dashed down into the hall and bounced on its cushioned buffers, throwing the occupant all awry, Subyrus looked up, unsmiling. He regarded the man who staggered from the cage clutching a satchel with none of the cruel arid expressions or gestures the man had obviously anticipated.

Subyrus' regard was compounded of pity, a vague inquiry, an intense drugged boredom.

It was, if anything, worse than sadism and savagery.

A melodramatic laugh and a glimpse of wolf-fangs would have been somehow preferable to those opaque and disenchanted eyes.

"Well?" Subyrus said. Less a question than a plea—*Oh, for the love of the gods, interest me in something.* The plea of a man (if he were that alone) to whom other men were insects, and their deeds pages of a book to be turned and turned in the vain hope of a quickening.

The man with the satchel quailed.

"Magician-Lord—I had heard—you wished marvels to be brought to you that you might… acquire them?"

Subyrus sighed.

"You heard correctly. What then have you brought?"

"In this satchel, lordly one, something beyond—"

"Beyond what?" Subyrus' sombre eyes widened, but only with disbelief at the tedium this salesman was causing him. "Beyond my wildest dreamings, perhaps you meant say? I have no wild dreamings. I should welcome them."

In a panic, the man with the satchel blurted something. The sort of overplay he might have used on an ordinary customer; it had become a habit with him to attempt startlement in order to gain the upper hand. But not here, where he should have left well alone.

"What did you say?" Subyrus asked.

"I said—I said—"

"Yes?"

"That the Lady Lunaria of Vaim—was wild dream enough."

Now the satchel-man stood transfixed at his own idiocy, his very bones knocking together in wretched fright. Indeed, Subyrus had lost his mask of boredom, but it had been replaced merely by an appalling contempt.

"Have I become a laughing stock in Vaim?"

The query was idle, mild. Suddenly the man with the satchel realised the contempt of the magician was self-directed. The man slumped and answered, truthfully: "No one would dare laugh, Magician-Lord, at anything of yours. The length of the river, men pale at your name. But the other thing—you can hardly blame them for envying you the Lady Lunaria." He glanced up. Had he said the right words, at last? The magician did not respond. The frightened satchel-man had space to brood on the story then current in the city, that the Master of the Ten Mechanicae had taken for his mistress the most famous whore this side of the northern ocean, and that Lunaria Vaimian ruled Subyrus as if he were a toothless lion, ordering him to this and that, demanding costly gifts, setting him errands, and even in the matter of the bedchamber, herself saying when. Some claimed the story was an invention of Lunaria's, a dangerous game she played with Subyrus' reputation. Others said that Subyrus himself had sent the fancy abroad to see if any dared mock him, so he might cut them down with sorcery in some vicious and perverse fashion.

But the satchel-man had come off the mountain roads to Vaim. A stranger, he had never seen Lunaria for himself, nor, till tonight, the magician-lord.

"Well?" Subyrus said drowsily.

The satchel-man jumped in his skin.

"I suggest," Subyrus said, "you show me this rare treasure beyond wild dreamings. You may mention its origin and how you came by it. You may state its ability, if any, and demonstrate. You may then name your price. But, I beg you, no more sales patter."

Shivering, the satchel-man undid the clasps and drew from the leather a padded bag. From the bag he produced a velvet box. In the box he revealed a sapphire glimmer wrapped in feathers. The feathers drifted to the floor as he lifted out a vase of blue crystal, about a foot in length, elongated of neck, with a broad base of oddly alternating swelling and tapering design. The castellated lip was sealed by a stopper that appeared to be a single rose-opal.

Prudently silent, and holding the vase before him like a talisman, the visitor approached Subyrus' chair.

"Charming," Subyrus said. "'But what does it do?"

"My lord," the satchel-man whispered, "my lord—I can simply recount what it is *supposed* to have done and to do. I myself have not the skill to test it."

"Then you must tell me immediately how you came by it. Look at me," Subyrus added. His voice was all at once no longer indolent but cool and terrible. Unwilling, but without choice, the satchel-man raised his head. Subyrus was turning a great black ring, round and round, on his finger. At first it was like a black snake darting in and out, then like a black eye, opening and closing.

Subyrus sighed again, depressed at the ease with which most human resistance could be overcome.

"Speak now."

The satchel-man dutifully began.

Mesmerised by the black ring, he spoke honestly, without either embroidery or omission.

2. The Satchel-Man's Tale

*A*n itinerant scavenger by trade, the satchel-man had happened on a remote town of the far north, and learned of a freakish enterprise taking place in the vicinity. The tomb of an ancient king had been located in the heart of one of the tall iron-blue crags that towered above the town. Scholars of the town, fascinated by the tomb's antiquity, had hired gangs of workmen to break into the inner chamber and prise off the lid of the sarcophagus. At this event, the satchel-man was a lurking bystander. He had made up to several of the scholars in the hope of some arcane jewel dropping into his paws. But in the end, all that had been discovered were dust, stench, decay and some brown grinning bones—clutched in the digits of which was a vase of blue crystal stoppered with a rose-opal.

The find being solitary, the scholars were obliged to offer it to the town's Tyrant.

He graciously accepted the vase, attempted to pull out the opal stopper; failed, attempted to smash the vase in order to release the stopper; failed, ordered various pounding devices to crush the vase—which also failed, called for one of the scholars and demanded he investigate the nature of the vase forthwith. This scholar, who had leanings in the sorcerous direction, had also become the host of the parasitic satchel-man. The satchel-man had spun some yarn of ill luck, which the scholar, an unworldly intellectual, credited.

So the satchel-man was informed as to the scholar's magical assaults on the vase. Not that the satchel-man actually attended the rituals first hand (as, but for the mesmerism, he would have assured Subyrus he had). Yet he was advised of them over supper, when the fraught scholar complained of his unsuccess. Then late one night, as the satchel-man sprawled on a couch with his host's brandy pitcher, a fearsome yell echoed through the house. A second or so later, pale as steamed fish, the scholar stumbled into the room, and collapsed whimpering on the ground.

The satchel-man gallantly revived the scholar with some of his own brandy. The scholar spoke.

"It is sorcery of the Brink, the Abyss. More lethal than the sword, and more dreadful. In the hands of a Power, what mischief could it not encompass? What mischief it *has* encompassed."

"Have a little more brandy," said the satchel-man, torn between curiosity, avarice and nerves. "Say more."

The scholar drank deep, grew sozzled, and elaborated in such a way that the hairs bristled on the satchel-man's unclean neck.

Searching an antique book, the scholar had discovered an unusual spell of Opening. This he had performed, and the rose-opal had jumped free of the mouth of the vase. Such a whirling had then occurred inside it that the scholar had become alarmed. The crystal seemed full of milk on the boil and milky lather foamed in the opening of the castellated mouth. In consternation, the scholar had given vent to numerous rhetorical questions, such as: "What shall I do?" and "What in the world does this bubbling portend?" Finally he voiced a rhetorical question that utilised the name of the ancient king: "What can King So-and-so have performed with such an artefact?"

Rhetorical questions do not expect answers. But to this question an answer came.

No sooner was the king's name uttered than the frothing in the vase erupted outwards. A strand of this froth, proceeding higher than the rest from the vase's mouth, gradually solidified. Within the space of half a minute, there balanced in the atmosphere above the vase, deadly white but perfectly formed, the foot-high figure of a man, lavishly bearded and elaborately clad, a barbaric diadem on his head. With a minute sneer, this figure addressed the scholar:

"Normally, further ritual with greater accuracy is required. But since I was the last to enter, and since I have been within a mere four centuries, I respond to my name. Well, what do you wish, O absurd and gigantic fool?"

A dialogue then ensued which had to do with the scholar's astonishment and disbelief, and the white midget king's utter irritation at, and scorn of, the scholar. In the course of this dialogue, however, the nature of the vase was specified.

A magician had made it, though when and how was unsure. Its purpose was original, providing the correct magic had been activated by rite and incantation. That done, whoever might die—or whoever might he slain—in the close neighbourhood of the vase, their soul would be sucked into the crystal and imprisoned there till the ending of time, or at least time as mortal men know it. Since its creation, countless magicians, and others who had learned the relevant sorcery, had used the vase in this way, catching inside it the souls or ghosts of enemies, lovers and kindred for personal solace or entertainment. It might be reckoned (the king casually told the scholar) that seven thousand souls now inhabited the core of the vase. ("How is there room for so many?" the scholar cried. The king laughed. "I am not bound to answer questions.

Therefore, I will do no more than assure you that room there is, and to spare.") It appeared that whoever could name the vase-trapped ghosts by their exact appellations, might call them forth.

They might then reply to interrogation—but only if the fancy took them to do so.

The scholar, overwhelmed, dithered. At length the miniature being demanded leave to return into the vase, which the scholar had weakly granted. He had then flown downstairs to seek comfort from the satchel-man.

The satchel-man was not comforting. He was insistent. The scholar must summon the king's ghost up once again. Positively, the king would be able to tell them where the hoards of his treasure had been buried, for all kings left treasure hoards at death, if not in their tombs, then in some other spot. Was the scholar not a magus? He must recall the ghost and somehow coerce it into malleability, thereby unearthing incredible secrets of lore and (better) cash.

The scholar, convinced by the satchel-man's persistence and the dregs of the brandy, eventually resummoned the king's ghost. Nothing happened. The scholar and the satchel-man strenuously reiterated the summons. Still nothing. It seemed the ghost had been right in hinting that the ritual was important. He had obeyed on the first occasion because his had been the last and newest soul in the vase, but he had no need to obey further without proper incentive.

Then the scholar fell to philosophising and the satchel-man fell to cursing him. Presently the scholar turned the satchel-man out of his house. That night, while the scholar snored in brandy-pickled slumber, the satchel-man regained entry and stole the vase. It was not his first robbery, and his exit was swift from practice.

Thereafter he wandered, endeavouring to locate a mage who knew the correct magic to name, draw forth, and browbeat the ghosts in the vase. Or even merely to draw out the rose-opal stopper with which the scholar had inconsiderately recorked it.

Months passed with the mission unaccomplished, and despair set in. Until the satchel-man caught word of the Magician-Lord Subyrus.

To begin with, the satchel-man may have indulged in a dream of enlisting Subyrus' aid, but rumour dissuaded him from this notion. In the long run, it seemed safer to sell the vase outright and be rid of the profitless item. If any mage alive could deal with the thing it was the

Master of the Ten Mechanicae. And somehow the salesman did not think Subyrus would share his knowledge. To accept payment in gold seemed the wisest course.

The satchel-man came to himself and saw the fire on the wide hearth had changed. It was green now, and perfumed with apples. The fire must be the third of the Mechanicae.

Subyrus had not changed. Not at all.

"And your price?" he gently murmured. His eyes were nearly shut.

"Considering the treasure I forego in giving up the vase to your lordship—" The satchel-man meant to sound bold, succeeded in a whining tone.

"And considering you will never reach that treasure, as you have no power over the vase yourself," Subryus amended, and shut his eyes totally from weariness.

"Seven thousand vaimii," stated the satchel-man querulously. "One for each of the seven thousand ghosts in the vase."

Subyrus' lids lifted. He stared at the satchel-man and the satchel-man felt his joints loosen in horror. Then Subyrus smiled. It was the smile of an old, old man, dying of ennui, his mood lightened for a split second by the antics of a beetle on the wall.

"That seems," said Subyrus, "quite reasonable."

One hand moved lazily and the fourth of the Mechanicae manifested itself; it was a brazen chest which sprang from between the charred-rose draperies. Subyrus spoke to the chest, a compartment shot out and deposited a paralysing quantity of gold coins on the rugs at the satchel-man's feet.

"Seven thousand vaimii," Subyrus said. "Count them."

"My lord, I would not suppose—"

"Count them," repeated the magician, without emphasis. Anxious not to offend, the satchel-man did as he was bid.

He was not a particularly far-sighted man. He did not realise how long it would take him.

A little over an hour later, fingers numb, eyes watering and spine unpleasantly locked, he slunk into the mechanical cage and was borne back to the surface. This time, his guts were left plastered to the lowermost floor of the hollow hill.

Musically clinking, and in terror lest he himself should be robbed, the satchel-man limped hurriedly away through the starry and beautiful night.

3. Proving the Vase

𝕿he fire burned warmly black, and smelled of musk and ambergris. This was the aspect of the fire which Subyrus used to recall Lunaria to him. The idea of her threaded his muscles, his very bones, with an elusive excitement, not quite sexual, not quite pleasing, not quite explicable. In this mood, he did not even visualize Lunaria Vaimian as a woman, or as any sort of object. Abstract, her memory possessed him and folded him round with an intoxicating, though distant and scarcely recognizable, agony.

It was quite true that she, of the entire city of Vaim, defied him. She asked him continually for gifts, but she would not accept money or jewels. She wanted the benefits of his status as a magician. So he gave her a rose which endlessly bloomed, gloves that changed colour and material, a ring that could detect the lies of others and whistle thinly, to their discomfort. He collected sorcerous trinkets and bought them for gold, to give to her. In response to these gifts, Lunaria Vaimian admitted Subyrus to her couch. But she also dallied with other men. Twice she had shut her doors to the Master of the Ten Mechanicae. Once, when he had smitten the doors wide, she had said to him: "Do I anger you, lord? Kill me, then. But if you lie with me against my will, I warn you, mighty Subyrus, it will be poor sport."

On various occasions, she had publicly mocked him, struck him in the face, reviled his aptitude both for magic and love. Witnesses had trembled. Subyrus' inaction surprised and misled them.

They reckoned him besotted with a lovely harlot, and wondered at it, that he found her so indispensable he must accept her whims and never rebuke her for them. In fact, Lunaria was indispensable to the Magician-Lord, but not after the general interpretation.

Her skin was like that dark brown spice called cinnamon, her eyes the darker shade of malt. On this sombreness was superimposed a blanching of blonde hair, streaked gold by sunlight and artifice in equal measure. Beautiful she was, but not much more beautiful than several women who had cast themselves at the feet of Subyrus, abject and yielding. Indeed, the entire metropolis and hinterland of Vaim knew and surrendered to him. All-powerful and all-feared and, with women who beheld his handsomeness and guessed at his intellect, all-worshipped. All that, save by Lunaria. Hence, her value. She was the challenge he might otherwise find in no person or sphere. The natural and the supernatural he could control, but not her. She was not abject nor easy. She did not yield. The exacerbation of her defiance quickened him and gave him a purpose, an excuse for his life, in which everything else might be won at a word.

But this self-analysis he concealed from himself with considerable cunning. He experienced only the pangs of her rejection and scorn, and winced as he savoured them like sour wine. Obsessed, he gazed at the vase of blue crystal, and pondered the toys of magic he had given her formerly.

The vase.

The stopper of rose-opal had already been removed by one of the spells of the *Forax Foramen*, a copy of which ancient book (there were but three copies on earth) was the property of Subyrus. At this spell, written in gold leaf on sheets of black bull's hide, Subyrus had barely glanced. His knowledge was vast and his sorcerous vocabulary extensive. The stopper leapt from the neck of the vase—Subyrus caught it and set it by. Inside the crystal there commenced the foaming and lathering which the scholar had described to the satchel-man.

At Subyrus' other hand lay a second tome. No exact copies of this book existed, for it was the task of each individual mage to compile his own version. The general title of such a compendium being 'Tabulas Mortem, Lists of the Dead'.

From these lists Subyrus had selected seventy names, a hundredth portion of the number of souls said to be trapped in the vase. They were accordingly names of those who had died in peculiar circumstances, and in an aura of shadows, such as might indicate the nearness at that time of the soul-snaring crystal and of someone who could operate its magic.

With each name there obtained attendant rituals of appeasement, summoning and other things that might apply when wishing to contact the dead. All were subtly different from each other, however similar seeming—to the uneducated eye.

The fire sank on the hearth now, paled, and began to smell of incense and moist rank soil.

Subyrus had performed the correct ritual and called the first name. He omitted from it the five inflections that would extend the summons beyond the world, since his intent was centered on the trapped ghosts of the vase. He had also discarded the name of the king from whose tomb the vase had been taken. Occult theory suggested that such a spirit, having been recently obedient to an inaccurate summons (such as the scholar's), could thereby increase its resistance to obeying any other summons for some while after. So the name Subyuus named was a fresh one. Nor, though the ritual was perfect, was it answered.

That soul, then, had never been encaged in the vase. Subyrus erased the name from his selection, and commenced the ritual for a second name.

In Vaim it was midnight, and over the hill above the magician's subculum the configurations of midnight were jewelled out in stars.

Subyrus spoke the nineteenth name.

And was answered.

The moistureless foam-clouds gathered and overspilled the vase. White bubbles and curlicues expanded on the air. From their midst flowed up a slender strand unlike the rest, which proceeded to form a recognizable shape. Presently, a foot-high figurine balanced on the air, just over the castellated lip of the vase. It was a warrior, like an intricately-sculptured chess piece, whose detail was intriguing on such a scale—the minute links of the mail, the chiseled cat that crouched on the helm, the sword like a woman's pin. And all of it matt-white as chalk.

"I am here," the warrior cried in bell-like miniature tones. "What do you want of me?"

"Tell me how you came to be imprisoned in the crystal."

"My city was at war with another. The enemy took me in battle, and strove to gain, by torture, knowledge of a way our defenses might he breached. When I would say nothing, a magician entered. He worked spells behind a screen. Then I was slain and my ghost sucked into the vase. Next moment, the magician summoned me forth, and they asked me again, and I told them everything."

"So," Subyrus remarked, "what you would not betray as a man, you revealed carelessly once you were a spirit."

"Exactly. Which was as the magician had foretold."

"Why? Because you were embittered at your psychic capture?"

"Not at all. But once within, human things ceased to matter to me. Old loyalties of the world, its creeds, yearnings and antipathies—these foibles are as dreams to those of us who dwell in the vase."

"Dwell? Is there room then, inside that little sphere, to dwell?"

"It would amaze you," said the warrior.

"No. But you may describe it."

"That is not normally one of the questions mortals ask when they summon us. They demand directions to our sepulchres, and ways to break in and come on our hoarded gold, or what hereditary defects afflict our line, in order that they may harm our descendants. Or they command us to carry out deeds of malevolence, to creep in small hidden areas and steal for them, or to frighten the nervous by our appearance."

"You have not replied to my question."

"Nor can I. The interior of this tiny vase houses seven thousand souls. To explain its microcosmic structure in mortal terms, even to one of the mighty Magician-Lords, would be as impossible as to describe color to the stone-blind or music to the stone-deaf."

"But you are content," said Subyrus.

The warrior laughed flamboyantly.

"I am."

"You may return," said Subyrus, and uttered the dismissing incantation.

Subyrus progressed to a twentieth name, a twenty-first, a twenty-second. The twenty-third answered. This time a white philosopher stood in the air, his head meekly bowed, his sequin eyes whitely gleaming with the arrogance of great learning.

"Tell me how you came to be imprisoned in the crystal."

"A Tyrant acquired this vase and its spell. He feared me and the teachings I imparted to his people. I was burned alive, the spell activated, and my ghost entered the vase. Thereafter, the Tyrant would call me forth and try to force me to enact degrading tricks to titillate him. But though we who inhabit the vase must respond to a summons, we need not obey otherwise. The Tyrant waxed disappointed. He attempted to smash the vase. At length he went mad. The next man who called me forth wished only to hear my philosophies. But I related gibberish, which troubled him."

"Describe the interior of the vase."

"I refuse."

"You understand, my arts are of the kind which can retain you here as long as I desire?"

"I understand. I pine, but still refuse."

"Go then." And Subyrus uttered again the dismissing incantation.

It was past three o'clock. Altogether, six white apparitions had evolved from the blue vase. Subyrus had reached the fortieth name selected from the 'Tabula Mortem'. He was almost too weary to speak it.

The atmosphere was feverish and heavy with rituals observed and magics pronounced. Subyrus' thin and beautiful hands shook slightly with fatigue, and his beautiful face had grown more skull-like. To these trivialities he was almost immune. Though exhaustion heightened his world-sated gravity.

He said the fortieth name, and the figure of a marvelous woman rose from the vase.

"Your death?" he asked her. She had been an empress in her day.

"My lover was slain. I had no wish to live. But the man who brought me poison brought also this vase under his cloak. When my soul was snared, he carried the vase to distant lands. He would call me up in the houses of lords and bid me dance for his patrons. I did this, for it amused me. He received much gold. Then, one night, in a prince's palace, I lost interest in the jest. The prince appropriated the vase. When I begged leave to rest, the prince recited the incantation of dismissal, which the whipped man had revealed. Ironically, the prince was not comparably adept at the phrases of summoning, and could never draw me forth again."

The woman smiled, and touched at the white hair which streamed about her white robe.

"Surely you miss the gorgeous mode of your earthly state?" Subyrus said.

"Not at all."

"Your prison suits you, then?"

"Wonderfully well."

"Describe it."

"Others have told me you asked a description of them."

"None obliged me. Will you?"

But the woman only smiled.

Broodingly, Subyrus effected her dismissal.

He pushed the further names aside, and taking up the stopper of rose-opal, replaced it in the Vase. The fermentation stilled within.

Slowly, the fire reproduced the darkness and scents that recalled Lunaria for the magician.

The vase was proven—and ready. The promise of such a thing would flatter even Lunaria. She had had toys before. But this—perverse, oblique, its potential elusive but limitless—it resembled Lunaria herself.

As the brazen bell-clocks of Vaim struck the fourth hour of black morning, an iron bird with chalcedony eyes (fifth of the Mechanicae) flew to the balconied windows of Lunaria's house.

The house stood at the crest of a hanging garden, on the eastern bank of the river.

Here Lunaria, honoring her name, made bright the dark, turning night into day with lamplight, singing, drums, harps and rattles. Her golden windows could be seen from miles off. "There is Lunaria's house," insomniacs or late-abroad thieves would say, chuckling, envious and disturbed. An odor of flowers and roast meats and uncorked wines floated over the spot, and sometimes firecrackers exploded, saffron, cinnabar and snow, above the roof and walls. But after sunrise the windows turned grey and the walls held silence, as if the house had burnt itself out during the night.

The iron bird rapped a pane with its beak.

Lunaria, heavy-eyed, opened her window. She was not astonished or dismayed. She had seen the bird before.

"My master asks when he may visit you."

Lunaria frowned.

"He knows my fee: a gift."

"He will pay."

"Let it be something unheard of, and unsafe."

"It is."

"Tomorrow then. At sunset."

4. Lunaria of Vaim

The sinking sun bobbed like a blazing boat on the river. Water and horizon had become a luminous scarlet, stippled with copper and tangerine. A fraction higher than the tallest towers of Vaim, this holocaust gave way to a dense mulberry afterglow, next to a denser blue, and finally, in the east, a strange hollow black, littered with stars.

Such a combination of colors and gems in the apparel of man or woman, or in any room of a house, would have been dubious. But in the infallible and faultless sky, were lovely beyond belief and almost beyond hearing.

Nevertheless, the sunset's beauty was lost on Subyrus, or rather, alleviated, dulled. At a finger's snap almost, he could command the illusion of such a sunset, or, impossibly, a more glorious one. It could not therefore impress or stimulate him, even though he rode directly through its red and mulberry radiance, on the back of a dragon of brass. The sixth of the Mechanicae, the dragon was equipped with seat and jewelled harness, and with two enormous wings that beat regularly up and down in a noise of metal hinges and slashed air. It caught the last light, and glittered like a fleck of the sun itself. In Vaim, presumably, citizens pointed, between admiration and terror.

A servant beat frantically on the door of Lunaria's bedchamber.

"Lady—*he* is here!"

"Who?" Lunaria inquired sleepily from within.

"The lord Subyrus," cried the servant, plainly appalled at her forgetfulness.

On the terrace before the house, the dragon alighted. Subyrus stilled it with a single word of power. He stepped from the jewelled harness, and contemplated the length of the hanging garden. Trees precariously leaned over under their mass of unpicked fruit, the jets of fountains pierced shadowy basins that in turn overflowed into more shadowy depths beneath. Trellised night flowers were opening and giving up their scent. In Lunaria's garden no day flowers bloomed, and no man could walk. Sometimes the gardeners, crawling about the slanted cliff of the hanging garden to tend the growth and the water courses, fell to their deaths on the thoroughfare eighty feet below. The only entrance to the house was through a secret door at the garden's foot, of whose location Lunaria informed her clients. Or from the sky.

The servant ran on to the terrace and cast himself on his knees.

"My lady is not yet ready—but she bids you enter." The servant was sallow with fear.

Subyrus stepped through the terrace doors, and beheld a richly clad man in maddened flight down a stairway.

Lunaria had kept one of her customers late in order that Subyrus should see him. This was but a variation on a theme she had played before.

Near the stair foot, about to rush to a new flight—for these stairs passed right the way to the interior side of the secret door—the customer paused, and looked up in a spasm of anguish.

"You have nothing to dread from me, sir," Subyrus remarked. But the man went on with his escape, gabbling in distress.

"And I. Am I not to dread you?"

Subyrus moved about, and there Lunaria Vaimian stood, dressed in a vermillion gown that complemented one aspect of the sunset sky, her blonde hair powdered with crushed gilt.

She stared at Subyrus boldly. When he did not speak, she nodded contemptuously at the dining room.

"I am not proud," she announced. "I will take my fee at dinner. I am certain you will grant me that interim between my previous visitor and yourself."

The red faded on gold salvers and crystal goblets. Lunaria was wealthy, and she had earned every vaimii.

They did not converse, she and her guest. Behind a screen, musicians performed love songs with wild and savage rhythms. Servitors came and went with skillfully prepared dishes. Lunaria selected morsels from many plates, but ate frugally. Subyrus touched nothing. Indeed, no one alive could remember ever having seen him eat, or raise more than a token cup to his lips. Occasionally, Lunaria talked, as if to a third person. For example:

"How solemn the magician is tonight. Though more solemn or less than when he came here before, I cannot say."

Subyrus never took his eyes from her. He sat motionless, wonderful, awful, and quite frozen, like some exquisite graveyard moth, crucified by a pin.

"Are you dead?" Lunaria said to him at length. "Come, do not grieve. I will always be yours for a price."

At that he stirred. He placed a casket on the table between them, murmured something. The casket was gone. The vase of blue crystal glimmered softly in the glow of the young candles.

Lunaria tapped the screen with a silver wand, and the musicians left off their music. In the quiet, they might be heard scrambling thankfully away into the house.

Lunaria and the magician were alone together, with sorcery.

"Well," Lunaria said, "there was a tale in the city today. A blue vase in which thousands of souls are trapped. Souls which can inform of fabulous treasures and unholy deeds of the past. Courtesans who will reveal wicked erotica from antique courts. Devotees of decadent sciences. Geniuses who will create new books and new inventions. If they can be correctly persuaded. Providing one can call them by name."

"I could teach you the method," Subyrus said.

"Teach me."

"And so buy a night of your life?" Subyrus smiled. It was a melancholy though torpid smile. "I mean to have more than that."

"A week of nights for such a gift," Lunaria said swiftly. Her eyes were wide now. "You shall have them."

"Yes, I shall. And more than those."

He had got up from his chair, and now walked around the table. He halted behind Lunaria's chair, and when she would have risen, lightly he rested his long fingers against her throat. She did not try to move again.

The scents of ambergris and musk floated from her hair.

His obsession. The gnawing and only motive for his existence.

Obscuring from himself his true desire—the pang of her indifference, her challenge—he saw the road before him, the box in which he might lock her up. Physically, he had possessed her frequently. Such possession no longer mattered. Possession of mind, of emotion, of soul had become everything. The joy of actual possession, the intriguing misery of never being able to actually possess her again. And his fingers tightened about the contours of her neck.

She did not struggle.

"What will you do?" she whispered.

"Presently, remove the stopper of the vase. It is already primed to receive another ghost. Whoever expires now in its close vicinity will be drawn in. Into that microcosm where seven thousand souls dwell content. That enchanted world. They come forth haughtily, and retreat gladly. It must be curious and fine. Perhaps you will be happy there."

"I never knew you to lie, previously," Lunaria said. "You said the vase was a gift for me."

"It is. It will be your new home. Your eternal home, I imagine."

She relaxed in his grip and said no more. She remained some while like this, in a sort of limbo, before she was aware that his hands, rather than blotting out her consciousness, had unaccountably slackened.

Suddenly, to her bewilderment, Subyrus let her go.

He went away from her, about the table once more, and stopped, confronting the vase from a different vantage. An extraordinary expression had rearranged his face.

154

"Am I blind?" he said, so low she hardly made him out.

Youth, and of all things, panic, seemed swirling up from the darkened closets behind his eyes. And with those, an intoxication, such as Lunaria had witnessed in him in the first night he had seen her, the first night she had refused him.

She rose and said sternly, "Will you not finish murdering me, my lord?

He glanced at her. She was startled. He viewed her with a novel and courteous indifference. Lunaria shrank. What an ultimate threat had not accomplished, this indifference could.

"I was mistaken," he said. "I have been too long gazing at leaves, and missed the tree."

"No," she said. "Wait," as he walked towards the terrace doors, where the brazen dragon grew vague and greenish in a damson twilight.

"Wait? No. There is no more need of waiting."

The vase was in his hand. Sapphire flashed, and then went out as the dusk enclosed him.

The dragon heaved itself, with brass creakings, upright and abruptly aloft. Lunaria, rooted to the ground, watched Subyrus vanish into the sky above Vaim.

5. In Solitude

Somewhere in the hollow hill, a lion roared. It was a beast of jointed electrum, the seventh of the Mechanicae, activated and set loose by Subyrus on his return. Its task to roam the chasm of the hill, a fierce guardian should any ever come there in the future, which was unlikely. It was unlikely because Subyrus, descending, had closed and sealed off the entrance to the hill by use of the eighth mechanism. The stone pavilion had folded and collapsed in unbroken and impenetrable slabs above the place. The periodic, inexhaustible roar of the lion from below was an added, really unnecessary deterrent.

And now Subyrus sat in his darkened hall, in his quartz chair. The fire did not burn. One lamp on a bronze tripod lit up the vase of blue crystal on a small table. The stopper lay beside it, and beside that a narrow phial with a fluid in it the color of clear water.

Subyrus picked up the phial, uncorked, and leisurely drained it. It had the taste of wine and aloes. It was the most deadly of the six deadly

155

poisons known on earth, but its nickname was Gentleness, for it slew without pain and in gradual, tactful, not unpleasant stages.

Subyrus rested in the chair, composed, and took the rose-opal stopper in his hand, and fixed his look on the vase.

He had exhausted the possibilities of the world long since. His intellect and body, both were sick with the sparse fare they must subsist on. There was no height he might not scale at a step, no ocean he might not dredge at a blink. No learning he had not devoured, no game he had not played. Thus, it had needed Lunaria to hold his horrified tedium in check, something so common and so ugly as a harlot's sneer to keep him vital and alive.

When the gate had opened, he had not seen it. He had nearly bypassed it altogether. He had sought a gift for Lunaria, then he had sought to trap her in the crystal, making her irrevocably his property and denying himself of her forever. Lunaria—he scarcely recalled her now.

Concentration on the minor issue had obscured the major. At the last instant, the truth had come to him, barely in time.

He had exhausted the world. Therefore he must find a second world of which he knew nothing. A world whose magic he had yet to learn, a world alien and unexplored, a world impossible to imagine—*the microcosm within the vase.*

Like a warm sleep, Gentleness stole over him. Primed to catch his ghost, the blue vase enigmatically waited. Perhaps nightmare crouched inside, perhaps a paradise. Even as the poison chilled it, Subyrus' blood raced with a heady excitement he had not felt for two decades and more.

In the shadows, a silver bell-clock struck a single dim note. It was the ninth of the Mechanicae, striking to mark the hour of the Magician-Lord's death.

And Subyrus sensed the moment of death come on him, as surely as he might gauge the supreme moment of love. He leaned forward to poise the rose-opal stopper above the lip of the vase. As the breath of life coursed from him, and the soul with it, unseen, was dashed into the trap of the crystal, the stopper dropped from his fingers to shut the gate behind him.

Subyrus, to whom existence had become mechanical, the tenth of his own Mechanicae, sat dead in his chair. And in the vase—

What?

Lunaria Vaimian had climbed the hill alone.

Below, at the hill's foot, uneasily, three or four attendants huddled about a gilded palanquin, disheveled by cool winds and sombre fancies.

Lunaria wore black, and her bright hair was veiled in black. She regarded the fallen stone of the pavilion. Her eyes were angry.

"It is foolish of me," she said, "to chide you that you used me. Many have done so. Foolish also to desire to curse you, for you are proof against my ill-wishing as finally you were proof against my allure. But how I hate you, hate you as I love you, as I hated and I loved you from the beginning, knowing there was but one way by which I could retain your interest in me; foreknowing that I should lose you in the end, whatever my tricks, and so I have."

Leaves were blowing from the woods in the wind, like yellow papers.

Lunaria watched them settle over the stone.

"A thousand falsehoods," she said. "A thousand pretenses. Men I compelled to visit me (how afraid they were of the Magician-Lord), only that you might behold them. Gifts I demanded, poses I upheld. To mask my love. To keep your attention. And all, now, for nothing. I would have been your ghost-slave gladly. I would have let you slay me and bind me in the vase. I would have—"

The electrum lion roared somewhere beneath her feet in the hollow hill.

"There it is," Lunaria muttered sullenly, "the voice of my fury and my pain that will hurt me till I die; my despair, but more adequately expressed. I need say nothing while that other says it for me."

And she went away down the hill through the blowing leaves and the blowing of her veil, and never spoke again as long as she lived.

After I Killed Her

When she comes to me, when I look at her beauty, tears still fill up my eyes.

My God, if they could see that in the taverns of the north. Would they even believe it? I must be under a spell, or a curse, they would say, and perhaps—perhaps I am.

In a way, it's only love. I'm in love with her. Not the carnal love I have known, those white women, with their sunburst hair, their thundercloud hair. Not that. And yet, it's love. Of course, it's love.

I remember the old man under the tower in the city, the old man they stoned, saying to us all that we were incestuous with ourselves. When the stone struck his head, he died, and the pigeon in his hands flew away.

My love; I will give you the sky, heaven, and earth. And you'll take them.

I'll make sure of it.

All my life, I've been a fighter. From the first brawls in the courts and backyards, to my training in the palace of a king. No one like me. I was proud of my body and my power. Arrogant with what I could do. But though I killed men in combat and on the field of battle, I also took them in friendship. I drank with them and went whoring, and when I wed, I was crazy for her, and my friends drained dry their cups wishing us well.

She perished inside a year. No one's fault, a sickness. But when she was gone it seemed to me all at once I'd never known her. She was like a summer leaf I'd held in my hands, admiring it, until it crumbled. And I was left with only her grave, and there I went sometimes, and talked to her, just as I had in life, about my plans, and my dreams, my fights and conquests, and never a word from her. Alive, had she ever spoken to me, beyond the smile, the look, the words of praise, her answers always yes. And finally her little sad whisper, "It hurts me."

So then I took myself off. I went wandering, selling my sword, as they say, which means I sold myself.

I was young and strong. I was tall and well-made. And I took credit for all of this. The death of my wife had been a blow to me, not only her loss, but the betrayal of my golden road, a pitfall the gods should not have set there, for I was lucky.

And still, I clove to people. I felt that in them was the hope of the world. I would love them for their adulation of me, as I had loved my wife, who even on her deathbed had told me I was beautiful, and must find another, she would not be jealous in the land of shadows.

Never idle, not I. When I was not in some war or contest, I assisted the farmers on their land. I laid down stones to build mansions. I filled nets with fish. And women I had, all the women I wanted. Then, glutted with my use of the world, on I went, to kill and love some more.

How many years?—not many. A dozen.

⟪T⟫he morning came, I rode down a mountain, and found a city by the lake.

Above, were groves of flowering trees, and smoke rose blue from thirty or more altars. The water of the lake was pale and full of clouds. The city white as snow.

Yet, there was something. I lingered, wondering what it could be. Everything exquisite, and yet, the seed of something terrible was there. I had learned this precognition from my dying wife.

At last I took the road that led to the gate of the city, which was a great gate of marble. Before I reached it, men came riding out, making to me the signals I knew so well, of respect, recognition, and the wish for my help.

I met them where the gate shadow came down on the road.

"Sir, we judge you to be a warrior."

"I am."

"We need you, then. Are you for hire? The work's heroic though deadly dangerous. We see from your bearing your reward shouldn't be pay, but honorable *recompense.*"

Maybe I smiled at that, they were treating me so charmingly. Or not. Can I remember?

But I said I'd go with them to their king.

When we got inside, I looked at the city. As I had expected from the outside, it was a glorious one. Huge marble buildings with gold on the cornices, carved pillars, deep shaded gardens behind high walls. The central avenue was lined by temples and statues, and fountains played into white basins. A pair of brazen lions guarded the palace doors. I'd seen no slums; but then, they take you by the pretty route, when they want you to like them. I was used to that. Anyway, I rose from a slum, and only returned to the hovel where I was born out of curiosity, my parents being dead. By which I mean, it seemed to me then men had no need to stay in the mud and muck even if generated there, since I had not.

The king received me as they do, among a few courtiers and guards. He was very easy, well-mannered, the way kings often are. He told me, once I'd drunk some of their snow-cooled wine, what was wanted.

It was a story I'd heard of, but never before myself come across. Indeed, it's less common now, and my kind are the reason for that.

They favored the Eastern science here, astronomy. And by use of it, their sages had learned of a peril. Across the lake lay a wasteland. It had been there centuries, and they seldom thought of it here, among their groves and vines and gardens. While the width of the lake made sure they did not even closely view the place. But now, something stirred in it. A dragon.

"At first," the king said to me, without ceremony, careful to be at one with me, "at first, we prayed there had been some error. We sacrificed to the gods. Then, less than a month ago, from the highest towers of the city, it became possible to see, by night, a red glow out in the waste. You'll know, sir, that a dragon evicts fire. It was the breath of the thing."

I said, "I've heard of dragons. I've seen their graves, here and there, and bones, once."

"We have an oracle," said the king. "A stream of water in a cave. We questioned it. The oracle told us this dragon would prey on us."

"That's usual with them," I said, "in the tales."

"Two nights back," said the king, "a fishing fleet was on the lake. As the moon came up, something rose out of the waste. Many saw it from the high places. A serpent creature with enormous wings. It flew over the moon and passing above the fleet, five boats in all, set light to them with a breath. As the vessels sank, the beast picked three screaming men from the fire, and flew away with them, back to the desert."

"You want me to kill it."

"The oracle, sir, promised a warrior would come."

"It can be done," I said. "But it's chancy. You know that, king."

"Of course. The wise-women make an ointment here used in rituals. It protects against fire—you will be shown proof."

"That's fair."

"We have," he said, "no fighter capable of this conflict. For a hundred years, we've devoted ourselves to the arts of peace. My soldiers are skilled in display. They lack the blood for killing."

I saw what, courteously, he told me. I was a killer, and they were not. I had the knack of it, and the practice, as the slim scars on my arms could evidence, the weapons I carried. The very look of me. Perhaps some faint odor, also like fire.

They didn't want the job. They had never had to slaughter more than a wasp or a rat. Those polished men with swords and spears who stood about the chamber, they were nobles. Fight was play to them. Pretend.

Was I contemptuous? I think not. I believed in men, and there was nothing wrong with peace, although my trade had always been war.

Presently they took me to another room and showed me a cloth painted with the magical ointment put into a brazier, and it was only a little singed. I tried the brew on my left smallest finger, and in the heat, the hairs were taken from my skin, but no more.

When I said yes, like the bride, I was conducted about, shown the gorgeous city all over again from the high roofs of the palace, informed I could have anything I wanted if I won the battle with the dragon. And I was also led past areas with treasure in them, and very desirable women moved across near distances, with lemon yellow hair or hair like midnight down their backs, and that all woven with beryls and silver and pearls, and they smiled sweetly at me.

It seemed to me I could do worse than to settle in this heaven-on-earth. I wouldn't mind it, maybe, to be rich and famous and live in luxury. To get a son. To hang up the sword.

As for the dragon, it excited me, the thought of this combat. This was a rare opportunity, for, if it was the last fight, it would be the most memorable.

I'm not quite witless, I did grasp that I might die instead. But there was always that, since I lost my wife, I didn't want to go as she had had to. For me it will always be the lightning flash that's the end. I won't wait for torturing. To die sudden is to die best. Well, I shall learn one day if that is true.

There was a feast held for me in the afternoon. I recollect I continued impressed by the manners and means of the city, but already I was in that state—which some men get through drink or various drugs—the battle-readiness that fills with metallic flame, part fear, part rage, part ecstasy. And through this glow I saw them all, the scholarly king, the delicious women, the cunning musicians, the brilliant painted scenes on the walls.

They told me too, these people, precisely what the oracle had said to them, falling through its channel, and the priestess heeding its secret voice. That their fate depended upon me.

I rested after the feast, regretfully alone, but I wanted all my strength.

Three hours before sunset, I went down, and they took me to the dock on the lake. Here they made a sacrifice of white pigeons and a white lamb. The king himself touched my forehead with the blood.

There was a boat, and a man to row me over. The monster was nocturnal. He had time to get me across and himself home safe.

This man did not speak to me. I asked him not to. I prefer silence before I fight. But he looked at me, cautiously, under his brows. He was an artisan of the city by his dress, perhaps he'd been selected for the work by lot. It wasn't that he was afraid, he seemed brave enough, for he was no warrior and the dragon was there, somewhere, across the lake. He seemed to expect me to be what I was. And what was I to him? To them all? A machine for death. And this he put on to me. I felt him do it. My garment.

But I'd been used to that, had I not? To being what I was to all the people of the places through which I went.

The sun was low when he put me off, with sword and shield and javelin, at the farther lakeside. He had half an hour to get away. I didn't detain him.

He made a sign to me, a sort of blessing, and rowed off, the wake of the boat cutting through the golden reflection of declining day.

Then I looked about. The shore was dry, with little scrubby bushes, and rocks beyond. And after that, when I got up to it, a plain, rolling and parched, reddish in the sinking light, with shadows cast by isolate things, a withered tree, a stack of stone.

Straight I stood, catching gold myself on flesh and helm and weapons, the bitter scent of ointment all over me. It came to me, the godlike feeling that was with me then, in the instants before engagement. Is there any feeling so wondrous, so massive, so pure? Only the apex of lust, perhaps. But different, for with this power comes other power. I was a giant. A man of metals and lights.

I looked where the land darkened, and there, about a quarter mile from me, I saw a running line of low hills, and in these a gaping hole, black, though the sunfall fell behind it.

There were patches of white along the slope, strewn bones, and I marveled at my eyes which saw them so clearly, the remains of men.

*A*long with graves, and skeletons of vast girth, I'd seen pieces of their hide, the carapace of dragons. And truthfully, they're nothing. Great snakes, that's what they are, with wings of brittle skin, and ribs in those that may be fractured.

It's their size that terrifies, and their firebreath that does the murder. So I believed.

I went along quietly to my appointment. I meant to get the advantage of ground, if there was one. But when I reached the foot of the low hills, I saw there wasn't much. The thing must come out and down at me. My other choice could only have been to enter its cave and face it there. I'd had no relish for that, and no time besides. It was awake now, I heard it moving, for the plain was perfectly still, a sound like that a snake makes against a boulder, but very large.

The sky above was transparent, as it is, turning toward the opaque darkness, and the light was in the air but not the earth. A white star stood above the cave. I remember that well.

But when the dragon moved out, the last ember in the west caught it, showed it exact. Like me, it was a beast of metal—coppery gold, with the head and body of a serpent, and a lizard's legs. Only the wings dull and tawny, folded back.

It saw me at once—or scented me and so saw me. I think there would have been little point in trying to conceal myself.

The snake's face had amber eyes, shining up now as the dark began to arrive. It opened its jaws and a slight rift of fire passed out of them, melting up against the sky. But the fire lit the slope and in that peculiar moment, I noticed the bones on the ground weren't any bones at all, but great white flowers.

Then it began to steal down toward me. It had a creeping yet hurried gait, and the wings stayed shut.

Never before, in all my travels and fights, had I seen anything like the dragon. The battle-itch was on me, or I would have been mesmerized. Not fear. Amazement. I had no thoughts, for I don't think in words at such a time. But I'd heard a priest once speak of feeling the presence of the god descend into his shrine, and the priest threw himself flat, gave himself over, and so, he claimed, survived the hour. The dragon was like this. It was beyond all elements, all knowledge. Like the moon falling to earth. What can you do if it does?

Abruptly then it spread its wings and crouched, and the long slender muzzle opened and out came the storm of fire.

I flung up my shield, also anointed, and covered my head and chest.

The fire passed over and around and I grunted at its scald. I was not quite unscathed, but only pricked and pierced, not harmed much, more astonished, for the vitality of this fire wasn't only in its knack of burning up. There was a dazzle to it, galvanic, like lightning. It smelled—*holy*.

Despite the ointment and my reason telling me I hadn't been much hurt, I had rolled over, and now, leaping up again, found the shield had buckled out of shape, and so threw it aside.

The dragon poised, staring at me with its cat's eyes, readying itself for another blast.

As it did so, I balanced the javelin and cast it, with all my craft and strength, straight for the place below the glimmering throat. It went right in, making nothing of the smooth scales at all, and from the wound the wine of the blood came out, showering the ground and the flowers.

The dragon reared, and now its fire shot into heaven and for a second changed the star to red. Then it leaned over and went down.

I ran to it, and when I came to it, I plunged my sword into the side of its neck, where the heart vein goes up in most things of human shape. The blow was violent and sure and almost severed its head, though the neck was as thick as my chest; how many times have I said how strong I am. And the dragon, despite its size, delicate, in its way. It had been easy. Easier than I'd have prophesied, or than their oracle prophesied, no doubt.

When it's done, the battle, especially if it was quick and easy, there comes a shadow, like cold dew.

I stood above it, the terrible foe, and as I watched, beheld the light of evening and of life go from its eyes. It sighed, and closed them, and was dead.

Presently, I sat down at the side of the cadaver.

A few trickles of fire were burning out on the hill. Otherwise night had the plain, and a cool wind moved over in long breaths, stirring the ashes and the flowers, and the hair on my head now the helm was removed. Other stars appeared. And turning, I saw the vague sheen of the city's lamps far off, above the lake.

I need only take my trophy, which in a minute I would. One of the forefeet would do, with its claws like jasper. Some lord would prize it, or the king, although he hadn't struck me as being partial to such items.

The wind began to make a strange little crying noise. This can happen. The imagination of warriors isn't devoid of ghosts.

I sat there, looking at the dragon.

Its armor—useless though it had been when touched by my spear and sword—was immaculate. And the line of it, sinuous and slim and curving, and the belly, which now, as the beast had fallen, I could partly study, so burnished, unblemished. And so, finally I saw as well the unmistakable second aperture that told me it had been a female.

I'd killed a living female creature, under that hill. A female creature like a jewelry made for some huge and beautiful throat. The only thing that spoiled her, my dragon, was what I'd done to her. And what I would do, cutting off her forefoot to prove my victory.

I wouldn't do it, then. I'd show them my burns, and the blood on sword and javelin, when I'd wrenched them out of her. Her very absence would suffice to let them know that she was done.

Still I remained a long while, on the plain, sitting by her, looking—not at last at her body—but away into the distance, where the lamps shone, not seeing them at all.

I was conducted to the king in the dark, escorted by torches. He came in a bedrobe, to thank me. Apparently, he had been lying down.

In the morning, after I'd slept, had a bath in a large bronze cavity under a fountain, been stuffed with a breakfast of twenty dishes, by young beauties, one of whom I had, then I went before the nobles, and the evidence was displayed, the ruined shield, the bloody weapons.

One asked me straight out why I'd failed to bring some token.

Taking my stance in the fine frescoed room, I said, "In the north, sometimes, the lords have you cut off the hand or head of a man you've slain for them. But I never would do it. I won't now. She's dead. Go and see, if you don't believe me."

The king got up from his golden chair and walked over and put his ringed hand on my shoulder. He said I wasn't to be slighted. A hero and champion, I'd done what they'd requested. Then he looked me full in the face with clear eyes, the way kings are trained. "We can never thank you enough. What will you have? There's a delightful house with a garden. It was my brother's. Servants to wait on you. I give you the freedom of my city. Anything you want is yours. And of course, I've not yet shown my personal gratitude. Humor me, accept this poor cup—my own, as a pledge." The cup had fat emeralds in it.

I accepted it all. Of course I did. I'd made up my mind to have it. And I knew the courtly language, how to grab it nicely. I too had been trained in the palace of a king.

The house lay just outside the city gates. It had an estate, fields, vineyards, orchards, a forest full of game. On a terrace with marble pillars, two of the most lovely women I ever saw sang to me, brought me wine, and, in the soft velvet of those honey nights, danced willing and laughing to my bed.

When I went into the city, people came out to look at me. They were well-mannered, and murmured, and raised fervent little cheers, and held up their children to snatch a glimpse. Girls gave me flowers. Fishermen brought me their catch, and my attendants received it. "We'd have nothing," they said, with decorous frankness, "but for you, sir."

That was my heaven then. Almost one whole month. But the nightingales singing in my park by night and day didn't secure my dreams.

They weren't the sort you start from, crying out. Not even the dreams that gnaw until they touch the nerves, and wake you, stone-still, with a heart like ice. No, they were only dreams of something flying, graceful, not a bird, and the moon silver on her. And then her long skeleton, that very thing I'd seen before, when I half thought a dragon was a lie. Her living, and her death. Only that. Every night. Over and over.

In the last days of the month, instead of riding into the city in my new wealthy clothes, my collars of jewels, I strolled alone and plainly. I'd grown my beard. I kept a fold of my cloak over my head.

They didn't know me. I didn't look right. I was just another man. I watched them, as I'd always watched humankind, as I'd always had to.

They were no better, no worse. They gossiped and bickered, they made oaths by the gods and broke them. They kicked stray dogs, or beat their horses, slapped their wives—all of that lightly. Nothing serious. And the women passed it on, cuffing their children or shouting, or ordering their servants to cuff or shout. They brought flowers for their dinner parties and wine. Next day the flowers were thrown out on the street for the refuse carriers. The wine was a headache, or voided. They spoke the same as all men and women do. They wanted riches and more riches. They wanted safe comfort. They wished to have babies like pets or toys, or they wished the babies would stop arriving, like locusts. They liked this actor in their theatre because he could move them, despised that one because he was too young, or too old. They were scornfully sorry for others less well off. They hugged their own luck. They feared disease, poverty, lack of standing, or of recognition or respect. Most of all they feared death. If ill befell them they cried, "Why me of them all?" They said at reserves, "This isn't fair on me. Haven't I paid my taxes? Haven't I placated the gods?" When they were beautiful they were arrogant, cruel, intolerant, and uneasy. When they were not, they were jealous. The poorer hated the richer, the richer dreaded the poorer. They spoke politely and cursed each other in secret. They admired what was unusual, a surprising tune, a dark rose, a very large gem. Their children wished to be as they were. When they grew up, they too must be opulent, handsome, powerful. The same.

Even the two girls who were my lovers in the kingly house, seeing them together, unseen, I heard them talking of what they'd got and wanted. The presents I'd awarded. The garments they were to have. The babies they would bear—to me?—that they were young, by which, although, they didn't know it, they also said in shame and anger, that one day they would age.

This then, all of them. This marvelous city, better than many, just like the rest. And I, just like the rest. The race of mankind. All one.

And not one of us, not one, could fly.

In that other city, I'd seen the mob, and gone into it, and questioned them as to what went on.

"That old fool there," said a youth to me. "He's ranting at us. You see, he feeds the vermin, and fills the streets with their droppings. Filthy. Look, the tower's crusted with them. It could bring a plague."

I glanced at the ancient eccentric. He held a blue pigeon calmly in his hands. But he bellowed at us all in a huge wild voice. He said to us that we were enamored of ourselves and of the race of mankind and cared only for that. We killed the beasts not only to feed ourselves; but for sport, and where they inconvenienced us, we were merciless. We cut, too, their throats on the altars of our gods who—we assumed—were made in our own image and desired what we did. He declared he fed the pigeons and the mice because he loved *them*. But we were incestuously in love with our own species, and it would be our downfall.

Who threw the first stone I don't know. But it struck him and killed him outright, I think. The pigeon flew away as his hands loosed it. It looked like his soul going straight up to God.

To them, I said I had to make a journey. I'd be back in the spring. The two women wept. These were real tears. One was with child. But so what? It would only be another of us, like her and like me.

Probably I only meant to go on, roaming, as I'd done before.

But eventually I went around the great lake, went right around, it took me ten days, and came into the waste, and so back to the spot under the low hills, the place where I'd killed her, the dragon.

All the flowers were dead too. The summer had been very hot, although it occurred to me perhaps they'd been watered by her urine, and this had kept them growing.

What had I expected to find of her? What I found, I suppose. She'd rotted and the birds had been at her. Not much left. Only the flower-white bones that were already turning brown.

If they had ventured from the city to inspect her corpse—maybe they had, when they were sure—none had taken anything from her. Doubtless she stank by then. They were a very fastidious city.

For a while I circled her, gazing at her, the leavings. Then something made me go along the slope to the cave. It seemed I needed to see where she'd laired. It didn't and doesn't make any sense to me, not truly. But I climbed up anyway.

The cave was a big bare hole in the stone. There was nothing in it, or so I thought, and then I began to make out a sort of nest, and I took it for her bed. But it wasn't that.

When I stood right over it, I saw it was a tomb.

There were four of them, the little ones, young dragons. They were only the length of my forearm, not quite that. About, lay a few fragments, of stuff that might have been the remains of birth shell. No debris of the men she had carried off. She must have eaten those elsewhere, to stay her, while she fed her young.

They'd starved. Calling for her—that noise I'd heard, thought to be ghosts on the evening wind—they'd died.

Their snake-skin scales were like the palest copper. Their eyes were shut, and their hungry mouths, with just the tiniest buds of teeth, open, arid for her sustenance, scorched from crying out. Babies. Sons and daughters.

I lifted my head and gave a roar. It hit the roof of the cave and fell back on me and forced down my head again. And on the tomb bed of death and grasses, two eyes, the color of sunset rain, were looking up at me.

In wonder, numbed, stupefied, I reached down and put my finger against the slender mouth. The dragon child bit me, hard, and my blood ran. She sucked. She was female, for so I learned when I picked her up.

The others had lost their essence, were empty. But this one, this last daughter, had somehow survived. Her clutch was weak, but her drawing mouth knew what it did. I held her on my knees, and when she'd had enough, she let go of my flesh, and fell asleep. I could feel her heart drum through me like a summons to another battle.

I built my hut up here, and I hunt here, and in the more fertile land to the south. I cook the food for her now, because, like us, once weaned, dragons are accustomed to broiled or roasted meat. As yet, she can't breathe fire, but it will come. I see her trying. She puffs up, groaning like a bellows. Not a flame answers, yet from her emits the holy smell of fire's possibility. Then she gives up, and glides to me, and I play with her, rolling her over, rolling with her. I've tried to be brother and father, and mother, to her. She sleeps by me. Now the cold's come, we need each other's heat.

She's already the size of the king's largest hunting dog. But her wings are brawny enough for only little flutterings. She doesn't go far. At the rate of her growth, however, I believe that the late spring will see her aloft. And the fire will happen then, too.

Her beauty's painful. Sometimes I sing her songs, adapting the words to her. I even talk to her. She minds my voice. I can see her listening. She makes her own sounds, the notes of dragons.

When she's strong and full grown, she'll begin to prey on men. The city will be directly in her way. Probably she'll also range much further than that.

I knew this. I mean, not in the instants when I realized she lived, when I fed her my blood, not precisely then. But in the time after. How

169

shouldn't I know, who killed her mother for the identical act?

She must live. And like us, she has to live from killing things. But she does it, you old man, as well you would understand, from necessity, not sophistry or pleasure. And she hasn't any vices. She will kill and live and eat and sleep—and fly. And, if others of her race persist, she'll mate. She'll birth offspring who'll be the same as she is and want nothing else.

If enough of them come to be, they could destroy the world of men forever.

It's the revenge then, of her kind upon mine. And my revenge as well, upon the world, for making of me what I was.

And, on myself, of course. For I'll be the first. When the day dawns that she has that power, she'll slaughter me without hesitation. She won't think anything of it. The fire will bloom out of her, the lightning flash. If she devours me after, as I expect she will, that's good. I always believed I'd die in battle, wielding a murderous sword, a machine for death. But here, in this waste, I'll die and give life. Maybe not vengeance after all, but payment.

Or better—not pay—but honorable *recompense*.

Cold Spell

There came a time in the world when it was Winter all the year round. The lands were white as white mint candy from north to south, and from west to east they were white as congealed white wine. Where the seas had been, lay furrowed sheets like glass; only here and there were there channels of black water where the whales came up to breathe.

The great cities covered themselves with tiles like dragon-scales and found ways to keep warm by heating large furnaces in their cellars, and by focusing huge mirrors to refract down the rays of the feeble sun.

Meanwhile, in the villages, that had only poverty out of which to produce tiles and fires and mirrors, the people starved.

There lived a witch in the north. Her hair was the colour of yellow amber, and she wore it bound on her head in six thick burnished braids, secured by combs of green jasper, and over her shoulders was fastened a cloak of bearskin dyed scarlet, which the bear himself had left her on his death, since she had cast a spell for him once, when he was no more than a cub.

The witch would work magic for the villages round about, and tell fortunes with her cards, and the villagers would pay her. As the Winter grew more and more harsh and more and more permanent, however, no one could afford to pay a witch. Then she began to make magic without charging a penny for it. With her spells she contrived to get the poor houses as snug as she could. She magicked loose bricks back into walls and fallen chimneys back onto roofs. She cured the sick animals and the sick children, and brewed sorcerous broths, and said chants to deter the winds and the snows. But every year it became harder. The Winter was too adamant and cruel for just one village witch to keep it at bay, though she did her best. To be sure, she no longer told fortunes; what lay in the future was all too apparent.

She sold her combs of green jasper to travelling merchants from the cities, and next her scarlet bearskin, though it was of sentimental value. With the money she bought food for the villages, but soon the food was gone. Finally, the witch took down her yellow braids and cut off all her hair, leaving only an inch of it on her head, and she sold her hair to the merchants. After that, she could only sell her own person, and this, being a free soul, she could not bring herself to do.

Then Death began to visit.

First, he came and knocked on the doors of the houses where the elderly were dwelling; presently he took the animals from their pens, and the children from their cots. He would pass up and down the country in his inky cloak—even Death disliked the cold—and one night the witch felt him brush by her on a village street. She curtseyed and said:

"Lord Death, you come too often."

"Young lady," said Death, "I come only where the door is opened for me." And he showed her two babies curled up in his arm, looking fast asleep. "See how peacefully they rest. Their mother wept, but she was glad they should suffer no longer."

Then he went into a house and the witch followed him. Here a young woman lay on the bed.

"Come, daughter," said Death, "it is time to be going." And the woman smiled.

"Wait," said the witch. "Sister, tell this dark gentleman to be about his business."

"I am his business," said the woman. "And he is not dark to me, but a shining angel of light. I am that glad to leave my misery behind me. It is Winter I fear, not Death." And her spirit went to Death thankfully, and with a mocking bow to the witch, he strode away into the night.

"This will not do," said the witch. "Death knocks before his time and no one refuses him, for the Winter has made weaklings of all of us."

Then she pulled her cloak, which was made of coarse cloth now, closer about her and over her cropped head, and she sat thinking till the sun rose. And it seemed to her that she must find someone brave enough to fight the Winter and drive it back again to the grim lands it came from, and this someone must be a hero, such as antique stories mentioned, a tall strong man with armour of gold and sword of bronze.

Being a free soul, and a creature of impulse, the witch got up and went out into the dawn to search for one immediately.

The witch assumed that if there were heroes to be found, she would find them in the cities, and thus it was to the cities she journeyed. Along the way, she infrequently met men, the hungry and the sullen. Once, a pack of wolves hunted her, but she sent them away with a spell that made them see deer running.

It was a long road. When she came to the first city, her hair had already grown to her shoulders.

What a place it was. The roofs piled up against the leaden sky, crimson and gold; all the windows had coloured panes, and warm breezes blew about in the streets from the underground furnaces, and strange little stunted trees craned from pots along the pavement. Here and there men and women rode in carriages drawn by teams of tabby cats. The outer walls were of stone twenty feet thick.

The witch went to the market, and she put on a conjuring act. She plucked birds from thin air and changed a heap of hot-house apples into emeralds—it was all illusion, but she was applauded, and the people threw her coppers. The witch walked up and down the city, looking for a suitable hero. No one appeared tall or strong or daring enough. Inside the buildings were lamps that shone like the summer sun, and through the stained glass of the windows you could see no grey in the sky, because they altered everything to rose, lavender and green.

"You would never know there was a Winter at all," the witch said to a lady pruning a tiny oak tree in a vase.

"Winter?" squeaked the lady, giggling loudly. "What peculiar word is that? Why, we all know that it is forever Summer here." Quite a crowd had collected to learn what the joke was.

The witch said quietly, "Outside the walls it is forever Winter. It will take a hero to drive this cold season away."

When the crowd heard, they shouted furiously. A captain of police in splendid uniform came up and seized the witch by the arm.

"You must not use foul language in this city," he said. "Naturally, some citizens are too innocent to know that the word you uttered is obscene. However, I cannot overlook such vileness."

And the witch was cast into prison for saying 'Winter' in a public place.

When night came, the city grew gaudier still, and it was not until the ashy sunrise that the witch ventured to unbar her cell by magic, and stole out into the streets, where a few drunkards were singing of the beautiful summer morning. Demonstrably, there were no heroes to be had here, and the witch left the city by the quickest route.

The next city she came to was altogether different.

It was built of crystal and alabaster and gave the impression of having been constructed of the snow and ice themselves. Although the furnaces heated the thoroughfares and houses, a chill blue light burned in the lamps. Strolling ladies dazzled in diamonds, gentlemen rode albino mammoths with trappings like icicles.

The witch went to a tavern and put on a conjuring act. She turned the wine three separate colours and feathers rained from the ceiling. After the applause and the coppers, she sat and watched the young men closely, but none was much like a hero. They played chess idly and smoked incense.

"This is a wintry city," said the witch to the bartender. "But I have been looking for a man valiant enough to drive the Winter away."

"Drive it away!" exclaimed the bartender in horror, dropping several frosty goblets. A crowd gathered instantly. "Why, who is so stupid they cannot see the perfection of Winter?"

"Yes, indeed," agreed the young men. "There is such delicacy and artistry in snow and ice, we welcome them. Thank heavens the ghastly brash Summer does not show his face around here anymore." And they yawned and wandered back to their chessboards and pipes.

The witch left the city before sunset.

After these adventures, the witch was an age on the road. Her hair had grown down to her waist on the day she came to an enormous wall and a pair of iron gates which was the entrance to the third city.

Inside was an awesome scene.

About the streets of grotesque dwellings stood groups of silent, black-clad people. The roads themselves ran up to a vast edifice of granite and no sooner had the witch come in the gates than a thunderous cannon went off amidst clouds of smoke. At this terrifying signal, the people began to climb the streets towards the ominous building, chanting dolorously.

Overhead, the sun-reflectors turned with a dim whining sound, and underfoot growled the furnaces, but there seemed little warmth in the black city. The witch accompanied the throng and found herself in a menacing temple. Here the multitude threw themselves on the ground in front of a colossal statue half hidden behind curtaining, while priests in black beat gongs.

Then the High-Priest roared:

"O eternal master, pray hurt us as much as you have ever hurt us. Send the snow and the wind and the bitter weather. Pray destroy us if you wish, for we are your devoted slaves, and we give you homage."

The witch called to this priest, for she reverenced him not at all: "Who is this dreadful god you are worshipping?"

"Silence, blasphemer," said the priest, "and you shall gaze on the face of him we extol, none other than King Winter himself."

And he touched the curtain, which fell away.

What was revealed was unspeakably shocking. The statue was of a giant man; half his face was white, half black, his eyes—which had neither pupil nor iris—were red, and flickered with fires, and his hair of steel snakes writhed as if alive. In one hand he held a flail of iron, in the other hand, which was bloody, a doll resembling a dead child. At the sight of this vision most of the crowd buried their heads in their arms, and some fainted. Only the witch remained standing.

"Kneel and repent your pride," bellowed the priest. "Kneel before the lord of entire creation."

"I never will," said the witch, and she went right up to the statue. "Perhaps I am not strong enough to match you and perhaps I shall never find one who can, but neither will I call you lord." And the witch spat at the feet of the idol and went her way without another glance.

One dull noon, when the witch's hair had grown down as far as her ankles—long enough indeed to braid, if she had had combs to secure it—she heard a soft tinkling of bells.

Turning about, she noted a silver sled drawn by six white wolves, the leader of whom nodded and politely asked:

"Are you the young lady who has been inquiring after a hero sufficiently brave to fight Winter?"

"Most certainly I am," said the witch, who was not as tremendously surprised to come on a talking wolf as anyone else might be.

"Please to get into the sled," said the wolf.

This the witch did at once, and the wolves loped off, the bells on their harness singing.

Over the snow-fields and ice-meadows they went, under the shadow of high mountains whose toothed crowns were gnawing the sky, across a coagulated indigo sea, where miles off the witch saw the blue seals sliding on the ice and the whales blowing water at the lemon sun. Eventually the sled drew up outside a big pale tent with platinum tassels, and inside sat a young man in a chair of white bone. His hair was black as night, but his eyes were blue as sapphire, and he bowed slightly when

175

he saw the witch, stood up and bade her enter.

The witch was pleased to see him, for he looked strong and clever, and definitely of the material from which heroes are assembled. She was also aware of some bright armour on a peg, a helm of azure metal and a shining sword.

"Well," said the hero, beckoning her to a seat, "before we debate matters, maybe you will play a game of cards with me."

"Gladly," said the witch for, cards being part of her witch's craft, she had rather missed this aspect of her trade.

Soon a little table was set between them, and they began.

First they played two-handed whist and then they played quadrille, and after a while, euchre. The hero would win a game, but the witch would win the next, then the hero would win again, and then the witch again. Presently the sun was low, and they played cribbage and bezique, and when the dusk commenced, faro and fan-tan. And, for every game the hero won, the witch would beat him at the next.

When the glittering stars appeared, the hero lit the chandeliers in the roof of the tent, and laid down a board of squares, and they played rouge et noir, with untold magics as the stakes. The hero won; and the witch won. As the moon was rising, their score was still equal.

"I see how it is between us," said the hero. "Neither can best the other, and neither win. Your luck is unusually good. We had better discuss terms."

"My terms are these," said the witch, "if you will challenge King Winter and drive him from the land, then I will work witchery for you for as long as you wish, and do anything in my power to make you happy."

"You are very generous, young lady," said the hero, "but I think you have been misled. As we played cards, now and then our hands have touched. Tell me, have you noticed nothing strange?"

"Your hands," said the witch, "are very cold."

"Draw a card from the pack," said the hero, gravely, "and you shall know me."

This the witch did, and the card she drew was the king of diamonds. That was how she discovered that it was Winter himself she had been sitting with all afternoon. "You are not as they say you are," remarked the witch.

"Few things are as white as they are painted," said Winter. "This much agreed, it seems to me we must compromise. Since you have been resolute, courageous, and amusing enough to seek my destruction, I will listen to whatever you ask."

"I ask only that you be less harsh to men," said the witch.

"That I cannot help. It is my function and my destiny. I am as I am and have no choice. Cold all the way through. However, there is one thing will change me."

"And what is that?"

"You must kiss me, thrice, on the mouth."

"Is that then so hard to do?" asked the witch, for privately she thought him very handsome.

"You may find it is," admitted Winter.

Maybe the witch felt some foreboding, but she had spoken even to Death and not been afraid. She took Winter's face between her palms and kissed him three times on the lips.

At the first kiss, a little colour appeared in Winter's cheeks and the witch's cheeks became a little pale.

At the second kiss, the hands of Winter grew warmer, and the hands of the witch turned numb with cold.

At the third kiss, Winter smiled; outside there was a sharp yammer of ice cracking: the thaw had begun. A wind blew up from the south, and a mild rain scattered the earth. By midnight, the seas had started to groan and melt. The snow slid from the mountains, and at first light, the Spring had opened half of one green eye on the world she had not seen for a chiliad. Winter himself, with a mixed shout of annoyance and laughter, leapt on his sled. The white wolves dashed off to the north with him over the fast-dissolving pack-ice. The pallid tent blew away into the sky. Even the cards took flight.

Shortly, only a single item remained. An image made of glass, or was it solid rime? A pretty snow-woman. A witch, frozen by Winter's kiss.

What did she think? Perhaps she was too cold to think at all. Perhaps not. Perhaps she thought: *What a fool I have been.* Perhaps, as with the jasper combs, the bearskin cloak, her hair, she thought: *it has not been wasted.*

As for Winter, he raced back to his old palace in the middle of northern nowhere, without properly understanding he had been routed, trying to pretend everything was normal. The snows had settled in drifts in the draughty halls, and the aurora borealis in the lamps burned low.

He went upstairs and sat down to play at a piano with stalactites and stalagmites for keys. He was remembering the witch. Where he had made her cold, she had warmed him quite amazingly. His heart was almost human, and as he wished events had turned out differently, the piano became extremely loud.

Right through the spring, the witch stood petrified among the grass and the small flowers. The temperate weather was not enough to thaw her after the embrace of Winter himself.

One day, Death came by, black as a scowl. He glanced at the primroses and crocuses, and he murmured to them, "By Summer, you will have withered, and be growing in my kingdom." He tapped the glacial witch with his thumbnail, and he asked, "Yes?"

But there was no reply from within.

"Surely," said Death, "you do not wish to remain like this forever? What life do you have, young lady, frozen stiff as you are? The sophisticated and philosophical thing to do," added Death, "would be to renounce this shadow of your former self and come to me."

Still, there was no reply.

Death looked closely. He looked into the eyes of the witch and through her eyes, into her mind. Eyes and mind had not been frosted over, being too alert and too warm to freeze. When he stared, there came a flash inside them very like—Death arched his brows—scorn?

"Come now," said Death. "Do you suppose anyone else will bother with you? You have freed the earth of perpetual Winter, but does the earth thank you? Do the people run up and lay garlands at your feet and offer prayers for your recovery? No, indeed. As is generally the case, I am the only one with any time to spare for the sick, the only one who takes any sincere interest in them." And Death sighed heavily at his onerous task.

In the witch's mind, something laughed. Death ignored it.

"Consider what I have told you. Weigh the alternatives. You can enjoy a comfortable sojourn in my land, or a wretched eternity of this. Make your choice. I shall be back."

And Death strode off, whistling a dirge fortissimo.

But the sun shone, and the flowers faded and new flowers flourished, and soon he returned, this time with his black cloak over his arm, smartly dressed, and wearing a lot of rings. Behind him came a grave concert party, pale haggard minstrels with curious instruments; a mandolin made from a yellow skull and strung with human hair, hollow ivory tibias, a xylobone. This orchestra stationed itself before the witch and began to play bittersweet laments.

"There," said Death. "Listen to the pretty music. Think how the world will regret you at your passing. They will bring wreaths to your resting place, and weep and exclaim: 'If only we had shown more gratitude.' You, meanwhile, shall be my honoured guest. What do you say?"

Death looked into the witch's eyes. The witch's eyes said, "While there is hope there is life."

"Platitudes," said Death, offended. "Young lady, it is not usual, but since you are so ignorant of the joys of my domain, I will show them to you here and now."

Death's face darkened with concentration, and he made images enter the witch's brain. Thus, she saw her fourth city: Death's. Very grand it was, like a huge graveyard where only kings were buried. The palaces were mausoleums of white marble, mantled with ivy and lichen, the streets were paved with tombstones. A river ran through the city, black as the black sky, afloat with funeral barges draped in black velvet. People rode solemnly in them or walked up and down the streets discoursing learnedly.

The primroses which had withered from the earth pushed between the tombstones, but they were pale as paper and had no scent. Even the nightingales did not sing on the steeples but chimed like small silver knells.

A woman who had died of starvation sat on the river bank. "How good it is not to be hungry," she said.

Two travellers, who had perished of frostbite, played bat and ball in a courtyard. "How good it is not to be cold," they cried, "and to have all our fingers."

A boy and a wolf were drinking wine in a cemetery garden. "I do apologise for eating you," said the wolf, who had been killed by hunters that afternoon.

"Please think no more of it," said the boy.

Then Death showed the witch a room of green ceramic, lit by a hundred tapers, with silver bier, and chairs.

"Accept this chamber as yours," said Death graciously. "Contemplate the peace and serenity you will know there."

In the mind of the witch something said: "It is very kind of you, Lord Death, and I am glad your kingdom is of benefit to those who are ready for it. But I am not ready, and while I believe in my life and my freedom—for I am a free soul—I never shall be ready."

"Damnation!" shouted Death, inappropriately, for he knew there was no such thing. And, scattering the musicians, he stalked away, only growling over his shoulder, "I shall be back."

Months later, the witch in her shell felt the faintest glimmer of sunlight break through to her. She observed, coming along the road from the south, a tall man in gold armour with a sword of bronze. This, she thought, is the hero I was after finding in the first place.

It was Summer. He peered at her sheepishly, embarrassed because he had been in hiding such a great while. As he passed, the witch felt a Summer heat like a fire, but even this was not enough to thaw her after Winter's embrace.

Needless to say, Death was close behind.

He was wearing a mask of bones to frighten her. He rapped on her glassy surface and demanded, "Are you ready now? Even the Summer has not done the trick. Do you suppose anything else can warm you?" Then he shivered and put on his cloak. "This is too much," said Death, as up the sunny slope came walking a snow-storm with Winter in the middle of it.

Winter stepped out. He looked twice as sheepish as Summer had done, and much angrier than Death.

"This living-death is mine," said Death at once, pointing to the witch.

"No, mine," said Winter furiously. "She is nearly ice, and the ice belongs to me."

"Nearly ice: nearly belongs to you. Nearly dead, and nearly belongs to me."

They darted ferocious glances at the witch, whose eyes said, "To neither. I belong only to myself."

Death said, "I have shown the young lady the wonders I am able to lay at her feet. You had better inform her of what you have to offer. Apart, of course, from a cold palace and a nice view of some glaciers."

Winter scowled. "Being of a friendly and generous nature," he shouted, "I am prepared to offer myself." Then, growing calmer, "Listen to me, girl. If you will come and live in the north lands with me, I will try to help you."

The witch could only answer with her eyes. Her eyes said, "How can I refuse to let you salve your conscience?" But there was a smile there too, and quite suddenly some of the ice that imprisoned her melted.

Death stroked his chin, musingly, having sensibly taken off his mask.

"Yours I think, after all," said Death to Winter, "reluctant as I always am to admit defeat." And without another word, he gathered his cloak around him and went away to bide his time.

Accordingly, Winter carried the witch to his palace. As they went up the staircase, the lamps grew brighter and the furniture took on a more polished appearance.

About midnight, a whole lot more of the ice-crystal, affected by Winter's angrily affectionate looks, fell off with a crash. Winter frowned at the unaesthetic noise. It would be, he foresaw, a slow and tedious exercise, defrosting his beloved—she was his beloved, he could no longer very well deny it, much as he would have liked to.

What a dreadful irony, he thought, that he, coldest of all things, should have acquired a heart warm enough to thaw ice, which even the blazing heat of Summer could not melt. Every time he smiled at the witch, shattered rime would scatter the floor. He wondered grimly how long it would take before she was herself again.

One morning, mistily but unmistakably, she smiled back at him.

Unnoticed, Spring crept almost up to the very ramparts of Winter's palace. Winter went out secretly at dark of moon to pick a few primroses for his thawed witch, before he ragingly chased the Spring away into the south.

Beauty is the Beast

The land was in turmoil, and from the City of the Thousand Domes, the outlaws fled to the town of the Free North. "How shall we be received?" they said to each other, as they rode wearily at sunset through a province of vines, and sighted such a town of fine old houses and leaning walls. In the yellow light, the world seemed peaceful. But they knew otherwise. "We bring them unrest and trouble. War—if they listen and come to our help."

But Northfree, by her very name, knew the state of the land, and how terror ruled southward, from the Capital. The town opened her gates and welcomed the outlaws, gave them food and wine, and lamps; let them shine and speak out from their broken hearts and blazing rage.

It was a fact, the City of the Thousand Domes had become in these years, *altered*. In the North they had heard of the riotous insanity. The citizens had thrown down the law and the religion. They lived now by vice and cruelty, and made a fetish of dirt, rags, ugliness, for they said all things were made equal, must therefore be equal, nothing better than another thing, but only as nature intended—though, in the way of the fetish, they occasionally drew attention to a deformity by ornamenting it in some curious manner. Ravens perched on the towers by day and rats ran like rivers in the streets by night, exalting in the carnage. For the new deity of the metropolis, whom they called The Reasonable, was a goddess of blood and demanded frequent sacrifice. All this, the outlaws reviewed for the town of Northfree, standing in the lamplit square. A vast crowd had gathered, the windows and balconies, the very roofs were filled by silent watches, listening. Even the stars looked down.

"For a year we struggled," said the spokesman of the outlaws. "By such legal means as are still recognised there, and also by schemes and plots, to bring back some sense, some justice to our heaven-cursed City. But we failed, and in fear of our lives at last, we fled." Then he covered his face with his hands and wept, and the crowd murmured.

Another spoke. He told how the City was now ruled by strange petty kings, who abused their power but refused power's name—being, of course, equal to everyone else. Evil madmen, magicians, who could ensorcell the creatures of the city, human and otherwise, bending men and women to their will, enlisting the terrifying rats as their minions, the ravens as their spies.

"To the unmerciful mercy of these monsters we were forced to leave our comrades, those imprisoned in the black dungeons on the river. They warned us to escape and will give their lives for ours."

And then the outlaws talked of raising armies here in the North, to march against the vicious rabble of the City, cast it and its masters down, and bring the reign of terror to an end. "Though they are magicians there, they are mortal. They can be killed."

The speakers enlarged upon particular tyrants, and though Northfree had heard of many of them, their names and deeds, the news had now a dreadful emphasis. Especially there was one, Chaquoh he was called, who was already well-known and infamous.

It was said he wrote and uttered poison. Even to read a sentence he had penned could blind you. The malignity of his words slew, or sent mad. He stank of a terrible disease, which would long since have eaten him up, but that the disease of his *spite* was stronger. Or else it was the spite itself which furnished the disease—a parasite that thrived on him, but dared not finish him entirely.

A little before midnight, exhausted, the orators concluded. The crowd shouted instead. Hands were raised and vows sworn of loyalty and protection. The young men of the town sprang forward.

"We will be your army, and go with you, to blast this obscenity of a City from our country's earth. How shall we take it? Only tell us what to do."

Then there were fresh lamps lit, and bottles opened. The campaign began to be discussed.

It was only as faint colour started again to come in the sky that one of the outlaws—he who had wept—said to the townsman at his elbow, "Tell me, do you know the young woman who was standing, until a moment ago, up on that balcony there? At one point there was a tall man in white beside her, but he went away. She had only one old servant for company. But she was very remarkable."

"By your description, that is Maristarre," said the townsman.

"She will have grown tired and gone home to find rest, no doubt," said the outlaw, his thoughts straying somewhat from the honourable war, for she had been exceptionally beautiful, this Maristarre of Northfree. But then anger and pain and hope laid hold of him again, and he forgot her quite.

아ristarre of Northfree. It was true she was beautiful, with her whiteness like clear marble through which the light shines, her darkly polished hair, and darkly polished eyes that seemed always to see far off. There had been many offers, but she had not wished to leave her father, it would appear. Now she went home to one of the old houses of the town, and seating herself as the dawn bloomed, she wrote to him. "Forgive me," wrote Maristarre, "it has come to me what I must do. The young men will fight. They will form an army discernible from miles off, and all the power of the City will be turned against them. But I am one woman, and may pass unnoticed." (She was modest. At home, people turned always to look at her on the street. This very sunrise as she returned, a tall man in white had looked long after her, from the porch of a neighbouring church.)

It was also true that she was a visionary, this Maristarre. She did see far off. As the orators had poured forth their flaming passion, her spirit seemed to speak softly within her. She thought; *They would fight sorcerers. What if the sorcerers lie dead?* And she beheld Chaquoh the evil one, the Beast, perhaps mightiest of the great tyrant-masters of the City of the Thousand Domes. She saw his vileness conjured by the outcry of the outlaws. And herself also she saw. She, so purely fair, and he so hideous and steeped in venom. Opposites direly attracting. As if to a magnet she was drawn to this. All her years, where another might have looked into her mirror and grown proud, visionary Maristarre had simply been puzzled at herself. But now at once she understood. She was a clean bright sword, fashioned for one incredible stroke.

So in the earliest morning she left her father's house, and the town where she had lived all her life, and the province of vines. She found transport to a town farther south, and there transport to another more southerly. Until at length she boarded one of the rattling black chariots that hurled itself along the rutted roads to the City of the Thousand Domes.

She had dressed in plain slovenly garments, and her hair hung down to her waist, for so the women wore their hair in the Capital now, sometimes with a bloody flower tangled in it pinned through by a stiletto.

As the coach came near the City, Maristarre saw such things as these on the hills: burned fields, where corpses lay; trees with skulls tied in them by ribbons; tall garlanded gallows of ornate wrought-iron, with the hanged hanging. Once or twice a shepherdess drove her sheep across the road and the carriage halted. These girls carried pistols in their belts, and one a tall pike with a grinning painted mask fixed to the top. Their own faces were grinning and maleficent, and the sheep too were changed, scarlet or ochre in colour, with sharply pointed teeth. They did not bleat, but made a guttural sound, as if they were in the process of learning human speech, and half choked on it.

The sun had just gone down when they reached the City. Against a dying sky, Maristarre saw its thousand black domes, and all the points of light and rays of smoke that rose from its hell fires.

What a place was this, worse than any telling. But Maristarre was not dismayed. She knew her task, her destiny, her punishment even. She had accepted all, and had no need to be afraid.

At the gate of the City, men with broken teeth glared in, and bade her get out of the carriage. (One lacked an eye but wore a patch which read *Look! I have lost my eye!*, the words picked out in gems.)

"Your business, sister?" ('Sister, brother', these were the formal and only lawful modes of address in the Capital, where everyone-and-thing was equal.) These men were part of the city's Guard of Brotherhood, and they wore the blood-red insignia of The Reasonable One.

"I am here," said Maristarre, calmly, "to join the glorious free women of the City."

The Guard approved of this. They were fascinated by beauty, too, provided it was natural; though generally they regarded it with suspicion.

"Your hands are smooth," one said to her, "there's no mark on you."

"I shall gain scars of honour, in the service of Chaquoh," said Maristarre. "I have come to offer him my whole self, for even in the nothing-town where I was born, his words ring like an alarm-bell. I am his slave. I will lie at his feet."

At this, the men toasted her with a deadly inky brandy they were prone to drink, and she was allowed to go on into the City. The name 'Chaquoh' would be a safe conduct. No one would touch her, if they thought her due to be his.

So she passed through the streets. In the narrower alleys, which she avoided, she heard the gutters chuckling and guessed what moved along them and how like a ruby it shone under the lamps. On the wide roads carriages whirled by, loud with drunken voices. The buildings, high-roofed and impressive always, were now much blemished from the fighting that had gone on in the City at the beginning of its alteration.

185

Whole sections had been blasted from walls, and windows shattered, and all left gaping, so one could see in as if to a lighted picture. Quarrelling, debauch, and even manslaughter, these were the normal subject of everyone. Harlots went by, slender or bloated, feathers and knives in their nests of hair; and gangs of men, some of whom would have seized Maristarre, but she spoke the name of Chaquoh with such authority, they let her continue. Once, a hunchback questioned her. His humped shoulder was sprinkled with faceted jewels, though he wore foul rags. When she said she would serve Chaquoh, the hunchback laughed. He had served mighty brother Chaquoh too, he said.

On one street she came to a waxworks lit by torches, and doing fine business. The waxworks' specialty was to show lifelike images of many persons who had been killed in the City, their faces having been modelled from death-masks obtained immediately after murder or execution. Several were victims of the goddess, The Reasonable One. Maristarre did not falter.

She reached a square where a forge was smoking up thick overcast and sparks. She told the blacksmith she wanted to buy from him a knife.

"See," he said, "look what I am melting down—a church bell and a holy cup to be cannonballs and swords. But here is a knife could disembowel a spider. This will do for you. Do you mean to slit the throat of some rival?"

"No," said Maristarre. "I intend to put the knife to the service of Chaquoh."

Then the blacksmith fawned on her and gave her the knife without taking any money for it.

Maristarre crossed the stone bridge over the City's river. All the statues on the bridge had been smashed and lay in piles of rubble, over which each traveller picked his way with difficulty. On days of festival, the bridges were almost impassable, due to the corpses heaped there. Down in the black river, fish sometimes leapt to the surface; corpse-fed and swollen, they had grown as large as dogs, and had luminous pale eyes. From the river, too, the prisons of the City rose up out of the water, and with narrow pale eyes, not unlike those of the unnatural fish, they scanned the dark as if searching for prey. But still Maristarre did not falter. Nor when, leaving the bridge, a tall man in white seemed to bar her way—but then he moved aside and was gone.

Having gained the other bank, she walked up a long and unlit lane, where the rats might be heard rustling and cheeping, and sometimes there came the flash of eager rat-eyes. But Maristarre had only to whisper the name: *Chaquoh*. She knew the rats would let her alone.

She had had no need to ask the way. The dwellings of all the magician-masters had been described in detail. She found the house of Chaquoh with no trouble.

It was tall, and leaned heavily on both its neighbours, which were ruined and empty, but for the scurrying, glittering rats. From colossal chimneys, grown by overuse seemingly too big for the building, vapours glided into the starless night. One window dully glowed, high up: There he would be, at his work. But even now Maristarre did not falter.

She knocked on the door; its knocker was a severed human hand, or so it looked—but made of white stone.

At the knock a hundred voices seemed to moan and cry. A rat, itself big as a spaniel, slid to her ankle, and the rat spoke to Maristarre, though its speech was awkward and impeded.

"Whatseek?" said the rat.

"Chaquoh, my brother."

"Whyseek?"

"To be Chaquoh's slave."

"Allusissame. Noslave."

"True, brother. But let Chaquoh correct me."

"Thenshall."

And the rat licked the door, which grated and drew open.

Beyond the doors, an empty vestibule, its corners filled by stacks of yellowing paper, and hung throughout by curtains of dust and webs. All these, and the paper stacks too, had been carefully spangled with gold-leaf, so no iota of the muck should be overlooked. On the long, crooked stairway, the broken tiles were rimmed by gold.

Maristarre went up the steps. On each landing there were doors, fast shut, though in some cases the wood was cracked, it was possible to see through—but only to darkness. Finally it seemed she had reached the attic of the house. Instead of a door, the stair opened directly on a cramped anteroom. Nothing was in it but a hard, wooden chair, and a lamp. A statue held this lamp, a statue of rusty iron in the shape of a snake with a woman's head and hands. "What do you require, sister?" asked the snake-statue.

"To see my brother, Chaquoh."

"Chaquoh is bathing. You must wait."

"Thank you, sister," said Maristarre. She sat on the hard chair and folded her hands. The knife nestled at her breast.

An hour passed. Out in the City of the Thousand Domes a bell struck for midnight, but the bell had a human voice, and every one of the twelve chimes was some ominous word. Maristarre caught such sounds as seemed to be *Pestilence, Despair, Hatred, Lies, Strangling*—and several others that do not look well written down. From the streets, too, came shrieks and growls, stupid laughter and wicked laughter, and now and then the noise of clashing swords, or shots.

Eventually Maristarre rose.

"What do you require, sister?" asked the statue-snake again.

"May I now go in to my brother, Chaquoh?"

The statue waited, then it said, "Yes, go in."

At this, a hole appeared in the wall, a jagged rent as if cannon-blast had passed through there, but every fissure was set with a pearl or a topaz. Beyond the fissure, a disheartening stair leading down and down, as the first stair had led up and up. But Maristarre took the stair, and went down it, into a vague luminous dark.

Far down at the stair's foot, she found herself above a great sewer full of murky fluid, which led away through channels on every side, apparently out into the City. A slight greenish slime on the water gleamed and illuminated the area.

There was a platform at the stair-bottom, jutting out on the water. Even as Maristarre stepped down on it, a creature appeared, swimming in from one of the outlets. It moved swiftly toward her, and suddenly, grasping the platform, its upper half emerged from the slime. Here was Chaquoh, it could be no other.

He was a man still, but barely. Now you could perceive the nature of his disease, his body scaled and plated—he was turning gradually and maybe less gradually with every hour, into a sort of alligator. Yet his hands and pale face, and his bright red eyes—these were like a rat's.

"You must pardon me, sister," he murmured to Maristarre, "but it is only here I can find comfort for my body."

His red-cold eyes stared at her, all over. He put one of his little rat paws on her foot. Maristarre did not falter. "Why," he hissed, "why, pretty sister, are you here?"

"I bring you the names of the traitors who recently escaped you," said Maristarre.

"Ah," said Chaquoh with a smile or grimace, "good news. Wait. My pen…" And he drew from behind one pointed ear a dagger-bladed quill whose long, long feather seemed to touch the very ceiling far overhead under the attic. "And ink…" At which he stabbed the pen into his arm, and as the swarthy blood spurted, he dipped the pen and wrote on the air—which sizzled—*The Names of Traitors.* "I promise you," he said, "they shall die in agony."

Then Maristarre leaned close and with her knife she struck Chaquoh through the throat, where he was not yet scaled, down into the heart. He gave a thin scream, more like a whistle. And then he dragged himself upward on the platform and dropped on his side. The blood from his death-wound was not of the shade of the other blood; it was black, and where it fell the platform smoked. "You have killed me," said Chaquoh.

"Yes," said Maristarre.

"Now," said Chaquoh, "you are indeed my slave." And then he died.

But Maristarre spurned his body and his words alike. She turned from him and stood composed to wait her punishment.

Very soon there began to be a screaming and shouting and roaring on all sides. The City felt his death. Things plunged in the sewer. The great black rats spilled round and stared at her. She thought she would be torn in pieces, and prepared herself to suffer it. But then men came, and women, rushing down the stair with torches in their hands, weeping and screeching. They took her by the arms.

They called her terrible things. "To the goddess!" they cried. "The goddess shall have you."

"I am the sacrifice," said Maristarre. "I have done what I came to do. The beast is dead."

But she was dragged away into streaming fire and darkness. Battered and bruised, spat on, beaten and enchained, cast into a dungeon blacker than moonless night, in the depths of the prison in the river.

Before dawn, a voice cried her sentence out of the black. As they had told her, she must meet the goddess.

But Maristarre's eyes looked far away. Her whiteness shone in the blackness. She said nothing. She had done what she had come to do.

They took her, the next sunset, to the temple where their goddess was worshipped. It was an open amphitheatre, seating many thousands, and every seat filled. At its centre was a platform, and here rose two uprights of wood. They bound Maristarre between them so tightly she could not move. Then the Guard of Brotherhood, who had escorted her to the place, and bound her in it, hurried away to the edges of the arena. Drums began to beat and bugles to wail, and the multitude clapped and cawed, invoking The Reasonable One, entreating her to manifest and claim her due, this assassin of one of the City's holiest sons. The sky bled down and soon the night would come...

"How shall she know the goddess is near?" the guards had said, in grim banter, as they rode beside her chariot on the way. "A shadow and a sound of wings," another answered. "And then the sharp beak!"

All along the route, the people of the City had howled at Maristarre and cursed her and made gestures of rending her. But as she was to be given to the goddess, she escaped maiming. Others danced and sang about the vehicle, describing how it would be for her, to die, when the beak of the goddess slashed her apart. Children at the wayside ate sugar skulls. In some places, hawkers sold pigs' blood in which to dip various flowers, so they turned the proper tint.

But then, and now in the amphitheatre under the prescient sky, Maristarre showed no fear—and felt none? Between the upright stakes she stood in silence. Her eyes looked far away. *I am the clean sword, stained now by filthiness. Break me. I consent. Purity triumphs. The beast is dead. I am not their sacrifice. I die for the hope and beauty of the earth.*

Nevertheless, the far-seeing, far-off visionary eyes of Maristarre now glimpsed a man in the crowd, a tall man all in white, and she realised she had seen him twice, or maybe three times, before. Who could it be? Had he followed her all this way from the North? Some rescuer? No, such a rescue could not be possible.

And the last embers were crushed from the sun. The sky turned sable, a wind blew fiercely over the amphitheatre, shaking garments and hair, and rattling the chains that bound Maristarre.

"The goddess! The goddess arrives! The Reasonable!"

The crowd moaned and thundered. A shadow fell abysmal on Maristarre and she heard a sound of wings...

Cold pain passed through her—but she recognised it was only the dash of the air, her chains falling away—she was in the sky, held firmly in the arms of a man, taller than any man she had ever seen, almost a giant, with a mane of pale hair flaming behind him, and vast white wings spread out, healing like the wings of a swan, as he bore her upward.

"Rescue, then?" questioned Maristarre.

"You may say so," he gently said to her.

"Where now?" said Maristarre. She did not speak of Northfree. He was the angel of death, and this she knew.

"You have seen a city of Hell-on-Earth," said the angel, as they spun higher and higher on his swan's wings, so high the sun was again visible far beneath, like a guttering lamp under their feet. "Now you must see another earthly city."

They made one enormous circle. The night revolved and was flung away like a stone; the sun, having fallen, blossomed once more.

There below, among the green lands of summer, lay a City of shining roofs and cupolas, with a silver river dividing it.

The angel spoke some sacred charm, and became a snow-white pigeon, and Maristarre a pearl-grey dove. They flew down into the shining City together, and in her visionary heart, her dove's heart, Beauty thought, *This is my doing. Good is victorious. This is how it will be.*

In the meadows girls picked flowers, and the sheep played, their wool ambered and pinkened by sunlight, their square little teeth harmlessly full of grass. Trees had paper rosettes tied on them; even the scarecrows were garlanded. The City gates stood wide, and the brave young men in their uniforms, with many honours pinned to them, saluted courteously whoever went in or out. All the women were lovely, and the men fine. Their faces were full of patience and optimism, and as they went about their work, or walked to and fro, they sang sweet or gallant songs. A woman passed with a load. A man hastened after her and aided her with it. A child fell down and a score of persons ran to console it. To a shop selling bread the hungry came, and received the hot loaves without a coin asked of them. A girl with a silver ring gave it gladly in barter for a daisy.

There had been some damage done to the buildings, it must have been in a fighting past unlike this harmonious present. Now the busy workmen patched the bricks, and where the workmen had not yet come, they had hung out wreaths and plants in pots and birds in cages and hand-switched banners, to soften any ugliness.

An image-maker's shop stood on a thoroughfare, where might be seen living celebrities and deceased. It was a popular place, each figure having been modelled from the life, even in some instances after death, that no falsehood might be told or injustice done the subject.

On the glistening river, the tranquil barges floated up and down.

Lions of gold had been set on the bridges, from which the statues of oppressors had long since been removed. The golden lions reflected in the silver water. Each bore an inscription which said: *"Let us all be lions!"* But somewhere a bell had begun to dole with a melodious sadness.

Flying with the angel, Maristarre paused in the air, and looked down to see a massive procession winding along the riverbank. Girls in white and solemn musicians, incense uncurling to the sky, and green branches strewn. And a lament was rising, and on every side men and women standing to watch and weep.

"Is it a funeral procession? Who has died?"

"One who loved us and cared for us…"

Then flying lower, Maristarre the dove beheld a chair borne high in the middle of the procession, and seated in it, seeming only to sleep, a man whose handsome face was darkened by nobility, sorrow and death.

In awe conceivably, certainly with attention, Maristarre followed the bier, and all its thousands of mourners.

As the procession flowed on, she saw one on whose humped shoulder the tears of another's compassion sparkled like jewels, and a one-eyed man, on whose bandage was written *Gladly given for my country*. The roofs about were clustered with white pigeons, white hyacinths fell, dipped in wine. Children pressed white handkerchiefs to their lips, kissing the embroidered picture of the dead lamented one. Even the alley-rats, the knaves and thieves, stared after the cortege and wept. He forgave us. He knew poverty drove us on. He was our brother, and our master.

"Chaquoh!" they cried, and their tears ran like rivers to a sea of loss.

"He?" said Maristarre to the angel. "Have I misheard?"

"Even he," the angel said. "Remember, he wrote in his life's blood, without a qualm."

And presently, as the funeral wound away, Maristarre found herself standing again in the sky, above a scaffold. Her own body was being removed from it, taken away for burial.

"Their goddess, that they worship," said Maristarre.

"Again, you mistook the words you listened to," said the angel. "They called it, not Reason, but Razor. It is only a common axe, or very nearly."

Maristarre looked down and observed her body, and that it was no longer beautiful, or pristine, or whole, but ugly, crippled, the carcass of a frightful beast.

"Is this, then," said Maristarre, "the truth?"

"Each sees the truth is his own way. The City strives for one truth, which it believes to be as you have now had revealed to you. Those who oppose the City's values, or fear them, see everything as monstrous, and the architectural creation of monsters—as you have had it revealed to you formerly, and on which sight you have acted."

Maristarre looked behind her, and she saw a man approaching them over the sky. It was Chaquoh. He was neither handsome and noble, nor a scaled rat-alligator with red eyes. He was merely a man, worn out with labour and fury, with his own demons, and the world's. He glanced at Maristarre and passed her, walking on into the distance, which was not simply sky.

"It seems to me I must, in fact, follow and serve him. Is it so?" asked Maristarre.

"You took away his life."

"He erred in his life."

"His mistake. Yours is the robbery. Now you owe him the debt."

"Then I am to be his slave and he my master?"

"You have seen him as the City saw him, and yourself too, through their eyes. Forget such terms as Master, Magician, Slave. Forget the masks men wear. Go now, and try to see the truth, which is never easy."

So Maristarre ceased gazing far off. She fixed her eyes on Chaquoh and she walked after him. And as she walked, she thought how he *had* written in his life's blood, and said—not *"They will die in agony"*—but: *"They or we will die in agony."* (How much had she misheard as well as misseen?)

Dimly behind her she fancied she detected now the shock of war, the North risen, the very shores of the planet, and the City rocking at the blast, blood and soot and violence: tears, courage, songs—till only the weeping of the rain could wash clean the thousand domes of it.

But how far away it seemed.

Into Gold

I

Up behind Danuvius, the forests are black, and so stiff with black pork, black bears, and black-grey wolves, a man alone will feel himself jostled. Here and there you come on a native village, pointed houses of thatch with carved wooden posts, and smoke thick enough to cut with your knife. All day the birds call, and at night the owls come out. There are other things of earth and darkness, too. One ceases to be surprised at what may be found in the forests, or what may stray from them on occasion.

One morning, a Corn-King emerged, and pleased us no end. There had been some trouble, and some of the stores had gone up in flames. The ovens were standing empty and cold. It can take a year to get goods overland from the River, and our northern harvest was months off.

The old fort, that had been the palace then for twelve years, was built on high ground, scanning out across a mile of country strategically cleared of trees, to the forest cloud and a dream of distant mountains. Draco had called me up to the roof-walk, where we stood watching these mountains glow and fade, and come and go. It promised to be a fine day, and I had been planning a good long hunt, to exercise the men and give the breadless bellies solace. There is also a pine-nut meal they grind in the villages, accessible to barter. The loaves were not to everyone's taste, but we might have to come round to them. Since the armies pulled away, we had learned to improvise. I could scarcely remember the first days. The old men told you that everything, anyway, had been going down to chaos even then. Draco's father, holding on to a commander's power, assumed a prince's title which his orphaned warriors were glad enough to concede him. Discipline is its own ritual, and drug. As, lands and seas away, the centre of the world caved in, soldier-fashion they turned builders. They made the road to the fort, and soon began on the town, shoring it, for eternity, with strong walls. Next, they opened up the country, and got trade rights seen to that had gone by default decades ago. There was plenty of skirmishing as well to keep their swords bright. When the Commander died of a wound got fighting the Blue-Hair Tribe, a terror in those days, not seen for years since, Draco became the Prince in the Palace. He was eighteen then, and I five days older. We had known each other nearly all our lives, learned books and horses, drilled, hunted together. Though he was born elsewhere, he barely took that in, coming to this life when he could only just walk. For myself, I am lucky, perhaps, I never saw the Mother of Cities, and so never hanker after her, or lament her downfall.

That day on the roof-walk, certainly, nothing was further from my mind. Then Draco said, "*There* is something."

His clear-water eyes saw detail quicker and more finely than mine. When I looked, to me still it was only a blur and fuss on the forest's edge, and the odd sparking glint of things catching the early sun.

"Now, Skorous, do you suppose—?" said Draco.

"Someone has heard of our misfortune, and considerably changed his route," I replied.

We had got news a week before of a grain-caravan, but too far west to be of use. Conversely, it seemed the caravan had received news of our fire.

"Up goes the price of bread," said Draco.

By now I was sorting it out, the long rigmarole of mules and baggage-wagons, horses and men. He travelled in some style. Truly, a Corn-King, profiting always because he was worth his weight in gold amid the wilds of civilization. In Empire days, he would have weighed rather less.

We went down, and were in the square behind the east gate when the sentries brought him through. He left his people out on the parade before the gate, but one wagon had come up to the gateway, presumably his own, a huge conveyance, a regular travelling house, with six oxen in the shafts. Their straps were spangled with what I took for brass. On the side-leathers were pictures of grindstones and grain done in purple and yellow. He himself rode a tall horse, also spangled. He had a slim, snaky look, an Eastern look, with black brows and fawn skin. His fingers and ears were remarkable for their gold. And suddenly I began to wonder about the spangles. He bowed to Draco, the War-Leader and Prince. Then, to be quite safe, to me.

"Greetings, Miller," I said.

He smiled at this coy-honorific.

"Health and greetings, Captain. I think I am welcome?"

"My prince," I indicated Draco, "is always hospitable to wayfarers."

"Particularly to those with wares, in time of dearth."

"Which dearth is that?"

He put one golden finger to one golden earlobe.

"The trees whisper. This town of the Iron Shields has no bread."

Draco said mildly, "You should never listen to gossip."

I said, "If you've come out of your way, that would be a pity."

The Corn-King regarded me, not liking my arrogance—though I never saw the Mother of Cities, I have the blood—any more than I liked his slink and glitter.

As this went on, I gambling and he summing up the bluff, the tail of my eye caught another glimmering movement, from where his house wagon waited at the gate. I sensed some woman must be peering round the flap, the way the Eastern females do. The free girls of the town are prouder, even the wolf-girls of the brothel, and aristocrats use a veil only as a sunshade. Draco's own sisters, though decorous and well brought-up, can read and write, each handle a light chariot, and will stand and look a man straight in the face. But I took very little notice of the fleeting apparition, except to decide it too had gold about it. I kept my sight on my quarry, and presently he smiled again and drooped his eyelids, so I knew he would not risk calling me, and we had won.

"Perhaps," he said, "there might be a little consideration of the detour I, so foolishly, erroneously, made."

"We are always glad of fresh supplies. The fort is not insensible to its isolation. Rest assured."

"Too generous," he said. His eyes flared. But politely he added, "I have heard of your town. There is great culture here. You have a library, with scrolls from Hellas, and Semitic Byblos—I can read many tongues, and would like to ask permission of your lord to visit among his books."

I glanced at Draco, amused by the fellow's cheek, though all the East thinks itself a scholar. But Draco was staring at the wagon. Something worth a look, then, which I had missed.

"And we have excellent baths," I said to the Corn-King, letting him know in turn that the Empire's lost children think all the scholarly East to be also unwashed.

By midday, the whole caravan had come in through the walls and arranged itself in the marketplace, near the temple of Mars. The temple priests, some of whom had been serving with the Draconis Regiment when it arrived, old, old men, did not take to this influx. In spring and summer, traders were in and out the town like flies, and native men came to work in the forges and the tannery or with the horses, and built their muddy thatch huts behind the unfinished law-house—which huts winter rain always washed away again when their inhabitants were gone. To such events of passage the priests were accustomed. But this new show displeased them. The chief Salius came up to the fort, attended by his slaves leaning on his staff, and argued a while with Draco. Heathens, said the priest, with strange rituals, and dirtiness, would offend the patron god of the town. Draco seemed preoccupied.

I had put off the hunting-party, and now stayed to talk the Salius into a better humour. It would be a brief nuisance, and surely, they had been directed to us by the god himself, who did not want his warlike sons to go hungry? I assured the priest that, if the foreigners wanted to worship their own gods, they would have to be circumspect. Tolerance of every religious rag, as we knew, was unwise. They did not, I thought, worship Iusa. There would be no abominations. I then vowed a boar to Mars, if I could get one, and the dodderer tottered, pale and grim, away.

Meanwhile the grain was being seen to. The heathen god-offenders had sacks and jars of it, and ready flour besides. It seemed a heavy chancy load with which to journey, goods that might spoil if at all delayed, or if the weather went against them. And all that jangling of gold beside. They fairly bled gold. I had been right in my second thought on the bridle-decorations, there were even nuggets and bells hung on the wagons, and gold flowers; and the oxen had gilded horns. For the men, they were ringed and buckled and roped and tied with it. It was a marvel.

When I stepped over to the camp near sunset, I was on the lookout for anything amiss. But they had picketed their animals couthly enough, and the dazzle-fringed, clink-belled wagons stood quietly shadowing and gleaming in the westered light. Columns of spicy smoke rose, but only from their cooking. Boys dealt with that, and boys had drawn water from the well; neither I nor my men had seen any women.

Presently I was conducted to the Corn-King's wagon. He received me before it, where woven rugs, and cushions stitched with gold discs, were strewn on the ground. A tent of dark purple had been erected close by, its gilt-tasseled sides all down, shut as a box. A disc or two more winked yellow from the folds. Beyond, the plastered colonnades, the stone Mars Temple, stood equally closed and eyeless, refusing to see.

The Miller and I exchanged courtesies. He asked me to sit, so I sat. I was curious.

"It is pleasant," he said, "to be within safe walls."

"Yes, you must be often in some danger," I answered.

He smiled secretively now. "You mean our wealth? It is better to display than to hide. The thief kills, in his hurry, the man who conceals his gold. I have never been robbed. They think, 'Ah, this one shows all his riches. He must have some powerful demon to protect him'."

"And is that so?"

"Of course," he said.

I glanced at the temple, and then back at him meaningly. He said, "Your men drove a hard bargain for the grain and the flour. And I have been docile. I respect your gods, Captain. I respect all gods. That, too, is a protection."

Some drink came. I tasted it cautiously, for Easterners often eschew wine and concoct other disgusting muck. In the forests they ferment thorn berries, or the milk of their beasts, neither of which methods makes such a poor beverage, when you grow used to it. But of the Semites one hears all kinds of things. Still, the drink had a sweet hot sizzle that made me want more, so I swallowed some, then waited to see what else it would do to me.

"And your lord will allow me to enter his library?" said the Corn-King, after a host's proper pause.

"That may be possible," I said. I tried the drink again. "How do you manage without women?" I added, "You'll have seen the House of the Mother, with the she-wolf painted over the door? The girls there are fastidious and clever. If your men will spare the price, naturally."

The Corn-King looked at me, with his liquid man-snake's eyes, aware of all I said which had not been spoken.

"It is true," he said at last, "that we have no women with us."

"Excepting your own wagon."

"My daughter," he said.

I had known Draco, as I have said, almost all my life. He was for me what no other had ever been; I had followed his star gladly and without question, into scrapes, and battles, through very fire and steel. Very rarely would he impose on me some task I hated, loathed. When he did so it was done without design or malice, as a man sneezes. The bad times were generally to do with women. I had fought back to back with him, but I did not care to be his pander. Even so, I would not refuse. He had stood in the window that noon, looking at the black forest, and said in a dry low voice, carelessly apologetic, irrefutable, "He has a girl in that wagon. Get her for me." "Well, she may be his—" I started off. He cut me short. "Whatever she is. He sells things. He is accustomed to selling." "And if he won't?" I said. Then he looked at me, with his high-coloured translucent eyes. "Make him," he said, and next laughed, as if it were nothing at all, this choice mission. I had come out thinking glumly, she has witched him, put the Eye on him. But I had known him lust like this before. Nothing would do then but he must have. Women had never been that way for me. They were available, when one needed them. I like to this hour to see them here and there, *our* women, straight-limbed, graceful, clean. In the perilous seasons I would have died defending his sisters, as I would have died to defend him. That was that. It was a fact, the burning of our grain had come about through an old grievance, an idiot who kept score of something Draco had done half a year ago, about a native girl got on a raid.

I put down the golden cup, because the drink was going to my head. They had two ways, Easterners, with daughters. One was best left unspoken. The other kept them locked and bolted virgin. Mercurius bless the dice.

Then, before I could say anything, the Miller put my mind at rest.

"My daughter," he said, "is very accomplished. She is also very beautiful, but I speak now of the beauty of learning and art."

"Indeed. Indeed."

The sun was slipping over behind the walls. The far mountains were steeped in dyes. This glamour shone behind the Corn-King's head, gold in the sky for him, too. And he said, "Amongst other matters, she has studied the lore of Khemia—Old Aegyptus, you will understand."

"Ah, yes?"

"Now I will confide in you," he said. His tongue flickered on his lips. Was it forked? The damnable drink had fuddled me after all; that, and a shameful relief. "The practice of the Al-Khemia contains every science and sorcery. She can read the stars, she can heal the hurts of man. But best of all, my dear Captain, my daughter has learned the third great secret of the Tri-Magae."

"Oh, yes, indeed?"

"She can," he said, "change all manner of materials into gold."

II

"**S**ometimes. Skorous," Draco said, "you are a fool."

"Sometimes I am not alone in that."

Draco shrugged. He had never feared honest speaking. He never asked more of a title than his own name. But those two items were, in themselves, significant. He was what he was, a law above the law. The heart-legend of the City was down, and he a prince in a forest that ran all ways for ever.

"What do you think then she will do to me? Turn me into metal, too?"

We spoke in Greek, which tended to be the palace mode for private chat. It was fading out of use in the town.

"I don't believe in that kind of sorcery," I said.

"Well, he has offered to have her show us. Come along."

"It will be a trick."

"All the nicer. Perhaps he will find someone for you, too."

"I shall attend you," I said, "because I trust none of them. And fifteen of my men around the wagon."

"I must remember not to groan," he said, "or they'll be splitting the leather and tumbling in on us with swords."

"Draco," I said, "I'm asking myself why he boasted that she had the skill."

"All that gold: they didn't steal it or cheat for it. A witch *made* it for them."

"I have heard of the Al-Khemian arts."

"Oh yes," he said. "The devotees make gold, they predict the future, they raise the dead. She might be useful. Perhaps I should marry her. Wait till you see her," he said. "I suppose it was all prearranged. He will want paying again."

When we reached the camp, it was midnight. Our torches and theirs opened the dark, and the flame outside the Mars Temple burned faint. There were stars in the sky, no moon.

We had gone to them at their request, since the magery was intrinsic, required utensils, and was not to be moved to the fort without much effort. We arrived like a bridal procession. The show was not after all to be in the wagon, but the tent. The other Easterners had buried themselves from view. I gave the men their orders and stood them conspicuously about. Then a slave lifted the tent's purple drapery a chink and squinted up at us. Draco beckoned me after him, no one demurred. We both went into the pavilion.

To do that was to enter the East head-on. Expensive gums were burning with a dark hot perfume that put me in mind of the wine I had had earlier. The incense-burners were gold, tripods on leopards' feet, with swags of golden ivy. The floor was carpeted soft, like the pelt of some beast, and beast-skins were hung about, things I had not seen before, some of them, maned and spotted, striped and scaled, and some with heads and jewelry eyes and the teeth and claws gilded. Despite all the clutter of things, of polished mirrors and casks and chests, cushions and dead animals, and scent, there was a feeling of great space within that tent. The ceiling of it stretched taut and high, and three golden wheels depended, with oil-lights in little golden boats. The wheels turned idly now this way, now that, in a wind that came from nowhere and went to nowhere, a demon wind out of a desert. Across the space, wide as night, was an opaque dividing curtain, and on the curtain, a long parchment. It was figured with another mass of images, as if nothing in the place should be spare. A tree went up, with two birds at the roots, a white bird with a raven-black head, a soot-black bird with the head of an ape. A snake twined the tree too, round and round, and ended looking out of the lower branches where yellow fruit hung. The snake had the face of a maiden, and flowing hair. Above sat three figures, judges of the dead from Aegyptus, I would have thought, if I had thought about them, with a balance, and wands. The sun and the moon stood over the tree.

I put my hand to the hilt of my sword, and waited. Draco had seated himself on the cushions. A golden jug was to hand, and a cup. He reached forward, poured the liquor and made to take it, before—reluctantly—I snatched the vessel. "Let me first. Are you mad?"

He reclined, not interested as I tasted for him, then let him have the cup again.

Then the curtain parted down the middle and the parchment with it, directly through the serpent-tree. I had expected the Miller, but instead what entered was a black dog with a collar of gold. It had a wolf's shape, but more slender, and with a pointed muzzle and high carven pointed ears. Its eyes were also black. It stood calmly, like a steward, regarding us, then stepped aside and lay down, its head still raised to watch. And next the woman Draco wanted came in.

To me, she looked nothing in particular. She was pleasantly made, slim, but rounded, her bare arms and feet the colour of amber. Over her head, to her breast, covering her hair and face like a dusky smoke, was a veil, but it was transparent enough to see through it, to black locks and black aloe eyes, and a full tawny mouth. There was only a touch of gold on her, a rolled torque of soft metal at her throat, and one ring on her right hand. I was puzzled as to what had made her glimmer at the edge of my sight before, but perhaps she had dressed differently then, to make herself plain.

She bowed Eastern-wise to Draco, then to me. Then, in the purest Greek I ever heard, she addressed us.

"Lords, while I am at work, I must ask that you will please be still, or else you will disturb the currents of the act and so impair it. Be seated," she said to me as if I had only stood till then from courtesy. Her eyes were very black, black as the eyes of the jackal-dog, blacker than the night. Then she blinked, and her eyes flashed. The lids were painted with gold. And I found I had sat down.

What followed I instantly took for an hallucination, induced by the incense, and by other means less perceptible. That is not to say I did not think she was a witch. There was something of power to her I never met before. It pounded from her, like heat, or an aroma. It did not make her beautiful for me, but it held me quiet, though I swear never once did I lose my grip either on my senses or my sword.

First, and quite swiftly, I had the impression the whole tent blew upward, and we were in the open in fact, under a sky of a million stars that blazed and crackled like diamonds. Even so, the golden wheels stayed put, up in the sky now, and they spun, faster and faster, until each was a solid golden O of fire, three spinning suns in the heaven of midnight.

(I remember I thought flatly, *We have been spelled. So what now?* But in its own way, my stoicism was also suspect. My thoughts in any case flagged after that.)

There was a smell of lions, or of a land that had them. Do not ask me how I know, I never smelled or saw them, or such a spot. And there before us all stood a slanting wall of brick, at once much larger than I saw it, and smaller than it was. It seemed even so to lean into the sky. The woman raised her arms. She was apparent now as if rinsed all over by gilt, and one of the great stars seemed to sear on her forehead.

Forms began to come and go, on the lion-wind. If I knew then what they were, I forgot it later. Perhaps they were animals, like the skins in the tent, though some had wings.

She spoke to them. She did not use Greek anymore. It was the language of Khem, presumably, or we were intended to believe so. A liquid tongue, an Eastern tongue, no doubt.

Then there were other visions. The ribbed stems of flowers, broader than ten men around, wide petals pressed to the ether. A rainbow of mist that arched over, and touched the earth with its feet and its brow. And other mirages, many of which resembled effigies I had seen of the gods, but they walked.

The night began to close upon us slowly, narrowing and coming down. The stars still raged overhead and the gold wheels whirled, but some sense of enclosure had returned. As for the sloped angle of brick, it had huddled down into a sort of oven, and into this the woman was placing, with extreme care—of all things—long sceptres of corn, all brown and dry and withered, blighted to straw by some harvest like a curse.

I heard her whisper, then. I could not hear what.

Behind her, dim as shadows, I saw other women, who sat weaving, or who toiled at the grindstone, and one who shook a rattle upon which rings of gold sang out. Then the vision of these women was eclipsed. Something stood there, between the night and the Eastern witch. Tall as the roof, or tall as the sky, bird-headed maybe, with two of the stars for eyes. When I looked at this, this ultimate apparition, my blood froze and I could have howled out loud. It was not common fear, but terror such as the worst reality has never brought me, though sometimes subtle nightmares do.

Then there was a lightning, down the night. When it passed, we were enclosed in the tent, the huge night of the tent, and the brick oven burned before us, with a thin harsh fume coming from the aperture in its top.

"Sweet is truth," said the witch, in a wild and passionate voice, all music, like the notes of the gold rings on the rattle. "O Lord of the Word. The Word is, and the Word makes all things to be."

Then the oven cracked into two pieces, it simply fell away from itself, and there on a bank of red charcoal, which died to clinker even as I gazed at it, lay a sheaf of golden corn. *Golden* corn, smiths' work. It was pure and sound and rang like a bell when presently I went to it and struck it and flung it away.

The tent had positively resettled all around us. It was there. I felt queasy and stupid, but I was in my body and had my bearings again, the sword-hilt firm to my palm, though it was oddly hot to the touch, and my forehead burned, sweatless, as if I too had been seethed in a fire.

I had picked up the goldwork without asking her anything. She did not prevent me, nor when I slung it off.

When I looked up from that, she was kneeling by the curtain, where the black dog had been and was no more. Her eyes were downcast under her veil. I noted the torque was gone from her neck and the ring from her finger. Had she somehow managed her trick that way, melting gold on to the stalks of mummified corn— No, lunacy. Why nag at it? It was *all* a deception.

But Draco lay looking at her now, burned up by another fever. It was her personal gold he wanted.

"Out, Skorous," he said to me. "Out, now." Slurred and sure.

So I said to her, through my blunted lips and woolen tongue, "Listen carefully, girl. The witchery ends now. You know what he wants, and how to see to that, I suppose. Scratch him with your littlest nail, and you die."

Then, without getting to her feet, she looked up at me, only the second time. She spoke in Greek, as at the start. In the morning, when I was better able to think, I reckoned I had imagined what she said. It had seemed to be: "He is safe, for I desire him. It is my choice. If it were not my choice and my desire, where might you hide yourselves, and live?"

We kept watch round the tent, in the Easterners' camp, in the marketplace, until the ashes of the dawn. There was not a sound from anywhere, save the regular quiet passaging of sentries on the walls, and the cool black forest wind that turned grey near sunrise.

At sunup, the usual activity of any town began. The camp stirred and let its boys out quickly to the well to avoid the town's women. Some of the caravaneers even chose to stroll across to the public lavatories, though they had avoided the bathhouse.

An embarrassment came over me, that we should be standing there, in the foreigners' hive, to guard our prince through his night of lust. I looked sharply, to see how the men were taking it, but they had held together well. Presently Draco emerged. He appeared flushed and tumbled, very nearly shy, like some girl just out of a love-bed.

We went back to the fort in fair order, where he took me aside, thanked me, and sent me away again.

Bathed and shaved, and my fast broken, I began to feel more sanguine. It was over and done with. I would go down to the temple of Father Jupiter and give him something—why, I was not exactly sure. Then get my boar for Mars. The fresh-baked bread I had just eaten was tasty, and maybe worth all the worry.

Later, I heard the Miller had taken himself to our library and been let in. I gave orders he was to be searched on leaving. Draco's grandfather had started the collection of manuscripts, there were even scrolls said to have been rescued from Alexandrea. One could not be too wary.

In the evening, Draco called me up to his writing-room.

"Tomorrow," he said, "the Easterners will be leaving us."

"That's good news," I said.

"I thought it would please you. Zafra, however, is to remain. I'm taking her into my household."

"Zafra," I said.

"Well, they call her that. For the yellow-gold. Perhaps not her name. That might have been *Nefra*— Beautiful..."

"Well," I said, "if you want."

"Well," he said, "I never knew you before to be jealous of one of my women."

I said nothing, though the blood knocked about in my head. I had noted before, he had a woman's tongue himself, when he was put out. He was a spoiled brat as a child, I have to admit, but a mother's early death, and the life of a forest fortress, pared most of it from him.

"The Corn-King is not her father," he said now. "She told me. But he's stood by her as that some years. I shall send him something, in recompense."

He waited for my comment that I was amazed nothing had been asked for. He waited to see how I would jump. I wondered if he had paced about here, planning how he would put it to me. Not that he was required to. Now he said:

"We gain, Skorous, a healer and diviner. Not just my pleasure at night."

"Your pleasure at night is your own affair. There are plenty of girls about, I would have thought, to keep you content. As for anything else she can or cannot do, all three temples, particularly the Women's

Temple, will be up in arms. The Salius yesterday was only a sample. Do you think they are going to let some yellow-skinned harlot divine for you? Do you think that men who get hurt in a fight will want her near them?"

"You would not, plainly."

"No, I would not. As for the witchcraft, we were drugged and made monkeys of. An evening's fun is one thing."

"Yes, Skorous," he said. "Thanks for your opinion. Don't sulk too long. I shall miss your company."

An hour later, he sent, so I was informed, two of the scrolls from the library to the Corn-King in his wagon. They were two of the best, Greek, one transcribed by the hand, it was said, of a very great king. They went in a silver box, with jewel inlay. Gold would have been tactless, under the circumstances.

N ext day she was in the palace. She had rooms on the women's side, it had been the apartment of Draco's elder sister, before her marriage. He treated this one as nothing less than a relative from the first. When he was at leisure, on those occasions when the wives and women of his officers dined with them, there was she with him. When he hunted, she went with him, too, not to have any sport, but as a companion, in a litter between two horses that made each hunt into a farce from its onset. She was in his bed each night, for he did not go to her, her place was solely hers; the couch his father had shared only with his mother. And when he wanted advice, it was she gave it to him. He called on his soldiers and his priests afterwards. Though he always did so call, nobody lost face. He was wise and canny, she must have told him how to be at long last. And the charm he had always had. He even consulted me, and made much of me before everyone, because, very sensibly he realized, unless he meant to replace me, it would be foolish to let the men see I no longer counted a feather's weight with him. Besides, I might get notions of rebellion. I had my own following, my own men who would die for me if they thought me wronged. Probably that angered me more than the rest, that he might have the idea I would forgo my duty and loyalty, forget my honour, and try to pull him down. I could no more do that than put out one of my own eyes.

Since we lost our homeland, since we lost, more importantly, the spine of the Empire, there had been a disparity, a separation of men. Now I saw it, in those bitter golden months after she came among us.

206

He had been born in the Mother of Cities, but She had slipped from his skin like water. He was a new being, a creature of the world, that might be anything, of any country. But never having seen the roots of me, yet they had me fast. I was of the old order. I would stand until the fire had me, rather than tarnish my name, and my heart.

Gradually, the fort and town began to fill with gold. It was very nearly a silly thing. But we grew lovely and we shone. The temples did not hate her, as I had predicted. No, for she brought them glittering vessels, and laved the gods' feet with rare offerings, and the sweet spice also of her gift burned before Mars, and the Father, and the Mother, so every holy place smelled like Aegyptus, or Judea, or the brothels of Babylon for all I knew.

She came to walk in the streets with just one of the slaves at her heels, bold, the way our ladies did, and though she never left off her veil, she dressed in the stola and the palla, all clasped and cinched with the tiniest amounts of gold, while gold flooded everywhere else, and everyone looked forward to the summer heartily, for the trading. The harvest would be wondrous too. Already there were signs of astounding fruition. And in the forest, not a hint of any restless tribe, or any ill wish.

They called her by the name *Zafra*. They did not once call her "Easterner." One day, I saw three pregnant women at the gate, waiting for Zafra to come out and touch them. She was lucky. Even the soldiers had taken no offence. The old Salius had asked her for a balm for his rheumatism. It seemed the balm had worked.

Only I, then, hated her. I tried to let it go. I tried to remember she was only a woman, and, if a sorceress, did us good. I tried to see her as voluptuous and enticing, or as homely and harmless. But all I saw was some shuttered-up, close, fermenting thing, like mummy-dusts reviving in a tomb, or the lion-scent, and the tall shadow that had stood between her and the night, bird-headed, the Lord of the Word that made all things, or unmade them. What was she, under her disguise? Draco could not see it. Like the black dog she had kept, which walked by her on a leash, well-mannered and gentle, and which would probably tear out the throat of anyone who came at her with mischief on his mind— Under her honeyed wrappings, was it a doll of straw or gold, or a viper?

Eventually, Draco married her. That was no surprise. He did it in the proper style, with sacrifices to the Father, and all the forms, and a feast that filled the town. I saw her in colours then, that once, the saffron dress, the Flammeus, the fire-veil of the bride, and her face bare, and painted up like a lady's, pale, with rosy cheeks and lips. But it was still herself, still the Eastern Witch.

And dully that day, as in the tent that night, I thought, So what now?

III

In the late summer, I picked up some talk, among the servants in the palace. I was by the well-court, in the peach arbour, where I had paused to look at the peaches. They did not always come, but this year we had had one crop already, and now the second was blooming. As I stood there in the shade, sampling the fruit, a pair of the kitchen men met below by the well, and stayed to gossip in their argot. At first I paid no heed, then it came to me what they were saying, and I listened with all my ears.

When one went off, leaving the other, old Ursus, to fill his dipper, I came down the stair and greeted him. He started, and looked at me furtively.

"Yes, I heard you," I said. "But tell me, now."

I had always put a mask on, concerning the witch, with everyone but Draco, and afterwards with him too. I let it be seen I thought her nothing much, but if she was his choice, I would serve her. I was careful never to speak slightingly of her to any, since it would reflect on his honour, even to men I trusted, even in wine. Since he had married her, she had got my duty, too, unless it came to vie with my duty to him.

But Ursus had the servant's way, the slave's way, of holding back bad news for fear it should turn on him. I had to repeat a phrase or two of his own before he would come clean.

It seemed that some of the women had become aware that Zafra, a sorceress of great power, could summon to her, having its name, a mighty demon. Now she did not sleep every night with Draco, but in her own apartments, sometimes things had been glimpsed, or heard—

"Well, Ursus," I said, "you did right to tell me. But it's a lot of silly women's talk. Come, you're not going to give it credit?"

"The flames burn flat on the lamps, and change colour," he mumbled. "And the curtain rattled, but no one there. And Eunike says she felt some form brush by her in the corridor—"

"That is enough," I said. "Women will always fancy something is happening, to give themselves importance. You will know that. Then there's hysteria and they can believe and say anything. We are aware she has arts, and the science of Aegyptus. But demons are another matter."

I further admonished him and sent him off. I stood by the well, pondering. Rattled curtains, secretive forms—it crossed my thoughts she might have taken a lover, but it did not seem in keeping with her shrewdness. I do not really believe in such beasts as demons, except what the brain can bring forth. Then again, her brain might be capable of many things.

It turned out I attended Draco that evening, something to do with one of the villages that traded with us, something he still trusted me to understand. I asked myself if I should tell him about the gossip. Frankly, when I had found out—the way you always can—that he lay with her less frequently, I had had a sort of hope, but there was a qualm, too, and when the trade matter was dealt with, he stayed me over the wine, and he said: "You may be wondering about it, Skorous. If so, yes. I'm to be given a child."

I knew better now than to scowl. I drank a toast and suggested he might be happy to have got a boy on her.

"She says it will be a son."

"Then of course, it will be a son."

And, I thought, it may have her dark-yellow looks. It may be a magus too. And it will be your heir, Draco. My future Prince, and the master of the town. I wanted to hurl the wine cup through the wall, but I held my hand and my tongue, and after he had gone on a while trying to coax me to thrill at the joy of life, I excused myself and went away.

It was bound to come. It was another crack in the stones. It was the way of destiny, and of change. I wanted not to feel I must fight against it, or desire to send her poison, to kill her or abort her, or tear it, her womb's fruit, when born, in pieces.

For a long while I sat on my sleeping-couch and allowed my fury to sink down, to grow heavy and leaden, resigned, defeated.

When I was sure of that defeat, I lay flat and slept.

In sleep, I followed a demon along the corridor in the women's quarters, and saw it melt through her door. It was tall, long-legged, with the head of a bird, or perhaps of a dog. A wind blew, lion-tanged. I was under a tree hung thick with peaches, and a snake looked down from it with a girl's face framed by a flaming bridal-veil. Then there was a spinning fiery wheel, and golden corn flew off clashing from it. And next

I saw a glowing oven, and on the red charcoal lay a child of gold, burning and gleaming and asleep.

When I woke with a jump it was the middle of the night, and someone had arrived, and the slave was telling me so.

At first I took it for a joke. Then, became serious. Zafra, Draco's wife, an hour past midnight, had sent for me to attend her in her rooms. Naturally I suspected everything. She knew me for her adversary: she would lead me in, then say I had set on her to rape or somehow else abuse her. On the other hand, I must obey and go to her, not only for duty, now, but from sheer aggravation and raw curiosity. Though I had always told myself I misheard her words as I left her with him the first time, I had never forgotten them. Since then, beyond an infrequent politeness, we had not spoken.

I dressed as formally as I could, got two of my men, and went across to the women's side. The sentries along the route were my fellows too, but I made sure they learned I had been specifically summoned. Rather to my astonishment, they knew it already.

My men went with me right to her chamber door, with orders to keep alert there. Perhaps they would grin, asking each other if I was nervous. I was.

When I got into the room, I thought it was empty. Her women had been sent away. One brazier burned, near the entry, but I was used by now to the perfume of those aromatics. It was a night of full moon, and the blank light lay in a whole pane across the mosaic, colouring it faintly, but in the wrong, nocturnal, colours. The bed, narrow, low and chaste, stood on one wall, and her tiring table near it. Through the window under the moon, rested the tops of the forest, so black it made the indigo sky pale.

Then a red-golden light blushed out and I saw her, lighting the lamps on their stand from a taper. I could almost swear she had not been there a second before, but she could stay motionless a long while, and with her dark robe and hair, and all her other darkness, she was a natural thing for shadows.

"Captain," she said. (She never used my name, she must know I did not want it; a sorceress, she was well aware of the power of naming.) "There is no plot against you."

"That's good to know," I said, keeping my distance, glad of my sword, and of every visible insignia of who and what I was.

"You have been very honourable in the matter of me," she said. "You have done nothing against me, either openly or in secret, though you hated me from the beginning. I know what this has cost you. Do not spurn my gratitude solely because it is mine."

"Domina," I said (neither would I use her name, though the rest did in the manner of the town), "you're his. He has made you his wife. And—" I stopped.

"And the vessel of his child. Ah, do you think he did that alone?" She saw me stare with thoughts of demons, and she said, "He and I, Captain. He, and I."

"Then I serve you," I said. I added, and though I did not want to give her the satisfaction I could not keep back a tone of irony, "You have nothing to be anxious where I am concerned."

We were speaking Greek, hers clear as water in that voice of hers which I had to own was very beautiful.

"I remain," she said, "anxious."

"Then I can't help you, Dominia." There was a silence. She stood looking at me, through the veil I had only once seen dispensed with in exchange for a veil of paint. I wondered where the dog had gone, that had her match in eyes. I said, "But I would warn you. If you practice your business in here, there's begun to be some funny talk."

"They see a demon, do they?" she said.

All at once the hair rose up on my neck and scalp.

As if she read my mind, she said:

"I have not pronounced any name. Do not be afraid."

"The slaves are becoming afraid."

"No," she said. "They have always talked of me but they have never been afraid of me. None of them. Draco does not fear me, do you think? And the priests do not. Or the women and girls. Or the children, or the old men. Or the slaves. Or your soldiers. None of them fears me or what I am or what I do, the gold with which I fill the temples, or the golden harvests, or the healing I perform. None of them fears it. But you, Captain, you do fear, and you read your fear again and again in every glance, in every word they utter. But it is yours, not theirs."

I looked away from her, up to the ceiling from which the patterns had faded years before.

"Perhaps," I said. "I am not blind."

Then she sighed. As I listened to it, I thought of her, just for an instant, as a forlorn girl alone with strangers in a foreign land.

"I'm sorry," I said.

"It is true," she said, "you see more than most. But not your own error."

"Then that is how it is." My temper had risen and I must rein it.

"You will not," she said quietly, "be a friend to me."

"I cannot, and will not, be a friend to you. Neither am I your enemy, while you keep faith with him."

"But one scratch of my littlest nail," she said. Her musical voice was nearly playful.

"Only one," I said.

"Then I regret waking you, Captain," she said. "Health and slumber for your night."

As I was going back along the corridor, I confronted the black jackal-dog. It padded slowly towards me and I shivered, but one of the men stooped to rub its ears. It suffered him, and passed on, shadow to shadow, night to ebony night.

Summer went to winter, and soon enough the snows came. The trading and the harvests had shored us high against the cruelest weather, we could sit in our towers and be fat, and watch the wolves howl through the white forests. They came to the very gates that year. There were some odd stories, that wolfpacks had been fed of our bounty, things left for them, to tide them over. Our own she-wolves were supposed to have started it, the whorehouse girls. But when I mentioned the tale to one of them, she flared out laughing.

I recall that snow with an exaggerated brilliance, the way you sometimes do with some time that precedes an illness, or a deciding battle. Albino mornings with the edge of a broken vase, the smoke rising from hearths and temples, or steaming with the blood along the snow from the sacrifices of Year's Turn. The Wolf Feast with the races, and later the ivies and vines cut for the Mad Feast, and the old dark wine got out, the torches and a girl I had in a shed full of hay and pigs; and the spate of weddings that come after, very sensibly. The last snow twilights were thick as soup with blueness. Then spring, and the forest surging up from its slough, the first proper hunting, with the smell of sap and crushed freshness spraying out as if one waded in a river.

Draco's child was born one spring sunset, coming forth in the bloody golden light, crying its first cry to the evening star. It was a boy, as she had said.

I had kept even my thoughts off from her after that interview in her chamber. My feelings had been confused and displeasing. It seemed to me she had in some way tried to outwit me, throw me down. Then I had felt truly angry, and later, oddly shamed. I avoided, where I could, all places where I might have to see her. Then she was seen less, being big with the child.

After the successful birth all the usual things were done. In my turn, I beheld the boy. He was straight and flawlessly formed, with black hair, but a fair skin; he had Draco's eyes from the very start. So little of the mother. Had she contrived it, by some other witch's art, knowing that when at length we had to cleave to him, it would be Draco's line we wished to see? No scratch of a nail, there, none.

Nor had there been any more chat of demons. Or they made sure I never intercepted it.

I said to myself, she is a matron now, she will wear to our ways. She has borne him a strong boy.

But it was no use at all.

She was herself, and the baby was half of her.

They have a name now for her demon, her genius in the shadowlands of witchcraft. A scrambled name that does no harm. They call it, in the town's argot: *Rhamthibiscan.*

We claim so many of the Greek traditions; they know of Rhadamanthys from the Greek. A judge of the dead, he is connectable to Thot of Aegyptus, the Thrice-Mighty Thrice-Mage of the Al-Khemian Art. And because Thot the Ibis-Headed and Anpu the Jackal became mingled in it, along with Hermercurius, Prince of Thieves and Whores— who is, too, the guide of lost souls—an ibis and a dog were added to the brief itinerary. Rhadamanthys-Ibis-Canis. The full name even, has no power. It is a muddle, and a lie, and the invocation says: *Sweet is Truth.* Was it, though, ever sensible to claim to know what truth might be?

IV

"They know of her, and have sent begging for her. She's a healer and they're sick. It's not unreasonable. She isn't afraid. I have

213

seen her close an open wound by passing her hands above it. Yes, Skorous, perhaps she only made me see it, and the priests to see it, and the wounded man. But he recovered, as you remember. So I trust her to be able to cure these people and make them love us even better. She herself is immune to illness. Yes, Skorous, she only thinks she is. However, thinking so has apparently worked wonders. She was never once out of sorts with the child. The midwives were amazed—or not amazed, maybe—that she seemed to have no pain during the birth. Though they told me she wept when the child was put into her arms. Well, so did I." Draco frowned. He said, "So we'll let her do it, don't you agree, let her go to them and heal them. We may yet be able to open this country, make something of it, one day. Anything that is useful in winning them."

"She will be taking the child with her?"

"Of course. He's not weaned yet, and she won't let another woman nurse him."

"Through the forests. It's three days ride away, this village. And then we hardly know the details of the sickness. If your son—"

"He will be with his mother. She has never done a foolish thing."

"You let this bitch govern you. Very well. But don't risk the life of your heir, since your heir is what you have made him, this half-breed brat—"

I choked off the surge in horror. I had betrayed myself. It seemed to me instantly that I had been made to do it. *She* had made me. All the stored rage and impotent distrust, all the bitter frustrated *guile*—gone for nothing in a couple of sentences.

But Draco only shrugged, and smiled. He had learned to contain himself these past months. Her invaluable aid, no doubt, her rotten honey.

He said, "She has requested that, though I send a troop with her to guard her in our friendly woods, you, Skorous, do not go with them."

"I see."

"The reason which she gave was that, although there is no danger in the region at present, your love and spotless commitment to my well-being preclude you should be taken from my side." He put the smile away and said, "But possibly, too, she wishes to avoid your close company for so long, knowing as she must do you can barely keep your fingers from her throat. Did you know, Skorous," he said, and now it was the old Draco, I seemed somehow to have hauled him back, "that the first several months, I had her food always tasted. I thought you would try to see to her. I was so very astounded you never did. Or did you have some other, more clever plan, that failed?"

I swallowed the bile that had come into my mouth. I said, "You forget, Sir, if I quit you I have no other battalion to go to. The Mother of Cities is dead. If I leave your warriors, I am nothing. I am one of the scores who blow about the world like dying leaves, soldiers' sons of the lost Empire. If there were an option, I would go at once. There is none. You've spat in my face, and I can only wipe off the spit."

His eyes fell from me, and suddenly he cursed.

"I was wrong, Skorous. You would never have—"

"No, Sir. Never. Never in ten million years. But I regret you think I might. And I regret she thinks so. Once she was your wife, she could expect no less from me than I give one of your sisters."

"That bitch," he said, repeating for me my error, woman-like, "her half-breed brat—damn you, Skorous. He's my son."

"I could cut out my tongue that I said it. It's more than a year of holding it back before all others, I believe. Like vomit, Sir. I could not keep it down any longer."

"Stop saying *Sir* to me. You call her *Domina.* That's sufficient."

His eyes were wet. I wanted to slap him, the way you do a vicious stupid girl who claws at your face. But he was my prince, and the traitor was myself.

Presently, thankfully, he let me get out.

What I had said was true, if there had been any other life to go to that was thinkable—but there was not, any more. So, she would travel into the forest to heal, and I, faithful and unshakable, I would stay to guard him. And then she would come back. Year in and out, mist and rain, snow and sun. And bear him other brats to whom, in due course, I would swear my honour over. I had better practise harder, not to call her anything but *Lady.*

Somewhere in the night I came to myself and I knew. I saw it accurately, what went on, what was to be, and what I, so cunningly excluded, must do. Madness, they say, can show itself like that. Neither hot nor cold, with a steady hand, and every faculty honed bright.

The village with the sickness had sent its deputation to Draco yesterday. They had grand and blasphemous names for *her*, out there. She had said she must go, and at first light today would set out. Since the native villagers revered her, she might have made an arrangement with them, some itinerant acting as messenger. Or even, if the circumstance were actual, she would have been biding for such a chance. Or she herself had sent the malady to ensure it.

Her gods were the gods of her mystery. But the Semitic races have a custom ancient as their oldest altars, of giving a child to the god.

Perhaps Draco even knew—no, unthinkable. How then could she explain it? An accident, a straying, bears, wolves, the sickness after all... And she could give him other sons. She was like the magic oven of the Khemian Art. Put in, take out. So easy.

I got up when it was still pitch black and announced to my body-slave and the man at the door I was off hunting, alone. There was already a rumour of an abrasion between the Prince and his Captain. Draco himself would not think unduly of it, Skorous raging through the wood, slicing pigs. I could be gone the day before he considered.

I knew the tracks pretty well, having hunted them since I was ten. I had taken boar spears for the look, but no dogs. The horse I needed, but she was forest-trained and did as I instructed.

I lay off the thoroughfare, like an old fox, and let the witch's outing come down, and pass me. Five men were all the guard she had allowed, a cart with travelling stuff, and her medicines in a chest. There was one of her women, the thickest in with her, I thought, Eunike, riding on a mule. And Zafra herself, in the litter between the horses.

When they were properly off, I followed. There was no problem in the world. We moved silently and they made a noise. Their horses and mine were known to each other and, where they snuffed a familiar scent, thought nothing of it. As the journey progressed, and I met here and there with some native in the trees, he hailed me cheerily, supposing me an outrider, a rear-guard. At night I bivouacked above them; at sunrise their first rustlings and throat-clearings roused me. When they were gone we watered at their streams, and once I had a burned sausage forgotten in the ashes of their cookfire.

The third day, they came to the village. From high on the mantled slope, I saw the greetings and the going in, through the haze of foul smoke. The village did have a look of ailing, something in its shades and colours, and the way the people moved about. I wrapped a cloth over my nose and mouth before I sat down to wait.

216

Later, in the dusk, they began to have a brisker look. The witch was making magic, evidently, and all would be well. The smoke condensed and turned yellow from their fires as the night closed in. When full night had come, the village glowed stilly, enigmatically, cupped in the forest's darkness. My mental wanderings moved towards the insignificance, the smallness, of any lamp among the great shadows of the earth. A candle against the night, a fire in winter, a life flickering in eternity, now here, now gone forever.

But I slept before I had argued it out.

𝕴nside another day, the village was entirely renewed. Even the rusty straw thatch glinted like gold. She had worked her miracles. Now would come her own time.

A couple of the men had kept up sentry-go from the first evening out, and last night, patrolling the outskirts of the huts, they had even idled a minute under the tree where I was roosting. I had hidden my mare half a mile off, in a deserted bothy I had found, but tonight I kept her near, for speed. And this night, too, when one of the men came up the slope, making his rounds, I softly called his name.

He went to stone. I told him smartly who I was, but when I came from cover, his sword was drawn and eyes on stalks.

"I'm no forest demon," I said. Then I asked myself if he was alarmed for other reasons, a notion of the scheme Draco had accused me of. Then again, here and now, we might have come to such a pass. I needed a witness. I looked at the soldier, who saluted me slowly. "Has she cured them all?" I inquired. I added for his benefit, "Zafra."

"Yes," he said. "It was—worth seeing."

"I am sure of that. And how does the child fare?"

I saw him begin to conclude maybe Draco had sent me after all. "Bonny," he said.

"But she is leaving the village, with the child—" I had never thought she would risk her purpose among the huts, as she would not in the town, for all her hold on them. "Is that tonight?"

"Well, there's the old woman, she won't leave her own place, it seems."

"So Zafra told you?"

"Yes. And said she would go. It's close. She refused the litter and only took Carus with her. No harm. These savages are friendly enough—"

He ended, seeing my face.

I said, "She's gone already?"

"Yes, Skorous. About an hour—"

Another way from the village? But I had watched, I had skinned my eyes—pointlessly. Witchcraft could manage anything.

"And the child with her," I insisted.

"Oh, she never will part from the child, Eunike says—"

"Damn Eunike." He winced at me more than ever uncertain. "Listen," I said, and informed him of my suspicions. I did not say the child was half East, half spice and glisten and sins too strange to speak. I said *Draco's son*. And I did not mention sacrifice. I said there was some chance Zafra might wish to mutilate the boy for her gods. It was well known, many of the Eastern religions had such rites. The soldier was shocked, and disbelieving. His own mother—? I said, to her kind, it was not a deed of dishonour. She could not see it as we did. All the while we debated, my heart clutched and struggled in my side, I sweated. Finally he agreed we should go to look. Carus was there, and would dissuade her if she wanted to perform such a disgusting act. I asked where the old woman's hut was supposed to be, and my vision filmed a moment with relief when he located it for me as that very bothy where I had tethered my horse the previous night. I said, as I turned to run that way, "There's no old woman there. The place is a ruin."

We had both won at the winter racing, he and I. It did not take us long to achieve the spot. A god, I thought, must have guided me to it before, so I knew how the land fell. The trees were densely packed as wild grass, the hut wedged between, and an apron of bared weedy ground about the door where once the household fowls had pecked. The moon would enter there, too, but hardly anywhere else. You could come up on it, cloaked in forest and night. Besides, she had lit her stage for me. As we pushed among the last phalanx of trunks, I saw there was a fire burning, a sullen throb of red, before the ruin's gaping door.

Carus stood against a tree. His eyes were wide and beheld nothing. The other man punched him and hissed at him, but Carus was far off. He breathed and his heart drummed, but that was all.

"She's witched him," I said. Thank Arean Mars and Father Jupiter she had. It proved my case outright. I could see my witness thought this too. We went on stealthily, and stopped well clear of the tree-break, staring down.

Then I forgot my companion. I forgot the manner in which luck at last had thrown my dice for me. What I saw took all my mind.

It was like the oven of the hallucination in the tent, the thing she had made, yet open, the shape of a cauldron. Rough mud brick, smoothed and curved, and somehow altered. Inside, the fire burned. It had a wonderful colour, the fire, rubies, gold. To look at it did not seem to hurt the eyes, or dull them. The woman stood the other side of it, and her child in her grasp. Both appeared illumined into fire themselves, and the darkness of garments, of hair, the black gape of the doorway, of the forest and the night, these had grown warm as velvet. It is a sight often seen, a girl at a brazier or a hearth, her baby held by, as she stirs a pot, or throws on the kindling some further twig or cone. But in her golden arm the golden child stretched out his hands to the flames. And from her moving palm fell some invisible essence I could not see but only feel.

She was not alone. Others had gathered at her fireside. I was not sure of them, but I saw them, if only by their great height which seemed to rival the trees. A warrior there, his metal face-plate and the metal ribs of his breast just glimmering, and there a young woman, garlands, draperies and long curls, and a king who was bearded, with a brow of thunder and eyes of light, and near him another, a musician with wings starting from his forehead—they came and went as the fire danced and bowed. The child laughed, turning his head to see them, the deities of his father's side.

Then Zafra spoke the Name. It was so soft, no sound at all. And yet the roots of the forest moved at it. My entrails churned. I was on my knees. It seemed as though the wind came walking through the forest, to fold his robe beside the ring of golden red. I cannot recall the Name. It was not any of those I have written down, nor anything I might imagine. But it was the true one, and he came in answer to it. And from a mile away, from the heaven of planets, out of the pit of the earth, his hands descended and rose. He touched the child and the child was quiet. The child slept.

She drew Draco's son from his wrapping as a shining sword is drawn from the scabbard. She raised him up through the dark, and then she lowered him, and set him down in the holocaust of the oven, into the bath of flame, and the fires spilled up and covered him.

No longer on my knees, I was running. I plunged through black waves of heat, the amber pungence of incense, and the burning breath of lions. I yelled as I ran. I screamed the names of all the gods, and knew them powerless in my mouth, because I said them wrongly, knew them not, and so they would not answer. And then I ran against the magic, the Power, and broke through it. It was like smashing air. Experienced—inexperienceable.

Sword in hand, in the core of molten gold, I threw myself on, wading, smothered, and came to the cauldron of brick, the oven and dropped the sword and thrust in my hands and pulled him out—

He would be burned, he would be dead, a blackened little corpse, such as the Semite Karthaginians once made of their children, incinerating them in line upon line of ovens by the shores of the Inner Sea—

But I held in my grip only a child of jewel-work, of poreless perfect gold, and I sensed his gleam run into my hands, through my wrists, down my arms like scalding water to my heart.

Someone said to me then, with such gentle sadness, "Ah, Skorous. Ah, Skorous."

I lay somewhere not seeing. I said, "Crude sorcery, to turn the child, too, into gold."

"No," she said. "Gold is only the clue. For those things which are alive, laved by the flame, it is life. It is immortal and imperishable life. And you have torn the spell, which is all you think it to be. You have robbed him of it."

And then I opened my eyes and I saw her. There were no others, no Other, they had gone with the tearing. But she—she was no longer veiled. She was very tall, so beautiful I could not bear to look at her, and yet, could not take my eyes away. And she was golden. She was golden not in the form of metal, but as a dawn sky, as fire, and the sun itself. Even her black eyes—were of gold, and her midnight hair. And the tears she wept were stars.

I did not understand, but I whispered, "Forgive me. Tell me how to make it right."

"It is not to be," she said. Her voice was a harp, playing through the forest. "It is never to be. He is yours now, no longer mine. Take him. Be kind to him. He will know his loss all his days, all his mortal days. And never know it."

And then she relinquished her light, as a coal dies. She vanished.

I was lying on the ground before the ruined hut, holding the child close to me, trying to comfort him as he cried, and my tears fell with his.

The place was empty and hollow as if its very heart had bled away.

The soldier had run down to me, and was babbling. She had tried to immolate the baby, he had seen it. Carus had woken and seen it also. And, too, my valour in saving the boy from horrible death.

* * *

As one can set oneself to remember most things, so one can study to forget. Our sleeping dreams we dismiss on waking. Or, soon after.

They call her now, the Greek Woman. Or the Semite Witch. There has begun, in recent years, to be a story she was some man's wife, and in the end went back to him. It is generally thought she practiced against the child and the soldiers of her guard killed her.

Draco, when I returned half-dead of the fever I had caught from the contagion of the ruinous hut—where the village crone had died, it turned out, a week before—hesitated for my recovery, and then asked very little. A dazzle seemed to have lifted from his sight. He was afraid at what he might have said and done under the influence of sorceries and drugs.

"Is it a fact, what the men say? She put the child into a fire?"

"Yes," I said.

He had looked at me, gnawing his lips. He knew of Eastern rites, he had heard out the two men. And, long, long ago, he had relied only on me. He appeared never to grieve, only to be angry. He even sent men to search for her: A bitch who would burn her own child—let her be caught and suffer the fate instead.

It occurs to me now that, contrary to what they tell us, one does not age imperceptibly, finding one evening, with cold dismay, the strength has gone from one's arm, the lustre from one's heart. No, it comes at an hour, and is seen, like the laying down of a sword.

When I woke from the fever, and saw his look, all imploring on me, the look of a man who has gravely wronged you, not meaning to, who says—But I was blind—that was the hour, the evening, the moment when life's sword of youth was removed from my hand, and with no protest I let it go.

Thereafter the months moved away from us, the seasons, and next the years.

Draco continued to look about him, as if seeking the evil Eye that

221

might still hang there, in the atmosphere. Sometimes he was partly uneasy, saying he too had seen her dog, the black jackal. But it had vanished at the time she did, though for decades the woman Eunike claimed to meet it in the corridor of the women's quarters.

He clung to me, then, and ever since he has stayed my friend; I do not say, my suppliant. It is in any event the crusty friendship now of the middle years, where once it was the flaming blazoned friendship of childhood, the envious love of young men.

We share a secret, he and I, that neither has ever confided to the other. He remains uncomfortable with the boy. Now the princedom is larger, its borders fought out wider, and fortressed in, he sends him often away to the fostering of soldiers. It is I, without any rights, none, who love her child.

He is all Draco, to look at, but for the hair and brows. We have a dark-haired strain ourselves. Yet there is a sheen to him. They remark on it. What can it be? A brand of the gods (they make no reference, since she has fallen from their favour, to his mother). A light from within, a gloss, of gold. Leaving off his given name, they will call him for that effulgence more often, Ardorius. Already I have caught the murmur that he can draw iron through stone, yes, yes, they have seen him do it, though I have not. (From Draco they conceal such murmurings, as once from me.) He, too, has a look of something hidden, some deep and silent pain, as if he knows, as youth never does, that men die, and love, that too.

To me, he is always courteous, and fair. I can ask nothing else. I am, to him, an adjunct of his life. I should perhaps be glad that it should stay so.

In the deep nights, when summer heat or winter snow fill up the forest, I recollect a dream, and think how I robbed him, the child of gold. I wonder how much, how much it will matter, in the end.

The Truce

Dawn was already scarlet in the sky when Issla rose from the Prayer-Place. Issla had been there most of the night, not really praying, but finding some comfort from the unseen communion of the spirits of dead Ullakin. Today was the important and terrible day. So much rested upon the events of today that it was almost unbearable to think about it. Drael stood in the mouth of the Prayer-Place, spear in hand. Issla pressed herself to the known, loved body, seeking comfort, and at last the miserable and frightened tears welled out.

"Hush, darling," Drael said, "don't be afraid."

"I am, I am," Issla wept. "How can I not be afraid? I am carrying the burden of life on me today, and even you, who love me, will let me go to the Truce Place and suffer there."

"There'll be no suffering," Drael said sternly. "No one will hurt you. They must not break the Truce, even if they are beasts. I'll wait beside the cave mouth with my spear, and if you call out, I will kill the beast with you. Trust me." Issla's weeping grew less. "Come now," Drael said, "the Chief wants to bless you for the task."

They went up the slope, Drael's arm about Issla's shoulders. The way was steep, old grey rock, a few thorn trees thrust out here and there. The fortress of the Ullakin was built into this rock, safe from their enemies, but bleak and comfortless nevertheless.

The Chief stood outside the Big Cave, the Ullakin warriors spread around, spears in hand, waiting. Issla came with bowed head and was solemnly blessed. Then the Chief pointed away from the rock to the scarred defile below, where once an ancient river had dried itself out. And they were coming already, the dark and terrible Ullaks, the eternal enemy of the Ullakin, passing unharmed between the watching sentries perched on the rock walls, because today was the day of Truce. Issla whimpered.

"Courage," the Chief said. "Drael is pledged to protect you as we all are. Only be brave and you may save our race—and theirs, though our ancestors know that is a bad price to pay."

Issla stared at the approaching tribe and saw, after a while, that they were not as terrible as expected. Issla, who had never fought with the warriors, had never seen an Ullak close to, but they did not seem so very different from the Ullakin in fact, at least, not as different as the stories said. They were climbing the rough-hewn steps of the fortress now and arranging themselves on the plateau outside the sacred cave.

"Come," the Chief commanded, and the Ullakin went towards the plateau also, in the first heat of the day.

"I am not so afraid now," Issla said.

"That's good," said Drael. "Only remember, be on your guard. They're beasts, dirty sometimes in their ways of love." With a sudden weird jealous spite, Drael spat.

The sacred cave, the cave which was to be so important today, was set roughly in the centre of the rock wall leaning over the plateau. A whitish woven cloth painted with the ritualistic signs of the Ullakin rippled at the entrance, hiding the interior. To the right of it the enemy chief stood in front of the Ullak warriors. The skins they wore were badly cured and, coming this close to them, Issla became aware of their stink, a smell not only of the skins, but of their alien bodies and alien sweat.

I hate my enemy, Issla thought suddenly, the old traditional war vow, *but I must not hate. Not today.*

The two Chiefs went forward and confronted each other silently. The Ullak was bigger, grinning, leaning on a spear, deliberately ignoring the occasion's sanctity.

"You are my foe, but today I honour you," the Ullakin Chief said.

The Ullak repeated the Truce promise. They stood looking at each other.

Ralka, the Ullakin's Pronouncer, came forward and began to recite the already known reason for the coming together. And, although known, a great quiet hung on the plateau as every ear listened.

"We are met here, forgetting our enmity to save ourselves. It is told us that in the old times, young could be made by love, carried in the body and brought forth whole. Now, neither of our races can produce young by this means, and we have relied on the breeding machines and hatcheries left us by our ancestors, praised be they. Now the machines have ceased to function. The birth-eggs crack and the young die. It the same for both of us. It is told us that once the Ullak and the Ullakin were one people. Therefore, in answer to our prayers, our Oracle has told us to make Truce with you, and bring together one of our number and one of yours, hoping that a sign may be shown them, and that they may find some way of cross-breeding that will produce offspring. You have agreed to this." Ralka beckoned and Issla, trembling, went forward. "This is our Chosen One. Who is yours?" One of the Ullaks came shambling up. The large face Issla saw looming across the raw sunlight of the plateau seemed uneasy. Issla felt a sudden sympathy for this beast and fear diminished.

The Ullakin Chief said sternly:

"Let neither harm the other. You may kill our Chosen if harm comes to yours, and we claim the right to do likewise. Go now, into the cave."

Panicking, Issla stared back, and saw Drael's carved pale face and angry clenched hand on the spear. Drael's lips shaped the words, *Only call, and I will kill it.*

Then Issla was at the curtain, the Ullak was at the curtain, the woven stuff lifted, the gloom reached out, and they were inside together, alone in the dark and terrible cave.

Dried grasses lay over the floor. It was cool and dank. Little needles of muted light sewed through the tiny chinks in the rock's armour. Issla drew back against the cave wall and watched the Ullak draw back against another. After a minute, the Ullak spoke:

"I am called Kloll. How are you called?"

The voice was rough and different but the words formed were familiar.

"I am Issla."

"Let's sit down," Kloll said. "No don't be afraid. You sit there and I'll stay here. What a way for our ancestors to pay us out, isn't it?"

Issla gasped and made a quick sign to avert sacred anger. The Ullak laughed.

"You, Ullakin," Kloll went on. "You think you were the cream of the lost race, don't you? And the Ullaks were the degenerates, the morons, the deformed things, made out of spit and excrement?"

Issla sat wide-eyed, heart thudding.

"I'm sorry," Kloll said, "this isn't the way to go about it. Sacred Dark! What do they want us to do?"

"They hope our ancestors will grant us a sign," Issla whispered.

And the Ullak laughed.

They sat for a long while in silence.

Outside on the plateau the magic drums beat and religious smokes went up. The Chiefs would probably share an awkward meal at midday.

"Well," said Kloll eventually, "we'd better talk, perhaps. Tell me about yourself, Issla Ullakin."

Issla sat still not knowing what to say.

"Well," Kloll said, "don't you have a lover you want to praise to me?"

"Drael is my lover," Issla said, "one of the warriors. And you?"

"Oh, we're not so permanent as you. We chop and change. We have sacred orgies, too; I expect you've heard about them."

"Yes," Issla said, and repressed a shudder.

You must be strong, Issla's brain instructed.

Issla got up and moved closer to the Ullak, closer to the strangeness and alien smell, which now did not seem so repulsive. Presumably the Ullak must find the Ullakin odour equally obnoxious. Another silence fell and then after a while, the Ullak's great paw came out and touched Issla's hair. Issla trembled and found that the Ullak was trembling too.

"Don't be afraid," Kloll whispered, and the whisper was suddenly like Drael's whisper in the cup of the night, gentle, anxious and intimate. Issla moved closer to Kloll until their bodies touched. And in this closeness they waited for their ancestors to speak to them.

Day grew gold, and darker gold, passing on into the swift savagery of sunset. Firelight mounted on the plateau, and stars burst their shells overhead. Drael waited near the cave mouth, eyes fixed. Root wine had gone round and the two enemy tribes were friendlier now, soaking their worry in the drink. But when the cup came to Drael, Drael pushed it away.

And in the cave—

"I know you now," Kloll said suddenly.

"Yes," Issla said.

They had not spoken for hours, simply sat close, waiting; out of the trance that they had woven between them, the answer seemed now to be coming.

"I am no longer afraid," said Issla. "Why have we been enemies all this while when after all we are so alike?"

"Listen," Kloll said, "they tell us, long ago the young were made from love. Shall we pretend that we're lovers? Perhaps this is what our ancestors want."

But Issla had stiffened.

"Your ways of love are different from ours," Issla said.

"Perhaps that's what's needed." And the Ullak touched Issla softly, as Drael would have done, in the long night.

226

"This is right," Kloll whispered soon, "I feel this is right."

And Issla, washed away like a swimmer on the unexpected sea of the Ullak's hands, stirred, and seemed to know the strange lost hunger that possessed Kloll.

"Yes, this is right," Issla moaned, "yes, yes…"

And then, in the blackness, a wrongness, a pain.

"No," Issla hissed, "you're hurting me. No."

"Wait," Kloll pleaded. "This is as it must be. I feel it. I know."

But the Ullak had become again an enemy, and, after a moment of agonised terror, Issla screamed for Drael.

And Drael heard.

Drael's hands ripped aside the woven curtain, profaning the painted symbols. Drael paused one moment only, to ascertain which of the moving shadows was Issla and which the beast, and then the sharpened spear was thrust deep in the Ullak's back. With a small noise like despair, Kloll rolled over and died.

Drael lifted Issla.

"It's all right," Drael said, "I killed it as I said I would. Did it hurt you?"

"Yes," Issla wept.

Drael pulled the Ullak by the embedded spear, and dragged the corpse out on to the plateau. A cry went up, shock and rage. Several of the Ullaks bounded forward. Drael ripped out the spear and threatened them with it.

"Wait, you defiled things," Drael cried, "your Chosen broke the Truce. Your Chosen wounded Issla."

Issla came out of the cave, and there were red spots on the front of the Ullakin tunic from the wound Kloll had made. The Ullaks quietened, mumbled together.

Drael gazed at Issla a moment, then flung round to the Ullakin's chief.

"Let's kill them, these beasts, now, while we have them in the stronghold!"

The growling of anger and fear broke out again, but the Chief stepped forward and slapped Drael across the face.

"Fool," the Chief said, "our ancestors will always remember how you sought to dishonour us."

Drael fell back and turned away.

227

"Now," the Chief said, "Tribe of Ullak, go from us. Your Chosen has hurt our Chosen and, as it was agreed, we have killed. You cannot say we have not abided by our word. You Ullaks are the ones who broke the Truce."

The Ullak Chief stood glowering in the firelight. Then the glowering turned to a great sorrow, a great regret.

"I know it to be true," the Ullak said. "It is sadness to me, as it is to you, that we can never now find peace together. Our ancestors have proved to us cruelly that new life can never spring from the joining of our two races."

The Ullak Chief gestured to the Ullak warriors.

"We leave you now," the Chief said, "only give us Kloll's body so that we can bury it."

"Take it," the Ullakin Chief said, "go, like the ancient river, to die out from the face of the earth, as we too must die, now there is no hope."

So the tribe of men turned away into the darkness, carrying their dead one, leaving the fortress of women alone on their rock.

And Drael, her arms round the girl Issla, spat after them into the quiet night, "I hate my enemy," and pressed her mouth to Issla's hair.

The God Orkrem

How long I traveled I have no knowledge. When you have lost everything on earth for which you ever cared, distance—and time—become two foreign elements. To a man bereaved of all as I was, distance and time are only words.

For me then, and also now, only one word any more can exist: God.

The god Orkrem.

* * *

I think three seasons had fled over the lands, and by then I was far away from anything I had ever known. The leaves were falling thick and red as blood when the old woman met me on the path.

"Where you go, warrior?" she asked, flirting with her old eyes as crones do, as if she is your mother, or your aunt.

"North," I said.

"Oh," said she. "To the mountain towns."

It was beyond the towns I was heading, but I nodded. Then she said, "Watch for lizards, warrior."

"Yes, then."

"Never be impatient," she said, "with any that would help. Watch for lizards."

"Thank you, pretty auntie," carefully I said. For even then, sometimes I would take care.

But she only scowled. Behind her face of tree bark and black pearl eyes, I glimpsed a maiden with skin like snow and a rose for a mouth.

Then she was gone, and so was I.

Winter was coming on, and I had reached again another land when I met the second woman. And she was so ancient she made the first like a girl. She had no hair and her flesh was lacquered ivory. She was formed of bone and briar.

"Well then, warrior," she said. "These mountains are high enough."

I was past all the towns by then. The clouds often descended and touched the ground. I stood now in a cloud with her, and she and I peered at each other. Her eyes were not black pearl but the heads of white vipers—also blind she must be.

"Not quite so high," I found I said.

"So you must go still higher? Only the sky is there." I offered nothing. Then she said: "But the upper air is a country too. Beware of lions as you go."

Out it came before I had rein on it. "Not lizards then. Lions."

"Oh, there are lizards," she said. "But there are lions too."

"They will be no worse than life."

"Only one thing is worse," she softly said.

This was no question, nor did I answer. But in my head a voice spoke loudly as a beaten metal shield. The god is worse.

He. Orkrem is worse.

And she nodded, the ancient woman, as if she heard. And then she said, "If you were my grandson I would lesson and warn and train you, I would. But he died."

"Men die."

"And women die too," she replied. "The earth is all to die in, not to live. Not many know. But you have learned that, warrior?"

"Yes."

"Be on your way then, son."

I was not her son, nor her grandson. But her words cut me with the sharp blade of a terrible and unexpected tenderness. Kindness I did not want at all.

In the labyrinth of agony, no beauty must ever enter, not one single whisper of compassion. Or steel breaks like glass.

* * *

𝕿he mountains climbed like the crested backs of dragons, and I strove on. I knew very well where I must get to, if it were real.

Oh, since I was an infant I had heard them preach and sing of it.

In the stone temple I had sat with the other children, and by us our own *true* gods, our fathers and our mothers, all our kin. There we were instructed by the priests.

The world had been made for us by gods, of whom Orkrem was the greatest and the most inventive. He it was who had formed the clay of the earth, and dressed it with cunning pits and traps and varied dangers.

He it was too who had fashioned humankind out of some supernal wax, forming our ancestors with slow, spiteful pinches of his fingers that had viciously hurt them. So that, ever after, we knew pain first and best, and our own babies were born in pain, screaming and weeping even before they had the water for tears in them.

Orkrem was a harsh god.

Not a single priest said why—or knew not why to say. But the earth was to be our school of being harmed. We were to suffer here, and endure suffering. Other lesser gods, it was well known, had tried to make the earth beautiful, adorning it with charming and reassuring things—the loveliness of forests and seas, dawn and sunset, moon and stars, music of birdsong, flowers, honey and wine, and even the best gift of all, which was love. Animals too they had assembled in the world. But Orkrem, when he saw that, decreed animals must then feed on each other, and humankind must feed on the animals. To ensure the needfulness of that, Orkrem next adapted us so that we should have a physical necessity to devour meat, without which mostly we would not be healthy. Therefore even the animals came to harm and pain, and usually through us. Meanwhile Orkrem made certain otherwise we might not often, on any account, enjoy the beauties of the earth. He sent us diseases and anguishes; he sent us suspicion and jealousy and dread and murder. Even love he soured, turning it like cream, so it should fret us, and drive us mad in loss or denial. Suffer we must, and endure we must, and in the end die we must, most often in extremes of horror and agony. For pain was what we entered the earth to know, in all its forms, of body, mind and soul. Pain and despair.

And all the while, from screaming weeping birth to weeping shrieking death, we must praise, worship, and bless Orkrem, who was easily offended. So that any slight wrongdoing we committed, even as a reaction to his evil woundings, or in desperation, having no other recourse once his will was enacted on us, we should after death be punished for.

With such awareness I grew up. As all have grown who live upon this earth.

Though, when young, incredulously, I *doubted* it. I have no notion as to why, the proofs were already before me. But I was in my spring. My blood-red fall, my winter, still to come.

So Orkrem, the Great Artist, set on to show me the veracity of priestly teachings.

At seven years of age I saw my sister, along with others, perish of a scabrous plague. At ten I watched my mother die in childbirth, and the baby within her. At twelve an enemy came and destroyed our village. I witnessed my father's death. I and one brother were dragged away as slaves. In another place we were brutally versed in the arts of battle. We, like fools, and having no choice, allowed this, and came to shine. For these our conquering enemies then we grew up to fight as their champions, and helped win for them great renown. Freed at last due to our value, we achieved riches. We lived friendly among them, making ourselves forget they had slain our kin and were our foes. One day, I saw a young woman in the fields, gathering the sky-blue flowers for garlands. When she turned and gazed at me our hearts began to beat with the same tempo. It was the gift of the other god, who had brought love into the world, and at that time I so credited his power. Her skin was like *snow* and her mouth a rose, but her eyes were like the blue cornflowers. For her heart, Orkrem had made it. It was wax.

A few months after our wedding, she told me she was with child by me. And I rejoiced.

But as it happened, it was the child of my brother, since at him too had she gazed. And their hearts had also beaten as one. And this not fifty days after first I had her.

There are always those who will *see* and tell. They had seen, and soon they told. When the baby struggled out into the world it had the color of his hair, not mine. I let it live, as it screamed and tearlessly wept. Nor, as she screamed and shed her tears like a waterfall, did I kill her. Him though, my brother, him I meant to kill. But at the last I could not do it. I had killed so many men in my trade of war. And I had pictured *his* death, my brother's, too well and too often. There is some other lesser god who creates this magic. His name is *weakness*.

Then I must run. I ran.

Some while after, in another place again, I worked the land, and with the horses, and going one day to a temple I confessed my crime of hateful blasphemy. For this they did not punish me. They had no need. They told me Orkrem would himself see to it, since I had cursed his name. The world was made to torture men, and they must suffer it all and always bless him. One step from this path, and he would chastise them worse, during life, and after life, forever.

Later, I went on my way from that country. For years I kept my wandering course.

One other woman I met in that time, and loved. She was unlike the other, being dark, and her eyes the color of good beer. We lived in some pleasure with each other half a year, before the scabrous plague came on in those parts. Walking back beside me from the field one night, she suddenly fell down without a prelude, and was dead by daybreak. I saw to her funeral and went away. From the moment I had met with her, I believe by then, I guessed she and I would not have long.

I suffered, and all other men suffered, and sometimes, if only briefly, I or they prospered. And as I went on through all of that, I noted how most other men, and women too, proceeded always in the same fashion. All told, you could not press a slender stick between them for the misery and injustice to which they fell prey, and which in turn they dealt. We were all of us equal. We were damned.

Finally, about my thirtieth year, I reached a temple of another sort. They took me in when, all vitality spent, I dropped like the dead at their threshold. And they were kind to me—kindness which, even at that hour, not yet had I learned was the cruelest and sharpest of life's blades to cut and disable.

Presently the priest said quietly, "For us, we believe in that one god who brought love on to the earth. Believe in him, and nothing can defeat you."

"What of death?" I asked him.

"Death least of all," he told me. So sweet his face, and inwardly clean, as if his inmost soul had been washed in purest water. But less than a year after, I saw that face transfixed by a black-bleeding arrow, and all about a robber horde besieged the sacred house. I held him as in agony—what else—he died. And his weeping forgiveness of his god, the god of love, shattered what was left of any heart inside me.

When all had fallen then, black and burned, I fought away from the scene. And so went on with my wandering, going always north, and ever upward on the sloping land. For they had taught us in my youth that the master god, Orkrem, resides on the floor of the skies.

And Orkrem was, at that last, my only destination. If ever I had had any other goal, or could have done, seeing the ruling god in this world, any and all of it, the beginning and the end.

* * *

233

The tops of the mountains rose above the cloud, which I had not expected. The mountaintops were gray as sightless mirrors, and the skies, now winter began to stir its iron wings, far grayer.

Below, by day, those lower clouds yet nestled like forests of gray ash.

Above, by night, the stars were the razor tips of knives and swords, burnished and pointing through, every one hungrily focused on some human heart.

When last I had seen a green tree it had made me think of sickness, plague. When blue I had seen, the sky reminded me of faithless eyes.

And red was blood.

* * *

At last old woman met me on the track. And she was so old she had been wiped of anything, like as if she might have been a baby stretched like a string, and so peculiarly tall. Though her eyes were like dull yellow coins.

"None otherwhere to go, warrior," said she, "but up in the sky."

"Then that must be my road, granny," I told her.

"No use to warn you then," she said. "For you were warned of lizards and lions and paid no heed."

"Nor have I seen a single lizard since. Let alone any lion."

She spat on the earth, but her spit was wholesome, and only like a drop of bright water. It was almost like a courtesy when she spat. A tenderness that had no kindness, and could be borne.

"There have been lizards aplenty," she said. "They have run under your feet, and over your body as you lay sleeping. And *through* your body they have run, as if through a long cave or a deserted house, and through your brain they have run and in and out your dreams, as if through a high room in a tower. And many their lions have followed you, smearing the waste of their kill in your footsteps, and breathing their hot stinking breath into your nose and mouth when you slumbered, and *stood* on you they have, heavy as millstones, and torn your skin with their claws." She sighed, rustily. "But you saw and heard and felt nothing of any of it. The heavens crashed on your head and you missed it. The sea came up the hill and drowned you and you never even felt its wet. Go on then. Go up the sky."

"I shall, granny."

"I am never your grandmother. I am only the very final thing of humankind you will see before you meet your god."

Then she was gone, and so was I.

But I had learned not one thing from her, as nor had I from the other two.

* * *

No man can climb up the sky. Yet I reached the topmost peak and stood on its flat table, staring upward.

All round, beneath, the lands fell away together, but they were like a game-board, with their colors of plague and faithlessness and blood. The world no more real for me.

In the sky the higher clouds ascended like a stairway. I stretched up my arms, and for hours on end I bellowed, till my voice was gone. I called his name: *Orkrem! Orkrem!* And then I whispered his name: Orkrem.

Night bloomed its black poison-flower and the stabs of the stars pierced out.

Then a wind woke in the core of the sky.

It came forth on me like a giant bird, a dragon. Roaring, it clutched me, and whirled me off the peak.

No longer, me, with a voice to blaspheme him, only my whisper to say now he would dash me to earth and break me. But this was not the way of it.

The sky wind thrashed me not down but upward, through the cloud and through the basement of the sky itself, and flung me headlong on the floor of a huge echoing chamber that was black as the void, yet lit as if with torches.

And when the wind was gone, and the noise of it emptied from my ears, I looked and saw I was in some colossal place like a temple of pillars, but carved out of the night itself. Far away down a long avenue, the slender moon was rising, on its side like a white boat. Swollen planets the colors of sickness and betrayal and war moved slowly through the vault.

I was in Orkrem's house. The house of the god.

He did not come in for a while. Or he may have been there anyway,

235

unseen and unfelt. He might have hung in the tiniest drip of moonlight, like a spider in its web. Or curled about the pillars like a sort of night mist, visibly invisible to me.

But then he did come in.

He made no sound. He did not even manifest—appear, as a flame would, struck all at once on a lamp. He was not. Then he was.

I pulled myself off the floor of his house, which was a solid floor, like marble—but it was air. I stood and looked at him, in his face.

He was high as the house, wide as the house. Yet too he was only the height of a gigantic man, not that much—a span or two—taller and bigger in frame than I. But he was the lizard, and the lion. I can describe him no otherwise. I *fail* to be able to describe him. Only for that—lizard and lion—or that his face was a shout like the rumble of an earthquake. And his eyes put out the light of the razor stars.

And then my voice returned.

Did he give it me? For he spoke to me, and he asked *What do you want of me?*

And then I bellowed once more at him, bellowed as out on the mountain before the wind lifted me up.

"Orkrem—give me my life!"

The conflagration of his eyes flickered.

You live.

"No," I answered. I knew how to speak it. I had rehearsed my words so long. "No human thing can *live* in your world. Your world is death-alive, but *life* it never is. We are *born* into death, and *live* in death, until we die—in *death*—and if, after all these *dyings*, we are with you—then still it is *death*. Death through eternity, agony and anguish, terror and despair. Orkrem—*give me my life."*

When I grew silent I heard how the temple house rocked and rang from my uproar, and from my rage and grief, that too. No single man, even one lifted into the sky, could make such a passion and din. Instead it seemed I had brought with me the outcry of every human thing, and every beast, all the complaint of the earth that Orkrem had made for us to suffer horror in.

Time passed when I was done. But time, though still somewhat it seems I had measured it, meant nothing to me.

A moment or an hour or a night or a season went by.

And then the god was beside me, so near I might have stretched my hand and touched his lizard-lion form, or his face of earthquake and volcano.

I never touched.

But he put up one hand, or as it might be one scaled and taloned paw. He passed this once across the visage of his godhead.

And then I saw. What...*what* did I truly see?

I saw his boiling and frustrated anger and his wretched hurt, I saw his tears that dropped like blazing rains. I saw into his mouth to his tongue bitten through in agony beyond bearing.

To me then, soft as snow, he said this:

"Your life I gave you, nor therefore can I give you it again. But as you have seen, and dared to tell me, my task I have failed at. For this then, you shall have my task. You shall be me. You shall be a god. You shall make and plan and direct and rule and correct and master the world. It is all for you to do. To change as you will, to repair as you can, to alter hate to love and misery to happiness. To make a paradise on earth. It is with you. And now, at last, at last, I shall have peace." With this he left me. But not I him.

A vast while I balanced there on heaven's floor, between aether and earth. Enormous metamorphoses shook me, with a hideous gentleness. Yet as I took on the mantle and the sacraments of the immortal life he had cast off on me, I must consider what I had been shown.

Judging by what was evident in his wounds, and his wild prolonging sorrow, it must seem he had writhed in that way for aeons. He had not then, surely, as our teachings had it, *begun* with ill intent to us—or why mourn so, as if at the ruin, not the glory, of his work. Worse, it must seem he had been unable to put anything right, however the ruin had occurred. More likely I felt it to be, that at the start of all, he had tried to make all perfect in the world, and we perfect also, that we could be glad, and create there nothing ourselves but fine things.

Yet some happening there was—either in him, through the exhaustion of all his ceaseless care and labor, or even in us independently of him. And from that came the worm that gnawed on the honeycomb, till all was wormwood ever after. And he, god though he was, could not heal such sores.

That much I had sensed in the single instant when he uttered his ultimate word, which had been *peace*.

I have no means to grasp, even now I have not, if this were some ending trick he played on me. Or some *beginning* trick of my mind, transformed so fast from clay to supernal fire.

Nevertheless, just as my huge shout had done, that subtle ending word echoed on and on, here in the god house which is now mine, and which I have grown already great to fill.

* * *

I stand on the sky and the planets turn and the stars rip their long rents through the night. The moon will sink. The sun will rise.

I am the god.

I am the maker and master.

Before me I behold multitudinous possibilities, vista on vista, world on world. But so then, once, must he too have seen them, and tried them—maybe even to the giving of the gift of love—but he had *failed*. And then he wept and screamed and had bitten through his tongue. Until, finding me, he has taken me up, and shed on me the whole of what he could not do.

Such *power* is mine. Will I then work success here, where Orkrem never could, now I am Orkrem?

I am God.

I am Almighty.

I am afraid.

The Kingdoms of the Air

Who is he, that Knight riding by?

—His name is Cedrevir. He has been Questing.

—Pale as death, and his eyes looked blind. I thought, a good thing the horse knows its way. I thought, there is one wounded by unseen arrows.

—They are an ancient Fellowship, these Knights. It is in their vows to invite the Quest, whatever it may be, whatever its peril or strangeness. But many return home as you have seen.

—This Cedrevir: What Quest then was his? Do you know it?

—Yes, and I will tell it you.

At the Midsummer Feast they met, as it is usual for them to do, this Fellowship of Knights, up there in the Castle of Towers.

In the Castle's heart, there is a great hidden hall, the entrances to which are known only to an Initiate. The hall is built as a perfect circle, its floor and walls paved with blocks of polished stone. From the high dome of the roof hang down the thousand swords and shields, banners and devices, of all the Knights who are and have been of the Fellowship. High on the walls the torches burn in iron cages of curious shape, so they resemble the heads of serpents and monsters which breathe fire. In the floor is set, in fine mosaic, a huge round sun-disc, and on the rayed rim of it stand the Knights, repealing the circle of power a third time, in flesh and steel.

For each man comes to that place fully armed and in mail, though each surcote is of undyed and unembroidered linen, and the visor of each helm lowered, and though every man carries in his gauntleted hand a sword, it has no mark.

(There are ways of knowing a man, even under these circumstances. From his height and build, his voice, his manner, or by some expression in his eyes.)

There they stood, then; at this Midsummer near to midnight, in the dark light of the dragon-torches. They performed their rites and reaffirmed their vows. In turn they confessed any of their transgressions against God, Man, or the Fellowship. They told, in turn, of their feats, and furnished proofs, which might be anything, from a lady's scarf to the severed hand of an enemy.

There is one further property in that hall. On a tall stand to the east is a clock, in the form of a golden sword and a marble heart on water. As the liquid drips down through the basin, the weights go up, and all morning the golden sword lifts slowly, until, at noon, it strikes a golden chiming apple in the summit of the clock. Then, as the water gradually refills the basin, the weights sink, the marble heart floats up and the sword descends, until at midnight its yellow blade pierces through the heart, which gives out a long singing note.

Shortly before midnight at Midsummer, when the sword is just grazing the marble, an Invocation is spoken by all the Knights of the Circle. There are those that say a certain wine is then drunk, a wafer eaten, and an incense burned. Every man bows his head and awaits what will come to him.

Then the sword enters the marble heart, and the heart sweetly cries.

Cedrevir heard the note of the heart, as he had previously heard it, twelve times in all, for he had been six years a Knight of the Circle. At first, he had been strung, expectant and eager, but year by year these emotions dulled to patience. He had undertaken betweenwhiles many adventures, all successful. As a warrior he was valiant and accomplished, and as a priest—for the Initiate of the Fellowship is both—he was equally chaste, and passionate. He had done no wrong, he had fought with honour and skill, but yet nothing had come to him at midnight of Midsummer, or in the dark Midwinter either.

Now however, as the note faded from the water-clock, Cedrevir began to hear another sound so like, that for a moment he thought the heart cried out a second time. Then he became aware that what he heard was the voice of a maiden, singing. Her tones were pure and thin as beaten silver, and her words were these:

Primo dolens lancea est
Corona dolor de Dominus
Est secundo et tertio
Gradalis cruenta fulgero

The voice rang all round the hollow chamber, and in the hollows of helm and skull it rang.

Cedrevir raised his head, sure that every other Knight did in like fashion, and looked with wide grey eyes. There at the centre of the mosaic sunburst, a column of light so sheer and bright it dimmed the torches, rose up from floor to roof. Even as Cedrevir stared into this radiance, half dazzled, uncannily half not, he began to make out objects moving, there within the column. For a moment, he did not know what these things were. Then, though never before having seen them, he recognised each, and a low faint groan burst from him. He fell to his knees, and wild bells began to ring, and mildly, terribly, the aching voices sang: *Primo dolens lancea est corona dolor de Dominus est secundo et tertio gradalis cruenta fulgero.* And down the pillar of white fire came drifting like a cobweb a spear of silver with a burning tip that shone even more fiercely than the light, and from it fell ceaselessly petals of crimson that became butterflies as they faded. And after the burning bleeding spear, a garland of fiery thorns, which also bled, and as the drops burst from it they changed to roses of gold that opened on hearts like the moon and stars themselves. Lastly, there weightlessly fell a chalice of a deep clear flaming green, a colour whose depths seemed bottomless as the sea. And from the lip of the chalice there ran a stream of blood, but the blood was like liquid gold and it blazed brighter than the sun.

Then, another voice spoke at the Knight's right shoulder. It seemed to him it was the voice of a man, but before them, on the ground, a glowing shadow showed with folded wings. "Seek then these things, Cedrevir. The Lance of Pain, the Sorrowing Crown, the Cup of the Life's Blood. That is your Quest, and may you be true to it."

After that came darkness on the wide grey eyes of Cedrevir.

ℭedrevir knew well enough what he had had revealed to him in the vision. And when he came to himself in the Castle of Towers, and recounted what he had seen—for no other but himself had been made witness to it—no man of the fellowship was in ignorance.

In the great light had passed the three holy relics of the Sacrifice of Christ: the Spear that had pierced His side, the Thorn-Crown that had garlanded His brows, the Chalice in which had been shared the sacred blood-wine of the Last Supper, and in which the true blood of His wounds had subsequently been caught.

These articles, long reverenced as aspects of the Martyrdom, are, we say, supposed to have remained on earth. Indeed, their whereabouts, as you may hear, are known, though not by situation. A fortress, called the Castle of the Jewel of Goodness (which is, *Carba Bonem*), that is where they are lodged, and tended there by mysterious guardians. All about

Carba Bonem stretches a vast waste that has no seasons in it, save only heat or cold, but that is named, for its looks and barrenness, the Winterlands. And in the waste is a dead forest, as old as the world, which is named the Wood of the Savage Hart. But the way to it, the forest, the wasteland, the secret Castle of the Jewel of Goodness, they lie off the edge of any map, beyond the memory of any traveller. It is not possible to come to them either by accident or by design. And so the quiet priests told Cedrevir as he kneeled before them, with his dark head bowed and beautiful hands upon the hilt of the sword which bore his device, a couched *sarpafex*.

For many days then he fasted and watched, and kept by himself or with these learned ones from whom he sought counsel. All this while, the images of the vision stayed clear before him, as if he had seen them only a moment ago, and in his ears the voices sang *Dolens lancea. Corona dolor. Gradalis cruenta fulgero.* And the last voice told him, waking and sleeping and watching, *This is your Quest. Be true to it.*

Then at last there came an hour just before sunrise, when the birds piped over the meadows, and the sky was pale as a shell. And Cedrevir came from the Castle of Towers.

He rode as if to a battle, sword, shield and lance at their stations, clad in mail of steel. Both he and the blond horse were trapped and clad in his colour, the blue-grey of distances. And worked on the saddle-cloth, and enamelled on the shield and sword-hilt, the snake-lynx of his blazon, silver and blue and gilt.

In the fields, where the women and boys were labouring, they raised their heads among the tall corn, to watch Cedrevir go by. *There is a Knight of the fellowship*, they said, *he goes Questing.* For the look of setting forth is, though unlike, as unmistakable as that other look with which, often, they return.

So he rode across the Near Lands, towards the north, for north lies the House of Winter, and in the north there are mountains, the high places. And that was all the guide he had to find a spot that is of the earth but not on the earth; a spot that some wise men say is a myth, although also a certain truth.

Beyond the Near Lands lie others less known, but all were wrapped in the late richness of summer, and it may be supposed that human tasks went on there much as they do everywhere. In the orchards, vineyards and fields, they would be making ready for harvest, toiling on into evening under the wide golden skies. At the streams and wells, the women gathered with their washing and their buckets, and by the rivers they cut reeds. Where the castles stood up on the hills, or some massive tower thrust from the woods, the sentries would remark a riding Knight. Some challenge or greeting might be offered him. And now and then, at a lonely chapel, the priest would render lodging, blessing, bread and wine, most frequently in silence.

Perhaps two months Cedrevir travelled, going always northwards, questioning on the way those he met, where it seemed the sign of knowledge was on them, here a hermit in his cell, there an old peasant woman, or a little child even, with a freckle like a star on its forehead. Otherwise, sometimes, the Knight himself would be petitioned for his help, and so would fight, a champion against some wrong. And then again, there were those who sought to tempt him aside, to view a wonder, which might be a mysterious flower that grew in a ruined pagan temple, a thing which would work miracles, or a fountain that gushed from a rock at the striking of his fist. Or there were, from time to time, those who desired to corrupt, such as a white-shouldered woman in a red gown, who leaned from her window so her long hair, scented with strange spice, brushed the face of Cedrevir as he rode by. But her he did not stay for.

One dusk, when the light still hung like a dome of crystal high up in the vault of heaven though all the landscape darkened, Cedrevir came on a broken tower beside a lake. Through the windows of the tower the shining afterglow ran like spears, and the lake itself lay like a great pool of sky fallen on the earth. Not a breeze stirred and not a cloud marred the surface of air or water. Then the stars began to dew and daisy out, and one lit more brightly than the rest upon the strand against the lake. It was a torch that burned in a cage of bronze before a pavilion. And as Cedrevir rode close, other lights bloomed in the pavilion's heart, and turned it to a bulb of softest fire.

Presently two Knights stepped from the pavilion. They were of another fellowship, and on the shield of one was the device of a falcon, and on the other a white bull with wings.

"Where are you going, Knight-at-Arms?" said he of the falcon-shield.

"Northward," replied Cedrevir. "It is a Vowed Journey."

There is not a fellowship, they say, that does not honour the Quest, or the bond of it.

The two Knights nodded. He of the bull-shield spoke next. "We guard here the Lady Marismë, our sister."

"I do not challenge that, nor offer any threat to her."

"No. But she is a seeress, trained in the Luminous Arts," said the falcon-shield knight.

"If you would confer with this lady, our sister, I believe she will do her best to help you," said the bull-shield Knight. "Only this morning, by her art, she descried you, and said, 'Here we will linger and await a traveller from the south. He seeks a key to his Quest, which I maybe shall find for him'."

Now the two Knights stood in shadow beyond the torch, and their faces were bidden under their glistening and dark helms. It came to Cedrevir that he did not credit all that they had said to him, and yet they had spoken no lie. It was the deep shadow of occult things on them, but not of wickedness, as it was only night had darkened the lake.

Just then, the draperies of the pavilion parted with a flutter, and a woman came out. On her the torch shone full, and she was young, and fair, with clear wild eyes. Her white gown was bordered with gems like water-drops, and on her dim hair drifted a net like silver spray.

She said nothing to Cedrevir, and her eyes looked into him and through him. It was a terrible gaze, for she seemed to see his very birth and death, and all other matters that might come between. Then she beckoned, only once, and drew back into the pavilion.

"Follow her," said the falcon-shield Knight. "She is honourable, as are you. And if you were not, she is well able to protect herself. Besides, we are here."

So Cedrevir, in a sort of trance, for her eyes had curiously affected him, dismounted and entered the tent after the lady.

There was a woven carpet on the ground within the tent, and the lamps hung in clusters from posts of bronze. But the lady stood in the centre of the pavilion where there was a pedestal of carved wood. And on the pedestal before her, a golden bowl filled with water.

"Come here and see," said the Lady Marismë.

Cedrevir went to the pedestal, and looked down with her into the bowl.

At first there was only the clarity of the water over the gold. Then there came a turbulence that was in the water and not in it, and a veil seemed to be torn away. There in the bowl, as if miles off, a great host was fighting in the sky. It was a gorgeous and a fearsome battle, for a

244

setting sun, and also bolts of lightning, flashed upon the gems and metals of the warriors, caught upon swords that blazed with inlay, and catching the crests and banners showed devices so mystic and so strange they were not at once understandable. But the sun was going down and the clouds, amethyst and purple and scarlet as the trappings of the Knights, began to lower and smother the scene. Then a trumpet sounded, unheard—but perfectly to be viewed—a long line of fire as from some comet. At the signal, through the cloud-mass, there came riding two mighty lords, and all the host drew back away from them to give them room. And this was very dreadful, for it was plain at once that these two Knights were brothers. Each was golden, each as cleanly beautiful and as sparkling as something made of the sun itself, and as hard to look on. But one was clad all in gold and white, and on his helm was a crest like stars, and on his shield a device for which there was no name at all, it might not be expressed or written, yet Cedrevir, glimpsing it, was filled by joy and terror. The other Knight was arrayed in the colours of heat and fire, and in his crest burned a green jewel so marvellous the eye seemed to drink at it. His shield had no device, but on his banner, that one bore behind him, were embroidered the words: *Non Servian.*

They met with a clash, these two, that shook the sky, their lances splintered and the pieces rained down like blood and lava on the world. Each sword came from its scabbard like a lightning stroke that lit all heaven. And as they dashed once more upon each other, the last of the red sun fell, and on a cloth of gold, dead black yet shining bright, they fought, on and on, as the moon rose under their chargers' feet.

There was no telling how long the combat lasted, time had no meaning there. Cedrevir watched with awe and misgiving, in pity and dread and triumph. It was the First Battle, when the angels of God had fought together. The golden Knight was the Archangel Michael. He clothed like fire, whose banner proclaimed his rebellion—*I will not serve*—Lucifer, before his fall.

When the final blow sang home, ever expected, ever impossible, needful and terrible for all that, the sky seemed to crack from end to end. Cedrevir did not behold the fall of him, Prince Lucifer, yet he saw filing out from the clouds a green shooting-star. It smoked and flamed, tearing downward to the earth. Over hills and heights it ripped its path, and there the ocean spread, glittering and unresting in the moon's sway. And here, in the sea, the emerald meteor went down, hissing. It was the jewel from the helm of Lucifer, the Prince of Hell, quenched in water.

But it was only the clear water in the seeress' bowl that Cedrevir now saw, and the Lady Marismë standing the other side of it, who spoke to him. "That spiritual jewel was the green ruby, his pride and pleasure. It lay in the sea, lost to him, as all else had been lost, until, with the centuries, it was washed ashore. Men, seeing it a stone beyond price, fashioned therefrom a chalice. So to the lords of the earth it passed, after the fire, the air and the water. Solomon the Wise drank from it. And through a line of kings it entered the possession of the Prince of All, Jesus, the Christ. You are seeking His Grail. In the world or out of the world."

"Lady, I am. And have always wondered at the tale, that the ornament of Satan, the Evil One, should become the holy Cup of the Christ."

"But is He not," said Marismë, "called the Redeemer?"

Cedrevir bowed his head. "But," he said, "do you know the road to *Carba Bonem?*"

"I shall tell you its name," she said. "This road is called *I will.*"

Cedrevir sighed. Then, surprised a little, he saw the lamps had burned away and that the soft light in the tent was dawn coming in from without. The moments of the magical revelation had consumed an entire night.

"If you wish," said the Lady Marismë, "you may now accompany us to our kingdom."

Then she spoke a word, and the whole pavilion lifted as a ball of thistledown lifts. It blew up into the air, and all its appurtenances and furnishings with it, and vanished quite. There they were, then, on the strand of the lake, and nearby the lady's Knights leaning on their shields, while on the hill-slope under the old tower the blond horse cropped the grasses.

At this minute the sun rose between two eastern hills, and threw down its rosy sword point foremost straight across the lake. And out of the sun's glory, there might be seen a slender raft with a transparent sail coming slowly towards them, guided by no agency that Cedrevir could discern.

As Cedrevir stood pondering, the Knight of the winged-bull approached him and said, "Your horse is safely penned within an ancient wall, no longer visible, for this was the stronghold of magicians, and power remains. Come now with us, if you will."

Then the raft drew against the shore. The lady stepped on it, and after her the two Knight-brothers, and the three stayed, waiting courteously. So Cedrevir went after them, onto the raft, which hardly looked stout enough to uphold the lady alone. But when he was on it, it began to move again, its sail turning to the morning breeze, and went back the way it had come.

The lady was foremost of the craft, with the sunlight on her, and she said to Cedrevir, "You must know, that in time past we dwelled on shore, where the tower leans, which is all that remains of a great castle. One season, the waters of the lake rose and overwhelmed the land. We, swept away, outlasted the catastrophe. And now, live there."

"Where is that, lady?"

"Beneath your feet, bold Knight. Under the water."

The raft had reached the middle of the lake, and suddenly it stopped, with only its swan-white wake fading behind it.

Then Marismë laughed, and she went out, onto the very water, and after her, her two brothers. And the liquid of the lake buoyantly held them up, and then gently drew them in. And as she slowly sank, Marismë called to Cedrevir. "Bold Knight, will you make bold to follow? We are your protectors in this. I, by the Arts called Luminous, will ensure you against harm. But you must be trustful, fearless, and swift. Follow now or do not follow."

Then Cedrevir also laughed aloud. "Say then I will," said he. (But his eyes, by turns were black or blazing.)

Blithely as they, or so it seemed, he stepped onto the water, which held him upright with only a little motion, just such as the raft had done, then gradually began to take him in, in company with the other three. Thus they sank together under the mirror of the lake.

𝕿his was the curious property either of the lake, or of the lady's magic, that there was no sensation of wetness, only of a silken levity, and that Cedrevir found himself enabled, as did his hosts, freely to breathe the water. Also, that he might hear and see, touch and taste, and in every other way respond and act as if he were above the surface on dry land.

Yet everything was, too, transmuted, and different. All speech, for example, now sounded to him like the sweetest singing. (And he heard besides the songs of the fish, which darted here and there like linnets, as he descended.) As for vision, a dark radiance hung over all things, and proceeding through the kingdom beneath the lake, every movement was swathed in the sleeves, robes and veil of silver eddies.

Under the water was a land that, in many ways, resembled the country of the earth. There was a road there, which led to a castle on a hill, but the road was paved with great round pebbles, washed smooth and lucent as glass, and above, the castle glimmered green as peridot. All about the road were orchards and groves, where fruit grew shining, like apples of milky gold.

The fish sat singing in the branches of the trees, whose foliage was fine and etiolate as strands of a girl's hair. Under the castle clustered a town of stone, and sometimes men and women passed to and fro. Seeing the Lady Marismë, these persons bowed to her. There was also something shadow-like about them, and it seemed to Cedrevir that here, too, though nothing was hidden, yet all was not shown.

As they neared the castle, the doors of the building opened and a Knight rode forth. He was clad in black, even to the plumes of his helm's high crest. The horse he sat was black and thin, but it was armoured all over, and its legs braced by black iron. And when they climbed and came up with the Black Knight, he turned his head to look at them, and he had no face, only a skull.

"It is Death," said Marismë, and she saluted him, and her brothers with her.

Death nodded, and made to pass on. Then, apparently noting Cedrevir, he spoke to him. "I shall meet again with you, in another place," said Death. "But that is many years hence."

Cedrevir crossed himself. But he would not be shamed, and looked long on Death, and it began to seem to him that behind the skull, there was a man's face, and two sombre eyes that regarded him. No sooner did he think this, than the apparition raised his hand and lowered the black visor of his helm. Death rode away down the hill on the iron horse.

"Do not be concerned," said Marismë. "Our kind, though we live, are also numbered with the drowned. He has some rights over us, being in part our king." And in the open doorway of the citadel castle, she turned to Cedrevir and said; "There are three mighty citadels of Powers. The Powers of the water, which are inconstant and eternal. The Powers of earth and fire, which mingle, and are of the passions, and by which most wrong-doing is invoked. The Powers of the air, whereof there are many kingdoms, for they lie closest to God—not in that they are in the sky, but in their permeation of everything, and their invisibility like breath,

248

and life itself."

When she had said this, she went forward into the castle, entering a huge hall there that had looked empty and dark before, but lit up at her coming.

Presently, as it would happen in a sort of dream, Cedrevir found himself seated on a dais at the lady's right hand, before a board draped with damask. On this, every delicacy that might be got from the dry world, or that might be found in fresh water, was displayed on dishes of gold and silver, while servers processed ceaselessly through the hall, bearing jewelled trenchers and longnecked ewers of wine. And in that ambience of water, not a morsel of food was lost, or a drop of liquor spilled out or mixed in the currents of the lake, but flowed from beaker to cup, from cup to lip. Down from the roof hung gilded wheels, each with a score of flaming candles in them, and in the walls torches burned, and not a fire was quenched, though the smokes wove endless patterns through the water.

In the body of the hall, not a place was vacant at the long tables. A full company of Knights and ladies dined together. And while they dined, proud dogs with collars of pearls lay by the tables or prowled about for scraps. The servers carved and the pages hastened on their errands, and the minstrels woke their harps. And on everything lay the iridescence of the lake. But under everything there lay a dimness and a shadow.

Perhaps several hours passed at the feasting. After this time, a trumpet was sounded and a silence fell. Up the hall there walked a page clothed in black, pale as a plant of the deep woods, and carrying a dish of horn and onyx. On the dish lay a fruit from the aqueous orchards below the castle. Coming to Cedrevir, but no other, the boy kneeled: "Will you eat of this fruit, Knight?"

And Cedrevir hesitated. "Do you not come from Death?"

"If I do, it is not himself he sends you."

"What, then?"

"The fruit, which is not forbidden yet which is a fruit of knowledge. Perhaps a warning, perhaps a prophecy, perhaps a symbol or a test of heart or brain. Take the fruit, and see."

Then Cedrevir took the fruit, and at once the boy vanished. Cedrevir gazed long at the apple's satin skin, as he had outstared Death himself. And in the core of the fruit the Knight thought he saw a fire, but it was not impure or poisoned. So he put it before him and cut it open with his dagger.

Cedrevir started back in horror. For from the apple came a scaled worm, a serpent, which his knife had severed. Yet, it did not bleed, and both parts of it ended in a head, each having cold sad eyes that looked at him.

"You have wounded me," said the snake.

"Pardon me for that," the Knight answered, "I did not do it knowingly."

"You lie," said the snake.

"Not so."

"Do you not recognise me, then? I am the Serpent, that creature cursed of God and man. I am the Beguiler. I am Satan, your Enemy. Say now you do not wound me knowingly."

"If you are he," said Cedrevir, "then, knowingly, I would cut you from me, mind and body and soul, a hundred times over."

"It has been easy for you, this once," said the snake.

And then it shrank and shrivelled, until it was no wider than a thread, and the thread went to ashes and crumbled, and was gone.

"What is the message of this, lady?" asked Cedrevir of Marismë.

"That you are already on your road. For no tempter would come to you if you had not entered the sphere of his sight."

Then she rose to her feet and the great hall grew vague and silent, as if a huge cloak had been thrown over it, and every light was smoored.

But at her side her brothers waited.

Marismë took Cedrevir by the hand, and led him out of the hall, and up a curving flight of marble stairs, into the well of a tower. At its summit was a chamber, in which the windows were pillared by stone, but the casements were water where the fish swam in and out as they pleased. The two Knights took their stance, as at the pavilion, one either side the door, which then closed fast of itself.

"Now Cedrevir," said the Lady Marismë. "You are young and you are thralled in my spell. You are here with me, and blameless, and who is to see us?"

And she showed him a bed, scented with flowers and soft as snow, and hung with heavy curtains of silver stuff. Next, she threw off her gown, and stood in her shift, as translucent as the lake itself. But when she had done this, he saw through her, through shift and skin and flesh and hair, and she was made of bones, as the face of Death had been.

"Lady," he said, "I will lie beside you, but in no other way."

She nodded, as Death had done, and drawing back the covers of the bed, she revealed to him that a barrier of upturned blades ran down the middle of it, a palisade of steel. Marismë stretched herself one side of this, and he the other, the blades between them. And all at once Cedrevir slept, in that bed of swords, and in his sleep the fence grew higher and touched the roof of the chamber, which caught alight and fell down on him, and at that he woke.

He lay beside the lake, on the shore in the sunrise, and up the slope, where the ruin was, the patient horse cropped the grasses.

There was no sign of any other thing, for his hair and garments had no trace of wet. He was hungry and thirsty. The feast under the lake had not sustained him.

Yet, on opening his right hand, he found lying in the palm a little coal-black shell, and there fell from it one water drop, like a single tear.

The Knight of the Fellowship of the Circle rode northwards another month or more, and the summer waned from the land. He came among places of sterility, where the trees were thin as famine, a burned country. In the valleys they had long since stripped the white corn, and the sun had withered off the grass and leaves.

Only crows stood sentinel on the bald hilltops. In the north, miles distant, were clouds that did not move, and these Cedrevir took for the mountains.

One noon, when the barren heat was very great, Cedrevir saw a church below him in the downlands, by a stream. The banks were shaded by walnut trees, and the water was fresh. The fruits on the walnuts were like stones, however, and when he smote on the church door it sagged wide. No one was there but lizards that rushed away like the scorched leaves over the floor. A window shaped as a wheel hung in the east wall; before it an antique banner dipped from a rafter, dark red, the fringes rusty. The altar was singular, a block of quartz, and in the depths of it might imperfectly be seen a war-axe, though how it had come there, there was no telling.

Cedrevir, going out again, tethered his horse, and stretched himself among the trees to rest through the heat of the day.

No sooner had he closed his eyes than he heard a weird, wild pagan chanting, and shouts, and the tramp of feet coming toward him along the valley.

Cedrevir started up—and as he did so, the noises died on the air. Only the stream lilted in its narrow bed, and the horse whispered to the plants under the wall's shade.

Cedrevir sat down again, and leaned his head on his hand and shut his eyes. Instantly, he heard the chanting and the outcry, as before but louder still. Now he did not stir, but only waited, and presently shadows began to flicker and dance over his eyelids, as if a company of people passed.

Cedrevir opened his eyes a second time, and wide and grey they gazed on nothing but the arid afternoon.

A third time he withdrew his sight, and past him the people trampled, and bells rang and women shrilled. Now Marismë, the lady in the lake, had said to him: The name of your road is *I will*. So then Cedrevir said softly to himself, "It is to be seen if it is to be heard, and I will see this thing and what it is."

And as he had smitten on the church door, so he smote open his own eyes with the thought.

Then he saw this: across the valley floor, following the course of the stream, came a band of men and women. They were summer-tanned, lean and ragged, but they had garlanded their heads with twisted briars. The women rang bells and the men brandished staves. In the midst was a cart, which they pulled violently along, and in the cart was bound a young maiden, wan as if near death, though in her dark hair too was caught a crown, of vine-leaves and poppies. Plainly, she was to be a sacrifice.

Cedrevir got to his feet and loosened the sword in its sheath. It transpired that, as he had formerly not seen these people, they could not even now see him; he was invisible. Unhindered then he trod behind them, and when they mounted a nearby hill, kept after.

There, among the stubble, was a ring of lifeless trees, from which the carrion birds rose at their arrival like flung, screaking stones. The ground under the trees, where they had been feeding, was littered by bones and bits of rotted meat. The spot smelled of death. As the men lifted the girl from their cart, she began to weep, but she did not beg for any mercy, judging it, seemingly, beyond them. They tied her fast to one of the trunks. She drooped there like a dying lily on a black branch. The maddened crowd ran about the tree, wailing and calling, and then an ancient man, cackling at the curtailment of youth, crept round the ring, sprinkling from a censer on the ground. It contained blood, which smoked and stank, and the crows, which had returned to the upper boughs, clapped their wings in greed.

When the ancient had completed his ritual, the people plunged together and swirled suddenly away. They went by Cedrevir, where he waited at the tree-ring's edge, without a look, and some even stumbled against him, but paid no heed to it. Their noise, which now had something more of fear than celebration, diminished and was gone. A vast silence settled on the hill. At this, the girl raised her drenched eyes and looked all about her. Her tears fell and she shook with terror, but nor did she make any sound.

Then there came a rumbling in the earth, under their very feet, and Cedrevir unslung from his shoulder the shield fronted with the *sarpafex*, and drew his sword.

In another second, the ground bulged and split, and out of it there burst, flaming like a molten thing, a huge lizard, a dragon.

It was the colour of brass, and in size half the height again of a man. It bore up with it a fearful smell of sulphur and decayed matter, and as it grubbed and pawed, discarding the soil, searching for the accustomed offering, from its jaws ran venomous breath tinctured with fire.

Cedrevir stepped forward, and lifting his shield against the exhalation, called to it.

The dragon turned at once, and its orbs of eyes, that looked blind with unthinking malice, yet appeared to take him in.

"Before her, first you must be done with me, Devil-spawn," said the Knight. "Now God be at my side, in Christ's Name." And he went forward straight at the dragon, but, as he did so, covered his head and breast with the shield. A wave of the filthiness and heat seared Cedrevir like a furnace blast. Yet he came on, and struck with his sword, upward, against the underside of the ribs.

But the sword crashed on the scales of the beast, and under the scales the cage of ribs was a monumental thing. He bruised it, for the monster roared, and in the trees the waiting crows exclaimed and took flight. But no more than that he did.

Cedrevir fell back now, for the awful breath and fire of the dragon were greatly weakening.

It slunk after him, and raking at him with its forefeet continuously, inflicted instead horrid wounds in the earth, for he was too quick for it.

Then again, he struck at the beast, at its jaw that weaved above him, and one of the huge teeth in its mouth was broken at the blow.

Down the hill they passaged, the dragon sweeping with its claws and pouring out its bane-breath, Cedrevir avoiding its attack as he could—and here and there a tree stump or a boulder sprang alight in lieu of him, or cracked in pieces.

But it was in the thoughts of the Knight that he would lead it down, away from the damsel, to the stream below the church. The dragon's element was fire, but there lay water.

Among the walnut trees they passed, and Cedrevir stepped back into the stream and felt, through his mail, its blessed lesser warmth like coolness. The dragon baulked. It would not come on. It snarled, and the small stones of the walnuts might be heard popping and snapping.

"Is it water you spurn, or the holy church above?"

Then the dragon spoke to Cedrevir. "You have wounded me. Is that not enough? Let me return to the maiden who is meant for me. I would not slay you. I honour your valour. You did not mean to wound me."

"Is it you?" said Cedrevir. "You were before a little snake."

"I? Who knows me, or what I have been, or may be?" said the dragon. The words came from its mouth, in a pure voice, shining like an organ-note in the flaxen air. The words came from it, yet no men could be sure it was the dragon which uttered them.

Cedrevir answered: "You are the creature of Satan, let him protect you. I call upon my Lord. You are the weapon of the Enemy. Oh God!" cried out Cedrevir, "send me a weapon here to meet this foe."

At that, the ground quaked, even as it had when the dragon erupted out of it. Above the stream, where the church stood, there came a sound of rending, and up into the air shot a beam of light. Cedrevir did not turn, he held his eyes on the dragon, and covered himself over with his shield. But also he let fall his sword, and raising his right arm high, opened his hand. And into it there came a heavy rounded haft, and at the haft's end a wedge of brightness like a jewel. It was the axe he had seen bedded in the altar.

"I will," repeated Cedrevir. He lifted up the axe and whirled it.

The dragon coughed out a spurt of livid fire, which enveloped Cedrevir, and seemed to touch his heart and shatter it. But yet still he let the revolving axe fling free, and even as he sank down, he saw the axe-head meet the dragon's skull, and cleave it and become embedded in it. And he saw too that the skull seemed made of a substance like quartz.

The cool water laved the mail, the hair and flesh of Cedrevir. He lay under the stream, dreaming of the dragon's death. But he could not breathe the water of the stream as in the lake he had. He must rise up again and shake it from him.

He climbed the hill wearily, and the crows berated him high above. (The dragon's corpse would be difficult eating.) Going to the dead tree, he cut the ropes which bound the maiden. She saw him clearly, as she had seen the battle for her life. She dropped at his feet. She clasped his ankles, and the garland of poppies slid from her shadowy hair.

"You are at liberty," he said.

"Yes, and I thank and bless you for it. But do not leave me here, for those savages of the region will themselves kill me. They have worshipped the dragon all the years of their lives." And she looked at him with the blackest eyes, and her mouth was red as the poppies. "I am called Melasind. A great lord is kin to me. Take me only to his kingdom. It lies northward. It is not far."

$\mathfrak{C}$edrevir set the girl before him on the horse. She was slender and silent, no trouble to them, but for her beauty—which did trouble the Knight. For her beauty was of a subtle and uneasy sort, like smoke.

She gave no direction to the home of her kindred, the kingdom of that lord she had not named. Northward, she had said, northward they rode, and she was content. She did not question Cedrevir on any matter.

At night, they slept upon the ground, and gentle Melasind made no complaint. She wrapped herself in her mantle and lay down, her cheek pillowed in her hand. Her slumber was discreet, but her hair strayed as she slept, it coiled and shimmered on the earth. She had been the dragon's bride, and her power over desire came from that, her virginity burned under her skin.

By day the sky was brazen. The landscape became a desert, flat-tabled plains where drifts of minerals sparkled. Not a tree grew. Water, where it was to be had, lay still in the cups of stone and tasted of metal, granite, or cinders.

Then, as an evening came on after the sunset, the girl said to the Knight, "Do not pause now. For another hour's riding will bring us to the kingdom I told you of."

Cedrevir looked before them, to the north. He saw dim, folded plateaux and the vault of night. There was no sign of any road, any wall or tower.

"There, lady?"

"There," she said. "Where the stars are coming clear."

Then Cedrevir beheld a strangeness in the sky. On the height of it some stars were flashing out, a whole constellation, but it had a form which he had never seen before in any land, or place, nor ever heard spoken of.

It was like a spear or sword, but winged, the clustered stars thick like diamonds at its centre, raying away to glinting dust at the huge pinion-points, and the whole dazzling more fiercely than any other star of the sky, or the full moon even.

Cedrevir said nothing else to the maiden, and she nothing more to him. They rode on towards the winged sword of stars. And an hour passed, as she had said it must, but with no feature of the plain altering. Then, "Draw rein," said she. And when he had done so, she leaned forward and cried in a high voice thin as a wire:

"Ex orio per Nomine."

That done, she bowed her head meekly and clasped her hands. But on the plain a mighty wind rose up. It seemed to lift the very corners of the world up after it, shards and dusts flew into the air, and in the welter of these things, soundless as an opening flower, Cedrevir saw a castle rising out of the earth. Its battlements and towers were pierced with lights, and banners curled about the tops of it. All was stillness as the wind died down. Then from the castle's walks the trumpets clamoured.

"Do not delay, we are expected," said Melasind.

So they rode forward, and as they went, the starburst of the winged sword was eclipsed behind the stoneworks, its point seeming to stab slowly to the castle's heart.

There was a gate, with torched turrets either side. The portals of this now began to open, and a Knight rode out. In the torches' light he was dressed in red, his mail red as new copper, and he was mounted on a red horse.

"You are welcome," he said courteously, and to the Lady Melasind he bowed.

With great surprise, Cedrevir heard her give a shrill merry laugh, and felt her shrink away between his arms. He looked, and saw that as the torches found her now, Melasind was a slender girl-child, some seven or eight years of age. She turned to him her laughing face and said, "In the world, I am wise. But here, in the house of my kin, I am as a child. Help me get down, Sir Knight."

So Cedrevir dismounted and lifted her down.

With misgiving, yet ever with the purpose of the Quest, he followed her under the great gate, into the castle which had risen from the earth.

A night and a day, Cedrevir remained, the guest of an unknown host, in the Castle of Earth and Fire. And so it was. For by day, only the slightest sunlight entered through the embrasures, that were closed besides by panes of thick glass tinted with cinnabar. Constantly the lamps and torches and candles burned there. It was a place of great heat, and of leaping fire-cast shadows.

The servants of the Castle waited on Cedrevir, as, in the mansions of his own land, he was wont to be waited on. There seemed nothing uncommon in it, though they did not speak to him of anything, nor did he interrogate them. At the ending of that first day, sunset filled the windows, and the Knight in red mail came to Cedrevir, greeted him with all proper forms, and asked him to descend the Castle to a hall of feasting.

Together they went down countless wide stairs of burnished basalt, by passages and chambers red with sunset and fire, and going always lower, until Cedrevir believed they had now passed under the ground. But he made no remark upon this fact, nor did the Red Knight speak of it.

At length, the last stair ended at a door, which opened itself at their approach. Beyond lay a garden, most unusual and enigmatic in its looks. No daylight ever came there, it was far beneath the earth, but in the midst of it was a pool of ebony water from which proceeded a sourceless glowing light. On the water the whitest lilies rested, and sometimes, in the lighted dark, the gold fin of a fish would blink. The walks of the garden were laid with opals and other pallid fiery gems. Herbs and flowers stood in the beds, but they had no hue nor perfume. All across the garden, nevertheless, a tall rose tree had spread itself, and every rose on the tree was crimson. But when they came near to it, Cedrevir saw that these roses were made of rubies, garnets and spinels.

Beyond the tree was another door, and through the door a hall.

They left the garden and entered the hall, and stood on its threshold. A million candles were burning there, above tables covered with cloth-of-gold, and against hangings that ran with gold, on cups of sheerest crystal and platters trimmed with precious stones. But none sat down there, and presently Cedrevir perceived that the dust of years had gathered over everything. And, as the fish had winked in the pool, now and then a black rat would flicker under the draperies.

At the room's far end, the child Melasind sat on the flagstones. She wore now a gown of yellow scarlet, and her hair was crowned with the colourless flowers of the garden. In her lap she held an agate bowl and a knife of bone, and she wept.

Cedrevir went to her and kneeled down before her. "Lady," said he, "why are you crying so bitterly?"

"The lord, my kindred, is sick," said Melasind. "Only this bowl, brimmed by the blood of a virgin, can revive him at such times. See, I have been nerving myself to it, but am afraid."

Cedrevir frowned.

The Red Knight stood at his left shoulder and said, "It is as she tells you. For long ago my lord, who is the lord of this kingdom, received a grievous wound. It does not heal. Only virgin blood can make him well, and that only for a little while."

"I do not ask the nature of the wound, nor how he came to it," Cedrevir replied. "The voice of fate, shouting or murmuring, is always to be heard on such a journey as mine. My vow is also of chastity. I have never joined with a woman, or committed any carnal act. I am as virgin as this child, and far stronger. Therefore, I offer your lord instead my blood, without fear. For my soul is in profound safekeeping."

The lord's Knight, hearing this, bowed very low. "He will receive your gift with thanks," said he. And he withdrew from the hall. But the child-girl only stared at Cedrevir.

"You must attend me," he said. "When it is done, take your scarf and bind the cut tightly. Now give me the bowl, and if you wish, look away from what I do."

So Cedrevir opened a vein in his left arm with the bone knife, and filled the agate bowl with his blood. When the deed was finished, the child-girl ran to him and bound his arm tightly, not looking at the cut. But then, she dipped her finger in the blood.

"You shall take him this yourself," said Melasind. "I will guide you to my lord's chamber."

Cedrevir felt a little weakness from the loss of the blood, and he remembered how he had lain down in the stream after the dragon's death, and heard the water singing in his ears, but not as it had sung under the lake.

"Where does your lord lie?" asked Cedrevir. "In one of the great towers of the Castle?"

"No. He is below us, here."

Cedrevir followed her, as she bore the bowl of bright blood, and her steps were quick and light, his slower and less gladsome.

She took him through a narrow door, and beyond the passage sloped and widened, lit only by the raw torches in its walls. Till suddenly Cedrevir could see they were entering among huge hollow caves underground. Soon enough, the lighted corridor fell behind them, and on all sides unfurled the shining dark, like eternal night. Yet nevertheless he could tell their path, for a hot radiance beamed out from the agate bowl.

Shortly, Melasind led him over a bridge of flint, under which, miles down, an unseen river lashed its furious way. On the other side of the bridge was a front of granite, in which a tall door of dull metal stood weirdly ajar. Through this slit went the maiden-child with her bloody lamp, and Cedrevir after her.

At once, he seemed struck nearly blind. For though no light came out from the place beyond the door, yet light blazed there within. The means of the light Cedrevir could not discern, but the cause of its power he could barely miss. For the cavern that plunged away before him was piled with such treasure it would seem to beggar the richest kings of the world above.

"Come, follow still," said Melasind, and she led him on now up hills and along mountainsides of piled gold, made all of coins and chains and casks, crowns and swords and rings, and furnishings of every type. And through the gold ran streams of silver, and down its slopes rattled slips of jewels that their feet had disturbed. Until, coming over a ridge of this colossal wealth, Cedrevir looked upon a lake of sapphires, emeralds and rubies, so blue, so green, so bloodmost red, it seemed to boil and to flash lightnings. But in the centre of the lake, as the dragon lies upon its hoard, lay stretched a man on cushions of silk. And he was a giant, clad in black armour, his face turned away, so his locks of hair, that outshone the gold, flowed on the silk like fire.

Then Melasind gave a cry, and she ran down into the lake of jewels, and over it, and came to the giant and leaned above him. After a moment, she called to Cedrevir again: "Come, Sir knight."

So Cedrevir walked out across all the jewels and when he reached the giant, gazed in his face. It was a countenance of such hideousness that none could look at it unmoved, nor without shrinking. For it was not the ugliness of any fleshly deformity, its horror stemmed from some inner twisting and torture. Then the eyes opened, and filled the face instead with an appalling beauty, but it was the endless beauty of agony that never ends.

"So you behold me, Knight," said the fallen one, and at his voice, no more than a sigh, stone and metal, skin and bone, heart and mind, were ravished and trembled and grew shamed and sick. "See what I possess," said the Lord of the Castle of Earth and Fire, "see what is mine. And see what I am brought to, that a child must fetch me gruel. I thank you for your charity, Sir Knight. Say now, may I drink?"

"Drink," said Cedrevir, but he must turn away, and leaning on a mace of silver that protruded from the lake of jewels, he hid his eyes with his hand.

After a moment, though, the wondrous horror of the voice whispered again. "Your gift does me good. There is great vitality in you. Whom then, do you serve?"

"Only my Fellowship," answered Cedrevir. "And God."

The fallen giant drank again. The bowl was drained. He said, "I serve none. I will not serve, and so may never be free. Do you think my punishment has lasted sufficiently long? No, I am not punished. I need cry out humbly only once *Ut Libet*. But will not do it. It is my pride, not your *God*, that binds me. *Ut libet. Nunquam. Ut qui libentam.*"

Cedrevir, unable to prevent himself, had gazed once more into that awful face of a fallen dragon, and in the deeps of the golden eyes he saw printed those words—*Ut qui libentam*. (Seeing that I will.)

"Go now," said the mouth that had drunk his blood. "Go, take your reward with this damsel. For I would not see this special virtue of yours wasted on another after I have had benefit from it."

"Lord," Cedrevir replied, "you know I may not take any pleasure with her in that way."

"That is to be seen."

And then there came up in the golden eyes a redness, like two dead suns that rose underground, and over the mouth, and all the features, went a ghastly flaring, as if wax melted in flame, and the being roared, and all the cavern seemed to break apart and the jewels rushed up over their heads like a storm of water.

Melasind took to her heels, and catching at his hand, she pulled Cedrevir after her. And in his terror, which was like no other fear in the world, he allowed her to do it. Together they escaped the cavern of riches, and ran over the unillumined bridge above the unseen river, and up the slopes of stone into the passage, and so back into the banquet hall, with all its places laid and not a single guest. And beyond that they ran, to the subterranean garden, and here both the doors slammed on them, and cold silence fell.

Cedrevir felt a longing for water, and leaning to the lily-pool, he raised some to his face and lips. As the rings settled in the pool, he saw reflected, between the white chalices of the flowers, Melasind, and she was no longer a child, but a damsel again, with sweet high breasts and a rosy mouth, and hair that poured to her hips.

Then Cedrevir drew his sword and smote that image in the pool so it smashed in pieces.

The damsel laughed. "But did he not give me to you?" said she. "And here I am, and we are prisoners in this garden. Who is to see?"

"I should see it," replied Cedrevir. "I am both warrior and priest. I will not break the vows I made. They have fashioned me, in water and fire, on the anvil, as this sword was fashioned. Though I desire you, lady, which you, and he, both know too well, I have another duty, and a better lust than for your love."

"Alas," said Melasind, and she hurried to him, swift and sinuous as a snake, and threw her arms about him and sought his lips with hers. But he remembered her, how she had been a child, sexless and innocent, who cried at the notion of a wound. And desire left him, and he put her away, though the heat of her body burned him through. Lifting his voice, he cried out then, as she herself had done on the night plain: *"Ex orio per Nomine!"*

But the Name invoked was now Another's, and all the power and passion of Cedrevir, which that place had stirred, turned otherwise, tore wide the enchantment.

With a screeching and thunder, the Castle of Earth and Fire seemed to burst, and up from the garden rushed the whirlwind, and taking Cedrevir in its grasp, hurled him through disintegrated stone and iron, glass and fire, onto the surface of the tindered land.

And as he lay on the breast of the world, the ground shook, and on the horizon a fiery crack, the shape of a serpent and two or three miles in length, healed itself, and thereafter everything was darkest night, without a beacon or a star.

But transfixing his palm, even through the steel of the gauntlet, was a blood-red thorn. And plucking it out, it left no mark on him. (And the cut from which he had filled the agate bowl had also vanished, leaving only a scar, a broken circle like the sickle moon.)

𝕴n a dream, then, he heard the voices sing:

First the Sword of Paining,
Second the Sorrow's crowning,
Third the Blood-Grail shining.

As in the Castle of Towers they had sung, dulcet as silver bells.

And after these, he heard the seeress Lady Marismë, who said, "Water inconstant and eternal, earth and fire that mingle, and the many kingdoms of the air."

When he wakened, the land was changed, as if swept by a mighty broom that had tumbled boulders, and the sky of earliest day showed the strokes of the broom in long riven skeins of cloud.

But northward, now, he saw the mountains sharp and clear as swords. Partially transparent they seemed, and hard as forged steel. Yet before the mountains was a vast forest lying on the land like the smoke of an old burning.

Now, this might be that forest called the Wood of the Savage Hart, and since he looked on it and found it there, Cedrevir so named it. Mounting his horse, which wandered docile on the plain, he rode north again, and in a few hours entered under the tangled branches.

In the stories, the trees of that forest were all dead, but the towering trees of the forest Cedrevir had entered, though leafless and often leaning with half their clawed roots from the soil—which was itself only of dust and stones—yet they seemed to pulse and throb with liveness, as if with the very beat of hearts. And even those trees which had fallen seemed quickened by a strange force, and here and there the roots had driven back into the unnourishing ground.

There were no birds, nor any truly living thing which Cedrevir might see, or hunt for food. But, as a Knight of a fellowship he was accustomed to fasting. As the noiseless days and silent nights went by, his thoughts grew only flawless and crystalline, and for the horse, it survived by sometimes chewing on a kind of mastic that exuded from the trees. Of water there was no scarcity, for the nights were chill and brought a frost which, in the sunrise, melted in quantities, dripping off the boughs and gathered in the stones until midday.

The only flowers of that forest were the sun and the moon. There was too an overcast, which hid the stars, and also that constellation of the winged sword. But probably this had been, in any case, a sorcery.

One dawn he woke from a deep sleep, in which the bell-voices chimed. Not the length of a spear away, a creature was drinking at one of the water-puddles in the stones. It was a hart, cold white, but between the forked horns of it a gold blossom seemed stamped upon its forehead.

It appeared to Cedrevir that this was a magical beast, the genius of the wood, and so he rose and began to go towards it, but at that the hart tossed its head and ran away. Yet it ran only to a clearing some score of trees distant, and there again it stood, flickering in its whiteness like a candle-flame, as if awaiting him.

Accordingly, Cedrevir untethered and mounted his horse, and rode slowly after the hart, which seeing him come on began to trot before him.

In this manner, the morning and the noon passed, the Knight following and the white hart dancing before him. If Cedrevir should spur his horse, then the hart would run, so fleet the man seemed likely to lose it. However, if Cedrevir should lag or pause, the hart too stayed itself, browsing on the dark mastic of the tree as the horse did.

When the afternoon came down into the forest, still the hart went on and Knight rode after. It was a cheerless day, the season was no longer summer, nor anything, cool and dry, and without kindness.

There seemed no change in the woods, but for the natural alteration of the light. Later, a pale amber westering glow flowed through the trees.

Later yet, the dusk began.

Where did the creature lead him? In the crystal thoughts of Cedrevir, from which the fast too had sloughed most of the need for sleep or rest, the motive of the pursuit of the hart shone indivisible and immaculate. On a Vowed Journey, such things had all a reason.

Night won the land.

They had reached another of the hollow clearings, and now the hart stopped of its own accord and turned to face its pursuer. It gleamed dimly, even in the utter dark, and between its horned brows the golden flower was like a lingering speck of day. Then, a fearful metamorphosis occurred. The hart leapt abruptly high into the air, so its feet no longer touched the earth, and as it did this, it seemed to leap out of its own skin, which pleated away into nothing behind it. From the skin of the hart there emerged a huge white lion, with a grey hoary mane like the spun frost, and eyes of flame. And in midair it sprang at Cedrevir, for his throat, and for his soul too it seemed.

The horse neighed in terror and plunged aside. The lion-beast, meeting the horse's flanks in its spring, ripped with huge talons, but only the cloth and leather of the caparison were breached. The lion hung then from this vantage, glaring in the face of the Knight. And in the black silence of the forest, the hatred and blood-craving of the lion were like a torch. But Cedrevir had by now freed his sword. He swung it over and thrust it down, into the lion's jaws, until the hilt, where was engraved the sigil of the *sarpafex* grated on the fangs. And the eyes of the lion turned to blackened coals. It fell away, and lay on the earth, still faintly shining, so Cedrevir beheld it was now only a flaccid pelt, without sinews, flesh or bones.

Cedrevir did not marvel, for he had come into a state of the marvellous, where nothing surprised him. But he bowed his head and gave customary thanks to God. Lifting his eyes again, he saw glowworms in the wood, and then that they were not glowworms, but the lit tapers of a procession of men and women, which wandered through the trees into the glade. As they drew closer, he noted also that they were garbed, the men as priests, the women as nuns. Reaching the spot where the skin of the lion sprawled, two of the priests raised it and bore it off. They spared no glance to Cedrevir, but passed him, chanting softly some litany he could not recognise.

Cedrevir leaned from his horse. He caught at the mantle of one of the nuns. "Where is it that your mysterious company goes?"

She answered, "The earth is fading. The sky will fall. You may follow us, if you wish."

"But where, holy lady?"

"It is true, all places are as one in the world's death."

And with no more reply than that (though that perhaps reply enough), she slipped from him. And all of them had left him, the lion's skin carried in their midst.

Cedrevir dismounted and, leading the horse, went after.

Soon the way ascended. They climbed, the religious procession, and behind it Cedrevir. The trees thinned. The Knight looked about him, and saw they had emerged on a range of cliffs, which might be at the foot of the northern mountains, although these he could not make out. Though the forest had been stricken and non-verdurous, these cliffs were bare of everything but the rock itself. Presently, however, he might see the destination of the travellers. It was a skeletal chapel, roofless and wrecked.

A curious light came down. At first, Cedrevir took it for the glowworm sheen of the tapers. But then, thinking over the words the nun had spoken, he looked up to heaven. And there was a strange sight, and one which filled him with a deep and sorrowing fear.

The night above had become a canopy, opaque and impenetrable, empty of moon or stars. Yet it was a canopy wonderfully adorned. Across the whole length of it, which stretched to the twelve quarters, ran scrolls and frettings of gold and silver, not in motion but still, as if painted there. And as Cedrevir gazed at this, the whole of it seemed always sinking a little nearer, so that indeed the sky, or this entity of the sky, was falling, by slow inches on the earth below. And from it nothing alive could fly away, but must be crushed beneath. Yet so beautifully fashioned it was, the great black coffin-lid of heaven, that now he saw gems of exquisite lucidity set into the metal, lilies of pearl and asphodel of the clearest topaz, and hyacinths of such purple corundum he could hardly bear to look at them. In his heart, Cedrevir wept. God, dismayed by the unrelenting wickedness of Man, let down the sky to end His creation. Yet, too, he honoured it with beauty. Not cruel water nor ravening fire would be the quietus of mankind, but black air flowered with jewels. Yes, Cedrevir's heart wept, and overflowed with pity for the Creator, and love and an anguish of fear, and resignation, also.

And so he followed the company into the chapel, and here they doused their lights, and were illumined only by the falling slow lights of the sky.

But where they had laid the lion's skin, suddenly there was also a fire on the earth. The pelt blazed up, and the flames divided. Out of them came daintily stepping a little snowy fawn, with a golden cross between its brows. For a moment it was clearly visible, and then it vanished, and the glittering ashes of the fire snuffed out to nothing.

A wind blew through the chapel, among the silent watchers there. It was fierce yet strengthless, all the winds of the world flattened under the lid of the sky. After the wind had passed, dew or rain fell, but it died to dust even as it touched the ground.

Looking up again, through roofless walls, Cedrevir saw the canopy had come so close that every flower and decoration might be measured by the eye, huge in dimension, with gems set within gems. Then again, he bowed his head. And heaven fell.

There was neither heat nor cold, nor sound nor vision nor thought. There was no pain or smothering. A vast *un-ness* covered all, and all was absorbed in it.

After the darkness, there was light. After the death of sleep, a second awakening: The Knight Cedrevir was as you have yourself seen him, well-made, and fair to look on, and he stood as formerly, clad in mail and fully armed, but alone, upon a mountainside. The world lay far beneath, or it was gone entirely to a ring of palest most insubstantial brightness, like the sea.

The sky was all around, roseate blue with dawn, and clouds passed below and on all sides, moving leisurely as swans on a morning lake. And the sky too was full of golden flowers and silver flowers, like those which had fretted the lid of the Annihilation. But these flowers hung, as if woven in a tapestry, and as he began again to climb, now and then they brushed his face or shoulders, and they had only the touch of flowers, but they did not break or fall.

Above there was a castle, which grew up from the mountain, and as it grew it changed to gold, so it was a thing of fire like the sun, and he could not keep his eyes on it. There was a road also under his feet, and it was laid with lapis lazuli and sapphire. While, at the roadside, trees sprang out of the mountain, and their boughs were all blossom, yet fruit hung from them that shone like mirrors and gave off a perfume like no fruit or bloom of the earth.

By accident or by design it is not possible to come there, but by faith and will, sometimes, it is.

For Cedrevir had entered a kingdom of the Kingdoms of the Air, and before him rose *Carba Bonem*, blinding him with its glory.

As he approached the gate, a horn blew within the Castle, a long and liquid note, and the doors of the gate opened without a sound.

Within lay a court. It was paved with marble, and on every side the towers went up blazing, and one tower above the others like a shaft of flame, whose head was not to be distinguished.

At the centre of the court stood a tawny willow, the curved trunk of which was braced with silver. From its boughs depended the helms and swords, spears and shields and colours, of many scores of Knights, marked with their various devices, so it was a gaudy object, this brown tree. Under it, there waited a maiden dressed in sackcloth. Her hair was white as salt, and her eyes the pallid green-azure grey of glass, but she was thin and twisted, and her face beautiless.

"Stay, Knight," said she. "You must leave your weapons and your colours here."

"As others have," said Cedrevir, "and not reclaimed them."

"Not all reclaim them, it is true," said the maiden. "But you have entered the *Azori Mundi Regna*, the Kingdoms of the Air, and must obey their laws."

Cedrevir unsheathed his sword, and unslung the shield from his shoulder. These he gave her, with his war-helm. And she raised the items, as if they were no weight at all, and hung them on the tree.

"Who guards you, lady?" he asked her then, "are you alone, and still make this harsh demand of any man that comes here?"

"There is protection, though invisible. I am Morgainor, and it is I myself who guards this place, and its treasures, which you seek."

"So I do," he answered very low.

"Enter the tower then, the tallest of all, and go up the stair."

At these words, Cedrevir went pale, and his heart thundered. He said, "Is there no other preparation?"

"What is to be can only be."

So he left the maiden, who had called herself Morgainor, and crossed the court, and the door of that tallest of the towers opened for him. He saw beyond a stair ascending. It was of polished ebony, inlaid with ivory. And in the tower too, the flowers of gold and silver hung in the air, brushing his face and shoulders as again he climbed upward. And he was filled by feverish lightness, and tears stood in his eyes.

Now as he climbed the stair of ebony and ivory, it did begin to suggest itself to the Knight that, aside from the flowers, which he might see and feel, the air thickened with unseen presences and sometimes they too brushed him as if with draperies or wings. Where the stair curled about itself, as it did very often, it seemed to him he detected voices also, soft and melodious, but they spoke in a tongue he had never heard.

At last, he saw the light of the sky again before him, but, as he stepped off from the stair, he found the way was closed with a palisade the height of three men, and made from the bones of men, and the day streamed through them and through the eyeless skulls, which were very white and pure, as if fashioned of alabaster, but they were not.

This door would not open for Cedrevir. He paced before it, and saw dimly through its eyelets radiant day beyond.

Then a shadow moved in an inner corner of the door, and there was a stooped, gross woman there, dressed in sackcloth, her pale hair matted and her face very ugly, though her eyes were the eyes of the maiden in the court.

"You must give me a gift," said she, "or I may not open the way for you."

"What would you have? For I have nothing."

"Give me," she said, "a coal-black shell and a blood-red thorn."

Then he considered how he had remained true to himself, and to his vows, at the castle in the lake and the Castle of Earth and Fire, and how, waking, he had on both occasions found tokens left him, the shell and the thorn. So he took them from his belt and placed them on the ugly woman's palm.

At that she smiled, and she shook her head, and closed her hand upon the things. "I am Morgainor," she said. "Do you recollect? You have met me before."

"If you are Morgainor, then you are she. I have given you what you asked."

"Yours is a heart that has no stain, not any occlusion," she said. "I see through it, therefore. Alas, did you never question what you have been given, to give it up so easily in turn?"

"A shell," he said, "a thorn."

"Knight, I will render you one thing in exchange, and then will open the door of bone." And she held out to him her other hand, the right, and on the palm lay a golden needle. Cedrevir took this, and as he did so the door broke at its centre and folded wide for him to pass.

Beyond, the day was itself standing open, like a flower; it dazzled him, that upper sunshine.

The atmosphere was rare, thin as silk, and fragrant, and cold. The place was by the turret of the tower, its topmost roof, and so high a place the castle itself had now vanished in the cloud below. A pavement stretched on every side, a round space without a wall, and at the centre of the pavement was a ring of white stones, each about half the height of a man. That was all, and the sun's rays smote on the stones, the pavement, and the gold turret, so everything was caught in a brilliant haze.

Then, from the brilliancy, forms began to shape themselves. Cedrevir stood immobile, and next he kneeled, for these creatures, though never wholly seen, yet appeared like angels, gleaming, and clad in robes of samite, with great wings, and having every one a nimbus about its head. And these strange ethereal beings went to and fro in the air itself, not treading the pavement. (But they did not go inside the ring of stones.)

Cedrevir knelt and prayed then, for the dazzle of the sun and of the angel-beings had brought him all at once to a leaden weariness. As he prayed, too, every slight transgression, every weakness of his life, came into his mind, and he was ashamed. He began to believe that, like those others whose weapons and colours remained on the willow tree, he too would shrivel in this bath of light, and die. Flawed as man and as priest-warrior, he partly longed to leave the height, he could not bear the peerlessness he sensed hovering over him.

Then he heard the chime of bells, and startled, looked up. In the sky to the east he saw a sight.

A glistening barge came floating down the air. It had a sail that shone like red bronze, and the prow was carved like an eagle. A band of Knights rowed the barge through the ether with gilded oars, and young girls stood in the stern and rang bells in their white hands, and chanted dolefully.

Down and down the barge descended; it slipped over the ring of stones and landed weightless on the tower beneath the turret. When that was done, the Knights put up their oars. One, who was clothed in white, came from the barge, and with him an old, crippled hag-like woman, dressed in sackcloth, who hid her face behind a veil. These two approached, and while the White Knight stood aside, the hag addressed Cedrevir.

"I am Morgainor. We meet a third time. Will you give me back now the golden needle, for if you do, I will then instruct you in the mystery."

Cedrevir rose from his knees. He looked at the White Knight, whose face was as splendid as sunrise and as unearthly. Cedrevir looked at the hag, who peeped hideously from her veil with faded azure-green grey eyes.

"Lady, before, you seemed to warn me that I had given up to you too easily the shell and the thorn. Shall I relinquish as easily this needle?"

"You must. And since you must, you shall."

"I believe I have begun to guess the riddle," said Cedrevir. He lowered his eyes and said, "The shell was symbol of the Blood Cup, and the thorn symbol of the Sorrow Crown. The needle is the Lance of Pain. I am unworthy of the vision which was sent me and so, unwittingly, but at the design of God, resigned the key to these sacred relics. Nevertheless, this needle I still hold, and if I do not part with it, perhaps I shall be granted one further sight of the Lance. Or, I shall be granted clean death upon the lance of a Knight more worthy than I, maybe such a one as he that stands before me now."

Then the hag said this: "Cedrevir, you must not presume. If God has chosen you, how do you dare to judge yourself unworthy? What is your knowledge beside the knowledge of Him? You see into your heart, but He sees much more. It is your soul He sees. Whatever is said to you, whatever you gain or lose, what do such things matter? Did the Christ not promise Heaven to a wretched thief?"

Cedrevir sighed deeply. He said, "I am in God's hand." And he gave the hag Morgainor back her needle.

She took it. She said, "Go to the barge. That is the mystery and the last test. There is no more to say."

Cedrevir went towards the barge, and as he walked, the White Knight with the archangel's face fell into step with him. And the White Knight said, "in the barge lies one under a curse, and you may free her from it." But his voice was remote, like distant music.

"What curse is that?" inquired Cedrevir, expressionless, and his heart ached within him, at the words of the hag Morgainor, at doubt, and *because* of doubt. He was not uplifted or comforted. His eagerness lay spent.

"That you shall see, the nature of the cursing. But to break it is, of itself, most simple. One lies within the barge. Embrace her, and kiss her, on the lips. All shall be well."

"That I may not do," Cedrevir replied, dully. "All and every intimate connection with women is forbidden me."

But now they had reached the barge. The beaked prow craned above, and the sail had netted the sun. At the stern, the young girls stood with folded hands, bowed heads. The Knights were motionless. A ladder led into the midships of the vessel, and Cedrevir mounted it and stepped down into the barge. There lay a canopied bier, the hangings of which were blue silk.

"It is not to be, I can do nothing," said Cedrevir to the White Knight.

But, "Look on her. Perhaps you will pity her enough to do it."

Then, impelled, Cedrevir crossed to the bier and lifted aside its hangings. At the view, he recoiled, unable to repress a groan of darkest loathing.

Then again, disbelieving, he stared, and could not take his gaze away.

On the bier there spilled a faintly-stirring mass. If it was a female, it was the more terrible for that, for it was also reptile. The ripplings of its curded flesh, shapeless under a swathe of silk, gave way at the upper limbs to the little clutching arms of lizards, sheathed in lustreless metallic scales. And from the waist its lower part was a serpent, oozing in a slime. And round the whole slithered hair that lived, fatted worms, the snake-hair of a gorgon. The face grew from the torso that had no scales. It was in truth a woman's face, but old as a mummy, all fissured and crinkled, lipless and having no teeth but the four long fangs of its serpent side, these broken and discoloured. An evil stink arose from it, as it laboured there at life, half-torpid and half-awake. And finally Cedrevir, sick with horror, dragged away his stare from it, but just then it spoke.

"You are wounded by the sight," said the voice. "But I by the existence."

And it was the voice of a lost child, that tore his heart.

"That is undeniable, lady," he answered.

"But you, if you would, with one kiss, might set me free. How long does a brief kiss last? How long my life?"

Then Cedrevir looked again on the monster. His gorge rose, but now for the first he saw her eyes. They had no colour and seemed mostly blind, yet in the windows of them shone the well of the world's tears. A hundred centuries of direst misery. Perhaps a hundred more if he should stint compassion.

To kiss her was not lust or longing, to kiss her was a kind of fearful death, and never sin.

So Cedrevir, keeping wide his eyes on hers, leaned down into the stench, and shimmering shadow. He put his hand under her head, among the hair of worms, and he put his face to her face, and his lips upon her serpent mouth, and kissed her the kiss of all the love-desire in him that never once had he bestowed.

It was as if he had grasped lightning or the rushing sea. He opened his eyes yet wider, and lifted his head, and saw there in his grasp a maiden so lovely and so fair that not even the wonders of the Castle could outshine her. Her hair, flowing over his hands, was like spring sunshine on wild flax, her eyes were like marine turquoise, her lips were red and her clear-water skin as white as may. And all of her was slim and sweet and human, but quite perfect, so her gentle fingers that touched his brow fell there like petals, and with her perfumed breath she said to him, "Kiss me again." And in that moment he could not stay himself, and he did kiss her, in her beauty and in his great irreconcilable lust.

"I too am Morgainor," he heard her murmur then, as the earth and sky wheeled about him. "And now you have given up to me all."

There was no thunderclap or shaking of the stones, but the light entirely perished. Everything was gone. The tower, the sky, the angel forms, the Knights and maidens, and the barge. Morgainor too, melted like water from between his hands. And Cedrevir was left in anguish and the dark.

But not for long. For presently, a new lamp was kindled. It was like the intimation of sunrise under storm.

Cedrevir, in his despair, looked yearningly towards it, and held himself ready, nearly gladly, for chastisement.

Next, through the smokes of the cloud, he beheld a searing hint of gold, and then of silver, of crimson, and of a depthless ruby green. Up in the air, anchorless, they wafted. He saw them hang in space, as if a thousand miles away—the Spear, the Thorn Crown, and the Grail. And Cedrevir, in his agony, covered his face and wept aloud, for he knew very well that now the culmination of his Quest was denied him. Even as he thought it, and other things more bitter, a burning wind passed by and colours stained against his tight-closed lids. After which the dark returned, without, within.

From the dark a voice spoke at last, at his right shoulder, and it seemed to Cedrevir that he had already heard it once, at the coming of the vision on Midsummer Midnight. But nothing now was to be seen.

"Cedrevir, were you not warned, and did not heed? It is your presumption that has denied you the final prize."

"Lord," Cedrevir replied, "it is my sin which has kept it from me."

"Who are you, before God, to judge yourself or how you sin? Know this. In the moment of the second embrace, you had not lost the Quest. You lost it in the moment that you deemed yourself one fallen, and damned yourself."

"Fallen and damned I was. My vows were broken."

"And who are you to say you will never sin? Are you not a human man? Or are you a god, who is above sin?"

"I am a man. A sinner, and cast from grace."

"Since you must be perfect in your own eyes, Knight, perfect as God, it is your own grace that you have fallen from. It is not for you to know how God has judged you, blameless or to blame. But be assured of this, even the King of All cannot grant you what you stubbornly refuse to take. Go then, Knight. Go down again to the world. Believe this, your fault is forgiven, for a man has only to say *Forgive me* for his sins to be stripped from him. But you are proud. You say in your heart to God, Oh God, forgive me. But to yourself you say, *I* cannot forgive myself. *I will not.*"

After that, the voice was silent, and a wan twilight came, and in the twilight Cedrevir stumbled down from the high place, over the stair of ebony and ivory, perhaps for many hours, and came at length into the court, the darkness gone, and another lesser darkness come, for already night had shut its wings.

There the willow cascaded to the ground, and on its ghostly weft the trophies of the Knights eerily spangled and swung. No figure was near, but three times round the trunk of the tree was coiled a silvery snake, which hissed at him. When the snake did this, the shield and helm and sword of Cedrevir dropped to the marble. He went and took them up, and in heavy grief turned from the Castle and descended the mountains.

A night and a day he travelled, scarcely knowing what he did, and eventually he lost his way and his wits, and wandered some while. In a valley of the world, kindly people found him, restored him as best they might, and brought to him a horse that was his own, lean and sad, which they had come on similarly wandering the valley a month before.

Of the Forest of the Savage Hart there was no sign, and the valley was set in verdant hills, flowered with fields and orchard-land, though now the winter came on them.

Cedrevir rode south before the snow, which pressed behind him and covered the earth with its white cloak. So, turning his head, he could yet see the snowy northern mountaintops for several days, shining up in the sky like shed pieces of the winter moon.

He saw, however, no unusual sights, and no uncommon adventures befell him.

Cedrevir returned, as you yourself have noted. And as he seemed, so he is. The Quest is more often resolved in such failure than in death. For now he knows the colours and the weapons on the willow tree remained of those who journeyed on to some explicit bliss he is denied. Or that he has, as the angel told him, denied for ever to himself.

—But tell me, then, since you have told so much, how do you know it all? His journey and his grief and loss.

—How do I know? How could it be, but that I too, long, long ago, have gone Questing. I too have striven and failed and fallen. I too have heard those awful words and known—not in heart and mind, but in my soul—the truth of them. God it is not who is cruel. But we ourselves. *Mea culpa. Mea maxima culpa.* I, too.

The Latin used in this story is the Mediaeval 'cat' Latin of the Imperii Quattuorviri.

Made in the USA
Monee, IL
25 April 2023

32363216R00154